Drogheda, Ireland, 1864.

Ellen Cooney is fit to burst with happiness. Her sailor husband is on his way home from a long sea voyage. But devastation awaits on the quayside of her beloved Drogheda.

Crippled with grief, Ellen knows she must keep her young family out of the dreaded 'Poorhouse' at all costs.

In time, Ellen glimpses a spark of hope for the future. However it seems that circumstances, and an unimaginably malign force, may drive her to make the biggest mistake of her life. Options are few for a woman in such a man's world.

Are the rest of Ellen's days to be blighted by the choice she had to make? Peggy, Larry, Nicholas, who can she trust?

Can she find the strength and the means to calm the turbulent tide of her life and navigate her way to happiness?

It's time for her to take control.

This is Ellen's story.

As The Tide Turns At Tredagh

Caroline Lynch

Clay Hill Publishing

This novel is entirely a work of fiction. The names, characters and incidents portrayed in it are the work of the author's imagination. Some placenames may be used to evoke a setting. Any resemblance to actual persons, living or dead or to businesses, companies, events, or institutions is entirely coincidental.

ISBN 978-1-0686605-0-4

Published by: Clay Hill Publishing

Cover design by: Getcovers.com

Printed and bound by: Harvest Moon Print and Design, Killeshandra, Co. Cavan

www.caroline-lynch.com

To Mam - Mary Murphy Lynch.
Thanks for everything.

To Bess,

I hope you enjoy!

Best wishes

[illegible]

About the author

Caroline Lynch lives in Co. Meath, Ireland, with her husband, two sons and Sally, her very yappy but loveable fluff-ball terrier. She was previously employed in the world of enterprise development, but decided to change direction, and now happily works in the events and tourism industry. A voracious reader, this is her first novel. In her spare time, she likes nothing better than planning her next trip, catching up with friends, listening to music, lifting a few weights, walking, Zumba and plotting her next novel.

Some words of the time and place.

Tredagh - Old name for the town of Drogheda.

Acushla – An affectionate form of address.

A Stór - My love.

Asunder - Apart.

Childer - Children.

Cú Chulainn - An Irish warrior hero.

Dudeen - Small, short-stemmed tobacco pipe .

Gasson - A young boy.

Hames - Mess.

Handywoman - Midwife.

Poorhouse - Government-run facility for the needy.

Pucking - Hitting.

Upscuttling - Upsetting.

Black Maria – Police van.

Abhainn mor/beag – Big/small river.

Fenian Brotherhood – Irish Republican movement.

Prologue

On board the barque 'Swansea Lass'.

Off the coast of Chile, South Pacific Ocean.

16thJuly 1864.

The wind snatched every plaintive note from the young man's fiddle, blunting each one, making it hover for a second and then disappear into the black night. The lilting Irish lament assimilated itself into the deep, dark ocean. He put down the instrument which had been his father's and his grandfather's before him and gazed up at the ship's masts. The wind was rising. His fingers traced the outline of the St. Christopher medal around his neck. She had placed it there so tenderly on their wedding day, her sweet breath warm on his cheek, whispering that it was to keep him safe on his travels. She had made him promise that he would always come back to her, a fathomless love burning in her bright blue eyes. He had fervently promised that he would.

Tonight, the sea seemed like it was toying with the ship, tossing and pitching it around like a matchstick on a whirlpool. It seemed to have a growing malevolence about it, like it was just waiting to unleash some unimaginable fury. The young man thanked his lucky stars that he hadn't been sick at all on this voyage, not even when they had rounded Cape Horn with its vicious Williwaw winds, churning waters and unpredictable swell.

He was the only one of his fellow shipmates, excepting the captain, who had not taken to his bunk. A sense of pride surged through him, as this was the longest and most difficult voyage he had been on so far. An 'Able Seaman', at twenty-nine years of age, his experience up to now had been confined to short trips over and back from his home on the east coast of Ireland to England and Scotland. This voyage had brought him far, far away from his familiar world, and introduced him to sights and sounds that he would never forget, to be woven into the tapestry of his life.

The moon kept disappearing behind the clouds that had gathered rapidly over the past hour or so. The stars were playing hide and seek, waxing and waning, and the wind was gusting, buffeting his hair. The captain had said they were a week or so away from their destination, the port of Coquimbo. Once there, they would discharge their cargo of coal and fill the hold with copper. A week or two of rest and hopefully, a bit of decent grub, and they would be on their way home again. He was mightily sick of the ship's food. Chuckling, he recalled the moans and groans of some of his shipmates whose stomachs had made strange with the dried peas, beef and pork. Sure, they weren't men at all, with their whimpering. Mind you, they were as good a crew as you could hope to have. He was one of only two Irishmen on board. There were none of the usual jokes about the thick potato-eating savages, and he knew he and his compatriot were well respected.

He didn't mind doing the night watch. More often than not, he spent his time playing his fiddle - Irish tunes which reminded him of home – the beautiful emerald isle with its green patchwork fields, stone walls, soft rain and scudding clouds. And dreaming about his family waiting for him. What tales he would have to tell them when he returned!

Looking up again at the sails, he decided that they needed to be taken down. If the wind rose any more, they could be blown completely off course.

The captain would have something to say to him about that! Licking his lips, he tasted the salty tang of the Pacific Ocean and started to haul himself up the mast quickly and with practised ease, muscles tensing underneath his rough clothes. Pausing at the top, he laughed into the wind, feeling the sense of exhilaration that battling with nature's elements always gave him. He felt like he was on the top of the world. Invincible. A sudden ferocious gust caught the sail just as he was about to loosen it. With a yell of surprise, he lost his grip and toppled, hurtling towards the churning black water.

The inky sea closed over his head. He surfaced quickly. The cold was utterly shocking, causing him to gasp involuntarily and some water entered his lungs. He began to tread water, his clothes and boots weighing him down. After a few seconds, he gathered his wits and managed to find the breath to shout for help, praying that the wind would not be strong enough to snatch his words away, and that the captain had not had too many whiskeys before retiring to his bunk. Relief coursed through him as he saw a light emerge over the side of the ship. The captain's voice was roaring, 'man overboard!', rousing his shipmates to come and help. Heart beating at twice it's normal rate, his breathing ragged, the young man tried to grab a hold of the spar that the captain had thrust into the water. Feeling the cold seep through to his very marrow, his hands were clumsy. After two attempts, he managed to grab hold, but the sea decided to toss another vicious wave his way and he lost his grip.

'Come on man, grab it!' the captain shouted. With one more gigantic effort, the young man again reached out but before his hands could make purchase, the hull of the ship made a lunge towards him on the crest of a wave. He felt a searing pain as it struck his head. Stars burst before his eyes. As darkness engulfed him, all he could see was a pair of laughing blue eyes.

Part One

CHAPTER 1

Drogheda, Ireland

July 1864

Ellen didn't notice the bead of sweat that dripped off the end of her nose and joined the puddle on the floor. She was nearly beyond reason. The pains had been steadily getting worse all day. Another savage one grew and swelled inside her until she felt she was being torn asunder. She gripped the edge of the wooden table and bit so hard on the inside of her cheek that she tasted blood. Had it been this bad with Tommy? She didn't remember. Up to now, she had been trying very hard not to alarm her young son too much, but now, there was no room for anything else in her brain other than the fierce, unnatural pain that was trying to rip her apart. She tried to focus on the room where she could just see Tommy's worried little face emerge from the corner beside the open door. He walked slowly over to her, the bright sun framing his head and making him look like he had a halo. The spit of his Da, he was. His Da was never getting near her again.

Tommy's eyes were wide with terror as he looked at his Mam. She was usually so pretty, but today, she looked really scary. She had been walking up and down the room for ages and wouldn't sit down. Sometimes, she'd give a little low moan and then her face would screw up tight like she had a really bad pain in her belly. Maybe like the one he'd had the year before when he'd eaten too many blackberries? His Da had warned him not to, but they'd looked so juicy and had tasted so nice. His mouth got wet at the memory. A few minutes earlier, his Mam had done a wee on the floor and now she was bent over, making a noise that sounded like one of Mister Sarsfield's cows that were up in the paddock beside the mill. He approached his Mam softly, put his hand on her back and gave it a gentle, hesitant pat.

'Mam are you alright?' he whispered.

'Tommy, be a good boy and run up to Peggy. Tell her the baby's coming now. Quickly! Off you go!'

He didn't really want to leave his Mam, but she was scaring him. Maybe Peggy would make her better. His mind made up, he turned and ran as fast as his bare feet would carry him, out the door and down past the row of thatched cottages, the ground hot as coals. As he fled, he could hear his Mam letting out a terrible roar. It made him go even faster. His insides turned to jelly. He really needed to go to the privy.

Peggy Murphy had just dozed off in the chair beside the window of her single-roomed cottage. She wasn't one for the sun, and the hot July was playing havoc with her gouty toe. A trickle of drool was making its way down the left side of her slightly open mouth, and a sheen of perspiration coated her ruddy face. A few frizzy wisps of red hair had escaped from her bun, and she snored gently. Tommy burst through the open doorway and skidded to a halt in front of her. He hopped from one leg to the other. He needed to wake her up but was temporarily mesmerised by the big pimple on her chin that had a long, spiky hair growing out of it. Keeping one eye on the pimple, he poked Peggy on the arm. Nothing happened. He poked a bit harder, but all she did was move her head, which made her chins wobble. He counted three of them. They reminded him of the turkeys he had seen at the fair with his Da the Christmas before. He started to panic. What if she didn't wake up? What would happen his Mam then? His Da had told him before he went off in the big ship that he, Tommy, was the man of the house until his Da got back, and that he had to take care of his Mam. He wished his Da was here now because he'd know what to do. Would Peggy be cross with him for waking her up? His Da's face swam before him, urging Tommy to be brave. Maybe if he gave Peggy a 'Billy Molloy Special' she might wake up? That had been really, really sore and had left a red mark. But he hadn't cried. He'd get Billy back for that. His mind made up, Tommy reached forward and grabbed a fold of skin on Peggy's arm. He quickly pinched as hard as he could, digging in with his nails. Peggy let a roar that made Tommy duck behind the only other chair in the room, which was sitting beside a small, wooden table.

'What the blazes was that?'

Tommy emerged from his hiding place. Peggy put on the glasses that were hanging on the string around her neck, focusing on his anxious face.

'Tommy pet, I didn't see you there. Are you alright?'

'Mam says the baby's coming now. Can I use your privy please?'

If he didn't go soon, he'd wet his britches, and he didn't have another pair. His Mam would be cross at having to wash them before Saturday and that might make the pain in her belly even worse.

'Oh, the Lord save us, it's never coming already? I thought she'd wouldn't be calling on me until tomorrow – an early baby!' Peggy muttered to no one in particular as she heaved herself out of the wooden chair with a groan.

Every bit of her seemed to wobble. Tommy wondered what she meant about the baby being early. Sure, it was nearly teatime. The baby was very late, not early. He hoped he'd still be able to get his tea because his belly was rumbling fiercely.

'Can I *please* use your privy?' Tommy pleaded, hopping from one leg to the other.

'Sorry pet, of course you can. I'll go and see how your Mam is getting on. Don't you be worrying about her now. She'll be grand, and sure you'll have a new brother or sister very soon. Which would you like?'

A brother was what Tommy wanted. Ever since his Mam had told him there was a baby growing in her belly, he had imagined himself and his brother, when he was big enough, playing together, jumping off the old wall at the back of the Rope Walk, running through the fields down to the old tower, pretending they were soldiers, using big blackthorn sticks for guns. He definitely didn't want a sister. His best friend, Johnny said they were a pain in the arse. And he'd know because he had six of them. Tommy rolled the word 'arse' around in his head. He didn't dare say it out loud for clear of a clip around the ear from his Mam.

'I'd like a brother', Tommy shouted over his shoulder as he raced outside to the privy.

'Go and see Janey next door when you're done, and she'll show you the puppies.' Peggy said to his retreating back.

'Yes!' Tommy punched the air. He wondered if his Mam would let him bring a puppy home. She might be in a good mood if the baby came, and the pain stopped. He really hoped so. A little ripple of excitement ran up his spine. Him and Johnny would have such fun with a puppy! He'd call it *'Lucky'* because his Da always called him his *'lucky penny'*.

Peggy hurried as fast as her sore toe would allow, picking her way through the steaming horse droppings that peppered the potholed, uneven road as she made her way to Ellen Cooney's house. She wiped the beads of perspiration from her face with the hem of her apron. Squinting up at the sky, she couldn't see a trace of a cloud that might bring this blessed heatwave to an end. A good decent drop of rain was needed. Sure, the heat had everyone driven astray. And the stench! In summer, the smells from the river, the tannery and the brewery combined into something that would strip the hairs clean off the inside of your nose. Still, Drogheda was where she had been born and reared and she wouldn't like to live anywhere else, save perhaps in some nice big house by the sea, with large windows, big soft comfortable chairs and a feather bed to sink into where she could linger as long as she wanted. A big stove would be nice too, one of those new-fangled ones. And an inside privy. Now that would be heaven on earth! She could see herself in the garden of this big house, sitting in the shade of a leafy tree, with the sound of the sea washing over her. Someday, maybe.

Arriving at Ellen's cottage, she paused at the door, allowing her eyes to adjust to the dark interior. The room was small and cramped, like her own, with very little furniture, saving the bare essentials. Yet it had a homely feel. Living alone, Peggy didn't have the money or the inclination for fripperies. She heard Ellen before she saw her. The low, guttural noise the young woman was making sounded like it came from her very core. Peggy swept her eyes around the small room, and beyond the simple wooden table, she could see Ellen's slim frame bent over the chair, her eyes closed, and her face screwed up in agony.

'Ellen pet, Tommy says the baby's coming?'

'I can't do this Peggy. I'm being torn asunder!', Ellen gasped.

'Now, now, none of that talk. You've done it before *acushla,* and I'm here to help you. Can you walk over to the settle?'

Peggy guided the younger woman towards the straw bed in the corner. Ellen stopped half-way and roared like an animal caught in a trap.

'Oh, holy mother of God, I need to push!'

'Alright now, easy, easy lass. Lie yourself down and I'll have a little look to see how things are coming along.'

Peggy was well used to dealing with women in the throes of birthing agony as she was the area's *'Handywoman'*, something of which she was very proud. This baby wasn't one for waiting around. She could see the head.

'The worst is nearly over pet,' said Peggy. Now when I say so, I want you to push as if your life depended on it.'

'I can't', whimpered Ellen. 'I can't do this!'

'You can and you will.' Peggy's voice was just on the verge of stern.

'This baby has to come out right now! Think of little Tommy and how pleased he will be to have a new brother or sister. Now push!'

With a long, agonised bellow, Ellen pushed with all her might, and within seconds, Peggy caught the baby as it made its way into the world, mewling like a kitten.

Ellen collapsed back on the straw, exhausted.

'Is it ok?', she panted.

'As fine and healthy as a trout' answered Peggy with a chuckle. She produced some scissors from her voluminous skirt and deftly cut the cord. Then she swaddled the baby, placed it on Ellen's chest and waited for the afterbirth.

'Is it a wee boy or a girl?'

'God's truth, but I forgot to look!'

She put on her glasses and opened the cloth in which she had wrapped the baby.

'It's a wee lassie, pet! Congratulations, she'll be every bit as bonny as her Mammy, I have no doubt!'

'A girl', Ellen breathed, teary-eyed. 'Tommy will be disappointed. Where is he?'

'Don't fret, he's looking at the puppies with Janey. You have a gentleman's family now, with Tommy and this little lass. What name will you give her?'

'She'll be Alice Rose'.

'Alice Rose Cooney – a beautiful name if ever I heard one. Her daddy will be very proud when he gets home from his voyage.'

'He'll get a surprise for sure!'

Peggy knew that Jim Cooney had no idea, before he left on his voyage in January, that he was to be a father for the second time.

Ellen sighed. 'He said he'd be back by September.'

'Will you have a cup of tea and a slice of bread and dripping pet? You surely deserve it. They don't call it 'labour' for nothing!'

'Ooh yes please, that would be just lovely.'

Ellen reached out and squeezed the older woman's arm.

'Thanks Peggy. I don't know what I would have done without you.'

She'd lost two babies in the past few years and Peggy had been there to ease her physical and mental pain. Sometimes it was hard to accept God's will.

Seeing the gratitude swimming in Ellen's eyes and swatting away the compliment with a wave of her hand, Peggy turned to the fire and lifted off the permanently boiling kettle to make a pot of tea. Then, pulling up a chair beside the bed, she ran her eyes over Ellen, now relaxed and serene as she gazed adoringly at her new-born daughter. Peggy had seen so many women worn down by bearing child after child, barely nine months between some of them -exhausted with the stress of feeding and looking after their children, living in fear of the church which told them they had to keep having babies to add to God's family on earth. She thought of poor Cissie Mallon, gone to an early grave at the age of only thirty-four, having died in childbirth with her seventh. Some of her poor children were now in the workhouse. Father Flynn and his like had a lot to answer for, and no mistake. She didn't want a similar fate to befall Ellen who was so very vibrant and full of life. Hadn't she delivered her herself, twenty-six years earlier? She had watched her grow into a bonny lass and become a spirited young woman with a gentle soul - tall and graceful, with dark tumbling curls. It was no wonder she had caught the eye of Jim Cooney. Her and Jim seemed to be a match made in heaven. This young woman was like a daughter to her. She decided it was time to impart some of her wisdom.

'Now listen to me Ellen, hear me out', said Peggy, her expression a mixture of tenderness, concern and determination.

'I've seen the hardship that comes with having lots of children one after the other. It takes a terrible toll on a woman. You can tell me to mind my own business, but in my opinion, it would be a good idea for you to stop now that you have your two lovely little children. Don't pay any heed to Father Flynn and his preaching. If the men had to have the babies, sure there'd be none born!'

She looked over her shoulder as if to make sure they were alone and whispered to Ellen.'I can give you something to stop the babbies coming if you like. All you have to do is ask', she winked and tapped her nose.

Ellen grinned tiredly at Peggy.

'Thanks, I'll think about it.'

There was a sudden commotion at the door and a familiar little figure bounded into the room, dark hair flopping over one eye and with a smear of jam on his right cheek. He was followed closely by a curious, ruddy cheeked Janey. He halted a little bit away from his Mam's bed and stood stock-still.

'Come and meet your new sister Tommy.'

'I thought it was going to be a brother.'

Tommy sullenly cast a cursory glance at the little bundle latched onto his Mam. He sniffed and looked away.

'But a sister's good, she can still play with you. You can teach her to climb trees when she's older and she will always look up to you as her big brother.'

The little boy's face brightened up and then glancing at his Mam, a speculative look appeared in his eyes.

'Mam, can I have one of Janey's puppies?'

'We'll see when your Da gets back', Ellen replied fondly. 'Now come here and give me and your sister a kiss, but wipe that jam off your face first!'

Looking at the little family before her, a sudden shiver went up Peggy's spine. Suddenly, the room blurred, and she saw dark water, a flailing hand that dipped beneath the surface of the waves. A feeling of dread lodged itself in her gut as she experienced a terrible foreboding that Jim Cooney wouldn't be coming home from his sea voyage. She didn't welcome her *'visions.'* They caused her stomach to knot, because the blessed things kept coming true. She had been right about Jemser Moran that time he had gone missing. His body had been washed up on the beach a couple of miles outside the town. She had foreseen poor Bridie Farrelly's sickness which had wasted her away to nothing in a few short months. She damped down the feeling of dread, hoping with all her heart, that this time, her sixth sense was wrong.

CHAPTER 2

Ellen

Drogheda, September 1864

A fizz of excitement exploded inside Ellen. She felt like she might turn into a big ball of flames at any second. This must surely be the day. Jim had said he'd be home by September. She had no doubt that he would keep his word. He had never let her down before. Ever. Today was the seventh day of September and seven was her lucky number. Every day since the turn of the month, she had swaddled Alice and made her way down to the quayside as soon as it was bright, leaving Tommy with Peggy. She really didn't know what she would have done without Peggy these past few years. She was more like a mother to her than her own. Ellen sighed as an image of Brigid Sarsfield floated into her mind. Her mother's thin face, and sour, anxious expression were the result of thirty-odd years living with the bully that was Ellen's father. Giving herself a mental shake, Ellen dragged her thoughts back to the present. What a surprise was in store for her Jim! She giggled, inhaling the special scent of the little bundle nestled close to her heart. He would be so thrilled to find he had a daughter; she just knew it. She couldn't wait to introduce them to each other. She pictured how his laughing green eyes would light up, how the skin at the corners would crinkle, and how his two cheek dimples would appear. He really was the most deliciously handsome man. And he was all hers. Sometimes, she had to pinch herself.

'Just wait until your Da meets you' she whispered to Alice. 'He'll never let any harm come to you and he'll love you with all the fierceness a Da can. He'll never treat you the way mine has treated me. I can guarantee it, my love.'

Ellen's hair rippled in the slight breeze. She licked her lips and could taste the usual salty tang to be found down here at the river's edge. It put her in mind of the seaside. It was not that far away, but to go there was a rare treat. Jim, Tommy, Peggy, herself and little Alice would go next summer. Alice would most likely be walking by then.

The quayside was leaping with life as usual. All sorts of accents filled the air with curses and choice language. Ellen usually tried to steer Tommy away from the quay when the ships were being unloaded. He had such a love of words, but she didn't want him hearing this particular sort! Occasionally, a jeer or a laugh rose up as a load of coal fell into the water with a resounding splash, or someone burst into song. There were bangs and clatters as the business of unloading cargo got underway. Cattle bawled and emptied their bowels on the street as they were herded on to the steamer bound for Liverpool. Ellen shivered as she saw some of the poor souls who were leaving the country sitting out top because they couldn't afford the fare to go below deck. They would be rightly frozen by the time they got across the Irish sea. The creak of timber hulls was rhythmic as the ships moved gently with the motion of the tidal river. Ellen knew that coal came into Drogheda from Wales. Linen, from the mills that gave a good few of the people of the town their living, was bound for England. Ropes were thrown and caught deftly by the Badge Porters. A visit to the quays always made Ellen feel close to Jim whenever he was away. Not one for cursing like a typical sailor, he had a soft, gentle voice. He loved the sea and was popular amongst all the crews he had worked with. She literally couldn't wait to see him. He had been gone for such a long time. The latest voyage had taken him to the other side of the world. This had been the longest they had ever been apart since they married, but they needed the money.

A plaintive cry made Ellen turn around. Drogheda, for all its busyness, was like any other town. It had rich people, and poor. Ellen was grateful to be somewhere in between. A little girl of about ten years old was sitting with her back against the wall of the quay, crying loudly, her clothes ragged, her hair matted, her face pale, and streaked with dirt. Probably one of the poor orphans that roamed the town, Ellen thought. Or maybe she had legged it from the workhouse to try her luck on the street. Ellen had heard stories of *that place* up on the hill, across the river. The poor unfortunates that ended up there often created trouble so that they could be put into the town gaol where conditions were better. She shivered as she looked across at the dark tunnel that was the 'Poorhouse Alley.' She walked over to the little girl and gave her a halfpenny. The little one instantly stopped crying. Mumbling 'Thanks missus!', she took off like a scalded cat into town, no doubt to find a shop where she could buy a slice of bread or a bun.

Ellen raised her eyes to the horizon, willing Jim's ship to arrive. She thought she saw a shape emerging out of the mist. Sure enough, little by little, some tall masts appeared in her line of vision. She let out an excited squeak which Alice to startle.

'Sorry pet, I think this is your Da's ship coming. Oh, my Lord, how do I look?'

She grabbed a passing sailor as she smoothed down her hair.

'As pretty as a picture, lovely lady!' came the reply from the gap-toothed young man. 'He sure is a lucky fella, whoever he is!'

"He' is my husband, Jim' said Ellen proudly. 'And never a finer man has there been!' She tossed her head, making her dark hair ripple in the early morning sun that was doing its best to emerge from the mist.

'Why does the cursed thing have to be so slow?' Ellen was biting the inside of her lip with impatience. By the time the ship had finally docked, she was worked up into quite a frenzy. Most of Jim's trips so far had been short ones, mainly over and back to places like Glasgow, Cardiff and English ports. France was the furthest he had ever been. This latest journey, to Chile, was the longest and most distant yet. When in Liverpool the previous year, he had heard of a Captain Geoffrey Symonds, an Englishman who was looking for crew for his ship, which was to bring coal over to Chile and come back laden with copper. The *'Swansea Lass'*, measuring one hundred-and-eighteen feet long and twenty-seven feet deep was only a few years old, having been built in 1857 in Sunderland. Jim was to join the crew, and his shipmates would be from Cornwall, Swansea, Ipswich, Liverpool, Penzance, Devon, London and France. As *'Able Seaman'*, there would be no jokes about a backward, stupid Fenian at Jim's expense! Ellen recalled the proud tilt of his chin and the way his eyes had shone as he'd lifted her off the ground, twirling her around. He'd promised to get her the finest bonnet money could buy when he returned. She'd picked out the one she wanted already from the shop in town. Mrs. Cleary had put it behind the counter for her, with *'Ellen Cooney'* written in bold block letters on the cream and gold box. She couldn't wait to go and get it. She'd wear it to Mass on Sunday, and it would take the eyes clean out of the heads of all the silly women who kept fluttering their eyelashes at her Jim. As if she couldn't see what they were doing!

Straining to see, Ellen gave a gasp as she saw the name '*Swansea Lass*', written in big gold letters on the side of the ship. She kept her eyes trained on the deck, craning her neck. Jim was probably below, sprucing himself up and gathering his possessions. Remembering the smell of him, his rough, calloused hands and his deep, melodious voice, Ellen's insides stirred and twisted in a way they hadn't done for ages.

A bearded man, who looked to be in his fifties, threw down the gangplank with a resounding bang. She could see his eyes scanning the quayside crowd as he made his way slowly onto dry land. He was burly, with a nose that indicated fondness for a drink or two. Ellen watched him approach, as she scanned the ship behind him for the first glimpse of her Jim. Alice stirred in her sleep and gave out a little cry.

'Hush pet, your Da will be here any minute.'

'Ellen Cooney? Jim Cooney's wife?' the bearded man was talking to her.

'Yes sir, that's me' Ellen smiled a greeting. 'Mr. Symonds?'

She proffered her hand which Geoffrey Symonds took in his. She noticed it was rough and gnarly, no doubt from handling all the ropes on board. Ellen's eyes strayed again to the ship's deck where she could see numerous pairs of sombre, unsmiling faces looking in her direction. Why were all Jim's shipmates standing there, staring at her? She turned her gaze back to the man standing in front of her as a rattle of unease settled in her stomach.

'Geoffrey Symonds. Captain of the '*Swansea Lass*'. Pleased to meet you Mrs. Cooney. And who is this little one?' he asked.

'This is our daughter, Alice Rose Cooney' answered Ellen. 'Jim didn't even know that I was expecting when he left, so he's going to get a proper surprise!'

The words caught in Ellen's throat. She was beginning to think that something was badly amiss. It was in the way Captain Symonds was looking at her. He seemed a bit shifty and was having difficulty meeting her gaze. He closed his eyes and appeared to swallow hard. When he opened them again, they held an expression that made Ellen's heart thud in her chest and a pin prick of fear make its way from her gut to her fingertips and back again. It seemed like the quayside had hushed and was holding its breath.

'Mr. Symonds, where is Jim?' Ellen's voice was shriller than she would have liked, but she was past caring.

Symonds inhaled deeply and with a shuddering sigh said,

'I'm very sorry Mrs. Cooney, but...'

'No, no, no!' Ellen shook her head from side to side. 'You're sorry about what?' she gasped.

'Jim was drowned off the coast of Chile in July.'

Ellen looked at his lips which were still moving. His voice had been replaced by a harsh ringing sound in her ears. She felt her heart slow, give a powerful thud, and then speed up. With a whoosh of sound, she could hear again. He was saying things like 'heavy swell', 'sails flapping', 'knocked overboard' 'tried to reach him' 'hit his head against the hull' 'disappeared', 'pitch black', but they made absolutely no sense. His face swam back into focus in front of her.

'I'm so, so sorry, Mrs. Cooney. He was one of the finest seamen I ever did encounter. He was strong and brave and worked as hard as any man could. And there was no doubt that he loved you and your little lad like no others. He never stopped yabbering on about you.'

Was this man standing in front of her and telling her that Jim was gone? And saying he was 'sorry' like he had bumped into her at the market and spilled her bag of apples? A quiet scream was building inside Ellen, and she could feel it making its way from her lungs to the back of her throat. No, it couldn't be true. Her warm, strong, solid Jim couldn't be gone forever? Surely it wasn't real. Then, Mr. Symonds handed her a bag.

'Here's Jim's belongings.'

The stem of a fiddle poked its head out from a canvas bag. Symonds pressed an envelope into her hand.

'His wages, Mrs. Cooney, from the voyage.'

Geoffrey Symonds was not used to the female of the species. As an only child, his mother had died when he was very young, and his elderly father had not lasted long after that. His teenage years had been spent with a dour and uncommunicative uncle, so he had run off to sea as soon as he could. His time since, had been spent either away on a voyage, or in his little cottage in Penzance, with nothing but his little black dog for company. He had never felt the pull of a woman strongly enough to urge him out of bachelorhood and if he was honest, women were a bit of a mystery to him. He squeezed Ellen's hand, gave it an awkward pat and backed away.

As he turned to make his way back to the gangplank, the scream that had been building in Ellen finally made its way to the surface. Its piercing sound caused the gulls to lift and scatter in the wind, the men working at unloading the ships' cargoes to stop and stare and captain Symonds and his crew to bow their heads in sorrow. Ellen launched herself at Geoffrey Symond's back, pummeling it with all her might.

'You bastard!' Ellen screamed. 'You're sorry, you're sorry? You stand there and tell me my Jim is dead and that's all you can say! You hand me his things and walk away? Why didn't you save him? Why didn't some of those useless articles on board save him? He's at the bottom of the sea and all you can say is you're 'sorry'!?'

As suddenly as it had blown up, Ellen's rage receded, and she went limp like one of the ragdolls that they sold down at the Market Square. Geoffrey Symonds caught her awkwardly, looking around him for someone, anyone, to help him.

Mother and daughter wailed in unison as Ellen sank to her knees.

CHAPTER 3

Peggy

Peggy was itching to give the snooty young clerk in front of her a clip around the ear. Her dander was up. The little upstart had not even looked her in the eye since she had walked into the office. He was talking at her in a dull monotone voice, as if it was a supreme effort to rouse himself from whatever idle pursuit he had been engaged in before she had stepped into his dry, oppressive, dusty, domain. Evidence of his fondness for sweet things could not only been seen in his straining shirt buttons, but also on the dusting of sugar that coated his plump lips and the crumbs that he was now trying to remove from his paperwork. If she wasn't mistaken, he was the son of Hugh Matthews, himself a snooty 'speak to you one day and not the next' sort of man. The sort she couldn't abide. Sure, what made some people think they were better than others? Didn't the Queen of England still have to use the privy like everyone else? This young pup was not going to make her feel like a piece of dirt he had trodden on.

'I'm here to register a birth please, but I'll not talk to the top of your head young man. So, if you don't mind, I would appreciate it if you looked me in the eye as you deal with me.'

Peggy's voice was probably harsher than it should be, but she was bone-tired, and her patience was wearing thin. Having to care for wee Alice and young Tommy, whilst trying to pierce the bubble of grief that surrounded Ellen was taking its toll on her. She was no spring chicken, after all. Her body felt every one of its two-score and ten years. Trying to keep it all together for the little family, trying to cook something to whet Ellen's appetite and looking after the childer would put a younger woman to the test. As her own waster of a husband and gone and died of a heart attack five years previously, and with neither chick nor child of her own, when Jim had died, she had moved the few doors down Rope Walk and was now living with Ellen and her little family. She was all the poor craythurs had. Ellen's weak-chinned and weak-willed mother was no good to her daughter. Too afraid of her bully of a husband to disobey him and help her own flesh and blood. Ever since Jim had drowned a few weeks ago, Ellen had sunk into a terrible pit of despair; not eating, barely speaking, unable to care for herself, never mind her two children. Peggy shuddered to think what might have happened to them had she not moved in. The sadness in little Tommy's eyes would break your heart. It was as well that he had started school and had something to distract him for a couple of hours a day at least.

The clerk raised his eyes to gaze upon the woman who dared to take this tone with him. Something in Peggy's expression made him gulp and his Adam's apple wobbled.

'Yes ma'am, I'll certainly do that for you.' He dipped his quill into the ink well in front of him and poised it over a piece of paper looking at Peggy expectantly.

'Name'

'Alice Rose Cooney'

'Date of birth'

'16th July 1864.'

'Mother's name and maiden name?'

'Ellen Cooney, nee Sarsfield'

'Occupation?'

'Widow.'

The clerk glanced up at Peggy with a trace of surprise in his eyes.

'Father's name?'

'James Cooney'

'Occupation?'

Peggy rolled her eyes to heaven in exasperation. Could he really be that stupid?

'He's dead. I did say she was a *widow*. He drowned at sea on July 16$^{th.}$'

'I'm very sorry to hear that,' said Oliver Matthews, his piggy little eyes meeting Peggy's steely gaze.

After finalizing the last details, Peggy paid the fee and, tucking the birth certificate into her basket, wearily made her way back out into the cold October afternoon. At least Ellen wouldn't have to face a fine now for not registering Alice's birth as the new law demanded. Peggy supposed this was progress.

She had two more stops to make on her way back to Rope Walk. She checked her basket for her purse and then pulled her bonnet down over her ears as the wind did its best to dislodge it. She shivered and increased her pace as she wended her way down the narrow streets that led to the quays. She had heard that her contact was in town. She hoped he wouldn't keep her waiting too long as she could no longer feel her toes. She need not have worried. Niko wasn't wanting to hang about in the damp Irish weather. His brown eyes darted around as he greeted Peggy and handed her a brown paper package wrapped with string. With the other hand, he secreted the coins she had handed him.

'A pleasure doing business with you Senora' he said in his sing-song voice, inclining his head slightly.

'And you, Niko. Safe travels and enjoy your stay in Drogheda. Go carefully now.'

She winked at him, for she knew where he was headed next. To one of the many inns that dotted the streets around the quays which catered for the sailors and workers associated with the thriving town. She watched him as he set off briskly in the direction of the spill of light from Jem Clancy's bar, the home of the best whiskey in the area.

Peggy turned and walked in the opposite direction. Her next encounter wouldn't be so pleasant. Meeting Ellen's mother always left her in a bad mood, itching to shake the silly woman who was denied her daughter and grandchildren all because of her pride and her fear of her bloated buffoon of a husband. It was hard to believe that Ellen was the child of those two fools. Passing down West Street, Peggy stopped at the pawnbrokers. Holding her breath, she scanned the window display and then slowly exhaled. It was still there, her wedding ring that she had pawned out of necessity. Ellen had no money coming in now that Jim was gone. It really was a terrible state of affairs. She was going to have to get a bit tough with Ellen very soon as they couldn't go on much longer. The money she had received from Jim's final pay packet wouldn't last much beyond Christmas. Tommy was a growing lad, and Alice was hungrier by the day.

Panting slightly, Peggy made her way through the early morning crowds towards Bolton Square. As usual, the Drogheda streets were busy with folks of all shapes and sizes, ragged orphans, pedlars, sailors, furtive-looking miscreants, the rich and the working class like herself. They were all out today, Peggy noted, as a waft of cologne competed with the stench of an unwashed body. As she grew closer, the cacophony of sounds from the market square grew louder. The vendors were all trying to out-shout each other, dogs were barking, children laughing and squabbling. Neighbours gossiped and deals were done. A vagabond eyed up an unsuspecting woman, no doubt waiting for the opportunity to relieve her of her purse. Occasionally, the squawk of a cockerel, the quack of a duck or the squeal of a pig ripped through the din. The vegetable market was a completely open area bound by the Green Lanes, Magdalene Street and Fair Street. Peggy knew it had been used for military exercises down through the years, and she cast a glance up at the small army barracks that stood miserably on its own as if in protest at the noise. Rotting cabbage leaves, horse manure and other long-neglected rubbish formed a carpet on the ground. The smell of sweet hay, fish and the clay that cloaked mounds of potatoes, rose to tickle Peggy's nostrils. She scanned the crowd for the skinny frame of Ellen's mother. There she was, skulking at the back of one of the stalls. With a sigh, Peggy made her way over. Eyes darting furtively around in case anyone should see her, Brigid Sarsfield wrung her hands as Peggy approached.

'How is she? How are my grandchildren?'

'They are as good as can be expected.' answered Peggy.

Never one to beat about the bush, she added, 'But the money has nearly run out and Tommy is a growing lad. He'll be needing a pair of boots very soon. And his trousers are flapping around his shins. It's a poor lookout when his own flesh and blood couldn't be bothered to get to know him. A fine young lad he is'

'We've been through this before' whined Brigid, her expression a mixture of anxiety and defensiveness, her thin lips working their way into a bitter line of self-pity. 'Paddy won't hear tell of helping out. He says she made her bed and has to lie on it.'

A ball of fury was warming Peggy's innards. How these stupid people couldn't see what they were missing out on was beyond her. All because Ellen ran away and married Jim Cooney against their wishes. He had been a sailor, but that wasn't the problem. Patrick Sarsfield had made plenty of money from seafarers, having built a business around exporting candles and other general goods. Oh no, the trouble stemmed from where Jim Cooney had come from, not the man he was. Patrick Sarsfield had claimed Jim's father had cheated him out of money ten years previously. Ellen and Jim had eloped. Since then, she had been cut off by her parents. Brigid didn't have the gumption to stand up to the great Paddy Sarsfield and make him see the error of his ways. And now, even though his daughter was in mourning and her young family was in danger of starvation, he still wouldn't swallow his pride to help out.

'Take this, it's all I can spare. Paddy would notice anything more', Brigid thrust a few coins into Peggy's hand. And with that, she turned on her heel and walked away, keeping her head hidden under her brown woollen scarf. She was soon swallowed up by the crowd of traders and customers.

Peggy pocketed the coins and turned to face the hill that would bring her back home. It was getting harder to climb the bloody thing. Her right knee was giving her gyp. Tommy would be in from school soon and would need something hot to eat and Alice would need her milk, and a cuddle. She loved her little adopted family. Her dead husband had pickled himself in porter and whiskey and they had never been blessed with children of their own. Peggy prided herself on knowing a thing or two about herbs and potions. Even the various things she had secreted in his food down through the years had not been any help in her quest for a child of their own. So, now, Ellen, Tommy and Alice were her family. She had no patience with the clowns and shirkers of the world, but for the ones she cared about, she had a heart as big as the ocean. She slowly made her way home, stopping to chat occasionally with some of the townsfolk. She had bought a bag of apples at the market and her mouth watered at the thought of the way the juices would slide down the back of her throat. She needed something to wet her whistle as she was now panting like one of the steam engines that crossed the new railway bridge, bringing the wealthy from Dublin to Belfast. Turning onto Rope Walk, she prayed she could tempt Ellen to eat something. The poor lass was gone to skin and bone.

CHAPTER 4

Ellen

Ellen brought Jim's shirt to her nose and breathed in deeply. The cotton was beginning to lose its stiffness, as it had been scarcely out of her hands for the past number of weeks. She inhaled again, and a tendril of panic started to weave its way to her throat making her whimper.

'No, no!' Ellen rose quickly and went to rummage in the bag of Jim's belongings that Captain Symonds had given to her. She frantically took out garment after garment, sniffing each one with mounting hysteria. She couldn't get his scent from any of them. Two shirts, two pairs of pantaloons, a neckerchief, one woollen jumper and three pairs of socks. And not a trace of his smell remained on any of them. She fell to her knees sobbing, flung each item away with all the strength her weakened frame could muster.

The anger came on her in waves and at the most unexpected moments. She'd be absently stirring soup when all of a sudden, the urge to turn the whole pot upside down and hurl it at the wall would grip her fiercely. How could he leave her? How dare he? When they had such a happy future to look forward to! She had always felt anchored by his strength and solidness. The certainty that no matter what, he was hers and she, his. The world could throw what it liked at them, but they wouldn't falter. They were rock solid. He had been worth everything she had given up to be with him. Night after night, his tender whispers as they lay together, caused whatever annoyance the day had brought her to unfurl and dissipate like a wisp of smoke. How could she go on without him? How could it be so that the flesh of his arms, his chest, were being eaten away by fish; the bones of his sensitive fingers were leaching and crumbling at the bottom of the sea?

Almost as quickly as it had possessed her, the anger left, leaving Ellen spent. In the half-light from the only candle in the room, she saw Tommy standing stock-still near the settle. It looked like he was trying to figure out if it was safe to come close. She knew he needed comfort, that his whole world had been rocked to its foundations by his Da's death. But she hadn't the room in her head for his grief as well as her own. She turned her gaze from her son to the solid form of Peggy who was sleeping on the floor in the corner, dead to the world. She sensed, rather than saw Tommy steal quietly back into his bed. She knew he was probably lying there in the half light, bewildered and scared, but there was nothing she could do about it. With a sigh, she crossed the room to her infant daughter who had been awoken by the commotion and was working herself up into an indignant frenzy.

CHAPTER 5

Tommy

'Your Da's fish-food, your Da's fish food!' Billy Molloy's taunt rang out.

He was really in for it this time. Tommy was going to bash his brains out. No, even better, he was going to capture him, tie bunches of nettles all over his body and then squeeze him through his Mam's mangle until he was as flat as one of the horse manure pancakes on the street. He'd be sorry then!

'I bet he's inside a whale's belly! But the whale would spit him out because he tastes rotten!'

Ever since Tommy's Da had gone to heaven, Billy had been even worse than usual, waiting to trip Tommy up and giving him sneaky pinches and punches whenever he passed with his sidekicks, Joey and Crusty Christy. Three right ugly mugs they were. One long, one short with Billy in the middle. Billy had only one front tooth. One had been knocked out by the boyfriend of one of his sisters. He'd been caught looking at them kissing behind the tower near the mill. Tommy had heard Billy say that they had been making a slurping noise like the river made when it slapped up against the quayside.

Christy was long and lanky with a constantly dripping nose. Master O'Donnell was always telling him to blow it, but he never had a hanky, so he usually ended up with a hard crust of green stuff on his sleeve. Tommy was the one who had given him the name 'Crusty Christy'. Tommy seemed to be able to think of words more quickly than anyone else in his class. His Mam had taught him all his letters even before he'd started school. Billy called him 'teacher's pet' just because he could answer most of Master O'Donnell's questions and do his sums really quickly in his head. Johnny, Tommy's best friend reckoned that his cleverness was one of the reasons Billy hated him so much. And, also, because he looked older than nearly seven. He was as tall as some of the nine-year-olds in the school. Billy was shorter and sometimes went around on tippytoes to make himself look bigger.

At Billy's words, the dark feeling in Tommy's belly bubbled up and spilled uncontrollably to his chest, down his arms and legs, reaching his fists and feet. He launched himself at Billy, pummelling him faster and faster, harder and harder.

'DON'T. YOU. SAY. THAT. ABOUT. MY. DA!'

Tommy landed a blow for each word. It felt really good. It took Billy a second to react, and he swung his fist, hoping to land it in Tommy's gut. Johnny grabbed his arm before it got to land and twisted it behind his back. That left Tommy free to give Billy one final push. With Johnny's foot waiting behind to trip him over, Billy went sprawling to the ground. Tommy and Johnny had practiced this '*arm-push-trip*' movement many times when they were play-fighting up at the mill. The two friends sped off up the hill towards home, legs going like pistons, breath coming fast and hard. Billy was left in an angry heap on the ground as Joey and Crusty Christy stared after the duo with their mouths open. The knot that was in Tommy's chest felt just a tiny bit looser. Tommy and Johnny glanced over their shoulders as they ran. No sign of Billy and his two eejits.

'Coast's clear' declared Johnny.

'That showed him,' Tommy shouted as his breathing started to get back to normal, throwing a grateful glance over at his friend.

'He went down like a big ugly sack of grain', laughed Johnny, imitating Billy's fall.

Tommy knew his friend was trying very hard to make him laugh because he guessed he had looked really sad since his Da had drowned. Johnny's own Da was big, had hard muscles, and a wide, cheery smile. Johnny had said he couldn't imagine not seeing his Da ever again. Tommy could feel his sad face coming back the closer he got to his house. His Mam spent all her time crying or feeding Alice. Sometimes, his Mam's big tears dripped down onto Alice's face and made her squirm like a wriggly worm. No matter what he did, his Mam didn't seem to *see* Tommy. She didn't talk to him anymore. She didn't sing. He used to love it when she sang him a song when he was going to sleep. Like a lullaby. It was as if a storm had come and the wind had crept in under the door of their house and sucked the fun out of his Mam and left a sad person who didn't smile, didn't eat, barely spoke and when she did, it was in a whisper. She didn't even get mad these days. She just sat there, staring at the wall, or out the window. Peggy looked exasperated at times. He had learned that word recently. He'd seen it in a book. He'd asked Peggy if she was exasperated with his Mam. Or maybe with him? Peggy had taken him in her arms, hugging him to her big chest. She had told him that she could never be exasperated with him, that she was a teeny bit worried about his Mam, but that she was bound to get better soon. He really hoped so. It was bad enough that he had to feel so sad about his Da without feeling sad about his Mam as well. Alice smiled at him a lot, though. He even made her laugh when he pulled funny faces. She was alright, even if she was a girl.

Tommy reached his front door and turned to his pal. 'See ya tomorrow, Johnny. Thanks for helping with... ya know.'

'We are the kings of *Tredagh*!' shouted Johnny as he whooped and ran in a circle around Tommy. 'We will fight all our foes, including Billy Molloy, to the death!'

Laughing, Tommy watched his friend gallop off down the street, turn left and disappear around the corner. He was very lucky to have a good friend like Johnny. He knew Johnny would stick up for him no matter what. He drew in a deep breath of the damp November air. He hoped his Mam was in better form today. At least Alice would be pleased to see him.

CHAPTER 6

Larry

New York, September 1864

Laurence Clinton checked his reflection in the barber's mirror on Jacobus Street. He lifted his chin and turned it first to the left and then to the right, checking for stray stubble under his jawbone. He needn't have worried, for Jorge, the German barber took an obsessive pride in his work.

'Is gut, ja?' enquired Jorge, his blue eyes under a furrowed brow scrutinizing Larry's face for any trace of any rogue hair.

'Absolutely wonderful, my fine man' Larry winked at Jorge in the mirror, his brown eyes glinting in the sun that flooded the shop. *I need feeding up a bit,* thought Larry as he caught sight of the angles of his cheekbones. Jorge whipped the towel from around his neck and Larry stood up, filling the small space with his six-foot frame and broad shoulders. He took out his wallet to pay. As he left the shop, he flexed his biceps and a bolt of pure gratitude shot through him as he thought of all the poor men, who had lost limbs in the war between the Confederates and the Yankees. Oh yes, he was lucky to still have two arms and two legs of his own after the last four years.

Making sure his wallet was well secreted in his tweed jacket, he started whistling an Irish jig. You could be robbed in the blink of an eye in this city. It had happened to some of his mates. New York and his hometown, Drogheda, had a lot in common. They were both busy port towns, but New York was something else. Close to one million people lived here: different colours and creeds from all corners of the world. The Italians were coming in their hundreds, mixing with the Irish and the Jewish. Lots of his own countrymen and women had escaped famine-stricken Ireland in the 1840s and had settled in the hellish tenements. He had unwittingly wandered into that area a couple of weeks previously and had been utterly shocked by the squalor. That was not the life he wanted for himself. Some of the Irish had managed to upgrade their existence and move out of the slums. Anyone who was prepared to work could make something of themselves in this big city. There was work for all sorts of tradesmen. Larry had asked around if a stone mason might get a job. He was gratified to see they were in demand. There was a shop here, the biggest one that Larry had ever seen, a full city block with eight floors and nineteen departments, built by some man called Stewart. Larry had wandered in and had spent a couple of hours walking around, mesmerized at the fine wool and cotton scarves and shirts, the silk ties and kerchiefs in a rainbow of colours. He vowed that, in the not-too-distant future, he would have enough money to return and buy himself that peacock blue silk shirt that felt so deliciously soft to the touch. And one day, he would have a fine woman on his arm, just like the ones he saw browsing through the ladies' department. He was sure of it. He had had his share of female company down through the years in England and here in America but none of them had ever made him want to stay.

But first, he had to return home to Drogheda. He had been away for four long years. It had been hell at times, freezing cold during the winter, enough to make you think your toes and fingertips were never going to feel again, and hot enough in summertime to fry an egg on the sole of your boot. No doubt about it, America was a beautiful place. Mountains, creeks, rivers, an unbelievably blue sky. He'd had an encounter with a black bear once. The bear and himself had eyeballed each other from opposite sides of a fast-running creek. Larry had been washing and the bear had been fishing. Both had frozen. Larry's mate, Danny, had fired a shot into the air and the bear had turned and ambled away into the trees, its brown fur rippling in the sunlight. Larry had thanked Danny and his guardian angel for a lucky escape. The buzzards would have had no problem stripping the flesh from his bones. He knew he'd been spared because he had a job to do.

He might have the appearance of a gentleman, but he was well-versed in fighting now - well enough to return home and teach others what he'd learned. Other surviving Irishmen would be joining him in the weeks ahead; all, with one common cause in mind – to join the Fenian ranks and show the English what the Irish were made of. For too long, his people had been suppressed, impoverished, even starved to death by their nearest neighbours. It was time for the tide to turn. Next week, he would be setting sail, homeward bound. He felt his heart swell at the thought of seeing his beautiful homeland again with its green fields, bogs, mountains and holy wells. The only fly in the ointment was that he would have to let Nicholas know he was home. He felt the familiar surge of resentment which always assailed him when he thought of his older brother.

He increased his pace as he pushed through the crowded streets, a cacophony of sounds assaulting his ears. A rumble in his stomach reminded him that he hadn't eaten since morning. As if on cue, the smell of roasting meat reached his nostrils. Whatever it was, it smelled good. Literally following his nose, Larry turned towards a row of eating-houses, finding the best looking one. After he had filled his belly, he would take a wander down to the part of the city where he knew he might find someone with whom to while away a couple of hours. Patting his chest to make sure his wallet was still there, he thanked Mr. Lincoln for his wages. Ah yes, he was lucky. Life was good. He had a job to do when he got home. He had to make sure he was well fortified. The chicken brought out to him by a dark-haired beauty sure looked good. He felt the saliva wet his mouth. Oblivious to the admiring glances thrown his way, he sat down to satisfy his most pressing appetite. The other one would be satisfied later.

CHAPTER 7

Ellen

'Ah Peggy, it's no use. I just can't make it sit right!' Ellen scowled at her reflection in the small hand mirror she held. Peggy stifled a giggle.

'Are you laughing at me?', Ellen's tone was petulant.

'It's just that you look a bit like little Tommy when he's in a strop about something! Come here and I'll see what I can do about that wayward head of hair.'

Ellen's expression went from indignant to grateful in the space of a few seconds. The past few weeks had been so hard. It felt like her heart had been literally ripped out of her body before it was shoved back into her chest, but in the wrong place. It was still beating, but with a heavy, slow thud. She felt like she was wading through a bog, her feet heavy and leaden, every single movement a supreme effort.

She still couldn't believe she would never see her Jim again. He filled every thought from the moment she woke up until the moment she closed her eyes at night. Not that she was getting much sleep. Sorrow had seeped into every cell of her body and was now weighing her down, even making her skin sag. If it wasn't for Peggy, she dreaded to think where she would be. Probably at the bottom of the sea like her Jim.

She had fantasised about going down to the beach a few miles away and wading into the foamy water. In her dreams, she welcomed it reaching her ankles, her knees, making her skirt swirl and billow. It would cover her shoulders next, then her chin and eventually, her head. The noise in her ears would be deafening and then she would experience a sweet nothingness. The tide would bring her out to sea, and her body would somehow find Jim's in the middle of the Pacific Ocean where they would lie together for all eternity. Even the fact that she had two children who depended on her hadn't been enough at times to bring her out of the pit of despair she was in. The poor little craythurs didn't deserve the mother she had turned into this past couple of months. Peggy had stepped into the breach. Until one day, her friend had lost patience with her.

'Lass, you've got to snap out of this fug that you're in! You have two little ones relying on you. You're all they've got now.' Peggy had let out a sigh that had seemed to come from her boots. 'You have to be Mam and Da to them now. Poor Tommy is trying to be brave, but he's only six Ellen! A wee child. Don't turn your back on the little mite. I can't bear to see his eyes so sad.' Peggy was nearly in tears. Her words had been like a slap to Ellen's face.

'But, Peggy, I don't want to go on without Jim!".

'I know your heart is in pieces Ellen,' Peggy's blue eyes had filled up. 'You have to just put one foot in front of the other, take one breath at a time. If you keep practicing this, one day, you'll find that you can breathe easy by yourself for a whole day and that your legs are just that little bit lighter. You have to keep going for your children. It would break Jim's heart to think that his little loves were being neglected. Harsh words, I know but they have to be said.' Peggy put up a gnarled hand to stop Ellen retorting. 'Now, what are you going to do for money?'

'Rob the bank, maybe.' Ellen's response was wooden.

'I don't think you'd last too long down the gaol, lass. They'd shear off your hair and make you wear a sack of grey and it's not your colour.'

Ellen had thrown back her head and examined the work of a spider in the corner of the room. 'If only I were that spider', Ellen had sighed. 'He has nothing to worry about but where to spin his web.'

'Aye, but he will live this winter and maybe next and that'll be his lot. You have a lifetime to live yet, lass.'

'All right, Peggy, you win. I know I've not been a proper Mam to Tommy and Alice, and I promise to do better. You know I love them both more than anything? They're all I have left of Jim.' Squaring her shoulders, she had said. 'Now, have you any wild suggestions as to where I might get myself a job? I don't care if I eat, but Tommy and Alice have to get fed. You're right, Jim would never forgive me if I let them starve.'

Ellen had shivered as she thought of the workhouse across the river. She could never, ever allow things to get so bad that they ended up there. Families were separated once they passed through the big iron gates. Alice and Tommy would be taken off her. If that happened, there would be no point in living. She knew there wasn't much of Jim's last wages left in the jar on the mantlepiece. She needed to do something to earn money. She desperately wanted Tommy to stay at school. But, if she didn't find a job, he might have to leave and go to work. That would have broken Jim's heart. His eyes used to shine so proudly at how well Tommy knew his letters, and how quickly he could do sums in his head. No, she owed it to Jim to shake herself out of this fog of grief she was in and provide for her family. She would just have to find the backbone from somewhere.

'Now, that looks better.' Peggy had finally tamed Ellen's hair. 'I don't suppose you'd consider...?' Peggy's voice had faltered.

'Not a chance, Peggy. Don't even ask.' Ellen had absolutely no intention of asking her parents for help. Her Da was a bully and her Mam, a coward. She wanted nothing to do with them. She might reconsider if the poorhouse beckoned, but it would be a last resort.

'All right. Keep your hair on.' Peggy had patted Ellen gently on the hand and declared that she had a plan. Peggy was a great woman for a plan.

And so, here Ellen was, on a crisp November morning, a week after Peggy had given her the talking to, getting her hair and clothes all fixed up so that she could go up to the mill owned by Mr. Nicholas Clinton to look for a job. Clinton was one of four mill owners in the town. He was a widower, and Peggy had suggested Ellen try here first for employment as Clinton might have a bit of sympathy for her, having two daughters just a little bit younger than her. Also, the word on the street was that he was a kinder, more careful employer than some of the other mill owners in the town. There weren't as many accidents as his establishment.

Looking as presentable as possible, Ellen kissed Tommy and Alice in turn and left the house to walk to Clinton's mill, a good twenty minutes away. It was a very busy day in the town, with the usual early morning mixture of workers heading off for their daily shifts at the mills, the brewery, the tannery, the shipyard and the docks. Tall and small, some walked swiftly, some limped, some puffed and panted, occasionally hawking out fibres from their lungs onto the ground. Children, some of them barefoot, marched in twos and threes towards the school, the cold wind making them move a bit more smartly than usual. A steady stream of children also walked towards the mills. They were from families that couldn't afford the luxury of school when there was a wage to be earned, even though dodging in and out under the mill machinery was a very precarious way to make a few bob. Ellen joined the crowd heading east. She hurried along, her best mantle keeping some of the chill out.

As she turned a corner, facing into a bitter wind, Ellen stared down the street. *It couldn't be!* Breathing hard, she broke into a run, her boots making a ringing sound on the hard cobbles. People were milling all around her in the bright crisp sunshine, but she was impervious to them all.

'Watch yourself missus, you nearly knocked me over' an old man grumbled, righting himself and throwing her a grumpy glance.

'Jim, wait, Jim!' Ellen eventually caught up with the man she had spotted in the crowd. She put her hand on his arm, and he swung around in surprise. The look he gave her was quizzical.

'What you want missus?'

His eyes and the shape of his nose were all wrong. It wasn't Jim at all.

'I'm sorry, I thought you were someone else', Ellen mumbled. Her heart gave a few unsteady beats as she turned away, tears blinding her. She really needed to stop doing this – thinking that she could see Jim in every crowd. It was just that she was finding it hard to really believe that he was gone. She hadn't seen his body, hadn't had a proper funeral for him. Who's to say Captain Symonds was mistaken, and that Jim had found something to cling onto - a piece of driftwood, and he had been picked up by another ship and was making his way back to Drogheda?

It wasn't him today in the crowd and it hadn't been him last week at the docks. He wasn't coming home. She had to accept that. That man had looked at her just then as if she was a bit looney. She couldn't blame him. She would have to catch hold of herself. She couldn't have people thinking she was fit for the madhouse. What would happen to Tommy and Alice then?

Her heartbeat had almost returned to normal as she turned and joined the throng making its way up the hill to Clinton's Mill. She glanced up at the two big chimneys that dominated the skyline. The building looked unfriendly, aloof, like it was looking down its nose at her. Squaring her shoulders, Ellen stuck her tongue out at the white façade.

'You won't make me feel like I'm not good enough!' she said out loud. A few heads turned to look at the crazy woman who seemed to be talking to thin air. She made her way up to the stone steps and in the big wooden door that was painted dark green. It needed freshening up, she noticed.

The noise inside the mill was the loudest thing Ellen had ever heard. She had just walked into a seething den of noise and heat. Standing stock-still, she looked around her in bewilderment. People pushed past her, and she realized that if she didn't get out of the way she ran the risk of being knocked over. Finding a friendly face, she went over to a middle-aged man and shouted, 'Excuse me mister. I'm after a job.'

The man looked her up and down, paused for a second and then nodded his head in the direction of a wooden partition on the other side of the floor. 'Go over yonder and ask for Mr. Menton' he said with a nod.

Ellen made her way purposefully across the floor, trying to look more confident than she felt. Her nerve had nearly deserted her. She was about to knock on the partition, but her hand froze in mid-air. What was she doing? She had no experience, having been married to Jim since she was eighteen, and a mother just over a year later. Jim had prided himself in providing for his family and she hadn't had to leave the house to go to work like most of the other women she knew. She was a fool to think that anyone would want to employ her. Skill-less and spineless, that's what she was. She turned on her heel and had started to flee when she collided with a woman twice her size and with a shock of blonde, frizzy hair.

'Oi, watch where you're going!'

Winded, Ellen apologized. Between the shock of thinking she had seen Jim on the street, and now the mixture of emotions swirling in her gut, she was a wreck and on the verge of tears. As if sensing her fragile emotional state, the blonde woman stopped and looked properly at Ellen

'Are you alright?'

'I'm fine', Ellen sniffed, feeling a tear threatening in the corner of her eye and a tell-tale sob making its way from her chest up through her throat.

'You sure don't look it. Haven't seen you here before.'

The woman's eyes swept over Ellen. Her nerves raw, and fed-up at being scrutinized closely for the second time in as many minutes, Ellen felt a ripple of indignation rising up from her toes.

'What is it with all you mill workers that you have to look me up and down like that?' scowled Ellen. 'Anyone would swear that I had two heads!'

Time stood still for a moment while the woman decided whether she was going to take offence of not. A big belly laugh erupted from her, lighting up her face.

'Ah, sorry, I suppose it's working in the mill that does it. We're always eyeing up people's clothes and when we see a fine piece of fabric, we might examine it a bit more than is mannerly. Molly White's the name. What brings you here anyway?'

Sniffing, Ellen took the big, warm, chapped hand that was offered to her.

'I'm here to see about a job. I was told to go and speak with Mr. Menton.'

'Ah yes, he's in there, in his little kingdom,' she said nodding in the direction of the partition. Seeing Ellen's hesitation she said, 'Well, what are you waiting for? He doesn't bite. Remember, he's just a man!' With a gentle push, Molly propelled Ellen towards the partition and waited until Ellen rapped loudly.

'Enter!' bellowed a voice. Ellen peeked her way around the partition and was met by a pale, gaunt, pock-marked face. A pair of beady black eyes looked out at her from underneath a pair of very bushy eyebrows.

'Yes?' barked the man, looking up from a dusty looking ledger.

'I've come to see about a job,' muttered Ellen.

'What did you say?' he roared. 'I can't bloody lip-read. You'll have to speak up.'

Ellen cleared her throat and tried again. 'I've come to see about a job,' she said, raising her voice.

'A job, is it? And what experience might you have, missus?' The skinny man's eyes rested on the gold band around Ellen's finger. Nervously twisting the ring, Ellen admitted that she had none.

'Then what the hell are you doing wasting my time? This is a business I'm running in case you haven't noticed. We only take on experienced staff here unless you want to clean the privies?'

His mocking laugh and derisive snort made something spark in Ellen. How dare he make little of her. Jim would box his lights out if he were here. She drew herself up to her full height, looked him in the eye and stated: 'I can read and write, unlike most of the people out there on the floor, I'll wager. And I can do sums in my head quicker than anyone else I know.'

'Can you now?', a speculative look came over George Menton's face. Focusing on Ellen, he said. 'We may have just the job for a fine-looking woman like yourself' he declared. 'Come with me.'

He unfurled his spider-like legs and drew himself up to his full height, which Ellen guessed was six feet, even with the slight hump in his back. She followed him out onto the floor as he scuttled around, barking orders at some of the workers. She had to make sure she looked at where she was going as the ground was strewn with reels of thread, bales of linen and boxes. Small, skinny children ran in and out under the machines, dicing with death. She supposed the nimbler they were, the better they were at their job. She vowed that her Tommy and Alice would never have to do such a dangerous thing to earn a few bob. She caught Molly's eye and got a big wink and a cheeky smile. Ellen couldn't help but smile back.

She followed 'Spider' Menton, as she had named him, up a steep set of wooden stairs to an office. What with the heat and her nervousness, a bead of sweat was beginning to form on Ellen's top lip. They came to a wooden door with the name 'Nicholas Clinton' written on it in gold letters. 'Spider' rapped smartly on the door and entered without waiting for an invitation.

'Wait here,' he said. Through the gap in the open door, Ellen could see him speaking to the person in the room who Ellen knew was *The* Nicholas Clinton, mill owner and general 'rich-person-about-town'. She had seen him a few times over the years, mostly out and about with his two daughters, but had never made his acquaintance. Well, that was about to change.

'Well, don't just stand there, missus, come in!' Menton growled.

Ellen took a deep breath and walked into the room. It wasn't very big, but it was a man's room and no mistake. There were a couple of shelves with massive ledgers on them, some green, marked 'Debtors', and some red, marked 'Creditors'. A musky scent of cologne hung in the air. The furniture was sparse - just a big wooden desk with a chair in front. The desk was neat and tidy, with an inkwell, a fountain pen and a pad arranged neatly in formation. Behind the desk, sitting in a green leather chair was Nicholas Clinton. His russet hair was still abundant, despite the fact that Ellen guessed he must be near fifty. His waistline was still relatively slim, and his fashionable clothes were immaculate. He observed Ellen with a piercing gaze which she decided to meet with an equally steady one of her own.

'This woman is looking for a job and says she can read and write and do sums as good as anyone,' 'Spider' Menton broke the silence.

'And what is this young lady's name?' one russet eyebrow arched enquiringly at Ellen.

'It's Mrs. Ellen Cooney.'

She made sure that Clinton could see the gold wedding band around the third finger of her left hand. Something told her it wouldn't be a good idea to let this man know that she was a widow. Nicholas raised his eyes to meet Ellen's and paused before raising himself from his chair to proffer a hand.

'Pleased to make your acquaintance, Mrs. Cooney' he said smoothly.

Ellen didn't like the way he was looking at her. Certainly not in a fatherly way. Peggy had miscalculated that one! As Ellen shook the mill-owner's hand, 'Spider' Menton backed out of the room, silently, a satisfied look in his beady eyes.

CHAPTER 8

Clinton's Mill

Drogheda

Nicholas Clinton's eyes remained fastened on Ellen's as he gestured for her to have a seat. Ellen was well used to having men look her up and down and usually paid them no heed, but there was something disconcerting about the intensity of this man's stare. She wondered if, one hundred years from now, women like her would have to put up with such scrutiny on a daily basis. She knew she was pretty enough but wasn't one for using it to her advantage. But then, she might have to change her way of operating. Look at how her life had altered in such a short space of time. Here she was, a widow with two young children and having to look for a job to keep them all from starving. Jim's face swam before her eyes. *'Now don't be intimidated by this fella. He'd be lucky to have you.'* Ellen could hear his summary of the situation she found herself in, and it made her sit a little straighter in her seat and meet Clinton's gaze full on.

'So, you're looking for a job, Mrs. Cooney?'

'Yes, Mr. Clinton, I am.' Ellen unconsciously straightened her collar.

'Very well then, I shall conduct an interview, seeing as you have dressed for the occasion. Why don't you remove your mantle if you're too warm?' his tawny eyes held a hint of laughter.

Ellen was indeed feeling quite warm as the stove in the corner seemed to send out a heat that was rather overwhelming. She debated whether she should remove her mantle as she felt it was acting as a kind of protective shield. But she couldn't stand the heat any longer, so she stood gingerly, and placed it on the back of her chair. Sitting down again, she shivered involuntarily.

'Are you cold?'

'No, not at all. Perhaps I'm a little nervous as I have never been interviewed for a job before,' Ellen tried to muster up a confident looking smile.

'Ah, I see. So, you don't have much experience then, I take it? In that case, what makes you think that you would be an asset to my business?'

Nicholas sat back in his seat, his fingers in a steeple just under his nose. Ellen noticed that his fingernails were very clean, and his hands were peppered with little russet-coloured hair and freckles. Strong looking hands, but not rough like her Jim's had been. His had been permanently chapped, despite the lotions that Peggy had used to try and heal up the nicks and cuts the ropes inflicted on him every time he went to sea.

'I'm not afraid of hard work, I'm very trustworthy. I can read and write and do sums in my head as quick as a flash.'

Ellen looked at the ledgers on the shelves and the papers that seemed to have been hastily shoved into a drawer. Nicholas Clinton might seem to have everything under control, but she'd wager that it was all a bit of an act.

'If you don't mind me saying, Mr. Clinton, you could do with a bit of help with your filing system.'

'How very observant of you, Mrs. Cooney. My paperwork has indeed suffered a bit over the past few weeks since my last assistant had to leave.'

'Oh, was that a sudden departure?' Ellen enquired innocently, holding her breath for the answer. She figured that her predecessor most likely had had a very good reason for leaving and she wasn't at all sure she wanted to know why.

'Silly girl decided she wanted to go off and get married.'

Nicholas's eyes travelled once more down to the glinting band of gold on Ellen's finger. She decided honesty was the best policy,

'I'm a widow, Mr. Clinton. My husband Jim drowned at sea in July. I have two small children to take care of. I need a job, plain and simple, or we just might starve.'

Ellen couldn't get used to saying 'widow'. It was such a brutal and ugly word. The fact that she *was* one was something that she found very hard to believe. She took a breath, fully expecting to have Clinton send her on her way, as he would most likely consider a woman with two young children a liability. But instead, she caught a glimpse of sympathy in his gaze. He seemed to be making up his mind about something. After about ten seconds, he sat up straighter in his chair.

'Well, we can't have those wee ones of yours going hungry now, can we? How about you start here in the office tomorrow morning at 8 o'clock and we will see how you get on? I can't promise you a permanent job, but if we rub along nicely together, it just might work out. Do we have a deal?'

'A job here in the office?'

After mentioning what her wages would be, Nicholas put out his hand.

He chuckled. Ellen's surprise must have shown on her face. The most that she had hoped for, despite all her talk about being good at sums, was a job supervising the poor wee children out on the mill floor who risked life and limb every day, dodging in and out under the thundering machinery. Pulling herself together, she sat up a bit straighter and took his hand in hers. It was warm and dry.

'Yes, Mr. Clinton. We have a deal. I promise, you won't regret it.'

Ellen firmly shook his hand to seal the deal and smiled for the first time in what seemed like weeks. Relief coursed through her veins. She had come up to the mill to ask for a job on the floor and here she was, after landing one as the boss's assistant! It really was quite a stroke of luck. She supposed she had 'Spider' Menton to thank for that one. And her Jim. He must be looking down on her. Just wait until she told Peggy and Tommy. They'd be thrilled! She'd have to get herself a couple of respectable dresses to wear in the office. The wages would be enough to keep them from the poorhouse, but she might need to think about some other way to earn a few bob.

Nicholas stood up to signal that the meeting was at an end. As Ellen busied herself with donning her mantle and buttoning it up, he let his eyes swarm all over her. She really was a very gorgeous creature. So, she was the widow of the young fella who had drowned out foreign. He had heard about the tragedy but couldn't picture Jim Cooney's face. Ah well, the Lord moved in mysterious ways. He had Him to thank for bringing Mrs. Ellen Cooney into his life. Bowing slightly, he wondered what it would be like to make her Mrs. Nicholas Clinton.

'Good day Mr. Clinton. I will see you tomorrow at eight.' Ellen's expression was warmer than when she had first arrived at the office. She turned to make her way towards the door.

'See you tomorrow, Mrs. Cooney. I shall look forward to working with you.' Ellen walked through the door with her head held at a proud tilt. Nicholas sank back into his chair. He stretched, with his hands behind his head, and for the next ten minutes, he was occupied by all sorts of scenarios playing out in his head. Ellen Cooney was front and centre in all of them. Snapping himself out of his daydream, he focused on his ledgers. He needed to concentrate on business now. These damned figures were not behaving themselves and he couldn't for the life of him figure out why.

CHAPTER 9

Larry

Drogheda, December 1864

'A pint, is it?'

'Yes, and make it a good one please. None of that stuff from the bottom of the barrel.'

'Right you be.'

The pint was served up to him and Larry downed it in one go.

'Another one if you don't mind.' The bar tender obliged with an obsequious bow. Licking his lips and relishing the way the liquid soothed the back of his throat, Larry looked around. The establishment was medium sized, with the usual wooden benches and tables, some of which bore the scars of drunken disagreements that had turned physical. There was a piece of sackcloth covering one of the windows. A big fire burned in the hearth, warming the room and heightening the smell of body odour that hung like a will 'o the wisp in the stale air. But still, this was probably one of the better alehouses in town. It was warm and had a mostly jolly air. Larry had yet to make acquaintance with the few new ones that had opened since the last time he had walked around the familiar streets of his hometown, which seemed like a lifetime ago.

It was crowded tonight, with everyone intent on drinking away the extra few shillings they had got in their Christmas pay. The atmosphere was rowdy, guffaws of laughter erupting every now and again and with much back slapping going on. In the gloom, he could make out some dusky-skinned men seated at one of the tables. They were gesticulating wildly and chattering away. Italians, he'd wager. Beside them, a few grizzled looking men were loudly discussing the price of the cattle they hoped to get at the next market day. Locals. One of them hawked noisily onto the sawdust covered floor. Shuddering, Larry turned away.

He savoured the second pint and felt his shoulders relax slightly. A loud bang caused him to automatically jump up from his seat and instinctively reach for the rifle slung over his left shoulder. But, of course, it wasn't there any longer. The bang was just the door being nearly taken off its hinges by a rowdy group of men. Welsh by the sounds of them. They brought a blast of icy air in with then. Forcing his breath in and out a few times to slow down his racing heart, Larry sat back down. He wondered if he was destined to be this jumpy for the rest of his life. The man behind the counter was filling glass after glass of ale for the newly arrived crew. They were a motley lot, in very good spirits and Larry watched and listened to the banter as he slowly sipped his drink. One of them was a bit quieter than the rest. Dark-haired and built like a barn, there was something furtive about the way he was darting his eyes around the room, as if he was looking for something or someone. The hairs on the back of Larry's neck prickled. The stranger's skin was swarthy and pockmarked. A pair of coal-black eyes locked on Larry. A bad one and no mistake Larry thought to himself. He had seen his type before. No doubt, a bit of a loner. Had probably suffered at the hands of a bully in his younger years. Wouldn't think anything of kicking a dog to death. The kind of man that would make a dangerous enemy. Larry was first to look away. He was here to relax after all. He wasn't looking for any trouble. The war in America had hardened him up for sure. It had also taught him to trust few and rely on himself. Stealing another glance at the man, Larry found the stranger's eyes still boring into him, but this time the other man was first to look away, a sneer on his thick lips.

'Will your little songbird be here tonight?' shouted a ruddy-faced man with a shock of red hair. 'Ah, indeed she will,' answered the alehouse owner with a broad grin. 'She will be here to warm the cockles of your heart with her sweet tones!'

A roar of approval went up from the men. A bit of entertainment would be nice, Larry thought. Whoever was coming to sing must be something special, judging by the charged atmosphere that had edged into the room at the mention of her. He would just sit back, relax and enjoy the festive cheer. Lord knows he could do with it after the last four Christmases spent freezing in various camps over in America.

'Give us a kiss, handsome!', Larry found himself face to face with a young woman with a shock of blonde hair but very few teeth in her head. She held a bunch of mistletoe over Larry's head.

'Not tonight, thanks', he politely declined.

Looking slightly disappointed, the woman wobbled over to another table where she was grabbed around the waist and hauled onto the lap of a portly-looking sailor with a grey beard. 'Give over with your tickling beard!' she shrieked, laughing.

Someone banged a glass with a spoon, the laughter subsided, and a hush descended on the room. Larry's eyes followed everyone else's to the corner near the fire. A slim figure in a mantle which obscured her face stood beside a man with a fiddle. Theatrically, as if aware of the effect she was having, the figure lowered the hood and slowly undid the bow on the mantle and with a flourish, threw it to one side. Larry's breath caught in his throat as his pulse quickened. Before him, stood the most beautiful woman he had ever seen in his life. Tumbling dark locks framed a sweet dewy-skinned face. Large, luminous eyes swept around the room as if commanding everyone to silence. Larry knew that what he was about to hear would be special. He wasn't disappointed. She took a deep breath and started to sing a ballad of love and loss.

'My bonny is a sailor lad,
He roams the briny sea,
As the tide turns at Tredagh,
Please bring him home to me.'

Her voice was strong and pure, and seemed to swell and fill the room. It was as if she had lived every word she sang. A tear trickled down her cheek, which she quickly wiped away. As the last note died, Larry realised that he had been holding his breath the whole time. He felt his grip tighten on his glass and an unfamiliar feeling flood his veins. The crowd erupted into applause and slowly, Larry joined in. The next song was a jaunty one, everyone clapping along. The next one and the next one, in the same vein. She finished off with '*Silent Night.*' Larry sat, mesmerised. There was something so raw and vulnerable about this young woman. He wanted to fold her into his arms and spend the rest of his life protecting her. There was also something spirited about the angle of her head. It was an intoxicating mixture.

To rapturous applause, she made her way over to the innkeeper who thrust some coins into her hand with a wink.

'Thanks Ellen. That was great, as usual. You really had them in the palm of your hand tonight!'

'Ah, sure, I enjoyed it too' the young woman chuckled.

She was so close to Larry. Sensing his nearness, she turned, and he could see that her eyes were the colour of the sky on a May Day after a shower of rain. A jolt of electricity passed through his body. With a barely perceptible nod, she turned away, and swiftly made her way to the door. Then she was gone. She seemed to take all the air out of the room with her.

The dark-haired man Larry had seen earlier was standing near the door and he slipped out into the night after Ellen. Larry quickly made his way through the throng and, glancing up and down the street, he could just make out the figure of the young woman up ahead and to his left. In the shadows, the man was a few steps behind. He could see her stop and look over her shoulder. She hurried on, the man following her, making ground until he was nearly upon her. Larry followed, the snow and frost underfoot, making it difficult to hurry. A sudden scream pierced the air as Larry saw the man reach out and grab the young woman's arm and swing her round to face him. He quickly put his big hand around her mouth. She was flailing wildly, kicking his shins, but she was no match for the brute. He pulled her into a dark alleyway to the right. Fury burst through Larry, and he felt the icy air burn his lungs as he rounded the corner. He spotted a piece of timber, and picking it up, he smashed it with all his strength on the back of the man's shoulder. With a roar, the man loosened his grip on his victim just enough for her to wriggle free. She landed a full-force kick on her assailant's shin, causing him to hop about, crying out in pain.

'Take that you low life scum!' she roared at him.

His eyes swivelled from Larry to the young woman and back to Larry again. Knowing when he was beaten, he cursed and limped off into the night, swearing noisily. Larry and the young woman turned to face each other. Their breaths mingled in the frosty air.

'Are you alright?'

'Yes, thanks to you. I don't think that encounter would have ended very well for me had you not shown up,' she smiled weakly. 'Still, I imagine he will have a few bruises for his trouble tomorrow!'

'He certainly will.' 'You have a vicious right foot!'

'Ellen Cooney. Pleased to make your acquaintance.' She held out a hand and gave Larry's a firm shake.

'Larry Clinton, delighted to make yours.'

'Well, thanks again Larry. You can let go of my hand now', she smiled. To Larry, it was like the sun had come out from behind a cloud.

Feeling foolish, he released her hand and stepped back.

'Forgive me, I am an idiot. May I see you home? We can't be sure that vagabond isn't lurking somewhere waiting to strike again.'

Ellen looked at Larry, glanced uncertainly over her shoulder and seemed to quickly come to a decision.

'Thank you, Larry Clinton, that would be most kind if it's not too much trouble. It's this way.'

'No trouble at all, Ellen Cooney,' Larry breathed. Together, they turned and walked up the hill towards Rope Walk.

CHAPTER 10

Nicholas

Nicholas Clinton tried to concentrate on the book in front of him, but the figures were swimming before his eyes. There was an intoxicating smell wafting its way up into his nose and making his senses reel. It came from Ellen's hair. She was seated in front of him, poring over one of his ledgers. It was all he could do not to lift a strand of her dark hair and inhale. God, but she was a gorgeous! It seemed she had relaxed slightly since starting work with him. Over the past few weeks, she had seemed to stand just that little bit taller and the look in her eyes wasn't as haunted. He was glad that work at the mill was contributing to her recovery, even though it was in a small way.

He definitely wasn't used to having a woman work in such close proximity to him. Ellen's predecessor hadn't lasted too long, and she had been a plain, slightly sour looking young woman. Nothing to get excited about. But this exquisite creature before him had just made his life worth living again. He couldn't wait to get into work these days, making sure he was there before her. He loved to sit and watch as she breezed her way into the office. He'd pretend he was looking at his ledgers. It was becoming increasingly hard to keep his feelings from showing, and he had to school himself to make his expression neutral whenever she addressed him or asked him a question. She was a quick learner. She asked intelligent questions about the working of the mill and its finances. She had already made a couple of good suggestions about how things could be improved. He suppressed a sigh and tried to concentrate on what Ellen was asking him. She turned her head and looked up at him with those startling blue eyes.

'So, it doesn't seem to make sense, don't you agree?' she said.

'Ahem, yes, Ellen, I see what you mean. Let me give it some thought.'

She opened her mouth as if to say something else, but then seemed to think better of it. She turned away with her lips pressed slightly together. Truth be told, he hadn't heard a word she had said. There had been a rushing sound in his ears brought on by her close proximity. It had been something about invoices and hours that the mill was in production. It was probably something that he would have to have a look at whenever he managed to get a bit of headspace. She was firmly lodged in his thoughts, and he had room for little else these days.

It wasn't as if he was an inexperienced businessman. He had run the linen mill in this town for ages. He had to close a few years previously when it seemed like the cotton industry was destined to take over, but he had re-opened in a fit of optimism a year and a half previously and had managed to resurrect a good bit of trade. George Menton had come down from the north of Ireland, highly recommended, and was now his right-hand man, managing most of the finances whilst Nicholas himself went out and sought new customers. He had probably extended himself a bit too much financially. But he had needed the loan to get the mill back up and running and had used some of his considerable charm to convince the bank manager that he was a safe bet. He was managing to pay it back, just about. He grimaced at the twinge of indigestion in his chest, right behind his breastbone. He gave the area a gentle rub. He'd have to stop eating so much rich food. It wasn't good for the waistline. And now that he was approaching middle age, he'd need to start looking after himself. Especially if he was to make Ellen a permanent feature in his life. He glanced down at the waistband of his trousers. It had become a little tight of late. He'd have to do something about that. Ellen was going to be his wife one day. He'd make damn sure of it. She wouldn't like a portly husband.

The image of another pair of blue eyes flitted across his mind. Paler than Ellen's. Capable of driving him insane with their needy, pitiful expression. That was something else he would have to sort out. He needed a plan. He turned smartly away from Ellen and with a deep sigh, sat down behind his mahogany desk, a present to himself that he had bought off one of the craftsmen in the town. It was ever so slightly too large for the office and probably looked out of place, but it made him feel good. He admired its shiny surface. He liked to keep it highly polished and was careful when he placed his ledgers on it. An image of a similar desk came into his mind. His father, complete with a big bushy beard and intelligent nut-brown eyes, was seated behind it. Clarence Clinton had been an astute businessman when he was alive. He had taught Nicholas all he knew and had been instrumental in him getting to where he was today.

'Never take no for an answer Nicholas.'

Felled by a heart attack at sixty-one, his sudden loss had been a huge blow to Nicholas. The mahogany desk was his way of keeping the memory of his father alive. It was classic, shiny with hidden depths. What you saw depended on what way you looked at it. Just like him. A swift knock came to the door and before Nicholas could open his mouth to invite whoever was there to enter, his eldest daughter sashayed into the office. She walked briskly over to his desk and stopped abruptly, her long woollen skirt swirling around her not unsubstantial hips.

'Goodness gracious Daddy, it's fierce warm in here' she said as she proffered one slightly pock marked cheek to Nicholas.

'Hello Clarice, lovely to see you.' Nicholas rose and embraced his daughter, placing a warm peck on her face.

'I didn't know you were in town. How is married life treating you? Tell that husband of yours that he'll have me to reckon with if he as much as puts a toe out of line.' Nicholas's face held a mock-stern expression.

'Oh, don't be silly, Stephen adores the ground I walk on. He would never treat me like anything other than a high queen. Besides, I think he's scared of you! I was in town to see the milliner. She's working on a new piece for me for the races in July. Wait until you see it!'

If it was anything like the concoction she currently had on her head, it was going to be a sight to behold, Nicholas tried not to roll his eyes. His first-born had a penchant for the strangest looking headpieces –she was the proud possessor of umpteen – ranging from wispy bits of lace and ribbon in all the colours of the rainbow, to large things, made from felt and complete with peacock feathers. Every time he saw her, she seemed to be sporting a different one. She certainly contributed handsomely to the fortunes of Meg Malone, the busiest milliner in the town. The day Clarice didn't have her head decked out in some fripperie was the day they would have to take her pulse.

'Well, it's lovely to see you and your hat, daughter.' Nicholas grinned.

He noticed that she hadn't so much as acknowledged Ellen's presence, nor looked her way since coming into the office. It wasn't as if she didn't know he had a new assistant. He had mentioned Ellen to both his daughters when he had them over for lunch a couple Sundays before. He had purposely said very little about Ellen, not wanting to raise his daughters' curiosity. His offspring were notorious matchmakers, always trying to hint at the possibility of him getting married again and coming up with suggestions of who might make a suitable wife. They frequently got exasperated with him as he never seemed to take the bait they dangled in front of him. None of the women they tried to pair him up with interested him. Occasionally, just for a quiet life, he would escort some lady to a dinner or a dance, but he rarely suggested a second meeting. The minute Ellen Cooney had walked into his office and his life, he had understood the reason why. It was because he had been waiting for her all along. She just needed to be convinced. He would bide his time. He needed to tread softly.

'This is Ellen Cooney, my new assistant,' said Nicholas as he touched Clarice on the elbow and nodded over to where Ellen sat at her small desk, nose stuck in a ledger.

'Ah, yes, Mrs. Cooney, I have heard about you. Very nice to meet you.'

Clarice held out a gloved hand. Ellen rose from her desk and took it in hers, giving it a very firm shake. 'And you too, Mrs....'

'Matthews, but please, do call me Clarice. It's hard to get used to calling myself Mrs. anything! I was very sorry to hear about your husband, Mrs. Cooney.'

Clarice arranged her features in what she obviously thought approximated something like sympathy.

'It must have been a terrible shock for you.' Clarice seemed gratified to see the slightly older woman stiffen.

'Thank you, Clarice. It was a great shock alright, but I'm very sure that Jim is looking down on us. And I'm convinced he had a hand in getting me a great job with such a lovely employer!' Ellen recovered her composure as she smiled genuinely at Nicholas's daughter.

'Well, Daddy dearest', Clarice dropped Ellen's hand abruptly and turned back to Nicholas. 'I think I should let you bring me out to lunch. I'm feeling hollow with hunger!'

Chuckling, Nicholas grabbed his coat and hat and ushered his daughter out the door. He didn't notice Clarice observing the look he gave Ellen. Nor did he know that she had filed the image away in her brain, ready to be resurrected and dissected when she was again in the company of her younger sister, Sarah. Or that her in her head she was screaming *'this will not do, it will not do at all!'*

CHAPTER 11

Peggy

'What's in your book Peggy?' Peggy started as she hadn't heard Tommy approaching. She had been concentrating hard. Her battered and worn little red book was open on the table in front of her. A short, stubby pencil was behind her ear and her face was screwed up as she tried to make out the handwriting on the bag she held in her hand. It was time to add this particular powder to her list. It seemed to be doing the trick. Ellen's mood had improved dramatically since Peggy started slipping it into her tea. She still had dark days, some of them very dark indeed, but she seemed to have climbed, part of the way at least, out of the pit of misery she had been in. And little Alice seemed more settled too. For that, Peggy was thankful. She had chanced moving back to her own house, and she wasn't sorry to once again have her own bed to flop her weary bones into every night. It had been like a knife in her heart watching Ellen struggle with her grief. And poor little Tommy. He was missing his Da badly and yet he was trying not to show it because his Mam was so sad already. At least now Ellen was taking notice of him again, the little craythur. He needed his Mam's love and attention, more than ever.

'Can you read what it says on this bag for me, pet?' Peggy lamented the fact that she once more couldn't find her glasses. She had put them down somewhere, either in her own house or here in Ellen's but she couldn't for the life of her remember where. Tommy's face took on a serious look. She knew he liked to be helpful, and she liked to make him feel important by asking him to help her with jobs around the house. He especially liked helping her read things. He seemed to get great satisfaction from making the letters into words. He was a bright boy and no mistake. A lot of it was down to Ellen of course.

'The first letter is S. Then there's a T and a full stop' ventured Tommy. 'That's the first word. What's that short for Peggy?'

'St. is short for 'saint',' Peggy said. 'What's next?'

She wrinkled her nose up and took her pencil from behind her ear as she waited, looking expectantly at Tommy.

'J-o-h-n – that's John!' said Tommy, delighted to have recognized his friend's name. 'Then w-o-r-t. What's that Peggy? I've never heard of that word. It sounds like 'word' but it's not.' 'St. John's Wort', murmured Peggy. 'Well, that's a new one on me!'

With her tongue between her teeth, she set about the task of writing the name in her book as best she could without her glasses. Beside it, she wrote '*lifts the mood and relieves melancholy.*' With a satisfied flourish, she underlined the last word and closed the book with a snap.

'Good man yourself. Where would I be without my little helper?'

She grabbed Tommy and started to tickle him. He squirmed and giggled, managed to give Peggy the slip and darted out of her reach.

'Now, what do you say we put another sod on the fire and make the room nice and warm for your Mam for when she gets in from work? It's nearly time for Alice's milk. I can hear her starting to stir.'

Right on cue, Alice started to snuffle in her crib and Peggy knew it wouldn't be long before she started to wail hungrily. She was a great little feeder and pretty as a picture. A swell of rage and disgust rose in Peggy's stomach as she thought of Tommy and Alice's grandparents. Stupid people. They were missing out on getting to know their two gorgeous grandchildren. All because of a ridiculous sense of pride. Peggy did her best every day to make the young ones feel special, but she wasn't their flesh and blood. That fool Patrick Sarsfield and his idiot of a wife should be slapped.

Peggy busied herself heating some milk on the hob and her mind wandered to Ellen. She seemed happy enough working at the mill. Still, there was something about Nicholas Clinton that made the hair on the back of Peggy's neck stand up. Oh, she knew of him, with his fancy clothes and proper appearance. She had often seen him about town with his two daughters, through the years, pretty little things they were. They had grown into fine young women it seemed, and Nicholas looked to be proud of them. They were always dressed in the finest fashion and, one of them in particular, seemed to have an array of startling headpieces that she liked to sport at Mass. The kind that would take the eye out of your head if you got too close. Still, she wore them well. The other daughter seemed slightly more reserved. Both had russet-coloured hair and brown eyes like their father. Peggy could barely remember their mother. She had died when the Clinton girls were very young and so, it was a credit to Nicholas how they had turned out, in the absence of a mother's guidance. She had to give him that. He had all the signs of a respectable businessman and there were many people in the town indebted to him for their employment down through the years. But there was something about him that Peggy couldn't put her finger on. Something that made her sixth sense vibrate and not in a good way.

She had a feeling that he had taken a shine to Ellen, and she wasn't at all sure that this was something to be welcomed. Maybe she was imagining it. Ellen had never mentioned him in anything other than business-like terms. He was her employer and nothing else. She seemed to have made a name for herself up at the mill. Not everyone wished her well, that Peggy did know. There were some very jealous people around and Peggy had tried to warn Ellen, without alarming her. There were always begrudgers. Most of them envied Ellen's good looks and the fact that she had landed herself a job with the boss, instead of having to put up with the daily grind that was the mill floor. Some would, no doubt, like to take Ellen down a peg or two given half the chance. Ellen usually scoffed at Peggy when she warned her to watch her back. That was half her problem, Peggy mused -not realizing how much covert attention she attracted. The door opened and Ellen swept in accompanied by an icy blast of wind.

'Lord save us, but it's freezing out there!' Her cheeks were pinched with the cold. She rushed over to the fire and extended her hands to the heat. She turned her head to look around the room and spotted Tommy lurking behind the table. 'Come here lad and give your Mam a hug. Have you been good today? How was school? Did you learn anything new?'

She turned from the fire and took off her mantle and bonnet, laying them over the back of one of the wooden chairs at the table. Tommy hesitated for a second and then slowly walked over to his Mam. She enveloped him in a hug and kissed the top of his dark head. She closed her eyes, and it seemed as if she was struggling with something. Probably regretting how callous she had been with the lad, Peggy thought. But sure, she had been in the depths of despair, the poor lass. By the look in Tommy's eyes, he had forgiven his mother, even if she hadn't forgiven herself.

'School was the same as usual.' Tommy said, with a lopsided grin. 'I learned that the letters 'St.' can be short for the word saint,' he piped up, eager to impress his Mam.

'Did you indeed, well now that's a really good thing to know,' said Ellen as she regarded her son with a serious expression. Tommy puffed up ever so slightly, basking in the warmth of his Mam's attention.

'Good boy. And how is my little girl in her crib?' Ellen took the two strides needed to cross the room and peered in at her baby daughter. She lifted her gingerly from the crib and held her to her chest, rocking her to-and-fro.

'Your Mam's here now, baby. Hush now. How about some nice milk?' Ellen crooned. She lowered herself into the chair by the fire and took the bottle offered by Peggy. Alice proceeded to swiftly devour its contents.

'A penny for your thoughts,' murmured Ellen to her friend.

Peggy started and gave a little shiver. She had been having one of her *'visions'*. This time she had seen Ellen and Nicholas Clinton together. Ellen's head was bowed, and Nicholas had a spittle of fury around his mouth. He was shouting at her, and his face was contorted with rage. Peggy gave herself a mental shake and tried to smile.

'They're not worth a penny my dear.' Peggy replied. 'Now, tell me what went on up there at the mill today.'

'Well, the funniest thing happened today. Old 'Spider' Menton got all fussed when I asked him a simple question about an invoice. He nearly jumped down my throat. He asked me what I would know about such things and me only a woman. Then he went off muttering something. I heard the words 'rue the day', but I'm not sure what exactly what day he was ruing! He's a strange fish that one, even though he looks more like a spider!'

Tommy giggled at his Mam's words and Peggy thought how wonderful it was to see the little family looking a bit more content than it had in a long time. Maybe things were about to turn a corner for them, and they could start to look to the future instead of spending the present mired in grief. But she would keep an eye on Nicholas Clinton all the same. She sighed deeply. There was always so much to keep her mind occupied. Sometimes she wished she didn't care so much.

CHAPTER 12

Larry

Drogheda, January 1865

Larry Clinton had encountered many stenches in his life, rotten food, fetid water, decaying flesh, but the one that was assailing his nostrils now was familiar and comforting in a strange sort of way. He breathed in deeply and felt the hairs on the inside of his nose contract with the cold air which bore the tangy scent of the river Boyne. As he leaned on the wall of the quay, he could see the dull reflection of the gas lamps in the water, weak spots of light barely making an impression on its dense black roiling surface. It was almost hypnotizing. He had grown up near the shores of this river in his beloved Drogheda, or *'Tredagh'* as it was known in days gone by.

As a lad, he had been told stories of the ancient people, some most likely his own ancestors, who worked here by the river, making their homes on its sacred banks, toiling, fishing, navigating, building, engineering. He had loved to pretend that he was one of the brave, strong warriors who had inhabited the lands around his hometown, descended from *Cu Chulainn* himself. A hugely staunch sense of pride, belonging and Irishness had invaded his soul from a very young age. His love for his country was present in every cell of his body. That was why he felt as though his heart was being torn in two with grief as he witnessed his countrymen and women having to bow to their neighbour across the Irish sea. The English had a lot to answer for. Sure, wasn't it only twenty years ago that almost two million had perished when the potato crops failed, and the English did little or nothing to help the starving masses? '*A visitation of providence, an expression of divine displeasure*' the English had declared the great hunger. Just because the Irish were Catholics. As far as Larry was concerned, there wasn't much difference between Catholics and Protestants – they believed in the same God – the two religions were like the same sweet - just different flavours. Larry had many Protestant friends. Some were of the same mind as him - that it was time for the English to be ejected from this country and for the land which had been so brutally taken to be given back to its rightful owners. And he had his own part to play in making that dream a reality. He was part of a movement, secret for now, that would, one day, in the not-too-distant future, help to throw off the shackles of English rule from Ireland. His chest swelled with pride at the thought.

But, tonight, he had to get his head back down from the clouds and concentrate on the job in hand. The others were looking to him for guidance. He turned away from the river, hauling the collar of his jacket up as far as it would go around his neck and pulling his cap down around his ears. He started to make his way through the shadows, staying close to the edges of the buildings. His breathing was slow and even, making a cloud around him in the frosty air. He had learned to control it during his time in America. He had learned to control a lot of things over the four years he had been away, his temper, his emotions, his tendency to be too trusting. He had gained vast experience in the business of war but had also had to learn the art of biting his tongue and suppressing his real emotions. Trying not to object to the orders being constantly barked at you by a foul-tempered sergeant major would do that to a man. He had come home subtly changed in many ways. He was more still now, more watchful, less fiery and all this would count in his favour when the time came for the next big battle. If he could instill some of this watchfulness amongst his men, and dampen some of their dangerous fervour, then he would have the makings of a fine little battalion of his own.

Tonight, they would be having a drill up in a yard near the market. It was a perfect night for it - still and dry. The cold would keep the men on their toes. There wouldn't be any slacking, as they would want to keep warm, and so should be easy enough to coax into drills. Apparently, there would be a few new recruits tonight. Larry was confident he would be able to size them up fairly well after an hour or so, and he would have no hesitation in sending the ones who wouldn't make the grade packing. That was another thing that being faced with the wrong end of a rifle taught you. Life was too short for dilly-dallying around. Decisions had to be made quickly and there was usually no going back. The memory of the pleading face of a young man, probably not much more than twenty, swam before Larry's eyes. In that hot, dusty, godforsaken place it had been either kill or be killed, and Larry knew that he had made the right decision. He had a mission to complete and that's why he had been spared, and the young American had been left to be eaten by the buzzards. Larry shuddered at the memory and shook his head. The past was the past, and what mattered now was the job he had to do tonight. He walked on steadily, passing the odd streetwalker. One of them tried to engage him in conversation. 'No thank you madam', he politely side-stepped her and continued up the street. He started climbing the hill steadily, not decreasing his pace despite the incline. He was proud of his trim, toned physique and took pleasure in doing something every day that challenged his muscles. He liked to feel his heart beating strongly, proof that he was alive and well, healthy and vibrant. He liked to run around the paddock at his lodging house four times every morning, hail, rain, snow, or shine. It was good for his head.

Stopping at a large wooden gate with peeling paint, he looked up and down the street, stooping as if to tie his lace. Once assured that there was no one about, he straightened up and knocked swiftly on the gate in the sequence he had devised himself. It was opened immediately, and he stepped through.

'You fool, you should have asked me the code word,' snapped Larry as he cuffed the young red-haired Sean Swan around the ear.

'Sorry boss, I keep forgetting!' Sean looked very annoyed with himself as he closed the gate.

Larry stood still and peered around the yard. Dudeens glowed red in the pitch black and gradually, the men revealed themselves to him. He counted thirteen in total. That was a good turnout.

'Who's new tonight then?'

Three men stepped forward straight away, with a further two half a step behind them.

'Names please.'

'Mattie Molloy.' 'Stephen Maher.' 'Will Curran.' 'Paddy Sarsfield.' 'Walter Greene.' The men's breath lingered in the frosty air. So, there was one Protestant among the new blood Larry though with satisfaction. It was always a good thing to have a bit of both types fighting for the cause. It bonded the men together, made them more tolerant of each other. Made them understand that they were all made from the same flesh. *Same sweet, just a different flavor.*

'Welcome men. And thank you for joining the cause. Now, let's get started. Swan, keep a look out. And keep your eyes peeled and ears fully alert' he warned the youngster who sloped off to his post by the gate.

After an hour, Larry was satisfied that a good night's work had been done. The men were getting the hang of the moves and manoeuvres he was teaching them. They would be ready in a couple of months, he was pretty sure. He would let the gaffer know of progress when next he saw him. One by one, they stole through the wooden door into the night, blending into the shadows, making their way back to the warmth of their beds. Then, all that were left were himself and young Swan.

'Sorry about earlier, boss.'

'It's alright Sean, just be more careful next time.'

With that, the younger man took off and disappeared into the night. Larry closed the gate behind him gently. He paused, straining his ears for any slight sound. A fog had rolled in along the river, spreading over the town, its tendrils curling around the lamp posts. The moisture hung on the frosty air. Larry could feel the cold seeping into his lungs, and he had to stifle a cough. Satisfied that he was unobserved, he took off across the road at a rapid pace. The fog made no difference to him as he knew his way around his town like the back of his hand. An excitement burned in his belly as thoughts of what lay ahead. It wouldn't be long now. His men would be drilled to perfection and would join up with the other groups who were also training around the country. The English wouldn't know what had hit them. He eventually reached the place where he had hidden his bicycle and mounted, swiftly heading toward home, unaware of the man that watched him as he disappeared into the foggy night.

CHAPTER 13

George

It was all George Menton could do to stop himself laughing out loud. The look on Nicholas Clinton's face was comical. His brother, Larry had stridden angrily into the office a few minutes previously, and now you could cut the atmosphere with a knife. George had watched the mill owner's expression go from placid, to bemused, to suspicious, to thunderous, all within the space of seconds. And all because of the look that had passed between Larry and Mrs. Ellen Cooney. Larry had obviously made her acquaintance somehow already, although she was only working for a relatively short time at the mill. Larry had blustered in, addressing Nicholas in, what George considered a not very brotherly fashion. He had opened his mouth to say something, but catching sight of Ellen seated at her desk, had been apparently rendered speechless. She had been concentrating on her ledgers, chewing on her bottom lip, two pin pricks of red high on her cheekbones, her brow furrowed. She had looked up at the sound of Larry entering the room and firstly, the colour had drained from her face and then she had flushed right up again. Her and Larry's eyes were locked together as Nicholas regarded them from behind his ridiculous desk. George Menton was good at addition, and it didn't take a genius to add two and two and get four. There was something going on between these two.

'Ellen, what are you doing here?' Larry's eyes held a puzzled expression.

Quick to regain her composure, Ellen's reply was clipped and swift.

'I work here. What are you doing here?'

There was a pause. George could see the realization dawning in her eyes as she looked from one man to the other. Both had the same colour hair, the same dark, tawny eyes and pale, freckled skin. Larry was a couple of inches taller than his older brother and a lot leaner. It was no wonder, George thought. He had heard all sorts of terrible tales of conditions in the war in America. The temperature in the room had gone up a degree or two, made all the warmer by the smouldering looks passing between Larry and Ellen.

'Oh, since when? I thought you worked at the...'

'I have been in Mr. Clinton's employment since November' Ellen interjected quickly, casting a glance over at Nicholas.

George stifled a grin at the look on the older man's face. Ellen looked slightly perplexed as she again addressed Larry.

'I am guessing that you two are brothers. It doesn't take a detective to work that out!'

Her laugh was slightly forced. She was clearly trying to diffuse the situation. Well, he wished her luck trying to diffuse Nicholas Clinton. Once he had a bee in his bonnet about something, it was very hard to dissuade him from a particular course of action. And woe betide anyone who crossed him. Any one of the local businessmen could tell you that for nothing.

'Ah, I see,' murmured Larry, finally wrenching his gaze from Ellen and glancing at Nicholas. 'And yes, we are brothers, although by blood only. Any man that treats people so badly is no brother of mine' he spat, turning the full fury of his gaze on Nicholas.

George could see Larry's fists clenching and the sinews on his neck starting to bulge. As much as he liked to see a good scrap, now was not the time or place for a fist fight.

'Now, now, gentlemen, let's not get too worked up. I'm sure we can talk calmly about whatever it is that's bothering you, Larry.' George spoke soothingly in his practiced, conciliatory tone which he had honed to perfection over the years.

'It's hard not to get worked up when your own brother threatens to sack a young widow just because she's occasionally been a bit late for work! And she with four mouths to feed as well as her own!' Larry's look was scathing, his eyes flashing in fury.

George could see Ellen's eyes swiveling from one man to the other and back again. Her expression as she looked at Nicholas was slightly disgusted.

'*Is this true?*' her look enquired.

George could see a barrage of emotions crossing Nicholas's face. He cast his brother a look of pure hatred before taking a deep breath and arranging his features into a more pleasant configuration whilst turning to Ellen.

'Well, it's not easy being an employer. It has its responsibilities too, you know, bills to be paid and all that...' he blustered. He faltered at the look on Ellen's face. 'But I'm sure the widow-woman Keegan and myself can come to some arrangement. No need to concern yourself at all. It will be looked after'

Turning to Larry he said, 'Now if you wouldn't mind letting us get on with our work? We are quite busy you know. And next time, make an appointment.'

With a dismissive sniff, Nicholas returned to his letter-writing, signaling that it was time for his brother to leave. Larry unclenched his fists.

'You make sure you leave that woman alone. Or you'll have me to answer to,' growled Larry.

'Oh really, that sounds very like a threat to me!' Nicholas roared.

Ellen jumped in her seat. Nicholas was apoplectic, and the look he gave his brother was filled with pure venom. Then, as if realizing that this was not a side of himself that he wanted to advertise, he appeared to swallow his emotions and once more, his face donned a look of serenity.

'Just go, Lawrence. The woman will get no further threat from me.'

With one final glance in Ellen's direction, Larry strode out the door, leaving Ellen with a look of confusion and, dare George say it, longing on her face. It seemed she was rather taken with the younger Mr. Clinton. This was a very interesting situation indeed. George loved nothing more than a bit of drama. And it looked like there was plenty more to come if this little encounter was anything to go by! He silently retrieved the ledger he had come in for and scuttled out of the room on his long, spindly legs.

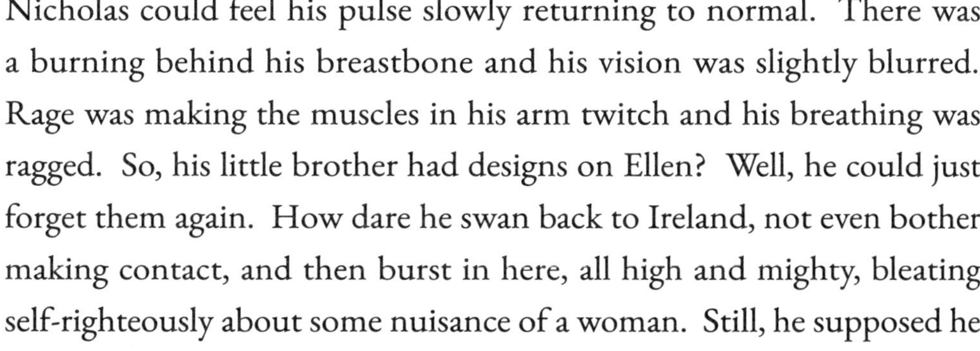

Nicholas could feel his pulse slowly returning to normal. There was a burning behind his breastbone and his vision was slightly blurred. Rage was making the muscles in his arm twitch and his breathing was ragged. So, his little brother had designs on Ellen? Well, he could just forget them again. How dare he swan back to Ireland, not even bother making contact, and then burst in here, all high and mighty, bleating self-righteously about some nuisance of a woman. Still, he supposed he had better watch his step. He hadn't had to come the heavy on anyone for a good while. And he had his reputation as a pillar of the community to consider. He didn't want to even think about the way Ellen had looked at Larry. It made his insides clench with fury that they seemed to know and like each other. Something would have to be done about this situation before it spiraled out of control. Ellen was to be his. He would have it no other way.

CHAPTER 14

Larry

The biting wind tried its best to burrow its way under Larry's collar and wrap its freezing fingers around his neck. He shivered and pulled his coat more tightly around himself, cursing that he had forgotten his scarf yet again. But his mind was not his own these days. It was consumed by thoughts of the person walking briskly by his side.

'There's no need for you to go out of your way to walk me home', Ellen cast him a glance from under her hat which was pulled right down over her ears.

The expression in her eyes seemed to portray a host of emotions. He dared to hope that one of these was pleasure. Ever since he had clapped eyes on her in the alehouse at Christmas, he had been filled with a sense of excitement, the likes of which he had never experienced before. No one had stirred his senses quite like Ellen did. It was like she had taken up residence in his brain and refused to leave him be. Every morning, on waking, he saw her face. It plagued him during the day, turning him vague and forgetful. It was the last thing he saw at night before sleep claimed him. His appetite, normally quite hearty, was as good as gone, as he had a permanently half sick feeling in his stomach. He had never been afflicted this way before by a woman and he was beginning to seriously think that he was in love.

'It's no problem. It's not safe for a woman on her own at this hour of the night. You'd never know what sort of animal might decide to follow you home. Remember the time at Christmas? I know the type that goes to that alehouse and they're not all there to hear your sweet voice.'

Larry hoped he portrayed the correct combination of concern and friendliness, as he didn't want to declare himself just yet. Better to try and see if his feelings might be reciprocated in some way in case he said something that made him look like a complete eejit. Still, his hope that perhaps Ellen might actually like his company had taken seed in his brain and was starting to bud with each look she threw him. He hoped he wasn't misinterpreting her shy glances. This was the second time he had walked her home since the night she was nearly attacked. It felt good to protect her. Better than all the promotions he had received in the army put together. He knew it was madness to feel this way so soon, but he wanted to look after her for the rest of her life, if she'd let him.

'You were in fine voice tonight, Ellen.' He loved saying her name. He loved it when she said his back to him.

'Why thank you Larry, that's very kind of you to say so.'

'Not kind, just stating the fact.' He was rewarded by the sound of her tinkling laughter as she turned her head to consider his profile.

'Are you always so sure of your facts?' she teased.

'I know talent when I hear it. And you have a rare one Ellen. Your voice can bring even the most hardened, gnarled old codger to the brink of tears. When you sang '*Oh Believe me of All those Endearing Young Charms*', you could have heard a pin drop.'

'It is a beautiful air alright. I like singing that one. But I like singing all the lively ones too.'

Larry detected a wistfulness in her tone, guessing that she was thinking of her late husband. His sources had told him she was a widow even though she hadn't mentioned it to him. Hopefully she would soon, as this would mean she felt comfortable enough with him to impart a little personal information. So far, their conversations on the fifteen-minute walk from the alehouse to her home had been limited to superficial things like the weather and her job. It irked him that his brother got to spend all day every day in her company. He intended to court her and had to figure out a way. He knew it was very soon after her husband's death and she might shy away like a frightened horse if he showed his hand too soon. He did not want to make a mess of this. She was too precious and becoming much too important to him.

They were approaching her door now. He wondered about her living in such a place. If she were his, he would bring her to live in a fine house, with as much comforts as he could afford to give her. His sources had told him that she had married for love. Her parents, being wealthy merchants, had cut her off since her marriage to Jim Cooney. His family had cheated Ellen's father out of some deal or other, so the rumour went. Larry always knew there were two sides to any story. And his time in the war had taught him that nothing was ever black and white. So, she lived here, with her two children, one only an infant. She had a close friend in Peggy Murphy but didn't seem to have many friends of her own age, save Molly White at the mill. Larry had done his homework. On the subject of Ellen Cooney, he had schooled himself very quickly. The cottage she lived in emerged from the gloom of the gas lights that lit the area poorly. A hungry looking mongrel eyed them dolefully and then disappeared into the night, his ribs visible beneath his mangy coat.

'Thanks for walking me home Larry. I appreciate it on such a horrible night.'

Ellen turned to meet his eyes. He could see the angles of her cheekbones. His eyes roamed all over her face, taking in the arching brows, smooth skin and slightly parted lips. It was all he could do not to swoop down and kiss her full on the mouth. Time seemed to stand still, and he imagined that her breath quickened slightly. She was first to break his gaze. He thought he saw a movement from behind the lace curtain at the window, but he couldn't be sure as the light from the gas lamp was very dim. All of a sudden, the door burst open and a young lad of seven or so flung himself at Ellen, wrapping his arms around her waist.

'Tommy, love, what are you doing still up at this hour of the night, or should I say, morning? You'll fall asleep at Mass tomorrow, and you won't be able to hear the sermon!'

Ellen wrapped her arms tightly around the young boy, who Larry presumed was her son. She had mentioned him before with pride.

'I was worried about you, Mam. It is so windy and cold and horrible out that I couldn't wait for you to come home.'

Tommy eyed Larry from beneath dark eyebrows, gripping his mother fiercely, staking his claim. There was a shadow of challenge in his eyes and Larry nearly felt as if the young lad could read his mind and knew how he felt.

'Tommy, this is Larry, a friend who walked me home from the alehouse tonight. So, you see, I was quite safe in his company. No one would dare say as much as 'boo' to me when I'm with this gentleman!'

Tommy regarded Larry silently.

'Where are your manners, young man?' Ellen admonished. Tommy stuck out his hand to shake Larry's and Larry pumped it up and down.

'Pleased to meet you Tommy,' Larry smiled, resolving to get on the good side of this lad. It was plain to see that he idolized his mother and so he would have to do a good job of winning him over if he was to make Ellen a permanent fixture in his life.

'I'd best get this little rascal in out of the cold,' said Ellen. 'Thanks again for walking me home.'

'No problem, Ellen. I might see you again at the alehouse next week?'

'Oh yes, I'll be there! I'll have to practice a few new songs during the week. Thanks again.'

Was it Larry's imagination, or did she seem to be reluctant to take her leave and go inside? Her mind was made up for her by a loud noise from the doorway. Peggy Murphy had cleared her throat and stood there, a disapproving look on her face and her hands on her hips.

'Get yourselves in out of the wind now. It's no night to be lingering on the doorstep.'

'You're absolutely right Peggy, time to get this young man back to his bed! Thank you very much for looking after them both for me. Will you be alright walking home?'

'I will escort Mrs. Murphy to her door,' offered Larry, thinking that this was another very important person in Ellen's life that he needed to get on his side.

'Sure, it's only down the road,' Peggy sniffed with a dismissive wave of her hand. 'I don't think anyone in their right mind would try to set upon me. They'd get the back of my hand if they did!'

'It's no problem, it would be my pleasure.' Larry bowed slightly and gave Peggy what he hoped was a winning grin. He was rewarded with a giggle from Ellen and with that, she turned, giving Larry one last glance before she went into the house, ushering her young son in front of her. The door was barely closed when Peggy hissed:

'Well, young man, I don't know what intentions you have for Ellen, but I have to warn you that she's very heart-sore at the moment with her husband hardly cold in his watery grave.'

'Hold your horses, Mrs. Murphy. What makes you think I have any intentions towards Ellen other than to make sure she gets home safely at night?'

Peggy snorted. 'I have been around quite some time, Larry Clinton, and I know a love-sick look when I see one. The way you cast your eyes at Ellen makes me think that you have taken a fancy to her. I'm warning you now, if you hurt so much as a hair on her head, you'll have me to answer to.'

'Oh, I don't intend to hurt her Peggy. It's the furthest thing from my mind.' He left her at the door of her house and bade her goodnight. He could feel her eyes boring into his back as he strode down the street. She could warn him off all she liked. He would bide his time, make sure Ellen's heart was fully mended before he made it his. Larry didn't feel the bitterly cold wind as he hurried home.

CHAPTER 15

Tommy

Tommy nodded to Johnny. This was their big chance. The woman in front of them had a brood of children gathered around her skirts and she didn't seem to be paying the blindest bit of attention to any of them as they chattered and jostled, pushing and shoving each other. She was too busy looking around her, taking in the red-bricked façade and arched windows of the brand-new Whitworth Hall.

'Here missus, keep some manners on those children of yours!', the red-faced caretaker seemed a bit overwhelmed as he puffed and panted, trying to put some order on the crowd that had gathered for the inaugural show in the town's splendid new hall. The woman paused in her gawping long enough to administer a cuff around the ear to the child that had the misfortune to be nearest. She didn't notice the extra two young lads that had tailed in behind her brood. Tommy and Johnny winked at each other. They were in!

Tommy came to an abrupt stop in the middle of the floor, and he felt Johnny pull him out of the way of the surging crowd.

'You look like a trout with your mouth wide open.' he heard his friend shout over the din of the crowd. 'Don't just stand there, you'll get trampled!'

Tommy barely registered what his friend had said to him. He had never in his life been in a place so splendid. He had thought the outside was grand, with its fancy arches and black iron railings, but the inside nearly took his breath away. The ceiling was so high. If you threw a marble up it would take ages to come down again. Johnny craned his neck to see. They both spotted the balcony at the same time. Tommy wondered if you would break both your legs if you jumped down from it. By the look on Johnny's face, he was wondering the same thing. It was beginning to fill up with people, all anxious to see the show that was being put on for free.

The hall had been built by a Mr. Whitworth and given to the people of the town. He had heard his Mam talking about it to Peggy. Imagine being that rich that you could pay for a hall like this one and then just give it away! Tommy's Mam didn't know he was here today. He didn't think she would mind that he had sneaked in, because she probably would have come herself if she hadn't been too sad. She liked to sing. Maybe she could get a job singing here instead of at the alehouse. At least she wouldn't have all those horrible men gawping at her. Being sure to stay close enough to the family they had come in with, Tommy and Johnny sat on two of the chairs that had been put out especially for the show. Seemingly, the place could hold nine hundred people! A loud bang made the boys turn around. It was the caretaker slamming the big wooden doors shut because the place was full. Tommy grinned and shook hands with Johnny at how their plan had worked. Pity the poor eejits outside on the street who hadn't managed to get in! Tommy sat back in his seat and let his gaze wander upwards to the high windows with the red velvet curtains and past them to the shiny timber ceiling. The place smelled of polish and paint, but it was the underlying scent of something else that made Tommy feel fizzy inside. He wasn't sure what it was. It was something he hadn't smelled before. There was a big stage up at the top of the room. In front of it, was the longest curtain of gold velvet material Tommy had ever seen. It shimmered in the sunlight pouring in through the windows. There were big lights hanging out of the ceiling. His Mam had called them 'chandeliers.' Tommy had practised writing that word down in his copy book. It wasn't spelled like you would expect it to be. The big lights twinkled in the sun and if you stared at them long enough, Tommy thought you would probably go a bit blind.

Suddenly, the caretaker and some other man with a shiny, bald head, a limp, and a face like Billy Molloy when he was really cross, lifted long wooden poles that had been lying on the ground and reached up to close the curtains on the windows. With the light gone, the place looked like a magical cave. A hush came over the crowd. Tommy peered up at the stage and saw a man peeping out from behind the velvet curtains. His hair was black and slicked back and looked very shiny, and he had funny eyebrows, a bit like he had taken a pencil and coloured them in. A moment later, the curtains were pulled back and the man was there, on the stage, dressed in a black suit and a white shirt. He announced in a really shouty voice that the show was about to commence. Tommy knew that meant it was about to start.

There was a group of about seven men playing instruments down at the front of the stage and to one side. There were a couple of fiddles and an accordion and a banjo. He felt something bubble inside him as the first act came out on stage. It was a man, singing a very lively song. Tommy felt himself clapping along with the audience and tapping his toes in time to the jolly music. The next song was slower and sounded sad. Tommy was glad when it was over because it made him think of his Da. After the man had finished up with another lively song, a funny man came out. Tommy and Johnny laughed at his antics until they thought their sides would burst. And then, the smallest man Tommy had ever seen in his life ran onto the stage. At first, Tommy thought it was a boy like himself until he heard his deep voice. The man, who it turned out was called 'Nicky Nebolshoy' was from Russia. Tommy had never seen anyone from Russia before. He was used to seeing dark-skinned Italians at the docks when they came to Drogheda to work on the marble altars of the town's churches, but Nicky Nebolshoy had white skin and very, very hairy arms. He had boots that went right up above his knees, were way too big for him and he did a dance on tippytoes. Tommy *'oohed'* and *'aahed'* along with the crowd, wondering how Nicky could stay standing, never mind dance.

The next act was a lady singing. She sang a couple of songs and winked at some of the men in the front of the room. Tommy thought she was good, but not as good as his Mam. She sang a cheerful little song that had words that rhymed and made Tommy laugh out loud. Then came the wonderful magician, 'The Great Lenny.' He had shiny, wavy hair and he wore a top hat. He also had a pointy beard, and he wore a jacket with tails and a big red sash around his waist. His trousers had a crease that looked like it would cut your finger if you touched it. He made his red silk handkerchief turn into a green one. He invited a boy up on stage to try and guess which cup the ball was under. He kept switching them around at a speed that made Tommy dizzy. The boy always got it wrong. And then, what did the Great Lenny do only pull a white rabbit out of his top hat! Tommy looked at Johnny and his eyes were wide as saucers. He and Tommy clapped until their hands were sore. *Janey-mack*, but this was the best!

And then, just like that, the show was over. With a final swish of the stage curtain, Tommy was back to reality. The caretaker and the cross man were opening the curtains with the long poles and trying to hoosh the crowd towards the front doors.

'That's it now folks! Show's over!' Tommy and Jonny started to make their way to the door. Johnny's face looked a bit red. He shouted over the noise.

'What did you think of the little man with the big shoes? He was my favourite!' 'Yeah, mine too', Tommy shouted over to his friend.

But really, his favourite had been the woman singing. Not because of her voice, but because of the song she had sung. It was funny, it rhymed and the lines of it kept going around and around in Tommy's head. Maybe, he would write a song like that someday, and his Mam could sing it on the stage. He would play the tune on his Da's fiddle for her, and Alice could dance along. Then it would be like they were all together again. This thought made Tommy feel all warm inside. He and Johnny went back out through the doors, into the bright sunlight of Laurence Street and made their way to Rope Walk, bellies rumbling, hungry for their tea.

His Mam was breathing very softly now. She had been kind of crying in her sleep before. Tommy had heard her call his Da's name and shout '*No! No*!' a couple of times. Nearly loud enough to wake Alice, but his sister just snuffled and gave a little wriggle in the crib beside the bed where his Mam and himself were snuggled up together. He guessed that his Mam had been having a sad dream about his Da. He had those too. But he bet she didn't have the really bad thought about his Da getting eaten by a big fish with teeth as sharp as knives. Tommy couldn't stop thinking about this ever since Billy Molloy had told him his Da was *fish food*. Every time the picture of a big, black fish with evil red eyes and yellow teeth came into his head, Tommy got a funny feeling in his stomach, and it made him want to go to the privy. To make it go away, he usually tried to think of something nice that his Da and he had done together when he was alive. Like the time they went to the fair in town and looked at every single one of the animals, making up silly names for them, his Da carrying him on his shoulders so that he felt like king of the world. Or the time they went out to Annagassan and stayed the whole day on the beach – running in and out of the waves. His Da had bought hot cockles from a stall and they had eaten them with their hands. They had licked their fingers and rubbed them on their trousers afterwards. Usually, these nice pictures in his head made the horrible ones go away, but they didn't always. Sometimes, the scary fish stayed in his mind until he thought his head would burst. The bad thoughts were usually worse when he woke up during the night. He didn't want to tell his Mam about them, because then she might start thinking about the fish too, and he didn't want her to be scared as well as sad.

He reached out and stroked her hair. It was lovely hair, so dark and shiny. He started to wind a bit around his finger like he used to do when he was three. It made him feel safe, but he couldn't do it when she was awake because he was seven now, and really, too big to do such a babyish thing. Peggy kept asking him if there was anything wrong. It was just that he was so tired all the time. Ever since his Da died, things were so horrible. His Mam was sad all the time. She got so cross when he asked if he could play his Da's fiddle. And she had to go out to the job in the mill and go singing in the alehouse at night. He had passed the door a couple of times during the day, and he had managed to have a quick peek inside. There were a lot of men in there, all shouting and falling over. It was very smelly too. He was scared for his Mam having to go in there and have all those men looking at her. So, he was kind of glad that Mister Clinton had started to walk home with her at night. She said his name was Larry and that he was a 'kind friend.' Tommy thought that he looked at her the same way his Da used to so he must be a special friend. But he wasn't his Da, and anyway, Tommy didn't want a new Da. He'd had a fantastic one and now he was dead.

Tommy sighed and looked up at the ceiling. He could see a spider's web and wondered what spiders were afraid of. They weren't afraid of the dark anyway, they seemed to like it. Tommy didn't. In the dark, he thought of all the things that scared him. Lately, he seemed to spend all his time afraid of something; the big fish, his Mam getting attacked by someone in that horrible alehouse, something happening to Peggy, and then him and his Mam and Alice would be all alone. He was afraid that he would wee in his sleep again too. His Mam hadn't minded, and she had told him not to worry about it. If Billy Molloy heard about it, he would tell everyone at school, and they would all laugh. He would punch Billy in the face if he did. Right, square on his nose and he would go down like a sack of spuds. Tommy clenched his fist at the thought, felt the muscle in his forearm twitch. He tried to fill his head with memories of all the wonderful things he had seen at the show earlier that day. But it was no use.

In her crib, Alice snuffled and sucked her thumb. Tommy thought she was a lovely baby really. When she was born, he had been sad that she wasn't a brother. But she was nice, even though she was a girl. She looked pretty like his Mam. She could sit up on her own now and Peggy said that she would soon be crawling and then she would be walking. He would be able to take her out next summer to the field to see Mr. Sarsfield's cows. She wouldn't be able to play ball with him though, until she was about two. She probably wouldn't be any good, but he'd try and teach her. Alice was saying '*dada*' now and sometimes he thought his Mam was about to cry when she said that. Tommy had secretly tried to teach her to say 'Mam' instead, but she couldn't do it yet. She was very smelly at times, and she cried a lot when she was getting her teeth. Tommy screwed his eyes up and tried to remember what it felt like to get his own teeth when he was a baby, but it was too far back.

Sometimes, he was mad at his brain for forgetting things. Like his Da's face or the sound of his voice. This was another thing that made Tommy very scared. He didn't want to forget his Da. He was scared at having to be the man of the house. He tried to protect his Mam and Alice, and he was afraid something might happen to them when he was asleep. So, he tried to stay awake sometimes. This made him very tired. Tommy turned over onto his side. He could see the table and chairs up close. There were shadows in the corner of the room and one of them looked like a big hairy monster with a hunched back. Tommy quickly closed his eyes and tried to remember what Peggy said about night-time monsters. She said that they weren't real, and they would disappear as soon as the morning came. He still thought they were scary though. He was tired of feeling scared all the time. He gave a big shuddering yawn that made his mouth open so wide that he felt his jaw crack. His eyes were all scratchy and sore. Rubbing them didn't even help.

Maybe if he did the job that Larry was asking him to do, he might get enough money that his Mam wouldn't have to sing in the alehouse anymore. Larry had been in his house for a cup of tea a few times now. He came on a Sunday after Mass and his Mam's voice always became cheery then. Sometimes, he brought two buns or some currant cake for Mam and him. Those currants were so juicy and fat and tasted nice. Tommy usually put butter on his slice, but his Mam preferred hers without. Larry would sit at the table and say: *'Well, aren't you the fine, handsome, big lad, Tommy?'* He said the same thing every single time he came. He would put his hand on Tommy's head and mess up his hair with his big rough hands. Tommy didn't really like Larry touching his hair. It felt like he thought he was his Da. But he wasn't. His Da had been strong and fierce and funny and lovely and …. Tommy felt his heart thumping in his chest. There was a big, massive lump in his throat, and it was hard to breathe. He didn't want to cry because it might wake his Mam. Sometimes, he went out to the privy and cried because no one could hear him out there. It was too cold to go there now. There was still a bit of snow on the ground, but it was horrible and slushy and brown. Tommy tried to swallow down the big lump and put his hands up to his eyes to stop the tears from falling. This usually worked. He took a deep breath like his Da had told him to do whenever he felt upset about something. Like the time when he was four and a half and his little puppy Fido had been kicked by a horse and died. He had taken so many deep breaths that day that he had ended up dizzy. But it had helped him not to cry. It was hard being a boy because you weren't supposed to cry whenever you were upset. It was well for Alice. She'd be able to cry whenever she wanted to, and no one would think she was a sissy. Girls had all the luck.

Larry had brought him outside one night to show him the stars in the sky and tell him the names of them. They had all sorts of funny names. When Tommy asked him how he knew them all, he said he had learned the names from a cowboy called *'Rifle Rick'* that he had met when he was in America. *'Rifle Rick'* had worn a big leather hat, a dirty scarf knotted around his neck, and he used to spit further than three feet. His Adam's apple had wobbled when he spoke, and he had told Larry all about the stars one night when they were around a campfire. Tommy thought that he would like to meet *'Rifle Rick'*. If he knew all about the stars, he was bound to know some other stuff about bears and wild dogs.

Larry had asked him if he would like to make some money to help his Mam so that she wouldn't have to work so hard. All he had to do, Larry had whispered, was to deliver some letters to people around the town. Tomorrow, he was to bring a letter to a man called Paddy who lived over near the Laurence's Gate. He would have to wait while Paddy read the letter and then Paddy would give him a message to bring back to Larry. He would have to make sure he hid the letter properly in his clothes and he was not allowed to show it to anyone. Tommy thought this would be an easy job to do. He would keep the money Larry gave him as a surprise for his Mam. Then she wouldn't have to sing in the alehouse anymore. Larry was to ask him tomorrow, after Mass, man to man, if he would take on the job. Tommy decided he would do it. Mind made up, he snuggled closer to his Mam's back and tried to breathe at the exact same time as she did. He closed his eyes and started counting back from three hundred. Ten minutes later, the spider scuttled across the floor, but Tommy didn't see him because he was fast asleep.

CHAPTER 16

Nicholas

Spring 1865

Nervousness was not something Nicolas Clinton usually suffered from. He was a man who was assured of his place in the world. People usually did his bidding, and it was uncommon for anyone to oppose him in any way. Being the eldest of two children, he had been doted upon by a simpering, and slightly feeble mother and he had, since his childhood, been convinced that the world revolved around him. His father had taken very little heed of him until he turned twelve and started to become someone who could be tutored to take over the family mill. Clarence Clinton had been a big noise in Drogheda in his day and wanted his son and heir to emulate him and carry on the family tradition of excellence in business. There was no room for sentiment in commerce. This had been drummed into Nicholas from a very early age. *'Profit is king!'* had been his father's mantra, and up until now, Nicholas thought he was doing a fairly good job of making his father proud, although it was hard to tell when his bones were resting up in the Cord cemetery.

A curious sensation was assailing Nicholas this morning as he strode down West St. on his way to the bank. Was it nerves? Drogheda was wide awake on this fine spring morning. People of all shapes and sizes rushed around him. He never ceased to be amazed how God bestowed such good looks on some people whilst others were afflicted with a limp, a cast eye or teeth like a rabbit. Nicholas preferred to rest his gaze upon the more attractive members of society. The others made him feel slightly queasy. He liked surrounding himself with nice things and beautiful people and up until now, he had managed to do that very nicely indeed. His home was, some might say, an ostentatious place, with fine furnishings and well-appointed rooms. He liked to think that it was a fitting space for a man of his position. The thought that he might lose it caused a tremor of something quite alien to lodge itself in Nicholas's gut. He side-stepped a lady, giving her the advantage of his best beaming smile, bowing slightly as she looked at him flirtatiously from under her eyelashes. He was well aware of the effect he usually had on the fairer sex - every one of them, except the one that mattered. Nicholas's false smile swiftly turned to a scowl and his pulse quickened slightly as he thought of Ellen and how she seemed impervious to his charms. She wasn't responding as he thought she might. And she seemed to be taken with his nuisance of a brother. It was time to try a different approach. He knew that he had to tread carefully as she was still in mourning for her sailor husband. He didn't want to frighten her off. He was not used to having to be cautious where women were concerned. He could usually take his pick, everything on his terms. It was perplexing, but he intended not to let it get the better of him. He was well used to turning a problem on its head and finding a solution. Being sent to boarding school had honed his negotiation skills, taught him how to dissuade his tormentors at first, and as he progressed, how to make his minions do his bidding. He would have Ellen if it was the last thing he did.

Right now, though, he had to concentrate on the task ahead of him - to persuade his oily bank manager, Mc Keown, not to foreclose on the loan he had taken out to get the mill out of trouble a couple of years previously. As the exterior of the bank loomed closer, Nicholas felt an eddy and swirl in his stomach again. He berated himself for being so anxious. It was just that he thought he had everything under control. He was in charge of attracting new customers and had had some success. Now that the cotton from America wasn't as plentiful as it had been, they had exported a lot of cloth to England. That war between the Yankees and the Confederates had been good for something at least. George Menton oversaw production and collecting the money. A job for which he was eminently qualified. So, Nicholas was at a bit of a loss as to why his account balance was shy of what it should be. It was putting a strain on his ability to pay back the loan. And now, the workers were getting a bit above themselves, demanding extra pay because they heard stories of how popular linen was becoming again. He hadn't given any worker a raise in a long time, so he supposed he would have to give some concession sooner or later. They were mostly young lassies though, so he might get away without being too much out of pocket.

He sighed deeply as he stopped in front of the bank. Giving himself a mental shake, he straightened his back, turned on his most charming smile, walked confidently up the three granite steps and pushed open the heavy wooden door. He could see his face in the brass handle. He didn't look like a man perplexed.

The interior of the bank was cool and ordered. The black and white tiles on the floor and the dark wooden paneling gave it an opulent look. The smell of beeswax made him shudder slightly as it brought back memories of his thirteen-year-old self and a certain very un-Christian brother. He mentally shook the image of Brother Marinan's lascivious face from his mind as he approached the clerk at the desk.

'Good morning, Mr. Arkins. I have an appointment with Mr. Mc Keown at nine o'clock.'

'Certainly Mr. Clinton. I'll let him know you're here.'

Donal Arkins shot off importantly in the direction of the bank manager's office, tapped lightly on the door and entered. Thirty seconds later, he was back, beaming at Nicholas.

'Mr. Mc Keown will see you now. This way please.'

'Mr. Arkins, I know my way to his office by now!' sneered Nicholas, dismissing him with a wave of his hand. Nicholas made his way towards the back of the bank where Thomas Mc Keown's office lay – with *'Thomas Mc Keown, Bank Manager'* written in fancy gold writing on the door. Nicholas swallowed a lump in his throat before knocking. *Pretentious old fart*, Nicholas thought. After a long ten seconds, Mc Keown called out 'Enter!' Typical of the old bastard to keep him waiting. Gathering himself, Nicholas replaced his scowl with a broad smile and opened the door. He held his hand out and the two men shook vigorously.

'Good to see you, good to see you,' boomed the manager. 'Take a seat.'

Mc Keown sat back in his green leather chair and regarded Nicholas from over his rimless glasses. He was wearing an expression that Nicholas couldn't quite fathom. He looked like he was doing some very complicated addition in his head.

'So, Nicholas, how's business?' Mc Keown steepled his fingers.

Nicholas noticed that his nails were long and ragged-looking and that there was a kink in each of his little fingers. He had large crops of white hairs in his nostrils and ears and the little hair he had on his head was slickly combed over his skin, which resembled a side of corned beef.

'Good. It's good! We have a whole host of new customers,' blurted Nicholas.

Calm down, you fool.

'What I mean is, we have increased client numbers substantially and have reason to believe that we will have a good steady source of income for the next couple of years.'

'Hmmm. Indeed.' Mc Keown appraised Nicholas with his cool blue eyes. Nicholas swallowed, and felt the starched collar of his shirt tighten slightly as a trickle of sweat made its way between his shoulder blades.

'So, Nicholas, can you tell me why the lodgments into your account have been down every month for the past six months? The way you're going, there won't be enough to meet your loan repayments very shortly.'

'Surely, things are not that bad Thomas?' Nicholas felt a flutter of apprehension.

'I'm afraid you will find they are. Here, has a look for yourself.'

Nicholas forced himself to look at the column of figures that Mc Keown presented to him. Week after week, the amount being lodged was going down gradually. He could see the balance in his account was dwindling, right enough.

'It's a mystery, a real mystery,' Nicholas muttered to himself as much as to Mc Keown. 'One I intend getting to the bottom of.'

He straightened his back, looking Mc Keown right in the eyes.

'I'll sort something out, but in the meantime, sure, what's a couple of repayments between friends, eh?' Nicholas smiled.

Mc Keown sat back and sighed deeply.

'Well, Nicholas. As you very well know, it's not that simple. I have a Board of Directors that I must keep happy. They are not as lenient as I am, nor as forgiving. They are all hardened businessmen, and they insist on me keeping the bank as profitable as it can possibly be. I have a duty to them.'

A duty to yourself, first and foremost, thought Nicholas. He could sense that the old scoundrel was angling for something.

'I see, Thomas. Of course, I totally understand that you must do your job. Is there anything, anything at all that I could do to make it a bit easier for you?'

It made his skin crawl to have to kowtow to Mc Keown. But it seemed like this was the direction in which the conversation was headed. Thomas Mc Keown leaned back in his chair and looked up at the ceiling, seemed to contemplate the plasterwork and gave a heavy sigh. Nicholas rode out the pregnant pause, trying to quell the bile that was rising in the back of his throat. With a dramatic sigh, Mc Keown fixed Nicholas with a steely gaze.

'Well, Nicholas, you know I'm not one for seeking favours.' Mc Keown pursed his thin lips.

'However...'

Here we go, thought Nicholas.

'However', repeated Mc Keown in his nasal drawl,

'If you could see your way of giving me a little assistance with the Ardee court-house project, then that would be something which would have a very positive impact on our relationship.'

Nicholas regarded Mc Keown's calculating gaze. He sighed mentally. He supposed it was a small enough price to pay for having the bank manager go easy on him until he could find out what was going wrong with his finances. He should be able to convince the other members of the Corporation to pick Mc Keown's construction company for the courthouse job. Even if the price was slightly above the others who had tendered. Mc Keown really was a conniving old git. Nicholas plastered a huge smile onto his face and extended his hand to shake the banker's.

'That will be no problem, Thomas, no problem at all.' The two men shook firmly to seal the deal.

'Good man, Nicholas. I appreciate your understanding in the matter.'

'And I yours, Thomas.'

Nicholas rose and bowed slightly, turned, and made his way out the door, back into the dimly lit exterior of the bank, walked straight past the line of clerks, oblivious to Donal Arkin's scowl, and out into the morning sunshine.

CHAPTER 17

Tommy

Tommy's breath came hard and fast as he hurried along Rope Walk. He looked anxiously over his shoulder to see if anyone was watching him. The boots his Mam had given him for Christmas were a size too big and he could feel a blister starting on his left heel. He should have worn the socks Peggy had knitted for him, but he had been in too much of a hurry to leave the house, waiting until his Mam was fully occupied with Alice before he made his escape. He muttered something about going to see Johnny as he slipped out, and she had answered him with a murmur, warning him not to be too long as it was bitterly cold outside.

Tommy pulled up the collar of his jacket against the biting wind. He hurried along Rope Walk, head down. He felt guilty about what he was doing as he hadn't told his Mam about it, but he also felt a tiny bit excited. Larry had given him the envelope for the man called Paddy last night when he had called to the house to see his Mam. He had slipped it to him when his Mam was outside in the privy.

'Now Tommy', Larry had said in an urgent whisper, 'I am trusting you with this very important job. I need you to deliver this to a man called Paddy O'Brien. He will be waiting for you at Laurence's Gate at nine o'clock tomorrow morning. He is tall, has dark hair and a bushy beard.

You are to wait until he reads the letter and gives you a message for me. You are to keep this letter safe at all costs. Hide it in your clothes. Try not to look scared or you might give the game away. Come straight back here and hide Paddy's letter somewhere in the house where your Mam won't find it. I will give you a shilling for doing this job for me.'

Tommy must have looked scared because Larry had taken him by the shoulders and given him a little shake and told him to think about how delighted his Mam would be when he gave her the money that he would earn. Of course, she was to think that he had earned the money at his market job, cleaning up after all the traders had finished for the day. That job didn't pay as well as Larry did.

As he made his way towards the centre of the town, he met lots of people, faces mostly thin and pinched with the cold. They were all probably on their way to work, some in the mills, some in the iron factory. Tommy thought about how he would leave Drogheda when he was older. He would explore the world like his Da had been doing on his ship. He would go out and meet *'Rifle Rick'* in America and learn all about the stars and bears and snakes. Then he would write about it all so that other people could learn. He would work hard and always have enough money so that he and his Mam and Alice and Peggy didn't have to be hungry. He would make his money doing something that didn't make him feel so worried - like this job was doing. He bumped into an old man that he hadn't seen shuffling around the corner.

'Watch where you're going young fella!'

'Sorry mister,' said Tommy, dodging the old man's fist and hurrying off down the road. He stepped over a pile of steaming horse dung and hurried across Peter Street past the chapel and the pawn shop. He stopped dead as he saw what he thought was a telescope in the window. His eyes widened in wonder as they roamed over the shiny brass and leather. His Da had shown him how to use one when he was five and Tommy really, really wanted one of his own. The stars had looked so close that you could nearly touch them. Tommy's hands tingled with longing. He wanted to hold that telescope, and run his hands down the shiny, smooth surface. If he owned one like that, he would never sell it to the pawn shop man. Tearing himself away from the window, Tommy made his way along the busy street, dodging the horses and carts that trundled up and down, weaving his way through the crowd, his legs pumping, and his hands shoved deep inside his pockets. He could feel the corner of the envelope that Larry had given him poking into his side. He had it tucked into the waistband of his trousers. He gave it a little pat. As he turned into St. Laurence Street, he could see the two stone towers joined by a bridge at the top. His Da had told him all about the gate. That it was built five hundred years ago. That the people of Drogheda climbed up the four floors inside one of the towers so that they could see any invaders coming up the river Boyne. There had been a look-out platform at the top of one of the towers for the soldiers to get up even higher. Tommy remembered his Da's eyes shining as he told him about how some bad people had tried to invade Drogheda a long time ago, but the soldiers had seen them coming and were ready for them. They had saved Drogheda. His Da had cheered and Tommy had cheered along with him, the two of them dancing around the kitchen with their arms up in the air. Mam had laughed at them and then Da had danced her around the kitchen too.

Tommy stopped in front of the stone towers and looked around. He looked up. They were very high. He couldn't see right up to the top now that he was beside them. He put his hand on the grey stone wall and looked around for Mr. O'Brien. He couldn't see anyone with a big bushy beard. Then he heard a loud '*pssst*' and looked to his left. Peeking out from a recess in the arch under the bridge that connected the two towers was a man with dark hair and a big beard.

'In here lad, quickly!' he motioned to Tommy to join him in the dark. Tommy saw that there was no one around, so he darted in under the arch and came to a stop in front of the man. It seemed the coast was clear, as the man asked Tommy immediately for the letter from Larry. Tommy fished out the envelope from his trousers and noticed that it was very warm. The big man grabbed it off him and tore it open, quickly scanning the page inside. He let out a sigh and it was all Tommy could do not to hold his nose. He thought the man really needed to clean his teeth. They were all brown and some were broken. He took out a piece of paper from his pocket and a pencil from behind his ear, licking it before he quickly wrote a few lines. He shoved it into an envelope and handed it back to Tommy who placed it in the waistband of his trousers again.

'Thanks, young lad. Now hurry back and don't let anyone except Larry get their hands on this letter.'

With a swift glance right and left, the man slipped out from under the arch and went off in the direction of the Cord Road, whistling tunelessly.

Tommy emerged from the gloom, blinking rapidly a couple of times and headed off in the opposite direction. He half-walked, half-ran home, anxious to get the letter hidden somewhere where no one else could find it. He had his head down when he collided, full force, with someone wearing dark blue trousers. Tommy's two arms were taken in an iron grip, and he found himself looking up into the face of a local constabulary man. His heart did two somersaults and a shot of pure panic raced up and down his spine.

'Careful young man, you nearly had my kneecap off then! Where are you off to in such a hurry?'

'I'm just going home to my Mam and sister.'

'And where might that be?'

'Rope Walk.'

'And what's your name?'

'Billy Molloy, mister.'

'Well Billy, off you go home now but be careful to look where you're going next time.'

The constabulary man released Tommy, and he stumbled off in the direction of home. *Janey-mack,* but that had nearly frightened the life out of him. He'd have to be more careful next time that Larry wanted him to deliver another message. Tommy rushed through the door into the safety of his house, breathing a huge, big sigh of relief. His Mam was there baking bread at the kitchen table. Alice was in her cot in the corner, her cheeks flushed, her fist shoved into her mouth and with drool running down her chin. She gave him a gummy smile when she saw him, her little face lighting up.

'Well, Tommy, you're back quickly pet. How is Johnny today?' his Mam asked.

'Johnny?' Tommy had a puzzled look on his face before he remembered he had told him Mam he was going to see his friend.

'Oh, he's fine. His sisters are annoying him as usual.' Tommy answered.

'No change then', his Mam chuckled.

Tommy felt huge relief followed by a ripple of pride in his chest. He had done as Larry had asked him. He had delivered his message and had the letter from Mr. O'Brien carefully tucked into trousers. Now he just had to find a safe place to hide it until tomorrow when Larry would call. He leaned over to Alice and gave her a tickle. At the same time, he dropped the envelope down behind the crib where it was out of sight.

CHAPTER 18

Peggy

Clogherhead, July 1865

Peggy took one last step towards the rippling water and lifted her skirt above her ankles. She welcomed the coolness of the gentle waves. She stood, luxuriating in it for twenty seconds with her eyes shut. She turned her face up to the sky. The heat of the July day had made the pain in her bunions almost unbearable. And the walk on the road from where the carriage had dropped them off hadn't helped her plight. She had high-tailed it as fast as her size and arthritic hip allowed over the scorching sand towards the water and was now in ecstasy as her feet cooled down and the piercing pain was soothed. She breathed in the salty air deeply and listened to the sounds of the summer day. All around, she heard childish shrieks, laughter, the cries of the seagulls, and the unrelenting, gentle whisper of the waves. The sea was quiet enough here on the east coast of Ireland. She had heard stories of the mountainous waves that were to be seen on the western coast. They would be nice to see, but probably not so nice to paddle in! Her feet feeling considerably better, Peggy shielded her eyes against the brightness of the sun and looked around her. There were little families dotted all around on the sand. Fathers lifted small children onto their shoulders, mothers doled out sandwiches and fruit to children who hopped from one foot to the other. The food was gulped down and the children ran, shrieking, into the waves. Young couples walked sedately along the shore. She saw two women in the new-fangled swimming costumes. She had seen one of them in the window in Meagher's shop in town. Some thought them a little vulgar, as they left little to the imagination when it came to a woman's shape, and they were like a pair of trousers. Peggy thought they were a wonderful invention. Cool and convenient. And if they had them in her size - and she could afford it - she would have bought one. She thought how nice it must be on a day like this one to immerse your whole body in the sea. She'd love to try, but only if the beach was deserted!

Over to her left, she could see Ellen, Tommy and Larry putting out scraps of linen to sit on whilst Alice toddled around and around in circles, trying to copy the seagulls in the sky, no doubt. All of a sudden, her chubby little legs collapsed, and she plopped down on the sand. She looked startled for a second and then her face broke out into a big smile, and a laugh erupted from her belly. She pointed up at the sky muttering some unintelligible babble. Her mother joined in her laughter. Little Alice was so like Ellen both in looks and in temperament. Both had sunny expressions and pretty faces with deep blue eyes and dark hair. Although poor Ellen had been in the doldrums for a good while after her lovely Jim drowned. She seemed to have perked up a bit lately. Probably thanks to the St. John's Wort Peggy had been secretly slipping into her tea. And, although it pained Peggy to say it, probably due to the attentions of Mr. Larry Clinton. Peggy still didn't know what to make of that fella. She was in no doubt that he had designs on Ellen. Any time she mentioned this, Ellen would pooh-pooh her and say that they were just friends. Sure, Jim was only a year dead, and she was in no way thinking of getting herself another husband. No-one could ever replace her first love. Whatever she might say, Peggy could tell Ellen was more than just friends with Larry. Peggy reckoned if he went and got himself a girlfriend, Ellen's nose would be rightly out of joint. Tommy seemed to like him though. She had caught the two of them as thick as thieves on many occasions, Larry seeming to whisper instructions about something to the boy. She thought she had seen him slip Tommy a coin once as if in payment for something.

Tommy certainly seemed to be blooming these days. She could still see the sadness in his eyes from time to time. But, overall, he seemed to be a bit happier in himself than he had been during the winter and early spring. It was as if he had taken on the role of man of the house, even though the gasson was only seven. He was standing taller. And he was growing like a weed. His trousers were flapping around his shins and his wrists were poking out of the sleeves of his shirt. He would have to get kitted out before he went back to school in September. Time enough to be thinking about this. The day was a blessing, and Peggy was hell-bent on enjoying herself. It was bliss to get away from the smells of Drogheda, which could be overpowering at times, and get the fresh, salty air down deep into her lungs. It would do the little ones the world of good also.

Peggy could feel the tip of her nose beginning to get very hot. She tilted the straw hat on her head to keep out the worst of the sun's rays and set off towards the others who had made their camp a short distance away on the sand. A young boy and girl of about eleven and twelve rushed past her, shrieking as they entered the shallows. In their excitement, they splashed water up onto Peggy's dress, causing her to gasp in shock as cold water ran in rivulets down her front.

'Sorry missus!' called the young lad.

'It's alright. Do me no harm to get cooled down a bit!', she answered, shaking her head at them.

Still laughing, she waddled across the sand. She eyed Larry as she approached. He had the same blood as Nicholas Clinton, and she didn't have much time for that schemer. He was all *'hail fellow well met'* on the street, him being a supposedly fair and generous employer and a member of the local Corporation. But even though she didn't have many dealings with him, there was something about Nicholas that she didn't trust. He was the kind of man who never did anything for nothing. There was always something he wanted in return. It was very possible that his brother was tarred with the same brush. Although, she knew the two of them didn't get on. Something to do with a will and property. It had left Nicholas relatively well-off and Larry needing to earn himself an income. She supposed that was why he had to work on the buildings and had gone off to America and joined the army. There was a decent wage to be had there by all accounts, even though there were also many dangers. She would try and get Larry on his own and ask him what his intentions were towards Ellen. Ever since she had warned him to tread carefully back in the beginning of the year, he seemed to be wary of her. And so he might! Ellen was like a daughter to her, and she loved the little ones fiercely. Woe betide anyone who might hurt them. They would feel the full force of her wrath.

'Well, that's a day sent from the heavens, for sure!' exclaimed Peggy as she approached.

'Tommy, budge up there and let Peggy sit down.' Ellen lifted her wriggling daughter onto her knee to make room for her friend.

'Oh, the lord save us, if I sit down, I might never get up again!' Peggy sank to the ground with a soft groan and arranged her skirt around her, squinting up again at the sky. She could feel a drop of sweat making its way down her spine and one forming on her upper lip. It was a curse being trapped in such a hot and sweaty body. Still, there was a nice breeze coming off the sea, so if she stayed still, and let it play gently on her skin, she would be able to survive the heat. She longed to strip off and run into the sea naked, but she would surely be arrested by the constabulary if she did that!

'Ellen, why don't you bring Tommy and Alice down to the water and let her have a paddle? This is her first time at the beach and the saltwater will strengthen her little muscles and help her get stronger.'

'Good idea Peggy,' said Ellen. Although now that she's walking, I won't have a minute's peace! Coming Tommy?'

'You bet!' he cried.

Peggy watched as the three made their way down to the waves, Tommy running ahead and Alice wobbling after him as fast as her little legs would carry her.

Larry sighed and lay back on the sand, hands beneath his head, a contented look on his face. Peggy studied him. He was a handsome devil and no mistake, despite the scar on his left cheek. He had russet hair that curled out from under his cap and skin that had turned brown in the sun. Numerous freckles were dotted across the bridge of his nose, and he had a wide, full mouth. His chin was on the determined side and was closely shaven. Peggy's eyes travelled over his broad shoulders, and she could see the muscles rippling underneath his light cotton shirt which was open at the neck. A tuft of reddish-brown hair peeped out from his collar. He had a lean torso and very long legs.

'Are you finished looking at me Peggy?' Larry's voice startled Peggy, and she frowned slightly at being caught examining him. She had thought his eyes were closed.

'I was sizing you up for a coffin because you'll be needing it if you upset my Ellen' sniffed Peggy.

A low rumble of laughter erupted from Larry, and he sat up on one arm and regarded Peggy appraisingly.

'I know you want the best for Ellen and the children and believe me, I do too. You know my brother has designs on her?'

'I had a feeling that might be the case alright,' she sighed.

'Well, he'll have her over my dead body.'

A steely glint came into Larry's eyes and Peggy shivered slightly.

'We don't want any dead bodies around here. There was enough tragedy this time last year. Ellen needs a bit of stability and peace of mind.'

'And I intend to offer her that.'

Larry's eyes wandered over to Ellen where she was jumping in and out of the waves with her two children. Peggy looked at the softening expression in his eyes. For once, she was sorry that she couldn't have one of her *'visions'* when it came to Larry Clinton. But her sixth sense remained stubbornly quiet when it came to this man. She hoped that was a good sign rather than a bad one.

CHAPTER 19

Ellen

Not for the first time, Ellen really wished that she had the luxury of a full-length mirror in her house. But one of those would cost almost two days' worth of the wages she got at the mill. And there were enough places for that money to be spent, with three mouths to feed, one of them insatiable. Tommy was sprouting up at a furious rate. And his feet were probably gone up a couple of sizes since the last time he'd worn shoes. She'd have to go to the drapers on West Street and see about getting him a new pair of trousers and a couple of shirts for school. She remembered only too well how her Jim had described the chilblains he used to suffer from not being wrapped up properly against the cold, and she didn't want that for her Tommy. The memory of Jim hit her like a punch in her stomach, winding her, and causing her to double over. It was a full year since he had drowned, and she still thought about him incessantly. She really wasn't sure that she should be contemplating doing what she was about to do, and it was causing a knot of anxiety to vie for attention with the butterflies in her stomach.

She had finally agreed to go for a walk out with Larry Clinton. He had been seeing her safely home from her Saturday night slot at the alehouse for months now and, so far, had been a real gentleman. She had had a feeling that he wanted to ask her for more than friendship but was afraid to because she was so recently widowed. Shortly after their trip to the seaside, he had asked her to consider going out, just the two of them. She had hesitated and said that she would think about it. She had done nothing else since. Hours spent agonizing over the feeling that she would be betraying her Jim if she went out with another man. She had been half afraid to discuss her feelings with Peggy but had plucked up the courage a week ago. Peggy had let out a big sigh.

'Does he make your heart beat faster pet?'

Ellen had shame-facedly confirmed that he did.

'Well, then, I think a pretty young woman like you with all of her life ahead of her deserves a bit of happiness and fun. And I'm sure Jim wouldn't want you to be pining for him forever. So, maybe you should give Larry a chance. He's been clean mad about you for ages, that I know.'

'Ah, go on out of that. He has only recently said that he wants more than friendship' countered Ellen.

'Well, we have to give him ten marks for patience!' declared Peggy. 'And you get none for observation!'

'I will always love Jim, but I think I do want to go out with Larry. He makes the world a little brighter for me.'

'Well then, go with him and see how you get on lass.'

That very night, Ellen had had a particularly vivid dream of Jim. He was sitting in his usual spot, the corner beside the fireplace, and he had an earnest expression in his green eyes. Taking Ellen's hand in his, he had lovingly traced a circle on the inside of her palm. She had felt the warmth of it radiate up through her arm and into her heart. His voice had been strong and yet soft. *'Ellen, it broke my heart to leave you and Tommy. I am at peace now. I want you to promise me that you will do whatever you need to be happy. If that means you want to love another man, then I give you my blessing. Be happy sweetheart.'* He had kissed her hand gently and then she had woken up, cheeks wet, feeling desperately sad. She didn't want to let him go, but she was torn between keeping his memory alive and making a new life for herself. The feeling of the dream had stayed with her for days afterwards. Eventually, the sadness faded to a dull ache.

So, here she was, getting ready to meet another man romantically, and she was all of a dither. She felt excited, but also hugely guilty. Looking in the mirror, she gave a lock of her dark, wavy hair a tug to try and show it who was boss, but it just flopped back into its original position. She looked down at her red dress with the daisy sprig print. It was quite shabby. Still, it was the best one she had, so it would have to do. She made a mental note to visit the fabric shop in town to see if they had any remnants that might do for a special occasion dress. She hadn't had much cause for nice clothes this past year, but if truth be told, she did feel a little lighter and brighter in her red dress. It had been Jim's favourite. He said the colour made her skin creamier and her eyes bluer. She remembered him removing it in rather a hurry on one occasion. Well, that wouldn't be happening this evening. Although, the thought made her feel a little bit hot.

'Where are you going, Mam?' Tommy regarded her with suspicion. He was old enough to know that something was afoot. Ellen had decided that there was no point in trying to pull the wool over his eyes or telling him an untruth.

'I'm going out for a walk with Larry. He asked me if I would go with him to the Whitehorse Hotel for a cup of tea and a sandwich.' Ellen smiled gaily at her young son. She could see a struggle going on behind his eyes. He was only seven, but sometimes Ellen thought he could read her mind.

'Is that alright with you Tommy?' He looked at her with his green eyes, so like his Da's.

'Just don't be home too late. You promised that we would go over to the river tomorrow, remember?'

Ellen stifled a laugh. He sounded like her father used to, with his instructions not to be late home whenever she had gone out as a young girl.

'Of course, I haven't forgotten our trip, Tommy. I am looking forward to it. Now, here's Peggy to look after you and Alice for the couple of hours I'm away.' Ellen abandoned the hand mirror as Peggy puffed in the door, red in the face even though her house was only a few doors up.

'Heavens above, but it's mighty warm out there. Well, aren't you a sight for sore eyes, lass. That dress is just lovely on you!'

'You don't think it's too much?' Ellen pulled at the cuffs self-consciously.

'You're just used to being in dark colours. You look a treat. Now, off you go and enjoy yourself. This pair of rascals will be fine with me' Peggy said as she scooped a tired Alice into her arms.

At that moment, there was a loud rap on the open door. Four pairs of eyes swivelled to see a large frame almost totally blocking out the sunlight.

'May I come in?' Larry's voice seemed to fill the small room.

'Of course, come on in.' Ellen replied in a slightly high-pitched tone.

'These are for you.'

'Oh, thank you they're very pretty.'

'Pretty flowers for a pretty lady,' replied Larry smoothly, running his eyes appreciatively over Ellen.

'Ah go on out of that!' Ellen could feel a blush rising from her neck up her cheeks and she laughed to hide her embarrassment.

Larry wrenched his eyes from Ellen and rested them on Tommy, kneeling down to his level.

'I promise to look after your Mam when we're out this evening. I will bring her home safely and will make sure that she has a lovely time. How does that sound?'

'It sounds good,' said Tommy.

'Good man.' Ellen didn't see the wink that Larry gave Tommy, but it wasn't lost on Peggy.

'Right then, my lady. Shall we go?'

Larry proffered his arm to Ellen, and giggling, she took it and walked out the door. On the way, she blew a kiss to Tommy. There was still a good deal of heat from the sun even at seven o'clock and Ellen felt it prickle her skin the minute she walked out from the gloom of her house onto Rope Walk. She was acutely conscious of the muscles of Larry's upper arm which she could feel under the cloth of his coat. Larry had a certain way of looking at her that made her senses swim. She had tried to ignore it up until now but there was something about this evening, and the way the sun was shining, that made her decide to allow free reign to the feelings she had been denying. She liked Larry Clinton more than just a little. So, she held his gaze longer than she had dared before. Each time she looked in his eyes, her stomach did a funny lurch like she was falling down a deep well. He certainly seemed to be delighted with her company as he could barely take his eyes off her. More than once, she had to laughingly guide him in a certain direction so as to stop him stepping in the horse manure that peppered the streets.

They strolled on, eventually, arriving at their destination. They were shown to their table for two, tucked inside a corner of the big dining-room, partially obscured from view by a big marble pillar. Ellen took in her surroundings. The bright furnishings gave the room a modern look and the tables each had a short white tablecloth. Pine chairs with gold cushions gave the room a sort of honied glow which was very pleasing to the eye. The whole room had a light, airy feel which was very much in keeping with how Ellen felt. After giving their order to a slightly portly waiter with a pronounced limp, Larry once again turned his gaze on Ellen. He reached across the table and took her hand in his. To her utter astonishment, he turned her palm upwards and began making circles on her skin, his touch featherlight and tantalizing. Ellen closed her eyes as the sensation was nearly too much. Before she could stop it, a tear had squeezed its way from under her eyelid. Larry stopped, a worried look on his face.

'What is it, Ellen?'

'Oh, it's nothing. It's just that Jim used to do the very same thing – trace circles in the palm of my hand.'

'I see,' maybe I shouldn't do that again, then?'

'Actually, no, it's quite nice.' Ellen took a shuddering breath, smiled and took Larry's hand in hers again. Once more, Larry, keeping his eyes locked firmly onto Ellen's began his gentle tracing of his finger on the palm of her hand. This time, she felt her breath quicken as she gave in to the delicious sensations his touch was arousing in her. She could see his pupils dilate and his nostrils flare. They were interrupted by the waiter who looked slightly disgusted at this public display of affection.

'Your tea, madam, sir.' He dumped the cups and tray of sandwiches on the table a little too abruptly to show his displeasure and walked away muttering to himself. Ellen and Larry dissolved into laughter as they regarded his retreating back. Larry poured, and Ellen sat back, happy to be waited on for once in her life.

'Ellen, I want you to know that I promise you two things,' putting down the teapot, Larry's expression turned serious for a moment. 'I do not want to make you forget Jim. I know how much you loved him, and I would never presume that I could replace him. I would very much like it if you would consider me as someone you might grow to love in time as I have loved you from the very first moment I clapped eyes on you in the alehouse.'

'What's the second thing?' Ellen's expression was soft and curious.

'I will never, ever let you down.'

They stayed there in their little cocoon until all the tea was drunk. The sandwiches lay untroubled on the plate.

CHAPTER 20

Ellen

Early February 1867

'*Oh no, not again! There couldn't possibly be anything left in my stomach.'* Ellen leaned over the edge of the bed and heaved and retched, her heart hammering in her chest, until she thought her whole body might turn itself inside out. There was nothing left but bile. This was turning out to be one of the longest nights of her life. She had felt a bit queasy earlier in the day and had put it down to having caught the sickness that was plaguing some of the workers at the mill. She was never usually sick. She lay there, panting, until another violent wave of nausea convulsed her body, and she leaned over the bed once more. Utterly spent, she wiped her mouth with the back of her hand. Even this minor movement was nearly too much for her. Opening her eyes, she looked to the window where she could see the first grey fingers of light starting to seep in through the light lace curtains. She turned her head to look at Tommy who lay beside her, sleeping peacefully. In profile, he looked so much like Jim, that a sob caught in her throat. The emotion caused her to be violently sick again. She decided that it was better for her if she didn't try to move at all or think. So, she made an attempt to empty her brain of anything except the movement of her chest as she breathed in and out. At least she hadn't woken the children. She would definitely have to call on Peggy today for help, even though it was Sunday. Thank God she didn't have to go to the mill today. 'Himself' would have to do without her at Mass today. She couldn't risk making a show of herself by vomiting all over the polished pews.

She lay there, trying not to budge, as any slight movement seemed to make the nausea worse. The sound of the lamplighter, as he came to extinguish the lights, drifted in from the street, along with an occasional clip clop and whicker from a passing horse. She could hear some of the neighbours call greetings to each other as they emerged from their houses, making their way to St. Peter's. In the corner, Alice snuffled, sighed and then Ellen could hear her sucking enthusiastically on her thumb. She really was such a good little girl. She was placid and smiled a lot. Well, most of the time. Except when she wanted to climb up onto the table and wasn't allowed. Then she could wail fit to split your ears! She had a fine set of lungs on her. Ellen could see her being a singer in years to come. She had her Da's green eyes and dark hair and sometimes, when she was laughing at something, her face held the ghost of his expression. And Tommy was growing into a fine young lad. He was nearly nine now and as tall as a boy two years older. He was getting on well at school, and was one of the cleverest there, according to the Master. She had beamed with pride. *'Oh Jim!, How I wish you could have lived to see them grow.'* In the two and a half years since his death, the anguish of losing him had changed from a sharp dagger-like pain to a dull throb. She still thought about him every day and sometimes dreamed about him at night. But, in her dreams lately, he appeared remote, always out of reach, heading over some hill, or around some corner, never looking back or waiting for her. It was as if he was fading from her life. Sometimes she found it hard to remember his voice, his touch, his eyes. She turned over to lie on her right side and immediately regretted the movement as nausea engulfed her once more. This time, she woke Tommy. Bleary-eyed, he turned his face towards her.

'Morning Mam.'

'Morning pet.'

The smell of his breath made her heave once more into the bucket beside the bed.

'Ah Mam, what's wrong? Why are you sick?' Tommy's hand cautiously patted her back, and she could hear the concern in his voice.

Taking a couple of deep breaths, she collapsed back onto the bed.

'It's probably that sickness that a lot of the mill workers have. I'll be as right as rain in a day or so pet. No need to worry about me.' She smoothed the fringe that tended to flop over his right eye away from his forehead and tried to look reassuring. He still looked worried, and rubbing the sleep from his eyes, he regarded her again.

'Will I get sick? And Alice?'

'I hope not sweetheart.'

'Good, because we will mind you until you're better.'

A sob caught in Ellen's throat. She was so lucky to have such a good-hearted little boy. She had been overwhelmed at Christmas when he had given her a present of a beautiful clip for her hair. *Mam, it has blue, sparkly stones that match your eyes, and it has a good sturdy clasp as your hair is so thick.* He had said all this as she had unwrapped it on Christmas Eve. She had nearly been afraid to ask him where he got it, but she needn't have worried. He had bought it from Mr. Mc Closkey in the pawn shop. Had been eyeing it up for weeks, saving hard from his job at the market. Then he had presented Alice with a wooden toy chicken, (which she had immediately called 'Cuk Cuk'), and Peggy with a pair of woollen mittens. He had bought nothing for himself.

'I don't need anything,' he had declared.

Some extra money had appeared in the tin above the fireplace also which Ellen figured must have been put there by Tommy. Her hard-working little boy was so kind. He seemed to be walking a bit taller lately, like he was happier in himself than he had been in a long time. And he and Larry were as thick as thieves. It was good for Tommy to have an older man in his life again. She knew he missed his Da terribly still, but Larry was teaching him all about the stars and really seemed to have taken him under his wing.

Larry had become quite a fixture in her life over the past year and a half and especially since she had agreed to walk out with him. He was extremely attentive, and had taken her to the hotel, to the seaside, to dances in the hall, or just for a picnic on the banks of the Boyne. He walked her home every single night she sang at the alehouse. She felt safe and protected in his presence. When Jim had died, she had felt unmoored, adrift, petrified for her future and that of her children. Larry made life a little colourful again. She looked forward to seeing him. He definitely made her pulse race. But she wasn't sure that she loved him yet. She might, some day. She knew he loved her. She could see it in the way he looked at her, the tender touch of his hand on the small of her back when they were out walking, his kisses. He was a generous man, both with his time and his attentions. But Ellen couldn't help feeling that there was some darkness in him, like he had another side that she hadn't yet seen. She saw the way women looked at him when they were out. Even the married ones. She knew he had eyes for no-one but her. The combination of his devotion and the hint of danger were intoxicating.

They had both gotten slightly drunk on Christmas Eve last. After her usual session at the alehouse, she had decided to throw caution to the wind and have a drink with Larry. Ellen wasn't used to drinking, but something had possessed her that night, apart from the alcohol –a recklessness that she couldn't quite account for. Larry hadn't been much better than her. He had drunk quite a few pints of ale, and they had stumbled home to her house, giggling like teenagers. Peggy had shushed them, frowning, as Tommy and Alice were fast asleep. Slightly chastened, Ellen had glanced over at her son and daughter and cautioned Larry to be quiet. Peggy hadn't wanted to leave them on their own in the house, but Ellen had assured her that after a quick cup of tea, Larry would be on his way. The older woman had reluctantly waddled out into the night, wishing them a Happy Christmas under her breath, whilst giving Larry a gimlet eye.

The memory of what had happened that night was still fresh in Ellen's mind. She had truly meant to send him on his way after the tea, but the alcohol had destroyed her inhibitions and increased his ardour. And so, he had stayed, and the very thing that Peggy had been afraid of had happened. That had been six weeks ago, and they hadn't had a repeat performance, but it was proving very difficult for them both to keep their hands off each other.

A bolt of molten terror shot through Ellen, and she stiffened in the bed.

Six weeks ago. Oh Jesus, Christ and all the saints!

She hadn't had a monthly since well before Christmas. She hadn't noticed because she was so busy with the children, working hard at the mill to get a big order out, and singing in the alehouse. She was normally as regular as clockwork. She frantically cast her mind back to the early days of her pregnancies with Tommy and Alice. She had been slightly queasy in the mornings, but nothing much. She couldn't be! Surely not after only doing it only once? Her breath became rapid and shallow, and she felt another huge wave of nausea rise up from deep inside her belly and this time, she couldn't swallow it down. Afterwards, she lay back, exhausted, covered her eyes with her hands and tried to breathe through her mounting horror.

'Tommy, would you run up and get Peggy to come down to me. Tell her I want to talk to her for a minute?'

Tommy left the warm bed, and pulling on his rough wool jacket and boots, trudged out the door, still wiping the sleep from his eyes. Ellen felt the room swim as she tried to calm her breath. Delicately, she felt her breasts. They were definitely bigger than they usually were, and they were quite hard. *'Oh sweet Jesus, no! What on earth am I going to do?'* She could taste her panic, coupled with her bile, and heaved again.

'Ah lass, what ails you?'

Peggy's bulk filled the doorway, and she waddled over to where Ellen lay on the bed. Peggy took one look at Ellen and asked Tommy to look after Alice who was just starting to wake up. She looked enquiringly from Ellen to the bucket beside the bed and back again.

'You're sick? What is it?'

'I'm not sure,' Ellen whispered, 'but I have a terrible feeling that I might be expecting.' Peggy's face crumpled in despair, and she closed her eyes.

'What did you just say?' she hissed. 'That Larry Clinton, I'll skin him alive with my own bare hands!'

'I was a willing participant.'

'When?'

'Christmas Eve.'

'I knew he was after more than a cup of tea that evening!' Peggy's fury was mounting. 'Ah lass, what am I going to do with you at all? He'll have to marry you. Will he be willing, do you think?'

'More than willing, I would think. But I'm not sure I want to marry him. Oh Peggy, I'm scared. I can't do this on my own. What if the sickness doesn't go away? What will I do then? I can't go on like this!'

'Hush pet, let me get you a cup of water and we'll put our thinking caps on. It will all work out. First things first. You'll have to tell Mr. Larry Clinton that he's going to be a father.'

As Peggy cradled a sobbing Ellen in her arms, she felt the familiar drifting feeling that always accompanied one of her *'visions'*. Ellen was in this one, but so was Nicholas Clinton and Larry was nowhere to be seen.

CHAPTER 21

Nicholas

'*What on earth is wrong with Ellen?'* Nicholas wondered to himself. His hand, full of a bacon sandwich, paused halfway to his mouth. She had been acting decidedly off for the past couple of weeks. And she looked extremely peaky. The usual healthy tinge to her creamy skin had been replaced by a sickly pallor, and she looked like the colour of cold porridge. Her hair was straggly and lank, lacking its usual lustrousness. Her lips, nearly bloodless. She seemed distracted a lot of the time and had made a couple of silly mistakes with the ledgers. He would have sacked anyone else for such carelessness, but of course, he wasn't going to sack the only good thing that had happened to him in years. She brightened his every day, and even though she wasn't his, at least he got to be in her presence. There she went again, rushing out of the office. He waited a minute and then followed her. As he suspected, she had rushed outside to the privy, and now he could hear her getting violently sick. She must have picked up the bug that had swept through the mill, striking down about fifty per cent of his workers. But most of them had recovered after a couple of days. Ellen's sickness seemed to be lasting a lot longer. Nicholas climbed the stairs back to his office and resumed sitting at his desk, as if he had never left.

A few minutes later, Ellen sat down at her desk, surreptitiously wiping the corner of her mouth with her sleeve. She took a deep breath and picked up her pencil once more. Nicholas could see that she was trying very hard to concentrate. She kept breathing in deeply. If she wasn't careful, she was going to pass out. He didn't want that to happen to Ellen.

'Ellen, are you feeling quite alright?'

'Yes, Mr. Clinton, I'm perfectly fine.' She looked at him directly but was first to drop her gaze.

'It's just that you seem to be a bit under the weather lately. Have you caught the sickness that was doing the rounds a couple of weeks ago?'

'Er, yes, I think that might be it.' Ellen flushed slightly as she studied the end of her pencil.

'Well, I think it might be a good idea for you to see the doctor, because it seems to be lasting a bit longer than it should.'

'Oh, I don't need a doctor to say what's ailing me.'

There was something in Ellen's tone – a bitterness – that made Nicholas sit up and take notice. Surely, she couldn't be? That dog of a brother of his. It wasn't enough that he was romantically seeing the woman that he, Nicholas, wanted, but could she now be carrying his child? A pure hot poker of rage ripped through Nicholas, and it was all he could do to keep calm.

'Very well my dear. You know best.' Nicholas stood up and put on his coat. 'People to see. I'm off out now. See you tomorrow.'

As he swept down the stairs, a plan began to take shape in his head. Maybe this situation could be turned to his advantage. Larry thought that no-one knew what he was up to, night after night, up in the old yard, drilling his troops to overthrow English rule. The fool hadn't been careful enough. It had been easy to have him followed on his nocturnal wanderings, and to figure out what he was planning and preparing for. Yes, Nicholas mused, there just might be a way for everything to work out to his advantage, and for him to engineer that Ellen Cooney be the next Mrs. Nicholas Clinton. Feeling quite proud of himself, Nicholas swept out the door of the mill and down the steps to his waiting carriage.

CHAPTER 22

Larry

5th March 1867

God, but he loved his country! Larry Clinton strode down West Street, feeling a surge of excitement in his belly. The town was busy today, despite the showers of hail that fell occasionally. Larry didn't feel the cold. There was a fire burning inside him. The time was nearly here. In a few short hours, all going to plan, the English would have something to talk about. They would have to sit up and take notice after tonight! For too long, Erin and her people had been subjugated by the pompous neighbours across the Irish sea. The only way to make them realise the error of their ways was by force. Larry, as chief *'Centre'* of the Drogheda Fenian brotherhood had been meticulous in his drilling of the troops. He felt they were ready. They would be joined by over fifty thousand comrades who would all launch their attacks tonight in various towns and villages -Cork, Tallaght, Limerick, Tipperary. It would be a concerted effort. The English would be taken completely by surprise, and before the night was out, Erin would be on the road to being reclaimed by her own people. The English would get their comeuppance.

A shot of elation coursed through Larry. And to think that he would play a major part in all of this! He had a good strong group of men, all ready for action tonight. At seven o'clock, young men and old would kiss their loved ones and leave their houses -all with one thing on their minds, all with one purpose - defeat of the enemy. This was what Larry had been preparing for since he was eighteen - ever since he had gone to England to study and became a stone mason; since he worked alongside many good Irish men in England, all with a burning love for their homeland, and a burning hatred for what England had done to the their people; since he had travelled to America to take part in the war, where he learned the art of fighting. All of this had been leading to this very night. Larry's pulse was fast. He nodded to two young men who passed him on the street. Edmonds and Curtis would be good additions to the group tonight. They were both young and seemed fearless. There was just one thing over which Larry had no control - how quickly the weapons would arrive. They had some, hidden in houses all over the town, and even in a monastery, but they needed a lot more to make the English quake in their boots. They *would* arrive on time. They had to. Larry was not going to accept defeat after all the effort he had put into making sure there were enough men to do what had to be done tonight. There would be bloodshed. He was well aware of the risk he was taking. He thought of Ellen and their unborn child. It had been such a shock when she had told him the news. And then, a warm glow of anticipation had begun to spread all over his body. He had taken her in his arms and promised to protect her and his son or daughter with his life. Now, more than ever, he had a reason to ensure a brighter future for his country. He swallowed hard. This was not the time for fear or doubts. No, he would be fine. Tonight, he would walk away, uninjured and triumphant. Tomorrow morning, Erin would be well on the way to freedom, and he could concentrate on making a family for himself -if Ellen agreed to his proposal, that was. He had purposely waited to ask her, in case things went wrong tonight. The way Larry was feeling, both were impossible. It would all go well, and she would say 'yes'.

He just hoped that there were no moles in the camp like there had been across the water in Chester last month, when his compatriot Rourke had tried to steal some arms. That had been a disaster. So far, Larry had been lucky and had escaped arrest. He liked to think that he had been clever also. Some of his Fenian brothers had been imprisoned. Some had been let go, as there wasn't enough evidence against them. But the constabulary were on alert, or at least, had been. But, tonight, they weren't expecting anything to happen. Larry was sure of this. So, there would be an element of surprise. Ha, they wouldn't know what had hit them!

West street was busy with the usual hustle and bustle. People seemed to have a sense of urgency about them. Maybe it was the weather, but Larry imagined that the town was holding its breath, waiting for nightfall. An RIC man, clad in his blue uniform, passed Larry and gave him a withering look.

'Good afternoon officer,' said Larry politely. He received a scowl in return. He felt the constabulary man's eyes boring into his back as he hurried down the street. He was heading home to have a light bite of food to shore him up. He honestly couldn't face a large meal, but he would need something for energy. Time enough tomorrow to sink a good feed when the work was done

Shit. They were rightly in the shit. Larry breathed hard as he ran down Magdalene Street. He could hear shouting - the constabulary, his troops. He had, five minutes previously, given the order to abandon the whole thing. He felt sick to his stomach. It had been a fiasco. The promised arms had not arrived on time, and without them, the whole plan had fallen apart. They had some rifles, some bayonets and some bottles of Greek Fire, but without proper arms, they had been finished before they had even started. At least two men had been wounded when the constabulary had opened fire. He wasn't sure how seriously. His breath came thick and fast. He could feel his lungs burning. His feet pounded, jarring his body, the vibrations going right up into his jaw.

He flew along Magdalene Street, turning left onto Sunday's Gate ...*faster, faster, must get away.* Heart pounding, blood coursing through his veins, muscles screaming. Panting, chest about to explode. Into Scarlet Street. Hail stones clawing at his face, stinging his skin. When he got his hands on the lousers who didn't turn up with the guns, he'd lynch them. Arms pumping, legs like pistons. Running out of steam. He had to slow down. His breath was coming in short bursts. *Breathe, breathe.* Heartrate slowing, Larry considered that he was reasonably safe now that he was far away from Market square. With a glance over his shoulder, he slowed his pace, removing his cap to wipe the sweat from under his fringe. Fury was pumping around his body like a steam engine. His every sinew and cell were alight with the redness of it. How had such well-laid plans gone so badly wrong? All that drilling and training, all the effort, all for nothing! How had the constabulary found out about the plan? There must be a traitor in the camp. In one of the camps. He would find him, and he would make him rue the day he was born. He probably should have stayed to help back at the Square, but the stupid fellows, those who he had trained painstakingly for months, had scattered to the wind at the first sign of trouble. Yellowbellies, the lot of them. They had ducked and dived up whatever alleyway they could find. Retreating like a pack of dogs with their tails between their legs. Larry had quickly decided that they were not worth losing his liberty over, especially as he had Ellen and the baby to think about, so after one exasperated look around, he had turned and fled. So much for saving Erin. Tonight, he had only saved his own skin.

'Mr. Clinton, I do believe.'

Larry had just turned the corner which would bring him down by the Cord cemetery. He stopped dead as a dark blue clad figure emerged from an alley to his right. He quickly turned around to retrace his steps and was met by another member of the police force, this one, bigger and broader than the first one. He swivelled around, and was met by another two, advancing on him with scowling expressions.

'I wouldn't attempt to run if I were you.'

Larry looked around him, evaluating all possible escape routes, sizing up each of the men, assessing any weaknesses. The war in America had taught him how to make decisions in a split instant. The first policeman didn't know what had hit him as Larry delivered a swift blow to his gut. He doubled over and went down like a sack of spuds. Two more launched themselves on Larry, but being lighter on his feet, he side-stepped one and planted a deft punch into the side of the head of the other one. Before either could gather themselves for a second attack, Larry swiftly head-butted the last remaining policeman and escaped down the street as fast as his tired legs would carry him. In his haste, and because his cap was slightly obscuring his view, he didn't see the patch of hail that had accumulated on the ground at the corner of the cemetery wall. The smooth sole of his boot slid on the surface, and he stumbled, catching the side of his head on a sharp piece of stone sticking out. Stars exploded in his field of vision before everything went black.

The four constabulary men who had been sent on a mission to make sure that one Mr. Larry Clinton was apprehended for his part in the Fenian Rising that night, skidded to a halt above his prone figure. It would not have been good for their reputations to have to admit that, between them, they had not been able to capture one man. So, nursing the various injuries inflicted upon them by the scumbag Clinton, they agreed that they would declare it had been an easy job to apprehend and arrest him for his part in the pathetic attempt made that night by a group of insolent wretches to try and overthrow the law of the great British Empire. They nodded at each other in agreement, brashly overlooking the fact that if it hadn't been for a convenient patch of hail, they might well have become a laughing stock in the town. And so, they picked up the unconscious Larry and hauled him off towards the town goal as quickly as they could before the bugger woke up.

CHAPTER 23

Larry

Drogheda Gaol

He was swimming in a vat of something dark and slimy. The scent of it was overpowering, crawling up his nostrils and lodging itself somewhere in the space between his nose and his eyes. Somehow, he could breathe, even though he was immersed in the wet, acidic dun-coloured mess. He could see Ellen swimming beside him, but she was in a bubble, beautiful and untouched by the foul-smelling stuff. She was saying something to him, but he couldn't hear what it was. Her expression was playful, slightly reprimanding, as she arched one of her dark eyebrows at him and looked at him quizzically. He really needed to hear what she was saying. He fixed his eyes on her beautiful pink lips. He had never mastered the art of lip reading, but he thought she was laughing at him – something about a stone wall. It didn't make any sense whatsoever. He swam around some more and Ellen's bubble floated off. He tried to swim towards it, but it stayed just out of reach. Larry looked around him to see if he could find a way out of the morass he was in. Sure enough, there was a pinprick of light directly overhead. He swam towards it, pulling as hard as he could against the liquid that surrounded him, using every bit of his strength and willpower to gradually inch closer and closer to the light. It was getting brighter. But then there was a large, swaying shadow in front of the light now, blotting it out.

Gradually, the shadow came into focus. Larry tried his best to concentrate on the pulsing, wavering image in front of him. A big, shiny head, with mottled skin, swam into view. Two deep-set eyes, a large *'whiskey'* nose and slobbering lips were surrounded by pock-marked skin. The creature smiled to reveal a mouth which contained the sum total of two blackened teeth. The head was attached to a body which looked like it was ravaged by malnutrition and drink. A man stood before Larry, looking at him with a sneering expression. His pot belly protruded from under a caved-in chest. His spindly legs looked barely strong enough to hold his frame up. The stench of the man's breath was rancid, and his body odour was sour.

'So, ya decided to wake up, then, did ya?' the ogre chuckled, an amused expression on his face which was inches away from Larry's.

'Get away from me!', Larry yelled at the man, giving him a shove. 'You stink man!'

He tried to sit up, but the pain in his head caused him to stop in his tracks as the room started to swim again. He sank once again onto the slimy, cold floor and waited for the room to stop its sickening motion. The throbbing in his head was a real, live thing, beating in time with his heart. After a few minutes, he attempted to open his eyes again, one by one. He could see that he was in a small, dark, damp room, bound on three sides by slimy brown walls. There was no furniture. The old man now lay slumped in the corner, muttering to himself, picking the skin off his head. Occasionally, he would examine a piece in his long, dirt- encrusted nails before throwing it to the floor. Larry's gaze turned towards what appeared to be a wooden door with a small hatch on the top. The sole light in the room came from a slit, high up in the back wall which let in a paltry amount.

'Where am I?' Larry groaned. He ran his hand over his forehead. He could feel a huge lump just at his hairline on the left. He winced as his fingers travelled its circumference. God's truth, it was a big one alright. He must have given it a right whack. He couldn't remember how, though. And how had he ended up in this hovel? He turned his head and looked at his companion in the corner.

'Where am I?' Larry yelled.

'Ya don't know where ya are?'

'I wouldn't be bloody well asking you if I knew!'

A spasm of mirth overcame the old man, and his bony shoulders shook beneath the thin fabric of his filthy shirt. The laughing swiftly turned to a coughing fit, and it was about sixty seconds before he could catch his breath. The coughing subsided and eventually, he fixed his rheumy eyes on Larry and announced.

'You, my son, are in GAOL!', he cackled, joyfully.

In gaol, how could he be in gaol? Larry looked incredulously at the old codger.

'That bump on your head must have messed up your memory. You don't recall how ya got it, or how ya got here?'

An image of buildings flashing by came back to Larry. The feeling of his breath coming hard and fast, his heart pumping. He could feel the sting of something cold hitting his cheeks and forehead. He remembered lashing out at someone, raining blows in quick succession. Sprinting off again, something slippery underfoot and then.... nothing.

'Are you one of them Fenian eejits? That's it, you're a Feejit!'

The old man laughed uproariously at his own joke.

'Are you one of them that tried to do a rising last night? I heard the constabulary talking about it this morning. A right hames ye made of it by all accounts. They are laughing up their sleeves at ye!'

Warming to his theme, the old man's eyes lit up as he recounted the snatches of conversation he had heard, embellishing as much as his pickled brain would allow.

'Oh yeah, there were thousands of ye. Brave men, all. Waiting with pikes and pitchforks, ready to overthrow the men of the Crown! But ye failed miserably, ye rotten toe-rags. Your guns didn't show up, you ran like yellow bellies back into the shadows when the constabulary stood up to ye! Back home to your Mammies and women folk. Useless articles. Wouldn't organize a cock fight in a chicken coop. I would have done better myself.'

He continued muttering, occasionally erupting into laughter when he said something to amuse himself, then scowling over at Larry, as if the hundreds of years of oppression by the English were all his fault, and that they had lost the best chance they would ever have of overthrowing foreign rule.

It was all coming back to Larry now. He had been fleeing. The old codger was right. He was a lily-livered, no good, useless article. So much for all the years in the army, the months and months of drilling in secret, the hopes of catching the English unawares, of claiming Erin for her people once more. Of purging the Sassenach from his green and verdant country, of giving the land back to the dispossessed, and booting out the landed gentry with a swift kick and sending them back across the Irish sea with their tails between their legs. And now, here he was, stuck in gaol with a withered old has-been, dreams crashed like broken crockery at his feet. And, captured to boot! With a groan, Larry realized that he was in a terrible pickle - one of his own making. He had survived threat after threat on his life for over four years, had faced bears, savage wild dogs, poisonous spiders, and the barrel of more than one shotgun, but he had been felled by a patch of lousy ice. He must have hit his head on the cemetery wall. Larry's fists curled into a ball in his lap. He lurched to his feet; the room swam slightly. He started banging on the door. The sound made his head throb even more. The old man was cackling away in the corner.

'Quit yer banging, ya young fool,' he shouted. 'It won't do any good you know.'

Ignoring him, Larry continued with his thumping of the wooden door. Eventually, he heard footsteps and the jangle of keys. The hatch shot back, and a pair of eyes appeared, so dark they were almost black.

'So, the Fenian bastard is awake, is he?'

'Watch your tongue.'

'You're in no position to tell me what to do, *Mister* Clinton.'

'I don't even know why I am in gaol. Why was I arrested? I haven't done anything wrong.'

'Oh, not a thing, except incitement to riot, concealment of arms, illegal drilling, all in the name of a Fenian rising!'

'You can't prove I was involved in any of those things.'

'I don't need to prove anything. I have the word of one of the most respected citizens of this town to go by. And you, my lad, are going on a very, very long holiday to the other side of the world. I hear Australia is very nice at this time of year.'

A shiver scuttled down Larry's spine as the guard's words sunk in. What was he talking about? Someone – a *'very respected citizen of the town'* was saying that he was involved in the Fenian rising. Who could that be? He had heard of convicts being transported against their will to the other side of the world for minor offences. Surely, he couldn't be bound for the same fate? He hadn't even been trialled or found guilty of any offence.

'What man says that I am guilty of these things?'

'Oh, someone you know quite well. They say blood is thicker than water, but the blood in your family must be a bit on the thin side.' The black eyes had an evil glint.

Larry could tell the gaoler was enjoying imparting this news. Larry looked at him quizzically through the hatch. Suddenly, it all fell into place in his brain, like the pieces of a jigsaw puzzle. The feeling that, over the past year, he was being watched, followed. The barely concealed animosity emanating from his brother every time their paths crossed. He had been set up. It wasn't just bad luck that had made him run into four constabulary men the night before. He had been deliberately targeted. By his own brother!

CHAPTER 24

Peggy

For once in her life, Peggy Murphy was at a complete loss as to what to do. She sat on a small stool beside Ellen's bed where the younger woman lay prostrate, her face blending in with the white-washed walls. She had lost count of the number of times Ellen had been sick already in the hour since little Tommy had run down to her, once again, to get help for his Mam. She glanced at the boy who was in the corner, an expression of concern on his face. He was playing with his little sister as he had been asked to do. She was giggling at whatever antics he was up to. He really was such a good little gasson. The poor craythur. He had seen too much strife in his young life so far. He wasn't even nine years old, for God's sake. He shouldn't have to be dealing with all this worry and anxiety. His only concern should be how many sweets to buy with the pennies he earned from working at the market. Instead, he had to deal with the death of his father, the worry of seeing his Mam trying to make ends meets, and now this sickness.

Peggy had seen many women feel unwell in the early stages of pregnancy, but this sickness was something else. It was like it had drained every last bit of strength and energy from Ellen and left her like a weak, wrung out shell. She had only nibbled on a slice of bread for the past few days. She even had trouble keeping water down. Peggy had tried everything her sailor contact had suggested when he had landed in town last week. Ginger in her tea, sweet smelling mint and sprigs of lavender, but nothing was working so far. She could see that Ellen had lost weight, and her face was gaunt. Her lips were bleached, and her eyes had dark shadows underneath. One of them was bloodshot with the force of her vomiting. She really was in a terrible state. Peggy sighed deeply as she once again wiped Ellen's brow with a cold, damp rag. She felt a sudden bolt of pure fury towards Larry Clinton. It was entirely his fault that Ellen was in this predicament. And where was the scoundrel now? On a ship somewhere to the other side of the world because he had been stupid enough to get caught on the night of the failed Rising. Oh, it was a fine sentiment alright. The Fenians' hearts were in the right place. But, to think Larry was one of them! And a leading light by all accounts! She had always had her reservations about him. Afraid that he would hurt Ellen, but never in her wildest dreams did she think Ellen would end up in this situation - with child, and the father banished to God only knew where. She took a deep breath to try and slow down her pounding heart.

'I know exactly what you're thinking', said Ellen, her voice not much more than a whisper. 'But it was my fault too.'

She clasped the older woman's hand.

'But tell me Peggy, what on earth am I going to do now? Larry's gone and he won't be back. I think my heart is going to break in two!'

A sob caught in Ellen's throat as she turned her face towards the wall. Seconds later, she once again had to turn and heave into the basin Peggy was holding.

'Hush, now, don't be upsetting yourself pet. It only makes the sickness worse. Would there be any way you could take a sip of water?'

Ellen nodded weakly, speech seeming too much, so Peggy held a cup to her lips and Ellen took two tiny sips. She lay back on the pillow as if even this minor movement had exhausted her. Peggy smoothed Ellen's dull, lank hair away from her face.

'Well, my darlin, we'll think of something. When do you think the babby is due?' Peggy enquired kindly, damping down the anger that was rattling around in her chest. There was no point in getting Ellen any more upset than she was already. Peggy knew it took two to make a new life, but the world was not fair on the women folk, because it was them that had to carry and bear the child, and the man could walk away after having his fun, if he chose. He could swan off to the alehouse any time he liked, leave the woman with a house full of bawling children, or even get himself arrested like that fool, Larry. He may well have done the right thing by Ellen if he hadn't been carted off, but he was gone and wasn't likely to be back any time soon, so it was up to her, Peggy, to help Ellen with the predicament that faced her.

'Now, don't get mad with me, but I suppose you want to keep the child?'

Peggy left the question hanging in the air. She knew there were ways and means of helping women who found themselves in this particular situation, even though she wasn't quite sure exactly how it worked. Peggy considered herself a woman of the world, but she had never witnessed an actual abortion, even though she had heard whispers about a couple of young lassies from the town who had travelled to Dublin when they found themselves in the family way. One had returned almost straight away and seemed none the worse for the experience, but the other had returned, wan and with a strained look on her face, doubled over with the pain. She had succumbed to a fever, and Peggy herself had been brought in to try and help with her herbs. She thought the lass was not long for this world, such a hold did the sickness have on her, but eventually, she had turned a corner and made a recovery. Physically, at least. The poor lass walked around town now in a daze, a sorrowful expression on her face. She had been transformed from a bright, lively young thing into a pale shadow of her former self. By all accounts whenever she saw a newborn baby, she erupted into tears. Some thought her a bit peculiar, but Peggy knew what lay at the heart of her sorrow. She knew what Ellen's answer would be before she had even asked the question, but she really was in a quandary as to how to help.

'I will *not* kill my baby.' Ellen turned her head, and Peggy saw the depth of emotion in her eyes, despite her weakened state.

'Imagine killing Tommy, or Alice. How could you even ask me that?' she hissed.

'All right, keep your hair on lass. I knew you wouldn't be thinking of doing it, but I had to ask, for I don't rightly know how we're going to cope with three childer and no man around to provide.'

Ellen's gaze softened as she looked at Peggy. 'You said 'we.''

'What are you on about?'

'You said you don't know how *'we'* are going to cope.'

'Of course I did. Sure, I'm not going to leave you to sort all this out on your own pet. You're like a daughter to me, and I might never have said it before, but I love you, Tommy and little Alice like you were my own. We'll think of some way out of this predicament. For now, you have to concentrate on trying to keep a little bit of food down and sipping on the water. You'll need to have the strength to go to work tomorrow. You'll have to keep earning, although, what will happen when you start showing, I don't know.' Peggy absentmindedly wrung her hands, chafing the already chilblained skin.

'I suppose Nicholas Clinton will throw you out on your ear when he sees that you're in the family way. It won't take him long to put two and two together and realise that the child is Larry's, I'll bet.'

'I suppose he probably will' Ellen sighed, putting her hands over her eyes as if trying to block out the reality of the mess she was in. She quietly started to sob.

'There, there lass, it's not the end of the world. You're young and clever, and together we'll think of something. I could talk to your Ma and Da? They'd surely soften if they thought there was another grandchild on the way?'

'Have you lost your reason Peggy? Don't on your life, go anywhere near my parents. They made it very clear that I wasn't their daughter any longer when I married Jim. Oh Jim, what have I done? I'm so sorry I'm making such a mess of my life. All you ever wanted was for me to be happy.'

Ellen was beginning to get herself wound up like a clock again and Peggy knew there was no sense in going down that way of thinking, for it would do no one any good.

'Hush now, Ellen. Jim doesn't think any the worse of you. You're right, he would want you to be happy and he might even help come up with a solution.' Peggy didn't believe that Jim was anywhere but at the bottom of the ocean, but she knew Ellen had faith that he was in heaven.

'You have to pull yourself together for the sake of them wee ones over in the corner. And for the little one growing in your belly. Imagine, you, a mother of three! And all the times when you thought you'd never fall again after young Tommy! I wonder will it be a lass or a wee lad, eh?'

Peggy was doing her best to try and get Ellen to see the positive side of the situation. She couldn't stay sick for much longer. In the meantime, Peggy would help out as best she could. She was also going to pay a visit to Mr. Nicholas Clinton. Seeing as his brother was the father and he was going to be of absolutely no use to Ellen from the other side of the world, she would appeal to him to help Ellen out. After all, the child would be his niece or nephew. He should at least let her keep her job and help financially. She would call on him tomorrow evening when Ellen was home from work and have a word or two in his ear. Peggy knew she could be very persuasive when she wanted to be, and now was the time for some plain, straight talking. Happy that some sort of a plan was settled in her mind, Peggy turned to Tommy and Alice in the corner.

'Now then, young ones, who's ready for a bit of tea?'

'Me, me, tea!' shouted Alice.

'Yes please' said Tommy quietly.

Peggy bustled about the kitchen, putting out a loaf of bread and a slab of butter on the table and getting the jam down from the shelf near the back door.

'Is Mam going to get better?' Tommy whispered in Peggy's ear.

'She'll be as right as rain Tommy; don't you fret pet.'

Peggy ruffled his hair and stole a glance over at Ellen.

'If I have my way, it will all work out just fine.'

Tommy ran over to give his mother a hug and then returned to the table to polish off three slices of bread and jam in quick succession.

CHAPTER 25

Nicholas

Nicholas was just about to sit back and allow a glass of very fine whiskey ease the strains and stresses of the day. It had been particularly trying. The lodgement to the bank had fallen short last week, and again today, and Nicholas was at a loss as to what was going on. He stiffened as a sharp pain hit between his shoulder blades. It didn't last too long, but he'd had one like that before, more than once. He pulled at his tie to loosen it and opened the top button of his starched white shirt. *Ah, that was better.* The pain eased and he once again let himself relax into his favourite armchair. It was a heavy, wine-coloured leather, and was well worn from use. It was an heirloom from his father's family. Nicholas looked around the room, which was his retreat. No one dared enter here, except if they were invited. Even Mrs. Mc Mahon, the housekeeper, knew to keep out unless he wanted her to bring him in a cup of tea. It was very much a man's room. Its four walls clad in a subtle shade of deep cream, the furniture masculine, and the only adornment being an oil lamp with a deep red lampshade and golden tassels, that stood in the corner beside the window. It cast a subtle glow over the room. A fire crackled in the hearth and its warmth began to seep into his bones. He took a sip from his glass and stared at the flickering flames.

He was lost in thought, running the sequence of events of the past week over in his mind. Larry, the fool, had been easy to get rid of. Him and his Fenian foot soldiers hadn't been that clever despite all their 'secret' preparations. It wasn't as though Nicholas didn't agree with the Fenian sentiment. It just didn't do to be public about it. He had more sense than that. It seemed his little brother wasn't quite as wise as he thought he was. It had been easy to have him followed, to find out where he was drilling with the other sympathisers, and to ascertain that they would be attempting a Rising on the night of March 5th. His informant had only wanted a small fee for relaying all the relevant information. It had been worth every penny. A quick word in a certain constabulary man's ear and Larry had been picked up as easily as one, two, three. Well, four. He had heard that four of them had been dispatched to bring Larry in. That was an extra pay packet that he hadn't been banking on, but sure, it was still worth it. Now that Larry was out of the way, he could concentrate on making Ellen his. He recalled the pure white rage that had rattled him from head to toe when he had heard that Larry and Ellen were courting. Of course, he had to hide it. Bide his time. Come up with a plan to ensure Larry was dispatched. Once he was out of the picture, Nicholas had no doubt that it wouldn't be long before Ellen realized that he, Nicholas, was a much better catch. He had to carefully consider his next move. She had been quite smitten with Larry, by all accounts, so no doubt, there would be a little crack in her heart to mend. Nicholas had yet to come across a woman who couldn't be considerably cheered up by an expense account in the local fashion house and an endless supply of hats. He was sure Ellen wasn't very different to the rest of them. And if his suspicions were correct, then she would, most likely, be more than happy to have a knight in shining armour come to her rescue. Even though she was extremely peaky looking at work and she had lost a bit of weight, she was still utterly gorgeous. He wouldn't be long putting a smile back on her face and restoring her glow. His reverie was interrupted by a quiet knock on the door. Irritation coursed through him. Could a man not enjoy a nice drink in peace?

'Yes. What is it?' he enquired rattily.

The door opened and the curly grey hair of his housekeeper, Mrs. Mc Mahon, made an appearance first, followed quickly by her face which was relatively line free for a woman of close to sixty. Nicholas had often overheard her boasting at how well she looked, putting it down to the fact that she had never married. She considered a husband and children to be the main stressors in any woman's life. Nicholas could tell by the expression on her face tonight that she was none too pleased at having been summoned to door by a visitor at this late hour. He hadn't heard the front doorbell, so whoever it was must have arrived at the back entrance.

'Mr. Clinton. There's someone to see you,' she sniffed, opening the door a crack.

'Come in, come in,' he ordered.

Mrs. Mc Mahon moved into the room and closed the door firmly behind her. She was a trim woman for her age. She still had a good shape, despite the little extra padding that had crept on over the past few years. Her features were arranged so that her annoyance was plain to be seen.

'Peggy Murphy is here to see you. She says she has to speak with you very urgently and that it's very important. I did ask her if it couldn't wait until tomorrow, but she says not.' Mrs. Mc Mahon sniffed, and her lips tightened into a straight line to show her disapproval.

Nicholas sat up straight, making the old leather on the chair creak. What did that woman want with him that was so urgent, he wondered? The only person they had in common was Ellen. It must be something to do with her. His interest was piqued.

'Well, don't just stand there, show her in!'

Mrs. Mc Mahon looked like she had been ready and waiting for him to tell her to send the Murphy woman packing. Her expression was a comical mixture of disappointment and disbelief. With a sniff, she turned back towards the door, opening it wide.

'You may come in now, Mrs. Murphy.'

Peggy sailed into the room.

'Thank you, Mrs. Mc Mahon', she smiled sweetly, giving her best toothy smile.

With a toss of her head, Mrs. Mc Mahon retreated out the door, closing it firmly behind her. Peggy smiled, then, pulling herself up to her full five feet four inches, she turned to face Nicholas.

'Good evening Mrs. Murphy, how are you? Please, do have a seat.'

Peggy appeared to examine the seat on the other side of the fireplace. It was a straight-backed chair, covered in a cream and wine brocade. She lowered herself onto the chair, wincing a bit, as if her knees were protesting. She rearranged her skirts and rested her hands loosely in her lap. She raised her eyes to meet him.

He looked at her enquiringly. 'To what do I owe the pleasure?'

Peggy cleared her throat and wriggled herself into a more comfortable position on the chair. She swallowed and began to speak.

'I've come to ask you something -a favour.'

A hot flush was beginning to wind its way up Peggy's neck, a combination of the heat of the fire and her discomfort, no doubt. Her gaze met his steadily.

'Aye, a favour. On behalf of Ellen, although she doesn't know I'm here. She wouldn't be best pleased with me if she knew. It's urgent. I'm hoping you can help.'

Ha, his plan was starting to come together! A sixth sense told him that something was about to change to his advantage. He felt a stab of excitement in his belly. He kept his features neutral as he asked Peggy.

'Urgent, you say. Is Ellen well? She has looked a bit off-colour lately at work. I did wonder about her health.'

'Well, she has had a big shock last week, with Larry being captured. She didn't suspect that he was involved with the Fenians. And to have him taken away so suddenly -she has no idea where he went. All she knows is that he was taken from the gaol the day after he was captured, and he could be anywhere by now, off in a Dublin goal, or maybe up the north. It's an awful worry to her.' Peggy's voice trailed off as she gazed into the fire. The furrow between her eyebrows deepened. 'I'm here to appeal to you to see if you can find out where he is and maybe get him pardoned. He is your brother, after all. You're a man of means and influence, I'm sure with a word in the right ear, you could find out where he is. It would mean such a lot to Ellen - would give her a bit of peace of mind. Poor little Tommy is distraught. Not only does he lose his father, but just as he is getting very fond of Larry, he disappears. I dread to think what this is doing to the little mite's head.' Peggy exhaled loudly and sat back in the chair, her colour heightened after her speech. She looked over at Nicholas expectantly.

Nicholas observed the woman before him. He knew she was the local 'Handywoman' who helped out with births around the area. She had a reputation for being a formidable character but was a champion of the women she looked after. She had been known to give many a new father a clip around the ear for not allowing his wife enough time to recover after giving birth. Although she didn't mix in the same circles as he did, he had done his research, and he'd wager he knew a lot more about Peggy Murphy than she did about him. Even though he was sure there were no flies on her, it didn't look like she suspected him of having anything to do with Larry's disappearance. Good, he wanted to keep it that way. Hopefully those constabulary men would keep their traps shut. They'd be sorry if they didn't. The Inspector was a good friend of his. He decided there was nothing to be gained from pretending he didn't know where Larry was.

'Mrs. Murphy, I'm sorry to have to tell you that Larry is, as we speak, on his way to Australia.'

The colour drained from Peggy's face and her mouth became a perfect O.

'Oh, holy mother of God, that can't be true? How on earth could he have been banished so quickly? Sure, there wasn't time to try him or find him guilty of anything! How on earth was he shipped off and without a word to Ellen? That is so cruel!'

'I did try to dissuade the authorities from sending him away, but they wouldn't listen to me.' Nicholas's face looked pained as he spread his hands wide in a gesture of helplessness.

'Ellen will get a terrible shock. It won't be good for her in her condition.'

It seemed Peggy realised her mistake as, wringing her hands, she looked over at Nicholas. So, his suspicions were correct. A slow trickle of satisfaction started to make his insides glow. The old woman before him seemed to deflate.

'Yes, she's with child, and it's Larry's. So now you see why his disappearance was such a shock. The poor craythur is beside herself with worry and with sickness. She hasn't been at all well these past few weeks.'

'Well, well, wasn't that very stupid of my brother to go and get himself captured?'

Nicholas's eyes were inscrutable as he looked into the flames.

'Very stupid indeed.'

A plan began to form in his mind. He would have to go and pay a visit to his friend, Fr. Mulroy. He would need a bit of persuasion, but Nicholas was one hundred percent sure that he would co-operate. Nicholas was very good at making people do what he wanted them to. Ah yes, things had just taken a turn for the very best. A bit faster than he had anticipated, which was all the better.

'Will you try and see if you can get Larry back here as soon as possible? Surely you must have some influence that you can bring to bear on the situation?' Peggy's voice interrupted Nicholas's thoughts. He had almost forgotten she was in the room.

'Mrs. Murphy, I will see what can be done, but I don't hold out too much hope. Try not to worry. I will do my best to look after Ellen.'

Peggy's expression looked doubtful, like she didn't know what he had in mind, and that she had a feeling that the person who would be well looked after would be none other than himself.

CHAPTER 26

Parochial House, Drogheda

March 1867

Father Alphonsus Mulroy had never liked his Christian name. When he was a boy, if he hadn't been so saintly, he would have cursed his parents for foisting it upon him. It was prone to getting shortened to *'Fonsie'* by all and sundry. The other boys in his class took great delight in calling him just that. But they didn't stop at 'Fonsie.' One day, a particularly cruel classmate, who seemed to have the ability to seek out weaknesses in others, and, indeed delighted in making the most of his discoveries, declared that from now on, Alphonsus would be called *'Fancy Fonsie'*. This had something to do with, at age thirteen, the slightly effeminate way in which Alphonsus conducted himself. It was as if the bully could see into his soul and identify something that Alphonsus himself wasn't quite aware of. The name had stuck. Alphonsus had indeed proved to be slightly 'fancy' but after a while, the bullies got tired of not getting a rise out of him and they turned to different prey. During his third year at the boarding school in the Irish midlands, Alphonsus had discovered that he was rather partial to the look of the younger boys.

The smaller, the better. There was something sweet and slightly exciting about the downy hair on a young cheek, the shape of shoulders as they started to broaden, the outline of muscles through a vest. But he was careful, and his little fantasies lived mainly in his head.

By the time he was in senior year, at age seventeen, he found his head turned by a member of the latest bunch of new boarders. Gerard Burke was just shy of his twelfth birthday - blonde, blue eyed, with painfully thin limbs and almost translucent skin. Alphonsus could not stop thinking about him. About how his skin would feel, what it would be like to sit him on his knee. He began to engineer reasons to be around the younger boy; pretended to take him under his wing. It was easy enough to do, as the older boys sometimes mentored the younger ones. No-one passed any remarks, at least that's what Alphonsus thought. But he had bargained without the observation skills of Nicholas Clinton. One day, Alphonsus managed to get Gerard on his own in the little disused summer house on the grounds of the school. It became a regular thing. Gerard began to withdraw into himself. One autumn evening, the gardener came across the lifeless body of the boy swinging from the apple tree at the very farthest part of the orchard. No one knew what had driven the poor lad to take his own life. If any of the Christian Brothers had their suspicions, they were not voiced, as there was nothing surer but that Alphonsus Mulroy, with his keen mind and love of the scripture, was destined for the priesthood. It would be an absolute shame to deny his parents the honour and privilege of having a man of the cloth in their family. Nothing should be allowed to get in the way of this. So, the death of little Gerard was considered a tragedy and remained a mystery to his heart-broken parents.

'Fonsie' was now parish priest in Drogheda. He had been moved from Clara in Co. Offaly the previous year. Drogheda suited him, as it was a lively town, and there was no shortage of fresh blood to be observed at regular intervals down at the quayside where he took his daily constitutional. He had a young curate to help him with his duties and had the ear of the bishop. Life was good. His housekeeper was a fine cook and was especially talented at making biscuits and fruit cakes. His parishioners were a reasonably generous lot, and mostly gave his Sunday sermons the respect they deserved. There weren't too many funerals, and he was currently having a rest from the wedding ceremonies, it being Lent.

The only fly in the ointment took the shape of one Mr. Nicholas Clinton. Their first encounter in over thirty years had been the previous summer when they had bumped into each other on the street. Nicholas had extended his hand, a knowing, calculating expression in his eyes, but his features arranged in a friendly greeting. Something had quivered inside Alphonsus as he wondered how much Nicholas might remember about their school days. They hadn't been alone in each other's company since that day, but now, Mrs. Lynch had just announced that Clinton was waiting in the parlour for him.

Alphonsus straightened his dog collar which suddenly felt a bit tight. He could see in the mirror that two spots of colour had appeared high on his cheeks. He rocked back and forth on his feet and wiped a bead of perspiration from his top lip. Well, he had better go and see what Clinton wanted. He would get rid of him as quickly as he could, for Sunday's sermon wouldn't write itself. The people of the parish needed to be reminded that Lent was a time for penance and cleansing the soul.

Alphonsus entered the parlour and closed the door firmly, but quietly behind him. He stood looking at Nicholas who appeared to be engrossed in a painting of a ship which adorned the wall beside the fireplace. He turned around when Alphonsus cleared his throat. He was a handsome man, no doubt about it, if a little rounded in the waist department. Alphonsus patted the gentle mound of his own stomach.

'Nicholas! Great to see you. To what do I owe the pleasure?'

Alphonsus ran his hand through his black, slightly greasy hair, before extending it to shake the other man's. Nicholas's grip was strong, his hands warm and dry.

'Alphonsus, or may I call you Fonsie?'

There was a challenge in Nicholas's eyes that caused a shiver of unease to course its way down Alphonsus's spine. He never liked meeting anyone from school. Not that he had met many, down through the years. From the particular crop of boys that had attended St. Cuthbert's with him, few had been lucky enough to have a vocation like him.

'I have come to ask you if you would perform a wedding ceremony.'

Alphonsus frowned. 'I thought both your daughters were married already Nicholas?'

'They are. It's me that's getting married again.'

The words settled into the atmosphere. Alphonsus's eyebrows were raised in surprise.

'Oh, well, congratulations Nicholas. And who is the lucky lady?'

'It's Ellen Cooney.'

Alphonsus knew the young widow to see. She wasn't his type, obviously, but he could appreciate that she was a fine-looking woman, although, far too young for this old goat standing in front of him.

'Ah, yes, the young widow-woman. I heard the very sad story of her husband drowning at sea. Out off the coast of South America, I believe? It was such a tragedy. It's great to hear that she's ready to move on now. And with a fine man like yourself!'

Wanting to get Nicholas out of his sight as soon as possible, he moved to his desk which was situated in the furthest corner away from the fire.

'Let me get my diary and see when I might be able to fit you in.'

He took the heavy black book in his hand and opened it, starting to thumb through the pages after Easter Sunday.

'When were you thinking of? I could do the first week in May if that was agreeable?'

Alphonsus raised his watery blue eyes from the pages of the book to be met by Nicholas's brown ones. Silence.

'Nicholas. Did you hear what I suggested? A May wedding is always nice. It's the start of the summer, and very often, the weather can be quite sunny and warm. Will I pencil you in?'

'Actually, Alphonsus, I was rather thinking that I might like to get married next week.'

'Next week?' spluttered the priest. 'But, my dear man, it's the middle of Lent. Marriage ceremonies are not permitted in Lent as you well know.'

'Well, of course, I know that it's not a common thing to have a wedding in Lent, but if it's something that one of your parishioners really, really wants, then surely, some arrangement could be made? After all, we go back quite a long way.... More than thirty years. And I have a very long memory. Is yours as long? We had quite the fun at St. Cuthberts, didn't we? I seem to remember you particularly enjoyed your time there, especially taking all the little fellas under your wing. Now, there was one that you seemed to favour above all the rest. What was his name?'

Nicholas made a fist with his hand, bringing it to his pursed lips, casting his eyes up to the ceiling as he appeared to try and recall the name of the little boy.

'Ah, yes, his name was Gerard Burke if I remember correctly.' Nicholas fixed his eyes on Alphonsus with a steady, dead stare that shook Alphonsus to the core.

'Ah, I don't really remember anyone called Gerard Burke.' Alphonsus could feel the blood draining from his face and had an urgent need to sit down.

'Oh, I think you do Alphonsus. I certainly remember you keeping his company quite a bit. You seemed particularly fond of the old summerhouse, if my memory serves me correctly. Not many people knew, but there was a hole in the wall which gave a direct line of vision into the back window of the summerhouse. It was very easy to see in.'

Nicholas let his words hang in the air. With a gulp, Alphonsus flicked through the pages of his diary, back to the month of March.

'Well then Nicholas. I don't see why an old friend can't help out another, even during Lent. When were you thinking of again? Would next Wednesday suit you by any chance? I think I might be able to fit you in.'

CHAPTER 27

Nicholas

'St. Jude's', Lytham St. Annes, England

March 1867

It was the smell of the place that always got to him. Like a mixture of whatever soap was used to clean the inhabitants, the remnants of the previous evening's meal and the polish they used on the very shiny floors. Nicholas pressed his lemon-scented linen handkerchief to his nose as he tried not to gag. He cast his gaze around the room. Nothing had changed in the past year. The narrow window, which had bars on the outside, let in very little light on the best of days, never mind on this cold, dreary March afternoon. The walls were painted a pasty shade of dun, and the putty-coloured brocade armchair with the straight back and timber arms, from which the polish was all but worn, still stood in the corner. On the wall, there was a painting of a pretty young woman sitting on top of a windswept hill, with a rapt expression on her face, flowers in her long blonde hair. It was nearly the only bit of colour in the lifeless room. He let his eyes rest on the figure lying on the bed. The change in his wife's appearance in the past year had come as quite a shock to Nicholas. She was wearing a blue cardigan that he had never seen before over the usual beige smock thing that they made them wear in this place. She appeared to be asleep, but it was probably the cocktail of medicine she was on that had her slack-jawed and drooling into her pillow.

Sighing, he sat down on the chair. He needed to get out of this place as quickly as possible. It always induced a feeling of anxiety in him, and an urgent desire to flee. It was easy enough to slip away across the water to Liverpool from Drogheda, but any more than once a year, and his pretence that it was a business trip might not be believed. Always, at the first glimpse of this building's forbidding stone façade, with its sloping roof and barred windows that looked like semi-shuttered eyes, he was counting the minutes until he could take his leave. He had to force himself down the long avenue and through the highly polished dark mahogany doors. The pattern on the orange and brown tiles in the hallway were enough to make your senses swim, or maybe it was the muffled screams and howls to be heard emanating from behind some of the closed doors on the long, dark hallway. The place gave him the shivers.

Taking a quick glance over his right shoulder to make sure the door was closed, he leaned in and gave his wife's midriff a prod with his finger. He needed to see with his own eyes what sort of a state she was in. There was plenty of flesh on her bones now. Not like when they had been newly married, more than twenty- five years before. She had been whip-thin then, intelligent, and sharp of tongue. They'd had many a stimulating conversation. Indeed, it had been her keen intellect that had attracted him to her. That and her hand-span waist and copper hair.

Now she looked like some of the bread-and -butter pudding he used to like. Plump and devoid of colour.

There was no response from her. Nicholas sighed and sat back in his chair. His mind wandered to the past. Their marriage had been good at first. Exciting. But then, Rosemary had been anxious about the impending birth of their first child. Inordinately so. She had tried his patience with her constant babble, wondering how she was going to cope. She had very slim hips and seemed to be carrying an extremely big baby. As her time drew near, she seemed to withdraw into herself. Nicholas had retreated to the spare room as he couldn't be doing with her tossing and turning. The woman seemed never to sleep. One spring day, after what seemed like a never-ending labour, she had given birth to their daughter, Clarice. He had thought that she would rally quickly and get back to being the woman he had married, but then the tears had started. She would cry at the drop of a hat. Some days, she didn't even want to get out of bed. She turned from the vivacious, lively conversationalist that he had married into a wisp of a woman - a shell of her former self. Nicholas hadn't known what to do with her. All he knew was that she was getting on his nerves.

He had decided that she needed another baby to keep her occupied. Surely, with two, she would have to pull herself together? She agreed, reluctantly, it seemed. Night after night, she just lay there like a rag doll as if a spectator in the act rather than a participant. It hadn't been much fun for him. Surely a man deserved a bit of acknowledgment for his efforts? A few months after the birth of Clarice, she had woodenly announced that he was to be a father for the second time. Nicholas was puffed up with pride and didn't hesitate in telling all and sundry. He had been convinced that he would have a boy this time. Someone to take over the family business.

Rosemary had taken to her room and had rarely come out for the remaining six months. It didn't bother Nicholas too much as he was very busy at the mill, and with building up the wholesale end of his business. He shuttled regularly from his house in Greenhills to the mill. He was a busy man. He needed his sleep and left his wife to deal with their toddler daughter. Mrs. Mc Mahon was a godsend at the time. He slipped her a few extra bob on top of her salary to ensure that she didn't get thoroughly fed up trying to cajole his wife into eating some food and trying to put a bit of a smile on her face. Was a smile too much to ask for? Apparently so.

Their second daughter came into the world one cold December night. The labour had been a bit shorter this time, but not much. He had entered the room to congratulate his wife and to have a look at the new arrival. His face hadn't quite been able to hide his disappointment that it was a girl. He had sat at his wife's bedside to peer in at the little scrap of humanity latched to her mother's breast. She was truly tiny, with a wisp of reddish-blonde hair adorning the top of her head. He had looked at Rosemary's face which held an expression of utter detachment. She had motioned with her head for him to come closer. He had thought that she wanted him to kiss her, but instead, she had turned her cheek and had spoken softly in his left ear.

'Nicholas. That was the very last time that I will give birth. I am telling you now in no uncertain terms. That part of our marriage is over.'

The steel in her voice had been a bit of a shock to him. He had sat back in his chair, puffed out his cheeks, and without any further comment, had removed himself from her room.

Over the next few months, the new baby, Sarah, had made her presence felt keenly in the house. She was crotchety and very hard to settle, bringing up bottle after bottle. Clarice, perhaps sensing the tension in the house, had turned into a little madam. Rosemary got more morose as the weeks went by, seeming to sink into a depression where no one could reach her. Mrs. Mc Mahon ended up looking after both babies. One day when the girls were three, and eighteen months, something snapped in Nicholas. He was living a half-life. His wife had disappeared into some crazy world of her own. He realized that nothing short of a miracle would get him his son and heir and, frankly, Rosemary was a huge embarrassment. He did his research. There was a place near Liverpool where he could commit Rosemary. He left the girls in the care of Mrs. Mc Mahon and set out, with Rosemary, one June evening, telling anyone who cared to ask that he was bringing his wife for a holiday. A change of scene might be good for her. She would most likely get some enjoyment from the beaches at Formby and Southport. The jolly seaside atmosphere would surely be infectious? The sea air could only do her good.

He had to admit, he had played the part of the grieving widower extremely well when he had come home on his own. *Yes, it had been a total shock to wake up and find his wife gone, her side of the bed cold. Yes, the people in the area had been so good, helping in the search for her around the beaches and yes, she had been beginning to make a slight recovery, in that her mood had lightened slightly. It was a total mystery how she had vanished into thin air. And what a tragedy to find her shoes beside a rock on St. Anne's beach. It would appear that her depression had led her to take her own life. Yes, he was worn out with the stress and worry of it all. Yes, he was young to be a widower. And yes, he would do his best to bring up his two small daughters as Rosemary would have liked.*

He had accepted all the handshakes and sympathetic pats on the arm from the people of Drogheda. Most didn't mention the shame he must be feeling. *It was just as well they hadn't found the body, as Nicholas wouldn't have been allowed to bury her in a Catholic graveyard, seeing as she had taken her own life.* He had thanked his lucky stars that his wife had no living relatives. Something good that had come out of the cholera epidemic of '32.

Rosemary had put up a bit of a struggle when he'd brought her to this place. He had assured her that he there were doctors there that could help her feel better. He had departed as quickly as he could, leaving her in that brown and orange hallway, with two no-nonsense orderlies, one on either side of her. She was a thin pathetic figure, as she was led away down the corridor. On his instruction, she had received the heaviest sedation available, and no attempt was made to treat her malaise. As long as he made regular donations to the hospital, his wish was the head doctor's command. After a few years of playing the grieving widower, and as it became clear that there was apparently no hope of Rosemary being found alive, he had obtained a death certificate from a very obliging clerk who wasn't averse to a bit of remuneration.

And now, here he was, just about to win himself a lovely new wife. Nothing was to be allowed to stand in his way. He was a man who liked things neat and tidy. There could be absolutely no possibility of Rosemary suddenly appearing on the scene, no matter how remote. Not when he was married to Ellen. She hadn't agreed to marry him yet, but she would.

Rosemary stirred in her slumber and Nicholas poked a bit harder. This time, her eyes opened, and she grunted. She slowly turned her head as if sensing Nicholas's presence in the room. Her light-blue, clouded eyes focused on him with difficulty. God, she really was out of it. There was a spot of white spittle on the corner of her mouth. The mouth that he had kissed many times was now turned down at the corners, and the lips were no longer full. He stared at the spider's web of fine lines on her jowls.

She really had gone to pot. She grunted again and frowned slightly, as if trying to remember who he was. He could see the struggle on her face, and it was as if she was chasing images and memories in her head, but they remained out of grasp. Good, it looked like she didn't recognize him. She was living a half-life here. It would actually be a mercy for her to be released from it.

Nicholas liked to figure things out for himself, see the proof with his own eyes. It made his decisions easier. Left no room for doubt or regret. Rosemary turned her head away from him, lapsing back into her drug-induced world. It really was good stuff they were giving her. Nicholas rose to his feet. He took one last look at his wife, moved to the door, opened it, closed it gently behind him and made his way swiftly down the tiled corridor.

Finding out that Freda Cooper, one of the nurses here at the hospital, was in dire financial straits had been a godsend. It was something to do with her wayward son who had gotten in with a bad lot and was in debt. He had told her that he had a lovely bride-to-be waiting for him back in Drogheda who knew about Rosemary, and who had suggested that if he truly loved her, Nicholas would 'look after the situation'. Being madly in love, he was a slave to her every wish. What was he to do? Freda had understood how young women could be so determined to get what they wanted these days. So, telling her what he wanted her to do, a price had been agreed. Freda seemed desperate for the money. She had named a steep enough fee, but Nicholas was willing to pay it. She had assured him she would take the details of the arrangement to her grave. It would look like Rosemary had died in her sleep. She would be buried in an unmarked grave in the grounds of the hospital.

Nicholas made his way swiftly towards the front door. Once outside, he breathed in a big lungful of cold air. Thank God he would never have to set foot in that place again. A solitary flake of snow found its way under his scarf and made him shiver. He pulled his collar tight and walked briskly down the avenue to hail a cab to bring him back to the hotel where he would spend the night, before making his way back to Drogheda, and his new life. He whistled as he increased his pace, a smile hovering on his lips.

CHAPTER 28

Nicholas

Drogheda

Nicholas slowed his stride as he walked up the hill towards the Rope Walk. It was funny, he observed, how you could grow up in a town and still not be fully familiar with all its lanes and alleys. He didn't have much occasion to travel to this particular street, most of his business being concentrated at the mill and down nearer the river at the Linen Hall, where he sold his cloth to the many merchants from around the country and, also, England and Scotland. He had decided to walk to Ellen's house as he had wanted a bit of head space to prepare himself for the conversation that lay ahead. A heavy, sleety rain was driving hard into his face and making it a bit hard to breathe. His breath came in short bursts, and he could feel a tightness in his chest. Probably the bitterly cold wind. It was March, but there was no sign of the blessed winter weather to ease. The daffodils which should have been waving their yellow heads at this stage of the year were nowhere to be seen. No doubt, biding their time until the sun's rays would start to gently warm the earth. Nicholas felt an unfamiliar sensation unfurling in his stomach.

He zoned in on it, examined it, surprised to find that it was actual fear. He was annoyed at himself for allowing anyone to make him feel this way. But it wasn't 'anyone'. It was Ellen Cooney who had his insides in turmoil.

The fear was caused by what he was about to do. He was minutes away from asking her to marry him and he didn't know what he would do with himself if she refused. There was a good possibility that she would. He knew she was a proud woman. He had seen this in her bearing, her insistence that she was perfectly capable of undertaking the many tasks he had thrown at her up at the mill without any help, *thank you very much*. But he knew she was feeling vulnerable. With his brother out of the picture, and with her expecting - and so sick, -he reckoned this was the perfect opportunity to offer her a way out of her dilemma. She should be grateful to him. She would be grateful. He just needed to approach her with the correct amount of sympathy for her plight and appeal to her pragmatic side. He knew she had one. If she accepted, he would have her down the aisle as quick as sticks. The thought of having her in his bed every night made his pulse increase, and a sweat started to break out on his brow, mingling with the sleet.

At last, he reached the corner where he would turn left and walk twenty yards to Ellen's house. The sun suddenly broke through the clouds, and the row of low, whitewashed cottages dazzled him for a second. He stopped and looked up and down the street, keeping a look out for any 'undesirables' who might suddenly decide he was worth mugging for the loose change in his pocket. He counted the cottages. Ellen lived in the sixth one on the right-hand side of the street. He made his way gingerly across the road, making sure not to step in any of the horse manure or dog mess which peppered his pathway. He would have a sharp word in the ear of the chairman of the Paving and Cleaning Committee of the Corporation. They needed to up their game. A mangy-looking mongrel stopped to sniff him, and he gave it the benefit of his right boot to see it on its way. There weren't many about on this blustery Sunday afternoon. He had watched Ellen struggle at work all week with her sickness. She had tried to hide it from him. It was all working out quite nicely. All Ellen needed was a bit of gentle persuasion. Her defences were down. Nicholas prided himself on knowing just when to swoop in a business deal, and this was no different. Only, the stakes were high this time. Higher than he had let himself realize. He reached the door of Ellen's house. The paintwork was peeling, and the small windows were slightly grimy. He raised his hand to knock, but the door was opened before he could make contact. Ellen's young lad, was it Johnny? No Tommy, stood before him with a look of curiosity on his handsome young face.

'Yes, Mister- can I help you?' He had manners too.

'Good afternoon young man. I am here to see Ellen Cooney. Is this the right house?'

'Yes, she lives here. I'm her son, Tommy.'

The boy extended his hand and Nicholas shook it, noticing the confident gaze of the young lad.

'Is she here?'

'Oh, sorry, yes she is, but she's not feeling very well at the moment.'

Tommy looked over his left shoulder into the gloom of the room. Nicholas tried to peer past him but couldn't make out anything except a couple of dull shapes in the shadows.

'Can I give her a message?'

'It's ok Tommy. This is Mr. Clinton from the mill. You can let him in.' Ellen called from the shadows. Her voice was weak and barely audible.

The young boy took another look at Nicholas and reluctantly, it seemed, opened the door to let him in. Nicholas stepped over the threshold and let the lad close the door behind him. Taking off his hat, he stood still, trying to get accustomed to the dark. He took in the small room, the crackling fire, the steaming kettle on the crook. A table and three chairs stood in the middle of the room and his eyes could just make out a settle bed at the back. It wasn't a whole lot warmer in here than it was outside. Sitting on the settle bed was Ellen, looking completely forlorn. She rose to her feet and swayed slightly. It only took Nicholas two strides to cross the room and grab her elbow to steady her.

'Are you alright my dear?' he enquired. 'You don't look the best, I must say.'

'I'm fine, just a bit tired.'

She looked from him to his hand, which still had a grip on her elbow. Taking the hint, he released it, and she straightened her back, tossing her head and looking at him directly.

'Mr. Clinton, what brings you to visit?' Even dulled with the sickness, her eyes still held a spark.

'I have been very concerned about you lately, Ellen. You haven't been yourself at all. I was in the area and decided to call on you to see if there is anything I can do. You are a very valuable employee, and I hate to see you suffer like this. The sickness seems to have taken quite a hold on you.'

'It's very tiresome, I can't seem to shake it off.'

Ellen suddenly went limp and sank onto one of the kitchen chairs, holding a handkerchief to her mouth. A dried-out, brittle looking sprig of lavender was clasped in one hand. Her head was bent, and she seemed to have trouble staying upright. She looked like she just wanted to collapse on the table and fall asleep.

'May I?' Nicholas enquired.

She nodded almost imperceptibly. With one movement, he took off his coat and sat down at the kitchen table. He clasped his hands together and leaning over the table towards her bent head until his lips were almost touching her hair, he whispered;

'I know.'

Her head shot up.

'Know what?' she enquired breathlessly.

'About the baby.'

His words hung in the air between them. She held her breath, staring at him, a look of pure terror on her face. She swallowed hard, and keeping her eyes on his face, she said to Tommy.

'Go down to Peggy and see how she is and if she needs anything, there's a good boy. I think it's stopped raining now, so you won't get wet.'

Seemingly reluctant to leave his Mam, Tommy slowly made his way to the door, keeping an eye on Nicholas. Ellen waited until he was gone before turning to Nicholas.

'How?'

'Peggy told me.' A look of complete surprise came over Ellen's stricken face.

'Peggy told you?'

'Well, more like she let it slip.'

'When?'

'She came to my house a few days ago to see if I could do anything to help Larry's plight, but I explained to her that I have no influence with the authorities. There's nothing I can do to help him, I'm afraid.'

Nicholas shrugged and put on his best pained expression.

'I believe you and he were quite the item? I presume it is his child you are carrying?'

'How dare you!' Ellen eyes blazed and two spots of colour appeared on her cheeks. 'Yes, it is Larry's child I'm carrying, for I haven't been with anyone else. How dare you insinuate otherwise!'

Nicholas held his hands up in a conciliatory gesture.

'I'm sorry if I offended you, Ellen. I just had to make sure before I say what I am about to say.'

Ellen looked totally bewildered.

'What on earth are you talking about?'

'Ellen Cooney, I have come to ask you if you will be my wife.' Nicholas continued despite Ellen's sharp intake of breath. 'I think we rub along quite nicely. I know you will find it extremely hard to be a mother of three young children with no man to support you. I'm sure you realise that, as soon as you start to show, it will not be possible for you to work in the mill any longer? I am a respectable man and have my reputation to consider. And to have an unmarried woman, who is with child, on my premises...... well, it wouldn't be quite the best thing for me, as I'm sure you can understand.'

Ellen looked like she was about to cry.

'I was hoping I could keep my job for as long as possible. The baby doesn't affect my brain! If only I could get rid of this sickness, I know I would be absolutely fine. I really need this job!' Ellen's voice was pleading, rising slightly with hysteria.

'My dear, I'm afraid that won't be possible. Surely an intelligent woman like you realizes that?'

Nicholas let the words hang in the air between them. He could see emotions scurrying across Ellen's face like the March clouds outside.

'But we hardly know each other. And why would you take me on? Knowing that I have your brother's child growing in my belly?'

Nicholas shrugged his shoulders, and his expression was one of open friendliness.

'I guess, I just have a big heart. I wouldn't like to see a Clinton child branded as illegitimate, it's as simple as that. I'm a realist and I know that Larry is bound for Australia. There is a distinct possibility he will never come back, Ellen. But I also think that we would get along very well together, me and you. I respect you greatly. You have a quick mind and a kind disposition. I would be quite happy to have you by my side as my wife. You would never have to worry again about putting food on the table, a roof over your head, about clothing young Tommy, or the other little one.'

Ellen glanced over into the corner where Alice lay curled up on the settle bed, her thumb in her mouth, rosy cheeked and lost in her own little dreams.

'Why, Mr. Clinton, this is an absolutely huge surprise as I'm sure you can appreciate.'

'Please, call me Nicholas. You will have to if we are to be man and wife!'

Ellen swallowed, and raising her eyes to his, said 'Nicholas. I'm sure you will give me a bit of time to think over your proposal as it has come completely out of the blue?'

'Of course, my dear. Of course. I wouldn't expect you to give me an answer straight away. But think on this. I am offering you a better life, a solution to your problems, a father for your child.' Nicholas glanced at Ellen's stomach and continued. 'A home for Tommy and your daughter, a lifeline for you.'

He paused to let his words sink in. 'And now, I will take my leave of you to let you ponder on my proposal. There's no need for you to come to work tomorrow as I don't think you're really fit to. Don't leave me waiting too long now.'

He plastered a sweet smile on his face and, rising to his feet, donned his coat and hat and backed out to the door, still smiling.

Closing the door gently behind him, he emerged onto the street. He took in a deep breath of air and filled his lungs. He felt exhilarated. That had gone better than he could have anticipated. It seemed the sickness had completely weakened her out, so much so that there wasn't a huge lot of fight in her. She was desperate, he could see that. And she was at her wits' end about how she would manage. Telling her that she would have to quit her job at the mill had been a master stroke. As far as she was concerned, he was very keen to uphold his standing in the community, being on the Corporation and a respectable businessman. He gave a low chuckle to himself. He could feel Ellen Cooney within his grasp. His secret desires would soon become a reality. He looked up as he started to walk smartly down the street. Hah, there was a rainbow. The colours had never looked more vibrant to Nicholas, nor had his future.

CHAPTER 29

Peggy

The ticking of the old clock on the mantle-shelf was the only sound to be heard in the small room. Peggy looked around. Her eyes rested on Jim's fiddle, the only piece of him that remained, the little rag doll with the worn and torn patchwork dress of which Alice never tired, the pencil and piece of paper which Tommy used to write down some scheme or dream. That young lad was always thinking, writing, plotting. Some clothes were airing on a piece of twine strung over the range. The curtain on the window needed washing. So did the window. Peggy could see that things had slipped a bit over the past few weeks. Ellen was normally so house- proud and kept her little patch of the world spick and span. The poor lass had an excuse for sure. Peggy had never seen a babby on the way make someone so sick. She had used every remedy in her repertoire to try and ease Ellen's sickness, but none had worked.

Her gaze rested on Ellen who sat slumped across the table from her with her head in her hands. Peggy looked at her hair. It needed a good wash by the looks of it. A delighted girlish squeal could be heard from outside where Tommy and Alice were playing in the spring sunshine. He was a good lad. He never complained when asked to play with his little sister. Not like some of the little scoundrels from further down the road. They were, more often than not, mean to their younger siblings, giving them sneaky little pinches when they thought no one was looking. Tommy didn't have a bad bone in his body. He had sensed that Peggy needed to have an adult conversation with his Mam and had bundled Alice out the door without question. With an enormous sigh, Peggy broke the silence.

'So, what are you thinking, pet?'

The younger woman gave an anguished groan which seemed to come up from her very toes. 'Oh Jesus, Mary and Joseph Peggy, I don't know! What do you think I should do?'

Ellen raised her ravaged face and Peggy thought she had never seen a person so tormented. Peggy reached out and took one of Ellen's hands in hers. She rubbed it swiftly, trying to warm it, for it was very cold to the touch.

Peggy gazed into the distance, mulling over the situation in her mind as she had done constantly since Ellen told her of Nicholas's proposal. That bastard had poor Ellen over a barrel. There was no way she could possibly cope with three children to support and no income. He knew that, of course. He had more or less told her that she couldn't continue to work at the mill in her current condition. Larry was on the other side of the world. Peggy was starting to think that Nicholas had had some hand in making sure his brother had been removed from the scene. Then there was the shame of being pregnant outside of marriage. It wouldn't be long before Ellen started showing and people started asking questions. Ellen was a proud woman, and although she gave the impression that she didn't care what others thought of her, Peggy knew that deep down, she craved approval. Probably the result of the way she had been shunned by her own parents in the past. That was bound to have an effect on a person. Peggy decided that the best way forward out of the dilemma was to make to lists. One, in favour of accepting the proposal and one, against. Reaching across the table, she picked up Tommy's pencil and paper.

'Right Ellen, here's what we are going to do. We are going to take a practical approach and write down the reasons why you should marry Nicholas and the reasons why you shouldn't. We'll see which list is longer, and then you can make up your mind. I know you're very sick pet, and your brain is probably scrambled with all this worry, so I'll help you out.'

Placing her glasses on her nose and licking the end of the pencil, Peggy divided the page in two with a thick line, and on the left-hand side, wrote the word 'FOR', and on the right, 'AGAINST'. She sat back expectantly and looked at Ellen.

'Now then, let's start with the reasons why you shouldn't marry him.'

'I don't love him. He's not Larry. I've never thought of him in that way. He's old.' A cloud passed over Ellen's face. 'Marriage is for life and that's a very long time to be unhappy.'

'Good points my dear. It'll take me a minute or two to write that lot down,' Peggy answered wryly.

She paused, looking over at Ellen.

'Although, you could argue that age doesn't really matter. It's not that much of a difference anyway. Sure, my Paddy, bad cess to him, was eight years older than me. Not that we were much of an advertisement for marriage. And who's to say that you wouldn't be happy? Love can take many routes. Sometimes, it hits you like a lightning bolt. I'm guessing that's the way it was for you and your Jim. And sometimes it's something that can grow from nothing much into something strong and lasting. It doesn't have to be all about birds singing in the trees and your heart skipping a beat. It can be built on respect and shared interests and values. Do you think you could share any of Nicholas's thoughts?'

'Well, I suppose we do have some interesting conversations at work about topics in the news' sighed Ellen. 'He asks my opinion on things and always listens to my answers.' Ellen started playing with a stray splinter on the surface of the table.

I'll bet he does, Peggy thought. The conniver knows how to make a good impression. The more she thought about Ellen's situation, the more she came to the conclusion that Ellen would have to accept Nicholas's proposal. She just needed to help her arrive at the very same realization. And she had to make her feel content, if not happy, with her decision. In the process, Peggy needed to convince herself that it was in the best interests of Ellen and her little family.

'Well, that's a good thing. There are not many men out there that take heed of what us women-folk think. If more did, then there would be less trouble and strife in the world and that's for sure. Now, before we move on to the reasons 'For', have you any more thoughts on why you shouldn't marry him?'

'I suppose not.' Ellen slumped back in her chair.

'Right, so, start talking to me about why you should.'

Ellen's gaze went to the window where she could hear Tommy's cheerful voice and Alice's babyish squeals of delight. 'There are two very good reasons right outside. And one in here.' She absentmindedly rubbed her belly.

'How right you are pet.' Peggy said softly. 'Three very good reasons. You would have a home for yourself and your lovelies. A warm, comfortable one at that. You'd want for nothing. No more having to work. No more worrying about where the next pennies are coming from. No more having to sing in that alehouse to make ends meet. There would be a huge weight lifted off your shoulders. And your new babby would have a pair of parents who are married to each other. I'm sure Nicholas will love this child as his own. It is his brother's after all.'

'A nice new home would be lovely.' Ellen said wistfully, looking around the room. 'This place has never been the same since Jim died. Not to have to worry about money would be such a relief.' Ellen's face took on a dreamy expression. 'I want Tommy and Alice to make something of themselves. Tommy is a really bright lad, and I know he could do something special with his life, given half a chance. And she'll be the same. As for this little one, well, she deserves the best chance in life.

'They are something special already, Ellen. You should be very proud of him and little Alice. And I'm sure the wee'un will be another bright little spark. You're thinking it's a wee lass?'

Ellen nodded. 'I can feel it in my water. It's a girl. A daughter for Larry. But one he will probably never get to see.' Ellen's pained expression was hard for Peggy to bear. 'You think I should say yes, don't you Peggy?'

The older woman looked at Ellen, opened her mouth as if to say something, and then thought the better of it.

'Please, Peggy, tell me straight what you think. I haven't got the energy for guessing games. I'm going to have to go and lie down in a few minutes.'

'What I was going to say is that, yes, I think that this is an opportunity for you to make the best of a tricky situation. Larry is gone. We have to face facts. It's great that Nicholas is stepping up to the mark and agreeing to support you and his brother's child, not to mention Tommy and Alice. Although, I will miss you greatly, pet. Rope Walk won't be the same without you and the childer.' Peggy felt a huge lump in her throat as a wave of pure sadness made her catch her breath. How would she cope without Ellen and her lovely little ones? Ellen always pronounced that she didn't know what she would do without Peggy, but truth be told, Peggy would be lost without them. They were her reason for getting up in the morning. Tommy was like the grandson she would never have, and Alice was a pure sweetheart. She felt a stab of grief at the thought of losing them from her life.

As if reading Peggy's thoughts, Ellen sat up straight. For a moment, she looked like her old self when she'd had a bright idea. Her eyes sparkled and a determined look stole across her face.

'I'll tell him 'yes', but on one condition.'

'Oh, tell me more, what condition?' Peggy was agog.

'You have to come with me. It's me and you, or else the whole thing is off!'

Peggy opened her mouth to say something but found she was temporarily mute. Her eyes swam with tears.

'You really want me to come with you?' she breathed.

'Peggy, I never wanted anything more. I think I will need an ally. You're my best friend. I couldn't imagine leaving you behind here. And Tommy and Alice would be so happy if you were there every day. It will be so strange for them, leaving the only home they have ever known. Oh Peggy, I would say yes much more happily if I thought you were coming with us! Please say you will?'

'Well, I have to admit, I'm flummoxed!' Peggy gave a deep chuckle. 'But I think it's a great idea!'

'Yes!' Ellen punched the air with her fist and smiled broadly.

'But what if he doesn't agree?'

'Oh, he'll agree alright.' A look of determination crossed Ellen's features. 'We're a package, you, me and the children Peggy. He can like it or lump it.'

This world was so much more generous to the male of the species, Peggy thought. A woman needed to exert control whenever, and in whatever way she could. If he agreed to Ellen's counter proposal, she would be able to keep a close eye on Mr. Nicholas Clinton whether he liked it or not. There was something about him that made her feel on edge. He wouldn't dare mistreat Ellen with her around. That was a satisfying thought and no mistake.

'Right so. I'll have to start thinking about packing my bags!' Peggy's chins wobbled as her eyes danced. She grabbed Ellen's hand, giving it a hard squeeze.

'It'll all work out for the best lass. I'll be with you every step of the way.'

Decision made, Ellen rose gingerly from the chair and shuffled to the door. 'I'd better tell Tommy and Alice that they're going to live in a big, fine house. And that they'll be able to have bread and jam every day if they wish!'

'Let's hope that bread and jam doesn't come at too high a price', thought Peggy.

CHAPTER 30

Ellen

Drogheda, March 1867

Ellen ran her hands, which were clad in the finest of white gloves, over her powder blue wool skirt. She felt trussed up like a chicken. Her waistband was very tight. She wriggled uncomfortably in her seat and ran a hand around the collar of her fitted jacket. The lace was so prickly and annoying. The jacket was straining at the buttons too. She inhaled as deeply as the restrictive outfit would allow, but only got to fill her lungs halfway. At least the nausea wasn't too bad so far this morning. It wouldn't do to throw up all over Father Mulroy's shiny shoes. She managed a half-smile at the image.

'What's tickling your fancy pet?' Peggy smiled.

Ellen glanced over at her friend who was resplendent in a navy two-piece and sported a felt hat with a light blue feather. She looked every bit as uncomfortable as Ellen felt. They had both bought their new finery in a bit of a hurry. Nicholas had wasted no time organising the wedding. As soon as Ellen had given him her answer, he had immediately started preparations. She had to hand it to him, he was a man who could make things happen. And very quickly.

'I was just hoping I don't get sick all over Father' Mulroy's shoes.'

'Oh, lass don't make me laugh. I can barely breathe in this costume as it is. I've never had such fine clothes in me life. And I get to keep it! That husband-to-be of yours is quite the generous man. That's one thing in his favour at least.'

'You look magnificent Peggy.'

Ellen, overcome suddenly with emotion, took her friend's hand which was encased in a navy leather glove and squeezed it gently.

'I can't tell you how much it means to me that you're here today, especially as ....'

An image of her mother and father swam in front of her eyes. By rights they should have been at the wedding, but she had been too proud to contact them. Ellen wondered what they would think of their daughter marrying one of the richest businessmen in Drogheda. No doubt they would try and get back in with her when they heard about her change in fortune. Ellen knew that stubbornness was one of many facets of her personality. But it wasn't always a bad thing. It had made her determined to stand on her own two feet when Jim had died. It had helped her get the job at the mill, and the one singing at the alehouse, for she wasn't one to take no for an answer when she set her mind to something. So, she shouldn't really be upset that they wouldn't be there. She hadn't asked them. She was just feeling sorry for herself because a woman's wedding day is supposed to be the happiest one of her life. It's supposed to be shared with family and close friends. Here she was on her *second* wedding day and her parents hadn't been at either one. Marrying Jim had felt like the happiest day of her life. Today was so different.

'I know I didn't want them here, but..'

'I know, I know. Now don't be upsetting yourself lass,' Peggy reached across the carriage and tucked a stray strand of hair behind Ellen's ear. 'It's probably the babby that's making you feel a bit over-emotional. Sure, some women spend the nine months crying.'

Looking out the carriage window, Peggy announced that they had nearly arrived at their destination. A spiral of panic started in Ellen's gut and rattled it way up her spine. Was she really doing the right thing? Her breath came in short gasps, and she felt slightly faint. Peggy rose as the carriage came to a stop outside the neat, perfectly proportioned, grey stone building. Ellen grabbed her hand again.

'I'm not sure I can go through with this, Peggy.'

Peggy plopped back down again into the seat and Ellen saw that her brow was furrowed.

'Well, pet, you don't have to if you really don't want to. We'll work something out. But, you know, marriage to Nicholas might be quite alright. He's clearly besotted with you, and he will give you and the childer a comfortable home. And I'll be with you to help you out with the new babby. You'll never want for anything again. Tommy and Alice will be able to go to the nice school in town. There's lot of good things to be said for being 'Mrs. Clinton'. But, if you really feel you can't do it, then I will get this good man to turn the carriage right around and we will go back to Rope Walk. Just say the word.'

Ellen drew in a deep breath in an effort to steady her heartbeat. What was it that Peggy had told her to do? Breathe in through the nose, and out through the mouth. Yes, that was it. Gradually the panic subsided. Everything Peggy said was true. Ellen knew marrying Nicholas made sense. Her head told her so. Her heart was an entirely different matter. It had belonged to Jim, and more recently, she had discovered, after he had left so abruptly, Larry had captured it, but in a different way. But both were gone and now she was making a choice. It had to be the right one, didn't it? She would have a home for her children. All three of them. She would be a respectable married woman when this little one she was carrying was born. It wouldn't have to endure any name-calling in the street. It was impossible for her to continue working at the mill. She wouldn't miss the alehouse either. She liked the singing, but she didn't like the clientele. Yes, she had made her choice and it was the right one for her family. She turned to Peggy who was looking at her with such an expression of concern that Ellen felt she had to reassure her.

'I'm alright now Peggy. I just had some last minutes nerves. You're right. It's the sensible thing to do. It will all be fine.'

Looking relieved, Peggy turned the door handle and started to try and manoeuvre herself out of the carriage and down the steps. The driver gave her a helping hand and then they both stood looking at Ellen as she alighted. The sun chose that moment to come out from behind one of the clouds that were scudding across the angry sky, and Ellen was temporarily blinded. For a split second, she fancied that she saw Jim's darling, handsome face. He was smiling at her. Ellen caught her breath and put her hand out to touch Jim's face one last time, but as soon as the sun went back behind the cloud, his image was gone. Stunned, she turned to Peggy who was looking at her askance.

'Are you quite alright pet? Ready for this?'

'I'm ready Peggy.'

Ellen blinked back the tears that threatened to spill, straightened her back, and together with her best friend and witness, started walking towards the house where the Dominican fathers lived. It was in the small oratory there that she and Nicholas were to get married. Father Mulroy, his friend from years ago, had agreed to marry them as soon as possible. He was a discreet man; Nicholas had assured Ellen. If he noticed that her skirt was a bit tight around the waist, he wouldn't mention it, and certainly wouldn't make Ellen feel awkward about her condition.

The two women climbed up the three granite steps, and just as Peggy went to knock on the black shiny door, it was opened from within by a small, contrary looking woman with grey hair, pulled so severely back in a bun, that it made her eyes appear slanted. The combination of this and the thin, sour lips made her look quite fierce, despite her diminutive size.

'Mrs. Brady, isn't it?' Peggy extended her hand. The other woman didn't take it.

'I suppose you'd better come with me,' Mrs. Brady sniffed, looking Ellen up and down. Her gaze rested on Ellen's belly for a split second and then she turned and walked down the corridor which had a brown mahogany floor, shone to perfection. Ellen and Peggy exchanged a glance, and it was all they could do not to giggle as they followed the sourpuss down the corridor, her sensible shoes making a rhythmic squeaking noise as she walked at a clip.

'Slow down woman. These shoes weren't made for fast walking!' Peggy mumbled under her breath.

Mrs. Brady led the way down a long corridor, past a number of white doors on either side. Ellen wondered what lay behind each one. Probably the priests' studies, the kitchen, the dining room. A right turn, followed by a quick left, and they had apparently reached their destination. The door to the oratory was brown mahogany and was adorned with a crucifix. Mrs. Brady crossed herself and genuflected, opening the door at the same time. She stood back to let the two women through, and then vanished, closing the door none- too gently as she went.

Nicholas stood at the top of the room, deep in conversation with Fr. Mulroy. To one side, fiddling with his cufflinks stood 'Spider' Menton.

He was to be the other witness, along with Peggy. Ellen had been surprised that Nicholas hadn't wanted his daughters to be at the wedding. But, no, he was insistent that he wanted to surprise them, that they would be absolutely delighted to welcome Ellen into the family, and that they would all get on like a house on fire. Ellen doubted that very much, as the few times that Ellen had met Clarice and Sarah up at the mill, she had found them both to be quite snooty and a bit condescending. Ah well, they would have to get used to their new stepmother being not that much older than themselves. Ellen's thoughts flew to Tommy and Alice who were being looked after by Janey for the duration of the ceremony. Tommy knew that she was getting married to Nicholas. Ellen had taken him aside and assured him that he wouldn't be expected to call Nicholas 'Da'. His Da had been Jim, and he could never be replaced. Nicholas could be his friend, and Ellen was sure that he would be someone Tommy could ask about the stars and the moon. Tommy's little face had held a pensive look. He had given Ellen a hug then and said that he was really pleased that she had found someone to make her happy again, and that she mightn't be sick anymore if she wasn't worried. That had made Ellen want to cry, and she had hugged her beloved son tight.

At the sound of the door closing, the three men turned around. George Menton looked as if he would rather be anywhere else but in the presence of God. Fr. Mulroy smiled benignly, but something in his expression, and the way he shuffled from one foot to the other, made Ellen think he was anxious to get this ceremony concluded as soon as possible. Nicholas appeared to catch his breath, taking in Ellen's tall, slender frame. The way he was looking at her made her feel like squirming. She didn't know him very well, and she really couldn't believe that she was going to be his wife in less than forty minutes, with all that entailed. Still, she had agreed, and she wouldn't go back on her word now.

The sunlight shone through the stained-glass windows, decorating the altar cloth with jewel-like colours. It glinted off the tabernacle and bounced off Fr. Mulroy's shoes which could be seen peeping out from under his vestments, and which were indeed, a very shiny black leather. Ellen took a deep breath, claimed Peggy's arm, meeting the older woman's enquiring glance with an almost imperceptible nod. She was ready for the next stage of her life as Mrs. Nicholas Clinton.

The two women walked the ten or so steps it took to reach the top of the room. The floor in here was some kind of highly polished tile. The walls were painted a light pink and bore the stations of the cross pictures, all with a very sorrowful-looking Christ, framed in highly polished mahogany. Candles flickered on the altar which faced four mahogany benches where, no doubt, the Dominican fathers in the community said their 'Office' and came to pray. There was a massive crucifix on the wall behind the tabernacle, and Jesus had his eyes rolled up to the heavens in agony, sunlight glinting off the gold tips on his crown of thorns. There was a faint smell of incense which was nearly Ellen's undoing.

'You look quite beautiful, my dear.' Nicholas took Ellen's hand in his. 'The suit is very becoming. Good choice', he whispered in her ear.

Ellen smiled shyly, taken aback by the compliment as much as by the expression in Nicholas's eyes. She could only describe it as 'hungry.' Her insides gave a quiver. She forced herself to return his smile, looking him square in the eye.

'Thank you, Nicholas. It was very good of you to give us free reign in Meagher's. Peggy and I really enjoyed our shopping trip.'

'There'll be as many of them as you wish, my dear. From now on, you will want for nothing.'

And so, Ellen made her promises before God, a rather nervous and sweaty looking Fr. Mulroy, a slightly wheezy Peggy, and a restless George Menton. Nicholas slipped the ring on her finger. It was a heavier, thicker gold band than the one Jim had given her. But whereas her heart had soared the day she had become Jim's wife, today, it felt like a little part of it had turned into stone. She had thought she might marry Larry and look at how that had turned out. Nicholas must know in his heart that she was only marrying him so that she could have an easier life. She was tired of struggling, worn out by sickness and worry. For the sake of her children, she would do her best to be the wife Nicholas wanted and keep her part of the bargain. She was a woman of her word.

CHAPTER 31

Ellen

Avoca, Co. Wicklow

Ellen closed her eyes and took a deep, shuddering breath. She felt slightly dizzy and had to hold on to the wooden door frame to stop the world around her spinning. Her rising panic mingled with nausea and did a dance along the bottom of her empty stomach. Another lungful of the fresh Wicklow air did nothing at all to alleviate her feelings of dread. Dread that she was after making a huge mistake that she would regret for the rest of her life. She forced her eyes to open. She had always faced up to whatever had been thrown at her so far, so there was no point burying her head in the sand. But, last night had been so....she shuddered again at the memory of her honeymoon night with Nicholas. She was now Mrs. Clinton, for better or worse. A tear welled up in her eye and she angrily wiped it away. Here she was, twenty-eight years of age, and already on her second honeymoon, but married to a man she didn't love. Most women enjoyed their honeymoon. At least, they were supposed to.

A cold finger of ice had slid its way down her spine the day before when she had made her vows to Nicholas. It had been all she could do make a run for it. The thoughts of Tommy and Alice kept her rooted to the spot in front of that toad, Father Mulroy. It had seemed like she was outside her own body when she'd said 'I do.' Then all of a sudden, the priest was saying '*you may kiss the bride,*' and she was brought back to reality with the sensation of Nicholas's cold lips on her cheek. He had smiled at her then, a light in his eyes that made her feel very uneasy. As if he had just won the biggest prize of his life. And like he was waiting to unwrap the best present he had ever received. Ellen had smiled weakly back at him, her dread like a pile of cold, hard stones in her belly.

The couple of mouthfuls she had eaten at the 'wedding breakfast' after the ceremony had felt like sawdust. She couldn't take her eyes off the shiny gold band that now adorned her ring finger. Peggy had the one Jim had given her for safe keeping, as she didn't think Nicholas was the type to stand for his wife having a piece of jewellery from another man about her person. Even if that man was dead at the bottom of the ocean. Before she knew it, herself and Nicholas had been on their way to Wicklow in the back of his carriage, on their way to spend two nights at the famous beauty spot where the *Abhainn Mhor* and the *Abhainn Bheag* joined together to form the Avoca River. Nicholas had kept up a steady flow of inane conversation, but she had found herself unable to respond very much. She had been paralysed with fear, keeping herself as far away from him as the carriage allowed. She was used to being in the same room as him at the mill but being in such close proximity to him as his *wife*, was so very strange and hugely unnerving. She knew there would be no getting away from him that night. Or for the rest of her life. Panic started to build, and she did what she always did when these feelings threatened to overcome her. She pictured Tommy and

Alice's faces. They were her world. She had sacrificed her happiness for theirs. As long as she had breath in her body, she would protect them. And if this meant marriage to a man she didn't love - and who had seemed to change from a pleasant, affable, charming man into a stranger, whose aura was getting darker the closer they got to their honeymoon destination - then so be it.

She had been right to be anxious. It turned out her husband didn't give a jot for the fact that she was feeling weak and exhausted by her pregnancy sickness. Afterwards, Ellen had lain beside him whilst he snored loudly, her body rigid and cold, her mind whirling. Just before dawn, she had fallen into a fitful sleep which lasted a couple of hours. She had taken care not to awaken Nicholas, had dressed silently, and slipped out of the bedroom, making her way to the front door of the inn where they were staying. This was a place she would have loved to have seen with Jim by her side. He would have appreciated the beauty of the rushing rivers as they converged, the pretty, white-washed cottages, and the backdrop of the magnificent mountains in the distance.

'Oh Jim, what have I done? I'm so sorry. I had to do it for the children. Don't you understand? I hope you can forgive me?' A sob wrenched its way from Ellen's aching throat.

'What's this? We can't have a bride unhappy on her honeymoon!'

Ellen swung around in surprise. She had been so absorbed in her grief and panic that she hadn't heard Nicholas walk up behind her. His eyes held a questioning look, but there was not much kindness in his expression. Rather, a barely concealed impatience. That and something else on which Ellen didn't want to dwell.

'Seeing as you're dressed already, why don't we go for breakfast? I don't know about you, but I am feeling especially hungry this morning!' He moved a step closer to Ellen. She could feel his breath warm on her cheek. He smelled of stale alcohol, and slightly of lemons, his cologne of choice. She tried not to flinch as he ran one finger down the line of her cheekbone with a feather-light touch.

'And I think perhaps it might be a good idea for us to repair to our room after we eat. I think we should both have another little lie down. It would not do for either of us to get indigestion, would it?' Stepping back, he offered his arm.

'Shall we, Mrs. Clinton?'

Fighting back bile, Ellen hesitated for a moment and then, with a huge effort, took his arm.

'Nicholas, we will go for breakfast, but I will be retiring to the room afterwards, *on my own*,' Ellen emphasized the last three words. She could see the battle in his nut-brown eyes as he considered whether to take exception to her challenge.

'As you wish, my dear. You must be exhausted by the excitement of yesterday.'

With a sinking stomach, Ellen wondered how she would have the strength for this type of encounter on a day-to-day basis. For she feared in her anxiety to find a way out of her predicament, she had just made a very big rod for her back.

CHAPTER 32

Larry

Dartmoor, England

Late September 1867

'Ah for the love of God man, can we not linger for a moment and enjoy the sunshine on our bones?'

Larry turned his face upwards, and had to shield his eyes, so bright was the sun. He had become accustomed to the gloom over the past six months in his prison cell. It had only a small window which let in precious little light. Larry had missed out on the whole of spring and summer. It was the first time in his life that he hadn't been able to witness his favourite seasons, as the trees began to bud, and flowers began to emerge from the soil. He felt cheated. He chose to focus on this loss, rather than the other much, much greater one that threatened to tear his heart to shreds. His anger was strictly channeled into small, daily slights and grievances. It was the only way he could survive, as to give in to the reality of what he had truly lost, might result in him losing his mind.

'Wanting a little bit of sunshine, are we?' sneered Jones, an ugly slab of a man with mottled skin, and less than half of his full complement of teeth. Those that hadn't been punched out, or had fallen out due to neglect, were badly stained from the red wine to which he was so partial. He was Larry's least favourite prison warder, and that was saying something. Jones seemed to delight in persecuting all the prisoners. Dartmoor was where Larry had ended up, after being removed abruptly from the gaol in Drogheda. Jones had taken an instant dislike to Larry on the very first night he had arrived. The feeling was mutual.

'You'll be getting plenty of that where you're going, Fenian bastard. I hope you fry and sizzle like a fucking pig on a spit. That's what you deserve.' He gave Larry a punch in the gut.

'Oi, enough, Jones. No need for that now. Let him have a look at the sun. He ain't seen much of it these past few months.'

Larry recognized the voice of Sadlier, another prison warder. One with slightly more humanity than Jones. He was Jones's superior. With a scowl, Jones gave Larry a violent shove in the back, moving him towards the forbidding-looking black wagon that was to be the mode of transport for Larry and his fellow convicts to the train station in Tavistock. From there, they would travel to Portland. Larry was to be the only Irish man. The other thirty-nine prisoners were English. Thieves and murderers, most of them. The carriage doors were open wide, the interior dark and gloomy. He was acutely aware that once he got on that train, there was no going back. They were bound for Portland, and from there, to a place called Freemantle in Australia. The other side of the world. As far as it was possible to be from Ellen, Tommy, Alice, his unborn child, Drogheda and his beloved Erin. Panic began to rise in Larry. How was he to face his life alone in a foreign land? Would he ever see Ireland again, or would his bones whiten the yellow Australian soil? How would he live the rest of his life without Ellen, in a land where he couldn't feel soft rain on his face, breathe in the smell of newly ploughed clay, or see the flicker of a rainbow reflected off the skin of a trout as it leaped in the river? How could his child grow up not knowing its father? How would Ellen even survive with three children to provide for?

These thoughts crowded his head, making his brain feel like it might explode. For now, Larry would concentrate on putting one foot in front of the other, getting through each minute, each hour, and each day. Bit by bit, his natural optimism had seeped out of him as he had stewed in Dartmoor prison. The last of it had trickled away the day he heard talk of 'Australia' and 'three months at sea.' It was then that the enormity of what faced him had struck home. Six weeks later, he was about to start the first leg of a journey that would lead him to a terribly foreign place, and a fate completely unknown.

'Look lively, we ain't got all day!' That was Sadlier again. He had a slightly kinder, softer voice than Jones. He and Jones, and the other two warders who Larry didn't know, began to urge their charges in through the doors of the carriage. It was slow progress, as the men were all chained, both at the wrists and the ankles. It wasn't easy to climb aboard. Eventually, they were all on, and almost immediately, the doors closed, and with a big bellow of steam and a long, shrill whistle, the big black engine started its journey south and then slightly east.

Portland, Larry guessed, was probably a town much like Drogheda, except a bit smaller. The sounds and sights put him in mind of Customhouse Quay. There was a cacophony of shouts, warning roars and banging, as goods were loaded and unloaded, the smell of horse manure mingling with the salty tang of the sea.

He raised his head to look at the name painted on the side of the ship. 'The Foxhoud'. So, this was to be his home for the next three months. It was a bigger ship than any he had seen before. Even on his voyages across the Atlantic. Three masts, and he estimated, at least eighteen sails. He hoped it was sturdy, as it had a long, long way to go. God only knew what lay ahead of him. Despite the bright sun, a shiver ran down Larry's spine. There was almost a fairground atmosphere on the quayside as the locals came out to see the prisoners all lined up in a row to be reviewed by a doctor and the captain of the ship.

It was a sombre line of men that boarded, dragging their feet up the gang plank. One Englishman bucked like a horse in protest and got a clatter across the ear. Larry was one of the last to board. The prisoners wore Drogheda linen uniforms, white, with red stripes and a black band. It mangled Larry's brain to think that his own brother's mill was where the cloth had originated. Whenever Larry thought of Nicholas, bile rose in his throat. How could his own flesh and blood betray him? He had no definite proof but was sure that Nicholas had had a hand in his capture and incarceration, especially after what the warder in the gaol in Drogheda had said.

He and Nicholas had never been particularly close, there being a good ten years between them in age. Larry had kind of hero-worshipped Nicholas when he was very young. His brother was a good businessman, he had to hand him that. He was charming in public, but he had a mean, manipulative side, and he could be as cold and hard as a lump of granite. Drogheda hadn't escaped the cholera epidemic that had swept the country, and when it took both their parents, Nicholas, at nineteen, had taken over the family business. Larry had been carted off to boarding school. There, he had learned how to fend for himself. Education finished, he had presumed he would join Nicholas at the mill, so it had been quite a shock to find that his older brother had no plans whatsoever to give him his share of the family finances. By then, Larry had grown quite independent, so head held high, he had decided to put some distance between himself and his brother, and he had left for England as it was booming, and there was money to be made in the trades. He had worked hard, and become a pretty good stone mason, even if he said so himself. But, clever and all as he thought himself, it hadn't stopped him getting caught and ending up facing a future that looked as bleak as his heart felt.

Out of the blue, Larry heard the unmistakable sound of an Irish accent. A short, wiry-looking man had just boarded the ship, cursing like a trooper at the rough handling he was getting from one of the warders. He was pushed over to where Larry was sitting.

The other man landed with a thump. 'Daniel Cash, proud Cork-man.'

Now that their shackles had been removed, Larry had been able to take his hand and gave it a firm shake. He told Larry he had been part of a rising in Co. Tipperary, that March night when everything had gone wrong, and had been captured and spent the last few months in a prison called 'Millbank' in London. He had been in solitary confinement, and now bore a wide grin at the prospect of having other people to talk to. Sixty-odd of the prisoners who had boarded the ship were Irishmen. Cash had quickly sized up the situation on board even though they hadn't yet set sail. He knew the English were to be in the very bottom of the hold, and all the Irish Fenians were to be one compartment above. In total, there were two hundred and eighty convicts on board. Then, there was the crew, the captain's wife, a doctor, and a Catholic priest. All the Irishmen introduced themselves, laughing, slapping each other on the back, delighting in company and fresh air after so long without both. At least it kept their minds off the fact that the ship had set sail, and they were headed into the unknown.

That first evening, despite the original glee at finding other Irish to talk to, the mood on board amongst them became dark and melancholic. One by one, they had fallen silent, all lost in their own thoughts of loved ones and home. Would they ever see any of them again? A lively and loud fellow from Wexford decided that they needed to cheer themselves up and put forward the idea of having a concert on board, where they could sing their songs of Ireland. A banjo, a whistle and a trumpet were unearthed from below deck. It was surprising how much melody they could get out of those three instruments. That night, after the concert, Larry found himself up on deck, the only sounds the lapping of the waves and the creaking of the masts. He stared down into the glassy black sea and then up at the stars. He saw Orion. The sight of it made his heart ache, because the last time he had studied it, Ellen had been in his arms.

Six days into the voyage, the ship began tossing around like a match-stick on the sea. They were in the Bay of Biscay. Nearly everyone on board was sick. The seas were mountainous, and the noise of thunder was almost drowned out by the violent rattling of the riggings. Eventually, after what seemed like an eternity, but what was only a day and a half, the storm abated, and the men began to surface from their cots, roused by the jolly chorus of the crew repairing the damage. One morning not long after, Larry was taking a salt-water shower on deck, when he saw the most beautiful sunrise. He was told that they were near the island of Madeira.

The Fenians had another concert. A merry, jolly affair that certainly helped them while away the hours and take their minds off the fact that with every hour that passed, their loved ones grew further and further away.

From there, their journey would take them across the Atlantic towards the coast of Brazil, and then back towards the Cape of Good Hope. These were exotic places Larry had heard about, but never thought he would see. The heat was stifling. Hot tar fell off the inside of the hold, burning the skin of the Englishmen in the very belly of the ship. The Irish were great ones for celebrating Hallowe'en, and they kept their daily ration of wine, (meant to keep scurvy away), for a night-time celebration below deck on October 31st. At one Richie O'Neill's rendition of the 'Last Rose of Summer', Larry had a lump in his throat and a single, salty tear made its way down his nose and landed with a plop in his tumbler of wine. Looking around him, he could see that all his companions were lost in their own sad and sorry thoughts.

They had games of chess, cards, and dominos. By day, they looked in awe at extinct volcanoes on the Cape Verde Islands. By night, below deck they danced to the likes of 'Garryowen'. Some of the men decided to compile a newspaper which they called 'The Wild Goose' in honour of all the Irishmen who left their country to soldier in other continental armies. They sat around in a circle, and listened to tales of Ireland, poetry, amusing pieces, designed to temporarily distract from the melancholy that was never far away. Orion was still there, but it was in an unfamiliar place in the sky.

In mid-November, they crossed the Equator. They were two hundred and fifty miles from the coast of Brazil. Then, near the island of Trindade, they looked in awe at cliffs of two thousand feet high. Larry had never felt as small and insignificant. A fierce squall blew up, and many feared they were all about to meet a watery end. It was over as quickly as it had started. Then, the whales appeared. Massive creatures, about thirty feet long. Four of them stayed with the ship for the best part of the day, their huge bodies, doing a graceful dance amongst the waves. He was amused by the men who spent hours on the lookout for the ghost ship, the '*Flying Dutchman*.'

Larry had never experienced wind so strong or seas so high as those in the 'Roaring Forties'. It was caused by the warm Indian Ocean meeting the cold Atlantic. The third edition of the 'Wild Goose' featured articles about what Australia might look like. Full of kangaroos and convicts! The rumour went around the ship that the Australians were very nervous about the Irish convicts' arrival, fearing that they would, being politically radicalized, cause mayhem and destruction. As he looked around him at his bunch of fellow Fenians, Larry thought this highly unlikely.

Willie O' Sullivan from Kilkenny caught an albatross, and they had it for Christmas dinner. It was the biggest bird Larry had ever seen, having a wingspan of at least ten feet across, wing tip to wing tip, and a body larger than a goose. The men all closed their eyes and sent messages of love and longing across the sea to loved ones in Ireland. They formed a circle and sang songs that reminded them of home. On January first, the ship's crew began cleaning in preparation for docking. The mood on the ship grew morose again. They would, very soon, be no longer suspended in a bubble, but forced to, once again, face the reality of imprisonment in a cold cell. The prisoners began to dread the prospect of the words 'land ahoy! A farewell concert was organized. They might never see each other again once the voyage came to an end. Yet, in a way, they couldn't wait for dry land for, after nearly three months at sea, they were heartily sick of the journey.

Finally, after eighty-nine days, *The Foxhound'* docked in Freemantle on January 10th, 1868. The Fenians were marched to the prison. The suspicious eyes of the townspeople were on them, silently following the procession of weary, thin men as they wound their way to the prison like a red, black and white striped snake.

Part Two

CHAPTER 33

Peggy

Drogheda 1873

Peggy was at her wit's end. Her colour was even higher than usual, and she could feel her toe throbbing, along with the index finger on her left hand. The gout seemed to flare up when she was under stress. And by God, was she peppering. That scoundrel, Nicholas Clinton was a knave and no mistake. He was all '*hail fellow well met*' in public, but in private, she suspected he was a bully with a mean streak. He was careful enough to hide it most of the time, but Peggy knew what he was really like. It was in the downward tilt of Ellen's mouth, the expression of helplessness she sometimes saw in the young woman's eyes, the droop of her shoulders that had once been so straight and confident. How she rued the day she stood by and allowed Ellen to marry Nicholas. She should have seen through him. But Ellen had been desperate at the time. Nicholas had seemed like the only solution to all her problems. Well, Ellen might have as many fancy hats and costumes as she wanted these days, and the respectability of being married to a wealthy businessman, but she had paid a high price for her material comforts. Ellen did her utmost to keep the good side out and be cheerful for the children. Peggy could hear her and Nicholas sniping at each other from time to time. There was no doubt that Ellen gave as good as she got, verbally. She was never shy about standing up for herself. If only she could give him the son he wanted. Then he might leave her alone.

In the seven years she had been married to Nicholas, Ellen had produced another three children. Well, two of his and one of his brother's. She was now a thirty-five-year-old mother of five, and all the childbearing had taken its toll on her body and mind. Peggy had tried to get Ellen to confide in her so many times but there was always a babby to be minded, another one on the way, washing, feeding and everything that went along with an expanding family to take care of. That, and the hopelessness of the situation, kept Ellen from admitting the enormity of the mistake she had made. But, despite her unhappiness, Peggy knew that Ellen didn't regret having a single one of her children. She had a heart big enough to love them all to distraction.

Liberty was Larry's daughter, born just six months after Ellen and Nicholas had been wed. A nice, quiet, thoughtful child, not unlike Tommy. Next came Gladys, a child that never sat still, always wanting things that she couldn't have. Contrary, even at such a young age. Then there was Rosena, more placid, with brown, beguiling eyes. That one would be a real beauty when she grew up. She would break a few hearts, Peggy wagered. Nicholas barely paid attention to any of them. They all had one fault in common. They were girls. Even though he seemed to have soured towards Ellen in the past couple of years, it was plain to see that Nicholas Clinton was going to keep trying until he got a son. He was obsessed. Each time Ellen was pregnant, he was full of anticipation, a spring in his step. He would speak to the bump, watching it get bigger, waiting for the day when Ellen would give birth, pacing outside the door until he heard the unmistakable cry of the new baby. He would rush into the room, his face wreathed in expectation. He had actually stormed out of the room in a temper when Rosena had been born. Poor, exhausted Ellen had sobbed her heart out, clinging to Peggy. Peggy didn't know what she could do to help. She couldn't interfere between a man and wife. She knew what she would like to do to Nicholas, but she wouldn't be much use to Ellen if she ended up in gaol.

'How are you feeling today, pet?' Peggy roamed her eyes over Ellen's face as she took her hand. She glanced at Ellen's swollen belly and sent up a silent prayer that this latest baby would be the boy that Nicholas so desperately wanted. Then he might leave Ellen alone for a while. Tommy knew his Mam was bothered by something, but at fifteen, he was still a little bit innocent. She saw the way he looked at Nicholas sometimes, with a mixture of hatred and disgust. Alice was a happy-go-lucky little girl, and, at nine years old, was becoming quite the madam. She always did what she wanted to do, which was never quite what she was asked to.

'It's a boy, Peggy, I can feel it in my bones. I feel as if I'm carrying him differently, more to the front this time. What do you think? Do you think it's a boy?'

There was something slightly feverish about Ellen. She had two red spots of colour high up on her cheeks. The look she gave Peggy was half excitement, half desperation. Peggy thought the best thing to do was to agree with Ellen's 'feeling', as there was no point in upsetting the poor craythur. To Peggy, she didn't look any different than she had done in her past pregnancies. But if there was a God in heaven, He would surely send a boy this time so that Ellen could get a bit of a rest.

'I'd say that you are right this time Ellen. It'll definitely be a wee lad. A brother for Tommy and the girls. You're right, your baby is lying differently.'

Peggy made a great show of cocking her head to one side and then the other, examining the bump from every angle, smiling encouragingly. She reached forward across the table, with its fashionable lace cloth, and patted Ellen's hand. She noticed that the skin was stretched taut, the rings swollen on her fingers. She hoped that Ellen would deliver soon, as she had seen other women with swollen fingers and ankles in pregnancy and it usually didn't bode well.

There were some things to be grateful for, she supposed. Living in Nicholas Clinton's house, they were never cold, never hungry. She was close to Ellen and the children. She still met with her sailor friend down by the docks to get her potions, although she hadn't much use for them of late. Well, save for the stuff she was currently putting into Nicholas's dinner every other day, mixed into the mashed potatoes he was so fond of. Apparently, it was supposed to cool the ardour of even the most passionate. Peggy had been giving it to him for the past couple of months. She was hoping that it would build up in his system so that, even if this new baby was a girl, he might leave Ellen alone. It was all she could do to help. She was used to being able to fix things for people, and it gave her a sense of some control. She would do anything for Ellen.

'It won't be long now, mark my words. And it will be no bother to you at all pet, it's your sixth child after all! Peggy didn't mention the three miscarriages Ellen had had in the four years since her youngest daughter had been born.

'Six children! Oh Lord, I never thought I'd be mother to half a dozen!' Ellen's laugh was slightly hysterical, her fingertips drumming on the tablecloth.

'And here's my darling boy now!'

Tommy walked through the door at that moment. He was tall and broad, the spit of his Da. He looked at his Mam with such love in his eyes. It never failed to catch at Peggy's heart strings.

'How was school today, young man? Have you taught the teachers everything they need to know yet?'

Ellen's delight at her son's cleverness was clear to be seen by the shining light of pride in her eyes. At least marriage to Nicholas had meant that Tommy and Alice had been able to stay at school, and not have to go to work at ten years old. Johnny, Tommy's friend, was working like a dog at the foundry, not having had the luxury. It seemed Ellen needed to keep reminding herself of this on a constant basis. The poor lass needed some justification for her decision to marry Nicholas. To disagree and say that they could have come up with a different solution six years earlier would have been cruel in the extreme.

'Ah Mam, will you quit!' laughed Tommy as he spun a squealing Alice around the kitchen. Alice was very fond of her big brother and had followed him around like a puppy since she had been able to walk. He was the only one who could get through to her, and often persuaded her from a particular course of action which would definitely get her into trouble. She adored him, and the feeling was mutual. Alice put up with her little sisters, treating them with contempt a lot of the time. Tommy had time and patience for all his younger siblings. He really was a very kind boy.

'Did you learn anything new today?'

Tommy put his head to one side and a grin crossed his features.

'Do you know what the Latin word for bottom is?'

'No, I do not!' laughed Ellen.

'Natus!'

Ellen picked up a tea-towel and reached over to whack Tommy on his behind.

'I'll warm your *natus* for you,' she laughed.

Then, suddenly, she screwed her face up in pain and drew in a sharp breath.

'Mam, are you alright?' the smile died from Tommy's face.

'I'm fine, love. I think I might just have pulled a muscle.'

Ellen met Peggy's eyes across the table in a silent communication that only the two women understood. It was the start of labour. Ellen had experienced it often enough to know. With a bit of luck, it would be short, and, with an even bigger stroke of luck, Nicholas Clinton would have his son before the dawn of the new morning.

CHAPTER 34

'Spider' Menton

George Menton was in a good mood. Things were finally going his way again. A hiatus in his scheme had lasted as long as Ellen Cooney had been employed at the mill. Cursed nuisance that she was. She was a fine-looking woman and, as he had planned, Nicholas's brains had been relegated to his trousers since she had first made an appearance at the mill. Nicholas had definitely taken his eye off the ball since her arrival. George had been reasonably confident that his little enterprise wouldn't be discovered, as Nicholas trusted him implicitly. His boss was too busy getting new markets for the mill's produce and eyeing up Ellen. He had left him the day-to-day shipments and payments to look after. But George hadn't bargained with Ellen having brains. The way her brow furrowed as she looked at the books had given him cause to hold his breath on more than one occasion. She would bite her tongue between her teeth in concentration as she looked at the rows of figures. It was as if she could see that they didn't add up, but she couldn't quite put her finger on why. He'd had to ease off his little game for a while. Then, by some stroke of luck, she had seemed to get distracted, had begun to arrive at work looking pale and wan. Her concentration wasn't what it had been, and he began to breathe a bit easier again. He might get away with it. If he knew the signs, she was with-child and would more than likely have to give up work before she started showing. He had seen her about town with Larry Clinton. George Menton prided himself on being able to spot a pregnancy a mile off - a funny thing for a single man to have in his repertoire of talents. It came from being the only boy in the family growing up amongst a plethora of very fertile older sisters.

He couldn't believe his luck when Nicholas announced to him quietly one evening after work that Ellen had agreed to be his wife and that she would no longer be working at the mill. George had assured Nicholas that he would be more than delighted to be his witness for the marriage. The strength of the handshake he gave Nicholas was not just congratulatory. There was a good deal of relief thrown into the vigorous pumping. She would be out of his hair now, and good riddance. He would be free to continue with his own business. He had been creaming off a little bit for himself for years. Nicholas didn't suspect a thing.

He badly needed to up his game now, though. His creditors were not the patient type. They had warned him, the last time they called to his front door, that he was on borrowed time, had twisted his arm behind his back until his bones crunched. That was just a taste of what was to come, apparently, if he didn't keep up his payments. He cursed the compulsion he had to gamble. When he was in the grip of the urge, he was like a leaf blowing in the autumn wind, completely powerless to decide his own direction. His last big flutter had been on a card game in Dublin. He should have known that he was moving into a bigger league than he was used to. His opponent was renowned for being ruthless in the collection of his winnings. The Dublin thugs he employed were a different breed to the ones in Drogheda. They had a savage hardness, and George didn't doubt them when they told him of the catalogue of injuries they would inflict, should he not come up with his regular payments. His eyes had watered at the prospect of what they said they would do to his nether regions. He couldn't afford for his balls to end up coming out his throat. He was too fond of them.

He was on the way to see his contact at the docks. A few rolls of linen out of every shipment weren't missed. It was to George's advantage that the clerks in the bank were a disorganized bunch and made it very hard for invoices and payments to be reconciled. George had been the one responsible for this job and had been extremely good at obfuscating the real situation.

His contact, Henry Parsons, appeared. Henry was a canny man. Liverpool born and bred. He had an air of respectability about him, but George got the sense that he was only one step above a common navvy. His gilt exterior thinly veiled what lay beneath; it was in the size of his fists, the hair that was just a little too long, and the eyes that were just a shade too hooded for handsomeness.

'Are we back into the big business?' the Liverpudlian accent, usually sing-song, sounded threatening coming from Parsons.

'Indeed, we are.' George's reply, in his northern lilt, was borderline obsequious.

'Good, because I was beginning to think that you were losing your balls man.'

Little did he know that retaining that particular piece of his anatomy was something that George was working very hard to do. The two men exchanged their paperwork. No one would know that five rolls of linen had somehow disappeared from the shipment as it made its way across the Irish sea. George had a second invoice book that he kept under lock and key in his office. Henry would sell the linen on the black market and split the money with George. It had worked out well so far. Henry needed the money because he had a wife and also a fancy-woman that he had to keep in the style to which they were both accustomed. It took less than thirty seconds to exchange the paperwork. Henry had his own little cubby hole on the ship where he hid the extra rolls of linen, and a contact waiting in Liverpool. The fabric would be whisked off to various locations, before it came to its final destination, adorning the table of some fine house in Belgravia, London. It was all quite satisfying in its simplicity.

With the deal done, George whistled to himself as he made his way back to his lodgings on the Cord Road. He would have a nice dram of whiskey to celebrate. He breathed in deeply. Drogheda was looking well this evening. Sunlight glinted off the new bridge, and now that spring was finally here, there was an air of jollity among the hard-working inhabitants of the town. *Ah yes*, things were looking up again. He would be able to keep those thugs from re-arranging his nether regions whilst he tried to get a grip on his gambling. It was time to shape up, or maybe ship out. George ran through all the various scenarios in his head until a plan began to form.

CHAPTER 35

Ellen

Michael Joseph Clinton was in a hurry to be born. After inflicting no more than two hours of labour on his mother, excruciating though it was, he arrived into the world. Silent at first, and then his little face screwing up in anger, as if being wrenched from his lovely, warm cocoon was totally unnecessary, and a huge inconvenience. He ignored the whoop of joy that came from Peggy Murphy. He didn't notice that his mother sank back onto her pillows with pure relief. He threw his arms out and worked himself into quite a fury, until Peggy swaddled him and placed him on his mother's chest, and he found what he was looking for. He started sucking voraciously and peace was restored to the room.

'Peggy, he's just adorable. I can't believe I have finally done it! Oh, thank God!'

Ellen looked at the perfect features of her new son and then, closing her eyes, threw back her head, breathing in and out deeply. The relief she felt was not just that the agony of childbirth was over, but also that she had finally managed to give Nicholas the son he so badly craved. Now he might leave her alone. A son and heir. Her path to freedom. Her body was spent with motherhood. She now had six children, and she swore there and then, that this would be her last. She had finally repaid her debt to Nicholas for saving her, Tommy and Alice from a life of hand-to-mouth existence.

'He's a dote alright – the image of you I'd say,' replied Peggy, taking the dark, downy head and pale skin. 'He's a right ravenous little fella and all!' she chuckled, her chins wobbling.

From her chair at the side of the bed, she rested her eyes on Ellen's face and took her hand.

'You've done it now lass. You've given him his son. I sincerely hope that you are done having children for that man now?'

'I swear, Peggy, that's it, I'm done. No more. I don't care what he says.'

Ellen had never revealed the full extent of Nicholas's cruelty to Peggy as she found it hard to admit, even to herself, to herself that her actions had led her to this half-life, where her material needs were met, but at a massive price.

'Glad to hear it young woman! Now, let's get that hair of yours brushed and tidy you up a bit so that the others can come and meet their new brother.'

Peggy waddled over to the mahogany dressing table and picked up the silver brush from amongst all the bottles and tubs that were strewn across its surface. Sitting back down by the bed with a poof of her skirts, she took some of Ellen's dark hair in her hand and began to brush. Ellen knew it was nowhere near as lustrous as it had been a few years ago. All those pregnancies had sucked a hell of a lot of goodness out of her body. Ellen watched Peggy's familiar and dear face. A sudden swell of gratitude made Ellen feel quite teary. The motion of the soft bristles of the brush was soothing. When she was satisfied with her handiwork, Peggy sat back in her chair.

'Now lass, you're looking better. Is that young lad finished his supper yet? Here, let me take him and you tidy yourself up, and then I'll call the childer.'

Ellen handed her new bundle to Peggy and began to arrange her clothes and the sheets on the bed into some semblance of tidiness. She stifled a groan as she tried to sit up. He was a big baby, probably almost nine pounds. She felt almost weightless with relief that it was all over, and suddenly energized for some reason that she couldn't quite put her finger on. The door opened slightly.

'Come in pets! Come and meet your new brother!'

The door opened wide, and Tommy and Alice, with their three sisters in tow, bundled into the room.

'Now, have a look at him. Isn't he a fine baby with his dark hair and scrunched up little face?'

Five pairs of eyes peered into the crib in which the latest addition to the family was lying serenely, mouth twitching, fists curled up either side of his dark head. Tommy looked at Ellen.

'Are you alright Mam?' he enquired softly.

'Come here pet.' Tommy walked over to the bed and sat down.

'I'm just fine love. It's all over and I'm grateful to have a healthy little lad – a brother for you at last! Sure, you'll be able to teach him everything you know, and he will adore you, just as I do.' Ellen touched her son's head, ruffling his hair like she used to do when he was very small.

'Stop Mam!', he pulled away with a grin on his face.

He looked relieved, seemed delighted to see his Mam sitting up with such a contented look on her face. One by one, the other children tore themselves away from observing their new brother and launched themselves at their mother's bed.

'Be careful will ye now!' Peggy admonished. Your Mam's only after having a baby, will ye go easy!'

'It's alright Peggy, sure they're just excited. 'Well,' she turned to Alice, what do you think of him?'

'He's alright, I suppose. He's a bit smelly.'

Ellen burst out laughing.

'You were smelly too when you filled your nappy!'

All seven of them got a fit of the giggles at this statement. The room was filled with childish laughter. Ellen thought she would remember this moment for years to come.

'What's all this noise and rumpus?'

A booming voice cut through the merriment in the room and all the children instantly stopped laughing. One by one, they peeled themselves away from their Mam and formed a straight line.

'Off you all go now to play or do whatever it is that you do.' They trooped out the door, a subdued bunch.

Nicholas stood at the crib and peered in at his newest child.

'Well, is it another girl?'

He swayed slightly unsteadily on his feet and Ellen thought how much he disgusted her. His once trim waistline had ballooned over the past few years. He had lost most of his vigour and his nose was now swollen and red. No wonder, based on the amount of alcohol he put away on a regular basis. He couldn't even stay sober on the day his wife was giving birth.

Trying to keep the loathing from her voice, she answered lightly.

'Actually, it's a boy.'

She waited for his reaction. He looked at her incredulously, then looked back to the cot. A slow smile crossed his face.

'A boy? I have a son? I really have a son?'

His words were slurred, and his eyes slightly glazed. Ellen almost felt sorry for him. He had the look of a child who had just been handed the most magnificent present.

'Yes, Nicholas, you have a son. Although you already have one in Tommy, don't forget.'

Nicholas didn't appear to hear the contempt in her voice.

'Well done, my dear. You have finally managed to do something right. Finally, finally. Now I must go and wet the baby's head. A son, I have a son!' He threw a glance at Peggy. 'Make sure you look after him properly.' And with that, he turned and walked unsteadily from the room.

The two women looked at each other. Both were determined that things were going to be different from now on. But one of them had more concrete plans than the other.

CHAPTER 36

Larry

Australian Outback, March 1873

'Missa cooeee! Missa cooeee!' the voice drifted in through the open window of the wooden hut. Larry snapped awake, opened his eyes and lay stock still, listening intently. No one else in the dormitory was awake. There was the usual snoring, grumbling, and mumbling to be heard, along with the occasional heavy sigh. Larry sat up in his hammock, pausing to look around the room. The air was cool on his skin, and a light breeze ruffled the net at the window which was supposed to keep the mosquitoes out. Giving his eyes another thirty seconds to get used to the dark, he slowly put his feet on the ground and padded softly over to where the sound had come from. His bare, calloused feet hardly felt the knots in the matting covering the floor. Pausing to take one more glance around him, he turned and looked out through the window. At first, he couldn't see anything, but then his Aboriginal friend, Minjarra emerged from the dark with a beaming smile, set in a round, friendly face. 'Cooee Missa!'

'Cooee Minjarra!' Larry couldn't help but return the huge grin. He could hear the sound of the guard's snoring coming from the front of the hut. He jerked his head in the guard's direction and threw his eyes up to the heavens. He didn't know any Aboriginal words and Minjarra didn't know any English, but they still managed to communicate reasonably well. The young man mimed putting a bottle to his lips and threw his head back as if taking a big, long drink. Then he broke into a fit of laughing. He seemed to find the guard's liquor-induced slumber highly amusing. Larry put his fingers to his lips, afraid the guard would wake at the sound of the merriment. Minjarra understood and gathered himself.

He rummaged in the bush behind him and produced a cloth bag which he held aloft. Larry could see the outline of its contents. He could feel the juices rising in his mouth in anticipation. It looked like Minjarra had been busy. This would keep them all going for a few days. The young boy's feet made absolutely no sound as he covered the few steps to the open window. He handed the bundle to Larry. Larry opened it. He counted twenty-three Gubinges. The little green fruit, smaller than an apple, had proven to be a lifesaver for Larry and his fellow convicts. It was hard to survive on the meagre rations of bread and hardtack that they got every day in this god-forsaken place. And they were expected to work for ten hours every day. Hard labour it was too. But, since they had started eating the little fruit that Minjarra brought him, they had all found a new strength. Their gums had stopped bleeding, and miraculously they had less aches and pains. Minjarra was a little miracle-worker, it seemed. But only Larry knew the identity of their benefactor. He didn't want his friend to get into trouble and he didn't trust the others not to accidentally reveal the young Aboriginal's kindness. He would be sure to be found and punished if the guards realized he was supplying food to the prisoners.

'Bunji Mate!' whispered Larry, handing him back the bag. 'Bunji!' smiled Minjarra. With a wave, he was off, stealing through the darkness like a cat. The moon glinted off the dark, shiny skin of his back as the night swallowed him up.

Larry carefully placed three of the little pieces of fruit in each hammock. His inmates would wake in the morning, exclaiming that the fruit fairy had been again in the night. They would wipe the juice from their beards and somehow, the miracle would make what lay ahead of them slightly more bearable.

Larry climbed back into his hammock. The ropes groaned slightly. Closing his eyes, he ran his fingers down the scar on his left cheek. He could still feel the stinging pain that Mc Intyre's knife had made when it had sliced into his flesh. A couple of years earlier, shortly after he had arrived in Australia, he had come across the guard beating the young Aboriginal, just for the fun of it. Minjarra's only crime had been to wander too close to the convicts out of curiosity. Larry had thought him to be about fourteen. He was lithe, but had yet to develop his man's physique, so he had been no match for the big brute of a guard. Larry had reacted suddenly, exploding from the trench he was digging and taking the guard by surprise. It was enough to make sure that Minjarra got away. He had fled into the bush at lightning speed, leaving a cloud of dust in his wake. Larry's punishment could have been worse but for another guard, who stopped Mc Intyre doing any more serious damage. Larry was stronger than most of the convicts in the camp, so they didn't want him incapacitated. There was a lot of work to be done.

After that, Minjarra had considered Larry his saviour. He hid in the bushes, peeking out at the convicts working, day after day. Sometimes, Larry would sense he was being watched, and sure enough, when he looked up, a pair of shining, brown eyes would stare back at him from the branches of a tree. Minjarra was like a curious little monkey looking down from his perch. Then, he had begun his nightly ritual of bringing the fruit to Larry as if in payment for saving him from Mc Intyre. 'Gubinge' it was called, and by God, it was tasty and juicy. And it seemed to have relieved the convicts of some of their ailments.

Rolling over with a sigh and closing his eyes, Larry turned his mind from Minjarra and the harsh Australian outback. As he slowly descended into sleep, his thoughts were of green fields, soft rain and the myriad streets of his hometown, dissected by the river Boyne. And Ellen, the love of his life, with the laughing blue eyes and soft hair, the colour of treacle. He would see her again one day. If he ever got out of this place. There had to be a way. He would find a back path to his Ellen and his child. A smile on his lips, sleep claimed him at last.

CHAPTER 37

Drogheda

New Year's Eve 1874

Ellen was sick and tired of Nicholas. She was fed up with his moods, his drunkenness, his indifference to Tommy, their daughters and to anyone but his beloved son, Michael. Tommy and Alice avoided him as much as possible. Liberty, Gladys and Rosena were afraid of him. Peggy despised him, and Ellen's own feelings weren't far behind. But she was trapped. At times she felt like she couldn't breathe. The pressure on her chest felt like a horse and cart had driven right over it. And it was all her own fault. If she hadn't met and fallen in love with Larry, if fate hadn't conspired to tear him away from her when she needed him most, if she hadn't agreed to marry Nicholas....if, if, if. Today was a day when these thoughts went round and round in her head with no solution. It was on days like these that she thought she might go mad. She had a life that many would consider privileged. She was sure many women would trade places with her in a heartbeat. She had a warm, comfortable home, a full belly, food for all her children, all the clothes she could wish for.

Tonight, she had to nod and smile and pretend that she was happy. It was becoming increasingly harder to keep up the charade.

The sudden stop of the carriage jolted Ellen from her black thoughts.

'We're here my dear.' Nicholas's voice dripped honey as was the case when anyone outside of the family was within earshot.

'My dear,' thought Ellen as her lips tightened slightly. You didn't treat someone you hold dear the way Nicholas treated her. She forced herself to meet her husband's eyes. They were bloodshot now, appearing smaller than they had been. Perhaps the puffiness of his cheeks had something to do with that. In them, she saw a challenge. *'Cross me at your peril',* they seemed to say.

'Now, before we disembark from the carriage, I'm sure you and I can agree that we are going to have the most splendid night in the company of good friends. Do you think you could muster that glorious smile of yours and keep it pinned onto your face for the next three hours? It is New Year's Eve after all!'

A swell of pure despair rose in Ellen's stomach. She felt her jaw tense. The beginning of a thumping headache was right behind her eyes. Baby Michael had been fretful for the past couple of days, and she hadn't had much sleep. A night out was the last thing that Ellen felt like. She had hated leaving the children and Peggy to go to the function.

Peggy had alarmed her last week. Her friend had dropped the big serving spoon on the floor of the kitchen. She had turned to see that Peggy had gone into a kind of daze, and she was that pale, she looked like she had seen a ghost. Thinking she was going to faint, Ellen had helped Peggy to a chair where she had collapsed, trying to loosen the collar of her blouse. She had puffed and panted and there had been a sheen of perspiration on her ruddy cheeks.

'What is it, Peggy. Are you alright?'

'No, no, it can't be true!' wailed Peggy.

'What can't be true? Peggy! You're scaring me now!'

Suddenly, Peggy seemed to come out of her daze, and she focused on Ellen.

'Ah lass,' was all she had said as she lifted her hand to Ellen's cheek. She caressed it lightly and there had been desolation in her eyes.

'What, is it Peggy, what did you see?' Ellen had witnessed Peggy having various *'visions'* down through the years, but never had she seen her friend so distressed. Peggy remained mute; her eyes had filled with tears. She shook her head as if trying to erase the image from her mind.

'Nothing lass, nothing at all.' She faced Ellen, looking like she was struggling to assemble her features in a more normal fashion.

'Twas just a little turn I had. Nothing for you to be worrying your pretty head about.'

'But I do worry about you Peggy. You're to let me know if you feel like this again. For a minute, I thought you were having one of your *'visions'*!'

'Ah, no pet, it wasn't one of them. I just felt a bit light-headed for a few moments. It's passed now. I'm fine.'

Peggy's eyes had wandered to the corner of the room and had settled on the newly acquired copper-framed *tintype* of the family which adorned the wall. It had been taken a couple of months after Michael had been born, and showed Nicholas, Ellen and all six children in a somewhat stiff formation. Ellen had been delighted with it. It was a moment in time when her children were gathered all around her. She was exceedingly proud of every one of them. There were times when she couldn't believe they were all hers. Tommy was such a handsome young man now. Alice looked just like her. But she had a wanton, sometimes wild look in her eyes that made Ellen worry about her future. No matter what warnings and advice Ellen gave her, it would be routinely ignored as if she, Alice, knew better. The other three little ladies were slowly but surely asserting their own personalities as each day passed. They were a hungry mob. Peggy was hard-pressed to keep them fed. They reminded Ellen sometimes of a nest of hungry baby birds, mouths constantly open, looking for someone to deposit the next meal. And as for little Michael. He was a cherub. A little pet with dimples in his cheeks, the fattest legs ever, and a smile that would melt the heart of the chilliest character. She adored him from the top of his dark curls to his stubby little toes. And how his Daddy idolised him! That was one redeeming feature in Nicholas's character. He loved his son with a passion that bordered on obsession. Since his birth, Michael had been the centre of Nicholas's world. He virtually ignored his little daughters now. It was a good job that Ellen loved them enough for two.

Ellen had had a sense of unease ever since Peggy's 'turn.' She had caught Peggy looking at the *tintype* a few times since, and then turning her gaze to little Michael. She had seemed to hug him extra tightly. Ellen tried to put the unsettling thoughts to the back of her mind as she met her husband's eyes.

'When have I ever let you down in public Nicholas?' she enquired, arching one shapely dark brow.

'You haven't my dear. Yet. And I would very much like to keep it that way. Now, shall we?'

He leaned over to open the carriage door. The smell of whiskey seemed to emanate from his pores. She wasn't sure if she could stomach another year of being married to him. Normally, people welcomed the new year with a spark of hope in their hearts for better things to come. But, as far as Ellen was concerned, the year ahead would just be more of the same. The feeling that she was trapped in a loveless marriage sometimes threatened to cause her to almost stop breathing. The image of Larry haunted her waking hours and invaded her sleep at night. She yearned for him - even after all these years. He was on the other side of the world, but if wishing alone could have helped him escape from his prison cell, then he would have flown to her side. In her more elaborate fantasies, Nicholas somehow disappeared, she and Larry took over the running of the business, and he became a father to all her children. It was just as well Nicholas didn't have the power to read her mind, as he would no doubt be incensed. His fury was something she was used to after seven years of marriage. It regularly bubbled up from deep inside him but was unpredictable in its severity. Some days, it was like a flash flood, over within seconds. Other days, it was like a mighty torrent, sweeping everything in its path and leaving devastation in its wake. She tried to protect the children from the worst of his moods, and to be fair to him, he generally kept the brunt of his ill temper for her. If he ever harmed a hair on any of her children's heads, then that was when all bets would be off.

Ellen and Nicholas descended from the carriage to the street, which was teeming with people. Carriages of all sizes and hues pulled up, as the well-connected of the town milled around, greeting each other loudly and ostentatiously, ready to see out the old and bring in the new with alacrity. A golden light spilled out from the windows of the West Hotel and the tantalising smell of roast beef was coming from inside. Scruffy young children were trying to get the gentlemen to buy flowers for their ladies. If Ellen hadn't married Nicholas, that could very well have been her Alice trying to earn a few bob, barefoot in the late December evening. Ellen gave a little shudder, and tried to remind herself she'd had no choice, all those years ago. Marriage to Nicholas had been the lesser of two evils.

Ellen took her husband's arm, and together they made their way into the brightly lit lobby of the hotel. Her stomach rumbled, and she realized she was looking forward to the sit-down meal. With any luck, she would be seated beside one of the least annoying wives tonight, and the evening would pass in a relatively pleasant fashion. She looked down at her ruby-red dress. That was one good thing about being married to a mill-owner, she supposed. There was never any shortage of money to buy material and she and the children were always very well turned out. Not that she had any idea how much was spent on clothing them. Nicholas looked after all the family finances. All she had to do was choose the fabric, and together with the dress-maker's fees, it all went down to the Clinton account. She admired the way the red rhinestones glittered in the lamplight of the ballroom. She knew she was looking well. She caught many of the men glancing in her direction. A few got their shins kicked, or arms pinched by their wives, who glared at Ellen, before scornfully turning, and steering their husbands away from her orbit. This was a source of amusement to Ellen. As if she would look at any of the men twice. Her heart had been captured by a russet-haired, tawny-eyed man nine years ago, and time had only served to make her feelings for him stronger.

The evening passed. The food was delicious. The conversation and the wine flowed. Nicholas downed drink after drink. His speech got ever so slightly slurred, his eyes turned a bit glassy, his nose, a touch redder. Ellen was glad to get sitting beside Mrs. Clogher, whose husband had a tannery in town. The band was tuning up in the corner. There would be dancing. But not for Ellen. She loved to dance, but Nicholas didn't. He felt that it made him look foolish. Ellen was quite happy not to have to spend any longer than she had to in close physical proximity to him.

Just halfway through the first dance of the night, Ellen heard a commotion coming from the doorway. There were shouts from the crowd.

'Watch yourself young lad!' 'Oi, be careful where you're going!'

Ellen turned from her conversation with Mrs. Clogher to see what was going on. A trickle of ice ran down her spine as she saw Tommy searching the room, his chest heaving and his face a mask of terror. She stood up, her eyes fastened on her eldest son. She waved to get his attention.

'Tommy, over here, love!'

Tommy spotted his Mam and rushed over to her, elbowing dancers out of his way. She ran to meet him, her heart in her mouth. They almost collided. She could see the sheen of sweat on his brow and that his green eyes were awash with fear.

'What's wrong?' Ellen felt her stomach do a somersault with dread.

'It's Michael. There's something wrong with him. Peggy told me to come and get you. I'm scared Mam. Michael doesn't look good. He went all floppy and Peggy couldn't rouse him. He has a rash on his belly too.'

'Sweet Jesus in heaven.' Ellen breathed. She ran over to Nicholas and told him that they had to go home straight away, that there was something wrong with Michael. Nicholas looked from Ellen to Tommy's stricken face and without a word, turned on his heel and strode towards the door. Collecting his and Ellen's coats and hats, all three ran to the front door. They climbed into the carriage and were soon racing towards home, the poor horse feeling the effects of having to make two journeys in rapid succession. Nicholas made Tommy repeat his story, and then the carriage descended into silence, save for the sound of Ellen muttering something under her breath, over and over again.

'Dear god in heaven, please let him be alright, please let him be alright.' Ellen could feel her heart hammering in her chest, her breath coming short and fast. She felt sick, light-headed. Tommy reached over and held her hand. Nicholas was staring straight ahead, his face stony, and his mouth in a grim line. Now and again, he bellowed at the driver to go faster. It was only a short journey, but it seemed to take forever. They finally arrived home, and Tommy caught Ellen as she stumbled into the house in Nicholas's wake.

Ellen wrenched her hat from her head and threw it, and her wool coat, in a heap on the hall floor. She started to run up the stairs and stumbled as she tripped on the hem of her gown. Cursing, she righted herself with the help of Tommy, who was in her wake. She had never really noticed the intricacies of the swirled pattern on the stair carpet before. Nor had her hearing ever seemed so acute. She could hear her own breath, coming raggedly from her chest, and the sound of Nicholas thundering across the wooden landing to the door of the nursery. She was ten steps behind him. She burst into the room. The look on Peggy's face made her stomach clench and heave. Her friend was standing by the side of the cot in which Michael lay. Ellen came to a stop beside Nicholas. Their son was lying there, in nothing but his cloth nappy, his little chest barely rising, as he took fitful, shallow breaths. His eyes were closed, and his little face was screwed up as if he was in pain. His face was deathly pale, apart from two spots of high colour on his cheeks. His torso was covered in blotches, which were clearly visible, even in the dull lamplight.

'What's wrong with him?' Nicholas bellowed. 'Have you called Doctor Murchin?'

He was addressing these questions to Peggy, although he never took his eyes from his son.

'He's on his way. I sent Tommy to call him. He should be here any minute.' Tommy nodded.

'Yes, I left him getting dressed in his outdoor clothes before I went to the hotel to get you both,' Tommy murmured.

Nicholas went to pick Michael up.

'No, leave him. He's burning up and the heat from your body wouldn't do him any good.' Peggy's voice brooked no argument.

The baby yowled, tossing his head from side to side. The sound tore at Ellen's insides.

'Peggy, what do you think is ailing him?'

Ellen was barely able to get the words out, as her throat was so dry. Her voice was at least two octaves higher than normal; such was the tide of terror that was threatening to engulf her. Michael had been fine before they left for their dinner dance. A little bit hot and grisly, but Ellen had put that down to the fact that he was probably getting his back teeth.

'I'm not sure Ellen', Peggy was biting her lip and refusing to meet Ellen's eyes.

'Peggy!' Ellen barked, 'Please tell me what you think is wrong. Is it serious?'

Ellen tore her gaze away from her son and was chilled to the marrow by the expression on Peggy's face.

'I think it might be brain fever.' Peggy exhaled slowly.

Ellen could see she was struggling to hold back tears.

'He was a little bit grumpy all evening, hot, and kept turning his head from side to side. I thought he either had a toothache or an earache, so I rubbed a little bit whiskey on his gums. The light of the lamp seemed to bother him, so I put him to bed. He didn't take much of his bottle. He felt a bit hot but settled well enough when I put him into the cot. He gave the odd whimper every so often, and when I went in to check on him half an hour ago, I couldn't rouse him. He was burning up, so I stripped him and that was when I saw the rash. I got Tommy to run and fetch Doctor Murchin and then he went for you.'

Peggy's head swivelled from Ellen to Michael and back to Ellen again. The older woman took Ellen's hand and gave it a squeeze.

'As I said, I think it might be brain fever which I have seen in children before. With a bit of medicine, he should be as right as rain. We have got to be hopeful.'

'Brain fever. But that's serious -not a trifle! How could you have thought he was teething, you stupid woman?'

Spittle formed at the corners of Nicholas's mouth and his face took on a mottled purple hue as he turned his vitriol on Peggy.

'Don't blame Peggy for this!' shouted Ellen.

She was fighting a losing battle with the panic that was slowly creeping outwards from her core into every single cell and nerve ending she possessed. She had seen children die of brain fever before back in Rope Walk. But she had also seen them recover. There were different strains of the fever. She prayed with all her might that the one Michael had was the less vicious kind. She couldn't possibly lose this beautiful child. He wasn't even two years old. Surely life could never be that ferociously cruel? She glanced over at Nicholas. He was swaying unsteadily on his feet, running his hand through his now receding hair. He loosened his cravat. Beads of sweat stood out on his brow and his upper lip. Ellen didn't know if it was from the belly-full he had drunk earlier, or panic that his pride and joy, his heir to the family business, his reason for living, was gravely ill. Her eyes met his, and for the first time in a long time, they were united - in their horror at the situation that they found themselves in, as their young son's breathing appeared to become more ragged.

Peggy continued sponging him down, her hands shaking. She was muttering something under her breath. Ellen would have sworn it was a prayer. She must be really scared of the outcome for Michael, as Ellen knew Peggy no longer believed in God. The sight of her friend's bloodless lips moving in silent utterance made Ellen feel like this was surreal. It could not be happening.

They all turned when they heard voices in the hallway. Doctor Murchin had arrived. Tommy had let him in, and he was now being ushered into the room. Ellen thought she had never seen such a welcome sight. The doctor was in his sixties, with a tall bearing, grey bushy hair, bright blue eyes, and a no-nonsense approach to sickness. He was also a compassionate man, as Ellen had witnessed many times since he became her family doctor. He had always been kindness personified to her children throughout the ups and downs of childhood illnesses. She had the utmost respect for him.

'Well then. What seems to be the problem with young Michael?'

The doctor took off his coat and placed his black leather bag down on the table beside the cot, opening it in one swift movement and removing a stethoscope.

'Tell the doctor every last detail and leave nothing out.'

Nicholas's gruff tone would normally make Peggy bristle, but now was not the time for taking affront. As the doctor listened to Michael's heartbeat, Peggy recounted the timeline of Michael's descent into a burning, semi-conscious little scrap. It was plain to hear that the boy's breathing was getting more and more laboured. The doctor took his temperature, and while they waited for the gadget to produce its reading, he examined the child, peering into his eyes, pressing on the rash and, occasionally, listening to his heartbeat again. Ellen noticed that his expression grew grimmer by the minute. Doctor Murchin peered at his thermometer. He turned his eyes to Ellen and then to Nicholas.

'I don't think there is any need for me to tell you that your son is extremely ill?'

'What is it doctor, what's wrong with him?'

Ellen felt a rising hysteria. Doctor Murchin had always come to the rescue before. Had always had the correct medicine, the right words to soothe Ellen's anxiety when one of her children was unwell. She saw something in his demeanour that made her nerves jangle and a block of ice wedge itself in her innards.

'It is my professional opinion that Michael has meningitis or 'Brain Fever' as it is more commonly known.'

Ellen felt herself sway as stars appeared before her eyes. She gripped the doctor's arm.

'But you can make him better, can't you? He has the curable one, yes? Say it isn't the worst kind, say it isn't!'

'Cornelius, you must cure my boy. You must!'

Nicholas's eyes were bloodshot. He grabbed hold of the doctor's other arm.

'I am heartily sorry to be the bearer of such bad news and to see little Michael so sick.'

The doctor peeled Nicholas's fingers one by one from his navy serge sleeve.

'There are no medical interventions of any worth that I can offer to you. It is true that there are different strains of meningitis, but I fear that it appears Michael has the worst one. In cases like this, the most we can do is as Mrs. Murphy here has been doing; keep the little lad sponged down to try and ease his temperature. And, after that, we wait.'

Cornelius's Murchin's expression was the gravest Ellen had ever seen it. She thought she saw a flicker of sympathy in his eyes as he looked from Michael to herself and back to Nicholas. It was as if he had given up on the little lad already. As if he could foresee the course this illness was to take. As if he held out little hope. A silent voice inside Ellen shrieked. *No, no, no, this cannot be happening to my little angel!* A series of images of him throughout his short life ran through her mind. The first time she had held him, the way he looked deep into her eyes when feeding, as if he believed that she should be so grateful he was lying in her arms; the dimple in his right cheek; the smell of him; the utterly delicious, round gorgeousness of his little body. Ellen had to remind herself to breathe. Her heart was hammering against her ribs. Peggy was holding her hand and stroking it, her bosom heaving heavily and erratically as she appeared to try and keep her own terror at bay.

The clock downstairs struck two. Was it only just over two hours since they had fled from the hotel? It seemed like a lifetime ago since they were making conversation with their acquaintances about trivial things. All that was to be heard in the room was Michael's laboured breathing, the occasional whimper from Peggy, and the clack of the doctor's stethoscope as he regularly listened to the little boy's heartbeat, his lips getting thinner each time, and his expression graver. The room grew stuffy. Ellen's back grew stiff, as she was ramrod straight, sitting on the left-hand side of the cot. Nicholas was on the other side, staring at his son as if he was trying to will his temperature downwards. Peggy kept up a constant ritual of sponging Michael, her lips moving almost imperceptibly. Ellen noticed that Michael's breathing had changed. It was even shallower and more rapid than before. He was now deathly pale, but still with the two bright spots on his cheeks. His little ribcage was fluttering, his stomach distended. Suddenly, his body went rigid, and he started to convulse. Ellen shrieked and leapt to her feet.

'What's happening to him now?' yelled Nicholas, his face almost as white as his son's.

'He's having a convulsion.'

The doctor picked the little boy up and rolled him over onto his front. Michael continued to twist and writhe in the doctor's arms for about ten seconds and then he went completely limp. It was the sight of his little fist slackening that caused Ellen to lose control. She let out a guttural howl and looked from her son's lifeless body to the doctor's face. It told her all she needed to know. He took the stethoscope out again and listened for a heartbeat. Again and again, he placed the instrument on the little mottled chest, but it seemed he could not find what he was looking for. Eventually, he removed it from his ears and with a sigh that seemed to come from his very core, he shook his head at Ellen.

'I'm so very sorry Ellen, Nicholas. I'm afraid Michael has lost his battle.'

Ellen wrenched her son from the doctor's arms and started to gently shake him.

'No, he can't be, I will not allow him to be dead! He's not even two! It's impossible! Doctor, give him something to wake him up. He must be just gone unconscious. Doctor, I'm speaking to you!'

Ellen raged at the doctor, but he just shook his head and sank into one of the chairs.

'Ellen, if I could do anything for him, I would. But I can't. It's too late. There was nothing any of us could have done.'

He looked from Ellen to Peggy to Nicholas and back to Ellen again.

'I'm so very sorry for your loss.'

'I'm sorry for your loss?'

Was the doctor really uttering these words and addressing them to her? Ellen stared incredulously at her son's lifeless face, feeling the dead weight of him in her arms. She could hear someone sobbing openly, then a rush of air as someone else strode from the room, the sound of footsteps heavy on the stairs, followed by the banging of the front door.

CHAPTER 38

Larry

'The Convict Establishment'

Freemantle Australia, March 1876,

It was St. Patrick's Day in Drogheda. The townspeople had removed their work-weary expressions for the day. The mill was silent, up on its perch, overlooking the town. There was no work of any kind to do, as all the factories and shops were closed. There was a sense of gaiety and fun about the place. The quays were thronged. All the lassies had green ribbons in their hair, the young lads had bunches of shamrock pinned onto their caps. And later, after Mass, musicians would suddenly appear on every street corner, with fiddles, accordions and bodhrans. It would be impossible to keep your feet from tapping and your hands from clapping to the merry beat. The bells of St. Peter's were tolling loudly, calling the townspeople to pray before they immersed themselves in the celebration of the national saint, who had banished all the snakes from Ireland.

'Wake up, Clinton. It's 4.30. Time to shake a leg.'

Larry was jolted from his dream of home by a vicious poke in the leg with a long stick, courtesy of Warder Prout, or 'Snout' as Larry and his mates called him. With his pink flabby face and squat nose, he was the image of a pig. Larry groaned as he realized that the bells he had heard were the prison's wake-up call. He let his eyes stay closed for ten more seconds before he dragged himself fully to consciousness. Prout had disappeared, whistling, before he prodded his next victim through the bars of another cell, his nasty laugh reverberating around the limestone walls. With a yawn, Larry sat up, rubbed his eyes, and swung his legs over the side of his bed. He missed his hammock. It was a darn site more comfortable than the hard bed he had now, which was barely long enough for him. His toes always stuck out from under the thin, grey blanket. At times, he nearly missed the other prison camp he had been in. Six years he had spent in the outback. Building a road that was to run from Albany to Perth. In this 'Convict Establishment,' his days still consisted of hard labour, but he was back in the company of his own countrymen. He had been delighted to see that five of the Irish he had met on the voyage were here. At least now, he had the company of people who understood what it was like to yearn with every fibre of your being for a soft mist on your face. And was heartily sick of all the warder's English accents.

After a hasty wash with the cold water in his basin, Larry joined the snake of men heading down the corridor towards the door that would lead to the parade ground. All around him, the inmates shuffled quietly, most still not properly awake, their striped linen trousers making a swishing sound. They all had sores on their ankles from the iron shackles they had to wear. Larry's wounds were causing a dull throb today. Occasionally, one of the warders barked at them to hurry up. He was almost used to the odour of unwashed bodies, mingled with the smell of the many chamber pots that had yet to be emptied after the night.

The cool air hit as he stepped outside and wrapped itself around him like a damp blanket. It was welcome. Still dark, the sun wouldn't rise for another hour and a half. That didn't stop the work. A lot would be done before breakfast, which would be the usual lumpy muck they called porridge. More work would follow, sometimes inside the walls of the *'Establishment'*, sometimes outside. Muster took place at twelve o'clock every day and this was when Larry allowed his mind to wander.

He was impervious at this stage to the high-pitched whining of the Comptroller General, a swollen midget of a man called Cooper, whose name was particularly apt, as he closely resembled a barrel. As Cooper reminded them all that they were worse than the dirt on his shoes, Larry's mind swooped and soared over oceans and land, mountains and rivers, until he was back by the beautiful Boyne, with the smell of salt in his nostrils, and the view of Millmount glinting in the summer sunshine. By God, he would get back there if it was the last thing he did. Seven years was too long to be away. He allowed himself to imagine the feel of Ellen's breath on his cheek, the touch of her hand in his. But only momentarily, for to dwell on all he had lost was the path to madness.

Many of the Fenians had been pardoned and had been sent to America. But he and five others remained. In his most despairing moments, Larry felt as if there was darkness and evil working against him. He had had ample time to ponder how he had been caught so easily that March evening in Drogheda all those years ago, when their plans to free Erin had gone so badly wrong. It was hard to believe that his own flesh and blood had betrayed him so badly. The knot in Larry's stomach grew harder. Back at work, he concentrated on lifting the pick and striking it as hard as he could into the block of limestone in front of him. It wasn't long until he was lost in a rhythm; strike, lift, repeat - until the muscles in his shoulders screamed for mercy. Later, at exercise time, Murphy, a tall, dark-haired man from Co. Cork, with hands the size of shovels, and a broad, intelligent face, sidled over to Larry.

'There's a whisper of an escape plan.'

Larry glanced at his friend. The man's face was impassive, his features blank. Larry thought he had imagined the words.

'Did you say *'escape plan'*?' Larry whispered, looking straight ahead. A bolt of energy had lit up his insides. Could it be possible?

'Aye, our friends in America have arranged for a whaling ship to come and get us. Finer details and instructions to be delivered later.'

'But, how? Where? Who?'

'Slater. Say nothing.'

John Slater was one of the warders who sympathized with the Fenian cause, even though he was an Englishman, originally from the city of Manchester. Unlike most of his compatriots, he didn't believe that it was the right of the English to conquer all they saw. He believed that Ireland should be owned and ruled by the Irish themselves. He had somehow received news from some powerful and rich Fenians in America, that the last remaining Irishmen were to be rescued from Freemantle Convict Establishment, on a ship purchased specially for the purpose. It would sail to Australia, under the guise of being a whaling ship. The Fenians were to await further instructions on where and how the rescue would happen. Jesus, Mary and all the saints. Would he really soon be free? It was all he could do to stop himself whooping out loud. But, under the beady eye of the warder, he and Murphy kept their expressions arranged in a way fitting to convicts who were contemplating the wrong they had inflicted on society and were happy to pay the price.

That evening, Larry barely tasted the meal of chewy meat, and vegetables which were boiled to within an inch of their lives. Nor the cocoa afterwards. A sliver of hope had lodged itself in his heart. That night, his dreams were full of sunlight, where he rode on the back of a whale, across the foam-tipped waves, all the way to Ireland, and up the mouth of the river at Mornington, triumphantly arriving at the quays in Drogheda, where Ellen was waiting for him with a green ribbon in her hair.

Larry wondered had the sky always been this particular shade of blue, and had the clouds always been so white? Had the sounds of the horses, clip-clopping past, always been so sharp, and the rumble of the carriage wheels always been so loud? He took a deep breath and tried to slow his heart, for it seemed in danger of coming out through his chest. He looked across at Murphy and caught his eye. The other man gave him the merest hint of a wink, and got back to wielding his pickaxe, the bright morning sun glinting on his black hair, giving it an almost green-blue hue. There were twelve of them here this morning, having been assigned to work just outside the walls of the Convict Establishment on construction of more housing for the prison warders. Murphy and himself were digging the foundations, which was back-breaking work. Larry paused for a moment and looked at the palms of his calloused hands. They had been released from their ankle chains for this job, as there was a bit of a rush on to get the work done.

There were ten men in total working on the job. Six Irishmen, all of them proud Fenian prisoners, and four English petty thieves. The English lads had the resigned look of men who had nothing to look forward to but ten hours of slave-labour and more stringy meat, pulped vegetables, and a bed as hard as stone. If anyone had cared to notice, there was something different about the Irish lads that morning. It was in the furtive glances they gave one another and the way they kept stopping briefly to look up from their work.

'Why do you keep looking at the clock, Irish?' demanded Scott, one of the warders, giving Larry a shove in the back.

'I'm just wondering when it will be time for a break.'

After another ten minutes, he dared glance at the clock that was built into the limestone arch over the entrance to the Establishment. The black iron hands told him it was 8.20am. Another ten minutes. Time to start getting everyone into position. He glanced down the street and caught his breath. About thirty yards away, a Black Maria had pulled up, having come from the direction of the town. It was stopped on the side of the road, the driver, having parked it up to give the horses a bit of feed and water. The road was busy, as it was the day of the Royal Perth Yacht Club Regatta. There was an air of gaiety, and a steady stream of well-dressed, jolly people made their way north. Warder Scott had drawn the short straw and had to work. Normally, he would have had at least one more colleague to help him keep an eye on the convicts. His face was a picture of resentment and sourness. *'Good enough for you, miserable bastard,'* thought Larry to himself. Scott hadn't a good bone in his body, and Larry was delighted that the escape of six Irish prisoners was going to happen on his watch. He hoped Scott would pay dearly. It would take a while for word to get to the Comptroller General as he was, no doubt, right at this minute, breakfasting on bacon, eggs and coffee, along with most of the staff. Larry's stomach rumbled. He hoped that Scott's punishment would be swift and hard. The others had seen the Black Maria too. At exactly 8.30am on the dot, Murphy feigned a collapse. The Black Maria moved off from the path.

The other five Irishmen crowded around Murphy, who was doing a very good job of writhing in agony, clutching his ankle. Now all six men were together in a group. The Black Maria picked up speed. Scott threw his eyes up to heaven and began a slow saunter over to see what the matter was. The sun was in his eyes.

Scott was just a few yards away from the knot of men now. Suddenly, the Maria veered off to the left, coming between him and the six Irish. Scott reared back in surprise, for fear of being trampled by the large bay and the equally powerful looking chestnut who were prancing and snorting. Before Scott had time to wonder what on earth was going on, the six Irishmen leaped on board the Black Maria from the other side, the driver cracked his whip over the ears of the two horses, and the carriage took off like the devil himself was chasing it. Scott was momentarily rendered paralysed by the enormity of what had just happened. His mouth open, he stared after the carriage, only coming to his senses when the other prisoners let up a mighty cheer at the Irish men's audacity. Fumbling for his whistle, Scott put it to his lips and blew as hard as his lungs would allow. They were a bit short of air, so the first peal was quite feeble. As the Black Maria disappeared around the bend, heading south, Scott finally gathered himself together enough to give a long sharp blow on his whistle. He couldn't leave the remaining prisoners on their own, so he had to wait until someone from inside the prison responded. By the time Warder Lewis poked his spiky-haired head out to see what was going on, Scott's face was an unhealthy shade of purple and his eyes were bulging.

'Code red, code red!' shouted Scott.

'Blimey, what went on?'

'The Irish are all bloody well gone! One of them faked an injury and then they all hopped onto this Black Maria that came from the north.

Bloody thing nearly ran me over! It took off like a bat out of hell, towards Coogee. I knew something like this was bound to happen when I was left on my own. That bloody regatta! It was waiting to happen, just waiting to happen......'

'Well man, don't just stand there like a clown, bring the others in and we'll get the wagons after them!' Lewis roared, running back into the prison complex towards the stables. Scott did his best to round up the remaining prisoners who were jeering and laughing at him. Ruddy impudent pups! He'd make sure they went without their supper this evening.

'Move!' he roared at them, his chins wobbling, spittle appearing at the corners of his mouth. The prisoners were in no hurry to move, enjoying the drama. The thought of what fate lay ahead for Scott, when the Comptroller General heard he had allowed six prisoners to escape, was enough to cheer even the most despondent amongst them. One by one, they picked up their picks and shovels and shuffled towards the gate of the prison. Scott abandoned them to another warder and then jumped on board one of the wagons which had stopped briefly for him. A sharp turn out the gate to the right, and they were off in the direction that the Black Maria had escaped.

A mile down the road, Larry and his fellow Irishmen were slapping each other on the back, whooping and cheering at how easy it had been to make their escape. And the look on Scott's face had been the icing on the cake! The Black Maria raced on, turning sharply around corners, so that the men were pitched about inside like corks on the sea. The plan had worked! They had their friends in America and their sympathisers here in Australia to thank for their salvation. Larry felt a sense of elation that made him light-headed. He allowed himself to picture Ellen as he had left her seven long years before. There was a glimmer of hope that he might get to see her again before the year was out. He would just have to be patient a while longer. But first, they had to make damned sure that they made it to the boat waiting for them in the bay.

'Burns, Mc Govern, Kiernan, Smith, Murphy and Clinton! Names that will go down in history!' Murphy's face was beaming like the beacon that was lit every St. Patrick's Day on the Hill of Slane near Drogheda. The others were also doing little jigs inside the small confines of the prison cart, which was no mean achievement. Larry was just as elated, but a bit more cautious, throwing a glance out of the small window on the door every so often, to see if they were being pursued. So far, so good. They had most likely gotten a few minutes headway on the prison warders. He imagined that Scott, once he got over his shock, would be hot in pursuit. He would have to try and save face with the Comptroller General.

It wasn't possible to talk to the driver up front. He knew how to handle the carriage and no mistake. Larry had been told he had been in town for a few weeks, having come over from America on the whaling ship bought especially by the brethren for the purpose of bringing home the last remaining six Fenian prisoners. Larry and the other five had been considered 'military Fenians' and there was no pardon on the horizon for them. So, they had taken matters into their own hands. Larry and Murphy had composed a letter between them, outlining their plight. It had been smuggled out of the prison, and given, unseen, to the man who was now driving the Black Maria. That had been six months ago. The driver had ensured that it got into the hands of John Boyle O'Reilly in America. The long, lonely nights in prison since were made slightly more bearable by the prospect of someone coming to their aid. It was a daring plan and so far, it had gone smoothly. But Larry knew he wouldn't relax until they were safely on that whaling ship, the *'Orca'*. It was anchored in international waters, two miles off the coast near Rockingham. They had to board a small tender to bring them out to it. A lot could still go wrong.

Larry stole another glance out the back of the cart. It was a good fifty minutes since they had bolted, and, by Larry's reckoning, they should be near the end of the road part of the journey. He wouldn't be sorry. It had been quite a bumpy ride. They had been lucky not to encounter much traffic, most locals being at the regatta. The others were quieter now. Five pairs of eyes stared at him from the gloom. He had become acquainted with all of these men on board *'The Foxhound'*. He knew they all had families at home in Ireland, north, south, east and west. Seven years of hardship had done nothing to dim the love for their homeland, but they would be going home changed men. Physically leaner, mentally tougher.

The cart began to slow. The men had stood up and were primed, poised ready to leap from the back of the prison wagon and look for a small tender bearing a flag with the red, blue, and white of America.

Suddenly, the carriage came to an abrupt halt and the driver banged heavily on the roof. Larry threw the doors open and was temporarily blinded by the bright light. It was still just 9.30am, but the sun was strong, and the day had the makings of a hell-fire hot one. They heard a shout from their left and, as one, the men turned to see someone waving frantically at them from a small boat, fifty yards away. The men sprinted towards the boat, adrenaline giving their tired bodies an extra boost.

Larry threw a glance over his shoulder to scan the horizon in the direction they had come from. In the shimmering haze, he could make out the shape of a horse and cart speeding towards them. There were two men on board. The sun glinted off something one of the men was wearing. A brass button. The prison warders were right behind them.

'Be quick. Scott is right behind us!' Larry roared. The men fell on board, panting and sweating and Larry cast off with one of the oars. Soon, they were in a rhythm, fighting with the swell of the sea. Scott and Lewis arrived at the shore and battled their way across the golden sand. They weren't as quick as the prisoners, encumbered by the bit of padding on their bodies and their heavy uniforms. Scott raised the rifle in his hand, steadied himself and took aim. A bullet whizzed past and landed in the water beside Larry with a splash. Then another one skimmed off the wooden hull of the boat. Faster, faster, they rowed, putting more distance between them and the shore. The sun beat down. The breeze was stiff. The next bullet landed feet away from the boat. The men let up a cheer. On the shore, the portly figure of Warder Scott raised his fist and shook it at the prisoners. 'Fenian bastards!' he roared. The seagulls seemed to laugh as they circled the boat.

They had done it! The shoreline was disappearing. Scott and Lewis were like stick-figures now. The men whooped and cheered.

'You're out-smarted, Scott! Ha!' Murphy roared as the others laughed with delight.

The men took it in turns to row as they wanted to reach the *'Orca'* as quickly as possible. Larry felt the muscles in his shoulders burn, his breath coming in short gasps. Five minutes at maximum effort. A rest for five, when some of the others took over, then back again, all rowing as if their lives depended on it. After thirty minutes, they could see the masts of the whaling ship coming into view. Larry had never seen such a welcome sight. Suddenly, one of the men shouted, 'look right!' Barely visible on the horizon was what looked like a cutter slicing through the water towards them, the sun bouncing off its white sails.

'Jesus, men! Effort, quick!'

Scott and Lewis must have raised the alarm and got the cutter mustered from the shore at Rockingham. The men groaned and rowed with every single fibre of their being. The cutter was gaining on them, having the advantage of a big sail. With one last herculean effort, they were suddenly alongside the whaleboat and one of the crew had lowered a rope ladder down from the side. One by one, they hauled themselves up on the side of the ship. Larry was the last to leave the rowing boat. The cutter was very close. A man was shouting through a megaphone. *'You are ordered to leave this ship immediately. I say, immediately. You are prisoners of Freemantle Convict Establishment, and you must leave the ship and return immediately.'*

The captain of the *'Orca'*, a man with a salt and pepper beard and a lively face, got his own megaphone out. He replied that the *'Orca'* was now in international waters and that the cutter was not entitled to make any such order unless Australia wanted to start a war with the American nation. With that, he raised the American flag right up to the top of the mast. Larry and the other men waited, exhausted from their rowing and barely daring to breathe. Silence from the cutter. The *'Orca'* raised its sails and was off at a swift clip over the foam-tipped waves, leaving the cutter with nothing to do but return to shore. The men on board whooped with delight. A surge of the most profound relief washed over

Larry. The first tendrils of hope started to wend their way from his brain into the rest of his body.

They began their journey west, away from the shoreline of Australia, heading for America. Larry inhaled and exhaled fully, feeding the tangy air right down into the very bottom of his lungs. This ship would take them to America, and then, if he had to swim the very Atlantic itself to get back to Ellen and his child, he would. But for now, he was looking forward to a sound night's sleep for the first time in over two and a half thousand nights.

CHAPTER 39

Peggy

Drogheda, June 1876

Peggy looked into the little blue box and quickly surveyed its contents. She bit her lip in concentration, then closed the lid and put the box back in its hiding place. She had discovered the little false door in the pantry wall a week after moving into this house in Greenhills, and for the past seven years, she had managed to keep it a secret from every other member of the household, even Ellen and the ever-inquisitive Alice. Turning to the window, she gazed out into the garden which was dappled by late June sunlight. It was a tranquil space. She and Ellen had strived very hard to make it so. Before they had arrived, it had been a mess, neglected by Nicholas who had no interest in it. His two daughters from his marriage to poor Rosemary had only cared about where their next costume was coming from, and Peggy doubted either of them had ever as much as dirtied their nails, never mind lifted a hoe or a rake to it.

The garden was a source of immense comfort to her. She had always dreamed of one day, owning her own plot of land, where she could grow flowers and vegetables, and have somewhere to sit under a big, broad tree. She never tired of the feel of the silky soil against her skin, the satisfaction of cooking a dinner using vegetables that she and Ellen had grown themselves. Little Rosena was showing interest, trailing along after her and Ellen from bed to bed, and throwing water on the plants from her own little jug. She was a bonny wee thing, getting more like her Mam every day.

As Peggy looked out at the big oak tree in the centre of the lawn, her eyes were drawn to the vegetable and herb patch. She deliberately kept control of what grew there herself, which was mostly parsley, sage, thyme, rosemary and dill. These all went into making flavoursome dishes that they whole family enjoyed. But she also grew *Valeriana Pyrenaica*. She told Ellen that she just liked it for its dense heads of tiny pale lilac flowers and its large heart-shaped, deeply veined leaves. Her swarthy-faced contact at the quays had told her of its calming properties, and the seeds he had given her had blossomed into a nice little crop that seemed to thrive in the partial shade of the stone wall. The good, strong roots of the plant were ground up fairly easily into a powder. Peggy had been secretly adding it to Nicholas's food for the past couple of years. On mornings when Ellen emerged from her and Nicholas's bedroom, pale and hollow-eyed, Peggy had slipped a little more Valerian into his tea or his dinner. Before poor little Michael had been born, he had been determined that Ellen would give him a son. For a while, life had been unbearable for her friend. Peggy could see it in her haunted expression and jutting cheekbones. Peggy couldn't do much to help Ellen other than try and cool Nicholas's ardour by slipping something into his food. It had worked for a while, and when Ellen had finally produced a son, he had been on an even keel. He had seemed to stop bothering Ellen. But then, when little Michael had died, things had taken a turn for the worst. Nicholas no longer seemed to care about anyone or anything, shouting at the youngsters whenever they crossed his path, drinking himself stupid every night in his study, barely going into the mill, some days not washing or shaving at all. He was looking every one of his fifty odd years. There was grey around his temples now, and his auburn hair had lost most of its depth of colour. More often than not, it hung limp and greasy around his bloated face.

It was time to harvest some more Valerian root, which would need to be dried before it could be used. The stash in her secret blue box was nearly empty. Nicholas needed a top up as his behaviour was becoming increasingly unpredictable. Peggy would protect Ellen and her brood if it was the last thing she did.

She turned her attention to gathering the ingredients for some soda bread. Sifting the flour into the big delph bowl she used for this task, her stomach contracted slightly when she thought of George Menton. He regularly called to the house to get Nicholas's signature on documents. But, when he had called the other afternoon, Peggy had had one of her 'visions'. She didn't get them that often these days, so she felt they warranted special attention when they did make an appearance. This one had involved George Menton, who was fleeing Drogheda, up the North Road, in a horse and carriage. He had a big black bag on his lap, but it was the expression on his face that had caught Peggy's breath. He looked like the cat that had gotten the cream, his long, bony legs crossed, and his arms circling the black bag protectively. Peggy had gotten the feeling that whatever was in that bag did not belong to him, and he looked like he was prepared to guard it with his life. She couldn't shake the feeling of unease that had clouded her for days afterwards. That long string of misery was up to no good. Of that, Peggy was sure. She was roused from her reverie by the sound of a loud crash from the sitting room.

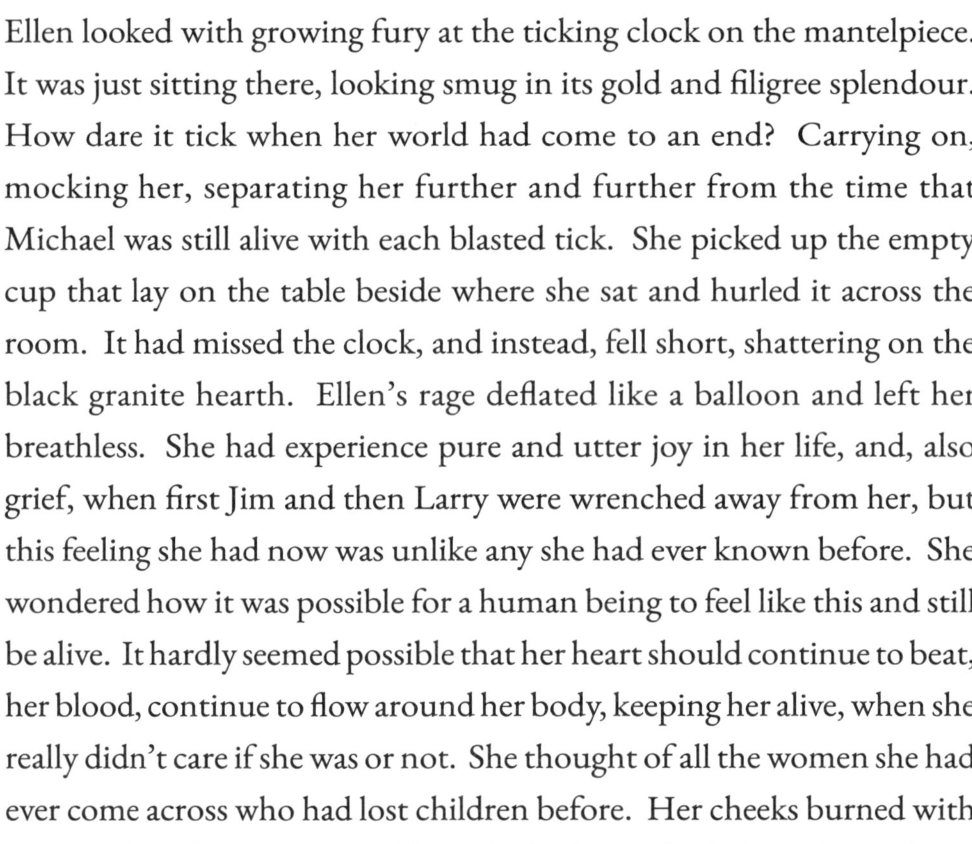

Ellen looked with growing fury at the ticking clock on the mantelpiece. It was just sitting there, looking smug in its gold and filigree splendour. How dare it tick when her world had come to an end? Carrying on, mocking her, separating her further and further from the time that Michael was still alive with each blasted tick. She picked up the empty cup that lay on the table beside where she sat and hurled it across the room. It had missed the clock, and instead, fell short, shattering on the black granite hearth. Ellen's rage deflated like a balloon and left her breathless. She had experience pure and utter joy in her life, and, also grief, when first Jim and then Larry were wrenched away from her, but this feeling she had now was unlike any she had ever known before. She wondered how it was possible for a human being to feel like this and still be alive. It hardly seemed possible that her heart should continue to beat, her blood, continue to flow around her body, keeping her alive, when she really didn't care if she was or not. She thought of all the women she had ever come across who had lost children before. Her cheeks burned with shame when she remembered how she had mouthed platitudes at them.

Why had she gone out to that ball on New Years' Eve? She hadn't wanted to, but Nicholas had insisted. She might have called the doctor more quickly. But Doctor Murchin had told her, time and time again, that nothing would have saved Michael that night. That she wasn't to blame herself, it was just one of those things. His blue eyes were kind, but his words did little to allay the feelings of guilt that weighed on her chest as if she were pinned beneath one of the wheels of the carriage outside.

She felt like the rag doll that Rosena dragged around after everywhere she went. Limp, hollow, not caring about anyone or anything. Peggy's voiced droned in her ears. Spouting about the other children, how they needed her, that she had to try and be there for them no matter how hard it was. Deep down, she knew her friend was right, but she wanted to grieve Michael fully and wholly for another while. It would be like letting him go if she carried on with everyday things - like she was consigning him to the past. How could he be past tense? She would never feel his warm little hand in hers ever again, hear his infectious laugh, rub his peachy cheek. She gasped with the shock of it.

Peggy swept into the sitting room and Ellen heard an almost imperceptible 'Tsk.' Peggy was her friend, but sometimes, she was such a pain in the posterior. Ellen knew Peggy was losing patience with her. But it had only been a year and a half since the day that her life had been turned upside-down. Ellen raised her eyes and was met with Peggy's stoniest stare.

'Have you something you want to say to me Peggy?' There was a challenge in her tone.

'Ah lass. I know you are hurting like you've never hurt before, for losing a child is surely the cruellest thing that life can throw at a body, but you have five others that need a Mam who pays them a bit of attention. Tommy is bewildered with not knowing how to help, Alice needs taking in hand, or she will run off with the first lad that shows her a bit of attention, and the little ones keep asking me why you are still so sad. Did you know that Liberty got all her sums right the other day at school? I tried to urge her to tell you, but she's afeared to. She thinks you will tell her to stop annoying you, the poor lass.'

Guilt made its way to the fore of Ellen's consciousness and temporarily gave the grief a back seat. This jostling of emotions was so tiring. Yet, she dreaded sleep. Michael filled her nightmares. He was always just out of reach. She woke most mornings with a sodden pillow.

'I know, Peggy.' Ellen let out a sigh. 'I haven't forgotten about them, but it's just so hard.'

'It is lass. It's the hardest thing you will ever have to do, to try and live the rest of your life without your baby son. Not to see him grow, send him off on his first day at school, hear his voice break, watch Tommy showing him how to have his first shave. But he's gone and I'm very much afraid that you must let him go. Bring his memories forward with you every day but try not be so permanently sad. Life is for living, and you have five other bonnie childer that are only peppering for their cheery Mam to return. Will you give it a go?'

The mole on Peggy's chin, with the now silver hair sprouting from it, was bigger than ever. Her eyes were earnest blue. With an enormous sigh, Ellen straightened her back, rose and put her hand on Peggy's shoulder.

'You're right Peggy. I have to pull myself together. I will try. From now on, I will do my very best to be a bit more cheerful. Thank you, Peggy.'

The hand that covered Ellen's was chafed from the rigours of the mangle, the nails had dirt under them from digging in the garden for vegetables, the knuckles starting to gnarl.

'Good girl. I'll be here for you whenever you need a little cry, but for the sake of the youngsters, I hope that you'll try and bury your feelings in front of them. They'll be so pleased to have their Mam back! Now, lass, will you come into the kitchen with me. I want to talk to you about Nicholas.'

Ellen's heels clacked on the black and white tiled floor as she followed Peggy into the kitchen. Through the large window, Ellen could see that the apple trees were in full bloom, their pink and white blossoms rippling in the gentle June breeze. The sun caught the copper pots hanging over the range, glinting and casting a sheen onto the big oak table in the middle of the room. Peggy had covered the chair seats in a red and white checked cloth. There was a permanently boiling black iron kettle on the hob, and always a tart or something sweet sitting in the middle of the table. It was Peggy's idea of heaven, to have at her constant disposal, the ingredients to whip up some nice, sweet things whenever the fancy took her. They usually didn't last very long with five permanently ravenous children in the vicinity.

Ellen followed Peggy's lead and sat down at the table. She noticed Peggy wince slightly as she gingerly lowered herself onto her chair and her heart was filled with a little pang of sadness at the fact that her friend was now in her sixties. Peggy's hands were clasped together, and her lips were pursing, a sure sign that she had something on her mind.

'What about Nicholas?'

'Have you noticed anything funny about him lately?'

'Funny?'

'Yes, strange, peculiar.'

'No more than usual. I haven't been paying him much attention, nor he me, thanks be to God.'

'Well, I have seen him looking mighty worried when the postman knocks every morning. I sometimes peep into his study if the door is open when I'm passing, and he usually looks like the weight of the world is on his shoulders whenever he is looking through his papers.'

'Oh.' This was news to Ellen. They had separate bedrooms now and he rarely bothered her, retiring most evenings after dinner to his study to drink into the wee hours. She supposed that was his way of dealing with Michael's loss. He might be many things, but she knew that he had loved his son with all his being. He was devastated at his loss; of that she was certain.

'And' Peggy faltered. Taking a gulp, she continued. 'I don't know if I'm imagining it, but he looks a bit white around the gills lately. Keeps rubbing his left arm. Have you noticed?'

'Peggy, you know I pay him very little heed these days. No, I haven't noticed any of the things you mention. Do you think he is unwell?'

'Quite possibly Ellen. I think that maybe you might need to talk to him to see if he'd pay a visit to the doctor.'

Ellen was taken aback at Peggy's sudden interest in Nicholas's well-being. The pair tolerated each other at best. She regarded her friend, who was wringing her hands now, an anxious expression in her eyes, her mole wobbling.

'Alright, if you think it's necessary, I will speak to him.' Ellen said slowly. 'But as you know, we rarely have a conversation these days about anything of any import.'

Ellen didn't relish the prospect a full-blown conversation with her husband. Let alone one where she had to feign interest in his physical well-being.

'Good, thanks lass.'

'Why are you worried about him anyway?'

'Well, he is the father of your children, and he does provide for all in this house.'

Peggy's eyes slid away from Ellen's, and she seemed to develop a keen interest in the steam rising from the kettle. Ellen regarded Peggy and wondered what was making her steady and fast friend look so unsettled.

CHAPTER 40

Nicholas

Nicholas heard his wife's soft tread on the landing outside his bedroom. As usual, there was no hesitation in her step. For the past couple of years, she had walked resolutely past his door to her own room. Not up for debate, not open to persuasion. Not that he wanted to persuade her to join him. It was hard to imagine how her mere presence had once made his body sing. Was it only nine years ago that they had married? It seemed like so much longer. He felt like an old man. It was as if the hands of time had fast-forwarded his body-clock at a rate three times quicker than it should have. He was in his fifties now. He really should be in the prime of his life, or at least feeling a damn sight healthier. These days, his legs were leaden, climbing the stairs raised his heartbeat to a rather uncomfortable tattoo. He slept fitfully at night. In the morning, he never felt refreshed. He had a permanent pain in his jaw. His teeth hurt. He absent-mindedly rubbed his face, feeling the rough stubble that was at least four days old. He couldn't remember when he had last shaved. He looked around his room. The big double bed was no longer inviting. It was where he tossed and turned, sometimes waking up with the sheets soaked and tangled. Sometimes he had to sit propped up, such was the discomfort in his stomach. He supposed that the amount he was drinking wasn't helping, but it was the only thing that gave him temporary reprieve from the emptiness that howled around his heart.

He glanced at himself in the mirror on his dressing table. He no longer cared what he looked like. Where once his eyes had sparked with interest at a business deal, or followed a good-looking woman around a room, now they stared back at him with a pale dullness. He was bloated, the puffiness of his cheeks making his skin taut. His hair was no longer shiny like a conker, but dull and greasy, longer than was fashionable. He saw the pulse jump in his throat and felt his head throb. He took a deep breath into his belly, trying to slow down his heartbeat. That was another thing that kept him awake at night. A familiar jab of pain ran from his chest bone down his left arm, into his neck, and finally came to a stop in his jaw. He probably should have a word with the doctor about it, but to be honest, he didn't really care enough. The light had permanently gone out of his life when Michael had died. Drink was the only thing that could soften the edges of the stabbing pain that gripped him when he pictured the soft, downy head, the dark curls, the dimpled cheeks. It was the only thing that could stop him re-living the horror of that night when Michael slipped away from them so cruelly, and with no warning. How could he have been laughing, drinking, chatting with the great and the good of Drogheda when a couple of miles away, life was slowly ebbing from his son's little body? How had he not known, how had he not felt it? Why had he insisted that he and Ellen go out that night? If only they had stayed at home. But Murchin had said there would have been no saving Michael. It was a swift and cruel sickness that had taken him, and nothing on earth could have stopped its progress. Nicholas slammed his hand so hard on the dressing table that his bottle of cologne rattled. He no longer believed in God. How could He, if He did exist, allow a warm, innocent little boy, with his whole life ahead of him die? When Nicholas closed his eyes, he could still feel the cold, stiffness of his son's body. He tried to remember the warmth of his embrace, but he was terribly afraid that he was forgetting what his son had looked like, what his little voice had sounded like when he cried '*Da Da*' and ran to meet him on wobbly legs.

Nicholas sighed, turned his head away from the mirror, rose stiffly and made his way towards his bed. Turning down the wine-coloured damask cover, he slipped underneath, still fully clothed, closed his eyes and waited for his thoughts to stop whirring, and for oblivion to come. He was hoping that the extra whiskey he had drunk would help. It would probably kill off a few more of his brain cells, but that was a few less with which to feel. Numb was good.

Nicholas's dreams that night were like a play in which he watched his life unfold. His childhood, schooldays, his many quarrels with Larry, his marriage to Rosemary, the births of Clarice and Sarah, Ellen with her flashing eyes and plump, upturned lips, Liberty, his younger daughters, and then Michael. Michael was there, just beyond his reach, his chubby little hand reaching towards his Daddy. '*Dada, come!*' Nicholas's heart expanded with love. Michael's head was suddenly surrounded by the most incredibly bright light. It was like a halo, and it engulfed his body. He turned and waddled away until Nicholas could no longer see him. There was no way he was letting his little boy out of his sight again. His heartbeat slowing, Nicholas walked into the light after his son.

CHAPTER 41

Ellen

Drogheda, July 1876

It was a good job that looks couldn't kill, Ellen thought, as she once more glanced in the direction of the young woman who was sitting in the chair across the silent, airless room. There was a poisonous flash in the eyes of Nicholas's eldest daughter, and the tight-lipped fury that was emanating from her was like a tangible thing. To Ellen it seemed to waft in waves across the space between them, mingling with the dust motes in the air, settling on her like a cloak. She absentmindedly waved her hand around her head, and then stopped immediately when she got an enquiring look from Tommy, who was sitting beside her. She gave him a watery smile. He took her hand surreptitiously and gave it a quick squeeze. She must have looked like a complete fool, waving her hands around like that. If anyone could read her mind, they'd surely commit her to the madhouse. Imagine thinking she could swipe away Clarice Matthews' venom. She must be losing her marbles. Well, it wouldn't be at all surprising. She had been through quite a bit in her thirty-seven years on this earth. She had thought that the worst thing imaginable was losing Jim, but that had been before little Michael had died. That still sliced through her like the cleaver that carved up the meat in the butcher's shop on West St. The pain was not lessening with time.

She gave an irritated sigh, deciding to send a nasty look right back at Clarice. Two could play at that game. Why that madam was so angry with her, she had no idea. Sure, hadn't she been doted upon by her darling Daddy until she had married that Matthews fella and moved down the country? Ellen knew that Nicholas had given both her and Sarah generous dowries when they had married. Neither of his two elder daughters had paid many visits to the Greenhills house since their father and Ellen had been together. Ellen had been too busy with her own brood to wonder why, or care much. She knew Nicholas had gone to meet his older girls occasionally, and sometimes stayed in their houses, but they had been both largely absent from the Clinton household in Drogheda and had only met their half-siblings a handful of times. That was their choice. They seemed to have a problem with Nicholas's second family. And with his young wife, for Ellen was only five years older than Clarice. Ellen tried to damp down the feeling of elation she experienced every time she realised anew that she was now free of one Mr. Nicholas Clinton and his ways. She tried not to smile, as a solicitor's office for the reading of her late husband's will was not exactly the place to exhibit such emotion.

She jumped as the door was roughly pushed open and a man crossed the room. He had a mop of fair hair, that she thought looked not dissimilar to the cocks of hay on the outskirts of town. Michael Cooke, of Cooke and Sons Solicitors, seemed in a hurry to sit down and get the business of the reading the will started. He shuffled the papers on his desk until he seemed to find what he was looking for.

'Ah, yes, here we are, here we are. Very good, very good.'

Perching a pair of glasses on the end of his large, red nose, he looked up from the document he was holding and looked at the people assembled before him for the first time. He glanced from Ellen to Clarice to Tommy and back to Ellen.

'Mrs. Clinton, I presume?' he raised his bushy eyebrows enquiringly in Ellen's direction.

'Yes, Ellen Clinton. Pleased to meet you. This is my son, Tommy.'

'Tommy, ah yes, young Cooney. I have heard you mentioned from time to time.'

The smile on his flaky lips didn't reach his icy blue eyes. This fella is a cool fish, Ellen thought to herself. He has the makings of a good solicitor. It didn't do to be too emotional in this job. He was probably sick and tired of reading wills to relatives, no doubt sometimes having to be a referee, or offer counsel. He had probably seen and heard it all down through the years.

He looked over at Clarice, who was sitting bold upright in her chair, her lips a tight white line in her face.

'Mrs. eh,' he looked down at a sheet of paper on his desk. 'Ah yes, Mrs. Matthews. Nice to meet you. Nicholas spoke very highly of you and your sister. Was she unavailable today?' He peered enquiringly over the rim of his glasses.

'Yes, I'm afraid she had other matters to attend to today.' Clarice's voice had lost any hint of a Drogheda accent it may have once had since she had moved to Tipperary.

'I see. Well, we can proceed without her in any case.' His tone was abrupt as he once again clutched the paper and cleared his throat.

'If you don't mind, ladies, and gentleman', he said nodding in Tommy's direction, 'we will get started. I have another appointment at twelve and it may prove to be a tricky one.' He absentmindedly rubbed his breastbone as if the thoughts of what was ahead of him was causing him some discomfort.

'Of course, carry on, Mr. Cooke,' said Ellen. She sensed another darting glance being thrown her way from Clarice. It seemed she wasn't allowed to speak at all! She stifled a snort with her handkerchief which smelled of lavender. Michael Cooke looked at her quizzically, then over at Clarice and, with a slight shake of his head, he took a deep breath and held up a sheaf of papers.

'As you will no doubt have guessed by now, this is the Last Will and Testament of Nicholas Clinton.'

He looked at the two women, ready to bask in their admiration. With a sniff, he re-arranged his glasses on his nose, which Ellen noticed, had a crop of very wiry looking fair hairs. He started to read.

'I, Nicholas Clinton of Greenhills in the town of Drogheda, in the County of Louth, do make this my last Will and Testament, hereby revoking all former Wills and other Testaments, dispositions by me of any time heretofore made...'

Well, that had all been quite underwhelming. Ellen stood up and walked across the room to retrieve her coat from the stand in the corner. She cast a glance at Clarice who was sitting bolt upright in her chair, staring straight ahead. The feather in the headpiece she was wearing seemed to vibrate. The younger woman appeared to be literally shaking with anger. Ellen felt a momentary pang of sympathy for Nicholas's eldest daughter. But it was fleeting, as Ellen reminded herself that Nicholas had already provided for his two eldest daughters. It seemed that they had both made good enough marriages and would want for nothing. Ellen had enough to be going on with. She had four young daughters at home and, was now, it seemed, the owner of a mill, complete with all its worries and concerns, not least the fact that she was now responsible for the jobs of all the employees. Nicholas had left everything to her on the proviso that she look after Gladys and Rosena. There had been absolutely no mention of Alice, Tommy or Liberty in the will. Nor Larry. She felt a surge of anger at this mean-spiritedness. She glanced over at Tommy who was, despite the fact that he had never seen eye to eye with Nicholas, bound to be smarting a bit from being overlooked in such an obvious fashion. He was old enough to understand the slight. She also felt fury at Nicholas's assumption that she needed to be ordered to look after his daughters. They were her daughters too.

Suddenly, Clarice rose and strode across the room to stand in front of Ellen, her navy gaberdine skirt making an aggressive swishing sound as she drew herself up to her full height and looked Ellen in the eye.

'Bad cess to the day my father ever laid eyes on you.'

A drop of Clarice's spittle landed on Ellen's cheek. She absent-mindedly wiped it away, baulking at the look of pure fury that was in Clarice's eyes. She realised, without doubt, that what had been in the cat was also in the kitten. Clarice seemed to blame Ellen for Nicholas's untimely death. Too much food, too much alcohol, the burden of keeping the mill running and Michael's death had been the actual culprits. But there was no point in trying to reason with Clarice. She had made her mind up about Ellen before she and Nicholas had even married. She had never attempted to give Ellen the benefit of the doubt and get to know her properly over the past years. True, her and Nicholas had not had a happy marriage, but the bulk of the blame for that lay at Nicholas's door. Oh well, she had more things to be thinking about than Clarice's spite. Before she could draw breath to reply, Clarice turned stiffly and left the room. Ellen and Tommy looked at each other.

'What's got the bee buzzing around her bonnet?' Tommy asked, staring after Clarice's retreating back. 'Sure, she hardly ever saw her father since you two got married.'

'Well son, pass no heed of her. You can never tell what's in someone's mind.' Ellen sighed, rubbing a hand over her face. 'It looks like you and I are the proud owners of a linen mill.'

'You and me?' Tommy looked slightly disturbed by this statement.

'Well, yes, what's mine is yours. It's not going to stop you going off to Maynooth University like you planned, but I might need a hand for a few weeks to get my head around everything.' Ellen reached up and gave her son's arm a squeeze. Her heart swelled with love for this boy, now a man, who looked more and more like his Da with every passing day.

'Sure Mam. I will give you a hand. Although, how I'm going to help you is a bit of a mystery to me.'

'Nonsense pet. Sure, there's a lot going on between those two ears of yours. It's a fine brain you have. Now, let's get home. I feel in need of one of Peggy's strong cups of tea after all that.'

Out in the bright July sunshine, turning from Shop Street into West Street, Ellen's heart gave a little leap. There were challenges ahead, of that she was sure, but she was finally free of Nicholas. Taking Tommy's arm, the two walked back towards home.

CHAPTER 42

Ellen

Ellen's could feel a drip of sweat rolling down her back. Her silk blouse was sticking to her. She licked her top lip nervously. She had barely made it safely in the door of the mill and up to the office without being accosted. The workers were nervous, and with good cause, it would seem. Ellen took a deep breath into her belly the way Peggy had taught her. It did little to calm her. How on earth had it come to this? And where was George Menton? Fear, shame, and disgust rattled around her in equal measures. She loosened the tie of her blouse in an attempt to lessen the choking feeling that was lodged in her throat. She shivered.

Sat behind Nicholas's old desk, she had a new perspective on the office. It was more-or-less as she remembered it when she had worked there. Except, not quite as neat and tidy. It had been patently obvious to her that Nicholas must have taken his eye off the ball somewhat over the past couple of years. Especially since Michael had died. But she'd had no idea that things were this bad. She'd been too busy giving birth and caring for the children to give a whole lot of thought to the business. With a groan, she slammed shut the ledger she was looking at and ran her hands through her hair. It just didn't add up. Any of it.

'Where the bloody hell is Menton!' she yelled, to no one in particular, snapping her head towards the door. As if on cue, Tommy burst into the office. He had accompanied her to the mill today, and just as well. She had been glad of his company when passing the sea of workers that met her on her arrival. Some had expressions of anxiety, some of anger. There was precious little sympathy to be seen.

'There's no sign of him. No one has seen him since before Nicholas died,' panted Tommy. His expression told Ellen that he was very unsettled by the air of thinly veiled aggression from the workers. He might be eighteen, but he was still like a child at times. Ellen decided she needed to pull herself together.

'Right, let's think this through. There's no sign of Menton. No-one has seen him since before the funeral. He was there that day. Does anyone know where he lives, I wonder? I must find Molly and ask her!'

Galvanised into action, Ellen ran from the office and descended the short stairs to the floor below. The noise was deafening as usual. She scanned the workers, looking for the tall, blonde woman whose acquaintance she had made when she first came to the mill. After a minute, she spotted Molly. Walking swiftly towards the other woman, Ellen tapped her on the shoulder. She tried to keep her expression neutral and friendly.

'Hello Molly, how are you? Can you come with me for a minute please?' Ellen turned and walked back the way she had come, trying to portray a confidence she didn't feel. She kept her poise, although her heart was hammering in her chest. The two women entered the office. Molly acknowledged Tommy with a smile.

'Please, sit down Molly.' Ellen tried to keep the wobble from her voice. She took a seat behind the desk she used to occupy and hauled out Nicholas's chair from behind his desk for Molly.

'I'm sorry for your trouble,' Molly said, her broad, open face full of sympathy.

'I know you are. Thank you, Molly. It was a big shock to us all. And especially to Peggy who found him dead in the bed.' Peggy had been beside herself at the time, wringing her hands repeatedly. Ellen had been quite taken aback at her reaction. Peggy had never been a fan of Nicholas Clinton.

Ellen regarded the other woman, who seemed uneasy. No doubt worried about where her wages were to come from this week. And who could blame her? The whole thing was a complete mess. Guilt ripped through Ellen when she realised that she had taken her eye off the ball also. She had known that things were amiss at the mill but hadn't bothered to investigate any further. Molly wouldn't have been aware of the situation, but she might know where George Menton lived at least. Ellen would visit him and ask to be fully appraised of the finances of the mill. Yes, that was what she would do. As Nicholas's widow, she was entitled to know what was going on. And she owed it to each and every one of the one hundred and twenty-two workers she now employed to figure it out.

'Molly, I need to have a word with George. Do you happen to know where he lives? I believe he hasn't been here since the funeral?'

'Aye, he lives up near the Marsh Road. Haven't seen the gangly yoke for the past few days. Mick has been opening and locking up every evening. Is everything alright?'

'Oh yes, everything is fine Molly. I just need to ask him a few details about how things are going. I'm surprised he hasn't been in touch. I just thought that he was keeping his distance for a couple of days out of respect. He has things under control, I'm sure? You've all been paid up to last week?' Ellen held her breath, half afraid of what her friend's answer would be.

'Yes, we were paid last week' Molly put her big rough hand on Ellen's.

'Don't you be worrying yourself now. I'm sure everything is fine. Perhaps George has been sick. Maybe he didn't have any way of getting a message to you or to Mick?'

'The Marsh Road, you said?'

'Yes, the fifth house on the left. It has a purple door.'

'And how are things on the floor? Production is running nicely?'

'A few little problems with some of the machines, but nothing Mick couldn't sort out. He's a wonder that fella.'

Ellen made a mental note to put a few pennies extra in Mick's next pay packet. Today was Thursday. The workers would be due their wages on Saturday. She had to make sure that no-one was left without their money. Ellen damped down a wave of panic that threatened to engulf her. Now that Nicholas was gone, it fell on her, his widow, to keep things going. She wasn't sure she capable, but she really didn't have a choice.

'Do you want me to come with you?' Molly asked.

Ellen gave her a smile. 'No, Molly, I'll be fine. I'll find out what's been wrong with him and make sure that he is ready to come back to work.'

'Right so, I'll get back to my station! Will we be seeing plenty of you here at the mill from now on?'

'Most likely, you will!' Ellen replied with a sinking heart. She wasn't sure she wanted to run the business, but what choice did she have? She would have to try and resurrect that part of her brain that enjoyed the figures, the planning, the challenge of getting new customers. But first things first. She was headed for the Marsh Road to find out exactly what was wrong with one Mr. George Menton. Molly turned at the door, gave Ellen a swift smile and was off, back to her workstation, her hips swinging as she went.

'Right Tommy, let's be off to find 'Spider'.'

'A good name for him!' Tommy smirked. Ellen gave her son a wink and the two of them swept from the mill, heads held high. Sometimes, you had to fake your confidence. If there was one thing Nicholas Clinton had taught Ellen, it was how to be a master at faking.

Ellen was very glad to have the support of her big, strong son as they made their way out into the bright July morning. She was feeling quite light-headed from the effort of trying to look like she had complete control. Tommy had grown more like his Da every day that passed. He was now an inch taller than Jim had been, and with the same dark hair that flopped over one eye. His expression could flicker from mischievous to compassionate in a heartbeat, but it was never, ever cruel. Tommy had been a clever boy and was now an intelligent and thoughtful young man. Ellen knew a mother wasn't supposed to have a favourite child, but Tommy occupied a corner of her heart that none of her other children did. He was her first- born and he was so like his Da that it was impossible not to love him just that little bit more. Tommy put his arm around her shoulder.

'Are you alright Mam?'

'I'm not sure son. I'll feel a bit better when I get to shake an explanation out of Menton. It's not good enough that he hasn't been looking after things at the mill. You and I have had enough to cope with these last few days.'

Ellen picked up her pace as she made her way down the hill towards the Marsh Road. She was feeling a bit stronger now, and she patted Tommy's hand as if to tell him it was alright to release her; that she wasn't going to collapse like a nincompoop with a fit of the vapours. She was stronger than that. Life had thrown some pretty horrible things her way, so confronting George, the slimy article of a man, should be no problem to her.

Mother and son continued to walk briskly, both wrapped up in their own thoughts, the smell of the river rising to greet them as they descended towards the quays. It was a good twenty-minute walk from the mill to 'Spider' Menton's lodgings. Ellen took the time to marshal her thoughts. She was very glad to have Tommy's company today. She was starting to have a funny feeling about Menton. She didn't know what she would find when she got to his door, but she had to be strong, whatever it was.

Turning onto the Marsh Road, Tommy straightened up, bringing himself to his full height. His face took on a set look. Ellen glanced at him, and a swell of pride rose inside her. She took his hand and squeezed it tightly.

'Thanks love.'

'For what Mam?'

'For being you. And for being with me today. I really appreciate it.'

'It's no problem. I wouldn't have you meeting this chancer on your own! And we need to find out what has been keeping him away from the mill. There is probably a reasonable explanation. Maybe he's been seeing some woman and she's kept him up night and day! The poor man could be exhausted!'

'Tommy Cooney. You're a scoundrel!' Ellen gave him a gentle slap on the arm as she laughed out loud. Tommy could always cheer her up.

Finally, there were at the door of George Menton's lodgings. The white-washed exterior had seen better days, and the purple paint was peeling off the door. Ellen thought she saw one of the curtains on the downstairs window twitching. Taking a deep breath, she gave the door a good rap. She stood back, craning her neck at the upstairs. She could hear children squealing and a baby crying somewhere. The screeching of the gulls overhead shredded her already rattled nerves. She could feel Tommy's strong presence beside her, protective, calming. He would make someone a really good husband someday. Maybe.

There was no stir from inside the house. So, this time, Tommy rapped loudly on the door, stepping back and craning his neck up at the windows. Ellen's heartbeat sped up. She was getting very annoyed. Where was the big, long string of misery? She rapped again, this time for longer. A snotty-nosed young lad passed by, staring at them, his clothes in rags.

'There's no one home.' Ellen felt dejected. She had built herself up for a showdown and now it looked like it wasn't going to happen. She sagged visibly and turned to look at Tommy. 'Come on son. Looks like we had a wasted journey. Lord knows what we'll do now, if he doesn't turn up to the mill tomorrow.'

Just as they turned to walk back in the direction of the river, the purple door opened a crack, and a long, skinny face peered out at them.

'What do you want? Banging on a person's door like that, loud enough to waken the dead!'

'We have come to speak to George Menton' Ellen announced, determination in her stance once more. 'Is he in?'

The door opened wider. The woman was tiny and bent nearly right over. Her hand that held the door was gnarled, with puffy joints, the skin stretched over them. Her face was criss-crossed with lines, her eyes like raisins, and a wisp of her grey hair escaped from underneath a bonnet.

She could have been any age from fifty to one hundred. A shawl covered her scrawny shoulders even though it was midsummer, and her chest was as flat as a pancake.

'Are you his landlady?' Ellen enquired.

'No, that's my daughter, Bridie. She looks after him. Or did.'

'Did?' Ellen's breath caught in her throat.

'Aye. The bastard's only gone and done a runner.'

Ellen felt the ground sway beneath her feet. A slow slide of panic started to grow in her stomach.

'What do you mean 'done a runner'?' asked Tommy, casting an anxious glance in his mother's direction.

'Took himself away, scattered, gone, in a puff of smoke', the old woman rippled her fingers in the air.

Ellen gulped. 'When was this?'

'The day 'afore yesterday if my memory serves me right. Left owing my lass last month's rent, the stingy bastard. High-tailed it out of here when she was off at the market. But, I seen him. Walking real fast down the street, with a big black bag in his arms. Looking around him in case he met someone he knew.'

She chewed on something in her mouth and then spat it out. A big brown globule landed between Ellen and Tommy's feet.

'Bad cess to him. I never liked the knave. Mean as anything. And you'd want to see the finery he'd buy for himself these past few years. New shoes and silk scarves and the like. And never a penny extra would he give to Bridie for herself, not even at Christmas. Like I said, a stingy bastard.' She raised her eyes to focus on Ellen. 'Does he owe you money too lass?'

'I'm not sure' Ellen whispered. The panicky feeling she'd had earlier was now firmly lodged in her gut, leaching its way into her bloodstream like a pot of spilled ink. She was vaguely aware of Tommy taking her arm, his deep voice thanking the old woman for the information, turning her to walk back down the Marsh Road.

'Well, it looks like Georgy-boy has disappeared, Mam. You and I will have to step in at the mill.'

Ellen was so grateful to Tommy that he had decided to share the problem of the disappeared manager with her. She had a sneaking suspicion that she would find the finances of the mill in disarray, and some instinct told her that she should go and see the bank manager as quickly as possible, and that she might not be able to protect her family from what was about to unfold.

CHAPTER 43

Ellen

Ellen scrutinised the bill in her hands for the umpteenth time. The figure at the bottom of the page remained resolutely the same. It had come that morning in the post. Meagher's Drapery in town was a fine place. She had shopped there ever since marrying Nicholas and loved the shop with its rows of fine clothes, wools, linens, cottons - all the latest colours and styles. Everything there was so crisp and new. She had clothed herself and her family well down through the years courtesy of the shop and had treated Peggy to a nice woollen scarf or a pair of leather gloves from time to time. Nicholas had been generous when it came to looking after them it that regard. Well, it fed into his reputation for being a good family man. Ellen had never had to worry about paying for any of the things she bought. It had all been taken care of. Only, now, it seemed that Meagher's were saying that the bill hadn't been paid for the past couple of years! Ellen had been sure it was a mistake at first, but now, waiting to see the Manager, Hugh Meagher, her conviction that there was an error was beginning to wane. She felt quite sick as she sat in the light and airy office of Drogheda's finest department store.

'Mrs. Clinton. Very nice to see you. I'm sorry for your trouble. Nicholas was a fine man.' Ellen took the hand offered by Hugh Meagher.

He had a pleasant, open face, a shock of dark hair and eyebrows that looked like the god's horses she sometimes saw in the vegetable garden in Greenhills.

'Ah, thank you Mr. Meagher.' Ellen didn't care to agree with his last statement, so she said no more. She cleared her throat as he sat down behind his walnut desk.

'It's very good of you to see me today. I'm here because I got this.... this bill.'

He seemed to wriggle uncomfortably in his seat and couldn't quite meet her gaze.

'Mr. Meagher. This bill. Surely there's been a mistake? We couldn't possibly owe this amount. I know Nicholas regularly cleared the account......' Ellen could see the man's colour was rising and he seemed to be having difficulty with the tightness of his shirt collar.

He remained silent.

'Mr. Meagher!' Ellen's voice was starting to sound a bit strangled as her heart was beating uncomfortably in her chest.

'Apologies Mrs. Clinton.' His expression was one of embarrassment, mixed with sympathy. 'I'm afraid that the figure is correct. In fact, we have knocked a bit off the total owed as a discount for being such good customers over the years. You see, Nicholas hasn't paid anything off the account for the past eighteen months.'

'Eighteen months? But that's impossible! I've been in here loads of times recently and no one breathed a word to me about owing so much money.'

'Well, no, they wouldn't Mrs. Clinton. Our staff here are trained to be professionals, so they would never, ever mention something like that on the shop floor to a customer.'

There was a pregnant pause. 'Look Mrs. Clinton, I'm very sorry that your husband has died. It must have been a huge shock. But I have to collect any money that's due to the shop. I have a family to feed myself. And your account is the largest one outstanding by far. There's the children's pinafores, shoes, winter coats, scarves, gloves, numerous items for yourself and a couple for Mrs. Murphy.....'

Ellen inhaled sharply at his words, stung with embarrassment. This couldn't be true. Once again, she kicked herself for turning into the type of woman who didn't keep an eye on the family finances. She had been content to let Nicholas take care of them. She looked at the man across the desk from her. He had an honest face. He didn't look like he was joking or trying to trick her. His expression was deadly serious. It must be true. Damn and blast Nicholas anyway. What the hell had he been at? Putting her in such an embarrassing position. If he was here, she'd give him a piece of her mind. She sighed inwardly and sat up straight.

'I'm very sorry Mr. Meagher. I honestly thought Nicholas looked after the account. I really don't know what to say. I'll make sure that you get paid as soon as possible. I had absolutely no idea....'

'Mrs. Clinton. I can see by your reaction that you are telling the truth. And I'm sorry that I had to send you the bill, but I couldn't let the situation go on any longer. I'm sure you can appreciate my position?'

'Of course, of course. As I said, you'll have your money as soon as possible. I'm very sorry that you've had to wait so long for it.'

Not wanting to spend another minute in the office, Ellen stood swiftly. She held out her hand to Hugh Meagher, pumped his strongly and left the room with as much dignity as she could muster. Ellen would have gladly high-tailed it out a side door, if there had been one. The walk from the office at the back of the shop to the front door seemed interminable. Everyone was staring at her. They must all know that she was someone who couldn't or wouldn't pay her way. Bad cess to Nicholas for making her feel like this. She was glad he was lying cold above in the Cord cemetery, for if he wasn't dead already, she would have cheerfully killed him for embarrassing her like this.

CHAPTER 44

Ellen

Dressed in her widow's weeds, Ellen swept into the red-bricked National Bank building on Shop Street. She was aware of the eyes of the clerks following her progress across the black and white tiled floor. She tried to keep the slight spring out of her step and her eyes downcast, in keeping with a woman who had lost her husband weeks before. Truth be told, there was an air of lightness in the house, now that they no longer had to watch their words, their actions or worry about what sort of mood himself would be in. Tommy's jaw had visibly unclenched. The girls were gradually relaxing, running around, no longer afraid of a terrifying roar from their father, their childish laughter echoing throughout the house. Alice, at thirteen was showing signs of having the potential to become quite a handful. Ellen didn't have the headspace to think about her. She cleared her throat as she approached the teller at the counter.

'Good afternoon, madam, how can I help you today?'

Ellen rounded her shoulders a touch, cocked her head to one side and answered in a solemn voice.

'I'm here to see Mr. Mc Keown. I have an appointment.'

'What is your name madam?'

Ellen damped down a sense of irritation. This man knew exactly who she was. Drogheda wasn't that big of a town.

'Ellen Clinton is my name.' she smiled sweetly.

'Very well Mrs. Clinton. I will let him know you're here. Please have a seat.'

He gestured to a red velvet covered chair outside Mc Keown's door the door.

'Thank you.' Ellen sank onto the chair gratefully. Her legs were feeling a bit shaky now. She tried to swallow down the sense of unease that was growing ever since the other day, when she had discovered that George Menton was gone missing. And then she had gotten the bill from Meagher's. She was still shaken from that one. She absolutely regretted now that she hadn't taken more of an interest in the business over the past few years. With his drinking, Nicholas probably hadn't been in a fit state to make sound financial decisions. She was about to find out just how bad things were.

The door opened with a squeak and the oily head of Thomas Mc Keown appeared. He stepped out of his office to usher Ellen in. She got a whiff of some sort of cologne as she squeezed in past him and noticed that the collar of his black jacket was peppered with dandruff. She had never been inside his office before. It was as she imagined a bank manager's office to be. Ellen bet Mc Keown spent a good deal of his time peeking out through his net curtain as, rumour had it, he was a great man for the gossip. No doubt, he felt that he could keep a finger on the pulse of the town from behind the piece of white lace. The desk was polished mahogany, and the paperwork on it was arranged exceedingly neatly, his fountain pen at a precise ninety-degree angle to the ledger which sat on his desk. There was a jug of water with two glasses in a prominent position on the desk beside a bottle of brandy. Ellen's stomach gave a lurch. Was that for her? Would she need it before the meeting was over? She sat down in the chair, feeling the leather cool beneath her skirt.

'Thank you for coming in today, Mrs. Clinton, Mc Keown regarded her from behind the steeple of his long, bony fingers. 'I am very sorry for your trouble. Nicholas was a fine man indeed and I'm sure you must be feeling his loss very keenly.' His watery blue eyes swept over Ellen's dress and then back to her face.

'Thank you, Mr. Mc Keown. Yes, it was a great shock. He was so young, you know.' Ellen lowered her eyes and sniffed. She pretended to gather herself together.

'Thank you for seeing me at such short notice, but I felt I must come. I have become very much concerned by my findings at the mill recently. I went up there after I had been alerted to the fact that George Menton had not been seen for a couple of days. Mick Matthews has been opening and closing up in the evening, but there is no one there now to look after the accounts and the customers. I went to Menton's house yesterday only to find that he has left, owing the landlady money.'

Was that a look of surprise in Mc Keown's eyes? With all his curtain-twitching he hadn't been party to that particular piece of gossip.

Ellen continued, 'So, it would seem that I will have to start to look after things up there now. I have come here to ascertain what the financial situation is. As no doubt you can appreciate, I have been busy over the past number of years with the children and I'm afraid to say that I didn't take as much interest in the mill as I could have.' Ellen tried a tinkle of a laugh, but it sounded wrong in these serious surroundings. 'So, I am here today in the hope that you can appraise me of how things stand.' Ellen gave him her sweetest smile and tried to ignore the mottled skin on the top of his head which reminded her of the slab of meat she saw whenever she passed the butcher's shop window.

Mc Keown cleared his throat, and Ellen could see a rogue hair that he had missed when shaving near his Adam's apple.

'Well, Mrs. Clinton. I...ah... I'm surprised to hear that George Menton has disappeared. That is somewhat irregular, certainly. To leave the town without appraising anyone of where he is going. Are you quite sure that he hasn't gone to visit family up north? I think he's from Belfast or somewhere near that city.'

'Well, he was seen leaving with a big black bag, and apparently, the room he used in his lodgings had been cleared of all his belongings. So, yes, it looks like he is gone for good.'

'I see.' Mc Keown closed his eyes.

The gold clock on the mantle-piece ticked away twenty seconds. If Ellen didn't know better, she would have though he was gone asleep. He straightened up and inhaled sharply, making the buttons on his waistcoat strain. He exhaled slowly. Ellen saw a range of emotions pass over his features. When he turned his face to hers again, his lips had formed a thin line.

'Well, Mrs. Clinton, I have to tell you that I have been quite concerned for some time about the finances of the mill.'

'Oh, how so?' Trying to keep her voice even, Ellen felt a tremor of foreboding wriggle its way down her spine.

'There have been some loans. It appears that Nicholas was struggling to get new customers. Prices have taken a bit of a dive. Cotton is becoming readily and cheaply available. There's not as much demand for linen. The lodgements that George was making were not as plentiful as they had been a couple of years ago.'

George Bloody Menton. The sneaky devil. Ellen had had her suspicions about him from the moment she clapped eyes on him all those years ago when she first got the job in the mill. She'd been about to mention to Nicholas that some of the information in the ledgers didn't add up when she had become pregnant with Larry's child and that was the end of her working life. After that, she had been busy with the girls, then Michael. It had all gone to the back of her mind. That black bag Menton had been seen leaving with was no doubt, filled to capacity with money. Her money. The bastard must have been systematically creaming off for himself, and Nicholas had been alternately too drunk and too grief stricken to notice or care. Bad cess to George Menton. Only God knew where he was now. No doubt, enjoying living on the contents of the black bag.

Slamming down her fury, Ellen said. 'So, what are you saying? How much exactly does Nicholas, I mean, do I owe?'

The man's face began to swim when he informed of her exactly how much was owed by the estate of the late Nicholas Clinton.

'Jesus, Mary and Joseph!' was all Ellen could utter. She felt winded. This was an even bigger shock that Nicholas's death had been.

'How long do I have to pay it off?', Ellen gulped, forcing herself to look at the man across the desk. He looked almost apologetic.

'That's just it, Mrs. Clinton. I'm afraid the trustees want the money back within six months or....' he shrugged his shoulders as if to say that it wasn't of his doing.

'Or what?' Ellen looked him square in the face, bracing herself for what he was about to say.

'Or the mill will have to be sold. And I'm afraid, that's not all.' His words dropped like a lead weight in the silence of the room. Ellen sagged into the chair, thoughts scurrying around her brain.

'What do you mean?'

'You see, the mill business wasn't doing very well for the past few years. I'm sorry to have to tell you this, but.... '

'But what?' Ellen could hear the near hysteria in her voice.

'Well, Nicholas mortgaged the house in Greenhills.' Mc. Keown's words hung like a will 'o the wisp in the air and slowly descended into Ellen's consciousness. The room seemed suddenly to suffocate her.

'Mr. Mc Keown, I would like a glass of brandy if you wouldn't mind.' Ellen forced herself to smile as the bank manager poured her a glass. She concentrated on sipping it slowly, willing her heartbeat to stop its racing. Things were worse than she could possibly have imagined. She and the children could soon be homeless! She didn't know how, right now, but she would think of a way out of this mess. She had to. The children and Peggy were depending on her.

CHAPTER 45

Ellen

January 1877

Ellen felt a piercing pain right behind her eyes, and her head was fit to burst. She was weary to her very bones, but she was nearly there. There was finally light at the end of the tunnel. She cursed Nicholas Clinton with feeling. But she couldn't let him take all the blame. Her rage mingled with a spike of shame.

Over the past six months, Ellen and Tommy had discovered the breadth and depth of neglect that Nicholas had inflicted on the business. They had discovered that he had more or less assigned complete control of the finances to George Menton after Michael had died. God only knew what he had been doing or where he had been going when he had left the house every day, because he certainly hadn't been paying any attention to the business. Menton had been systematically helping himself to money, collecting from customers and creaming a bit off for himself before lodging the balance. He had done this on every single order that had left the mill for the past few years.

They had survived the past six months. Between them, she and Tommy had managed to keep the mill running whilst Mc Keown looked for a buyer. She had kicked her brain into gear, done her research, and had come to the conclusion that there was no future in the linen business. She could have kept the mill going herself, but she was sure that to do so would have resulted in further financial heartache down the line. She hadn't the energy for that. No, she was very glad to offload it to Messrs. Jonathan Shanley and Sons, even though the price was rock-bottom. Let the new owners worry about the future. At least she didn't have the added guilt of letting all the workers go. That would have broken her completely. She had begun to despair, and then, on Christmas Eve, when she should have been at home with her family, thinking of nothing more than preparing for the next day's feast, and wrapping small trinkets for the children, a letter had been delivered to the mill containing an offer to buy it. She had lain her head down on Nicholas's old desk and wept in pure relief. The money would get Mc Keown off her back, with a small amount over. At least that. They could make a fresh start. She would try and get a job, though God only knew who would take on a woman of her age and circumstances. She had decided that she would put her worry on hold until the new year and try and create some happy memories with the children. They had had a lovely, peaceful Christmas, not missing Nicholas's sullen unpredictability. The children had shrieked and run around the house. Ellen had allowed them free rein to be as loud as they liked. Tommy had been quiet. He'd had plans to go to Maynooth College in Kildare to study poetry and literature, but now, that was all gone by the wayside. He had promised his Mam that he would find a job to earn some money. It nearly broke Ellen's heart to see her lovely boy losing out on his dream of being a writer. Instead, he would find himself doing labour for some slavedriver just to bring home money to help keep the family afloat. Ellen cursed the demons that had haunted Nicholas and reduced her family to paupers.

She sat up straight at the kitchen table, put the keys of the mill in an envelope and wrote the new owner's name on the outside. This evening, Mr. Shanley himself was calling around to collect them. Good luck to him. The last six months had taken its toll on her physically. She sometimes got a fright when she looked in the mirror. There were permanent dark shadows under her eyes. She was very pale, and the skin on her face was stretched over her cheekbones. She felt at least twenty years older than she was. So far in her life, she had loved two men and had married another one that she didn't love, granted, out of desperation at the time. Now, here she was, mother of six. She would always be a mother of six, even though she only had five living children. She had a home, but no means of supporting the four children who still needed to eat and be clothed. She supposed that Alice could leave school and look for a job. But she didn't want that for Jim's daughter. Ellen had seen Alice engaging in very animated conversation with young Murphy, a local coach driver. Even though she was only barely in her teens, she had a way of looking at him that made Ellen's blood run cold. She was going to be a handful. Ellen was sure of it. Well, there was no means of paying the driver anymore, so at least Alice wouldn't be given the chance to engage him in conversation now.

Just what Ellen was going to do for money she didn't know. If she had any, she would hire someone to track down that bastard Menton and wring his scrawny neck until he told them what he had done with her money. But that wasn't an option. Ellen took a deep breath and rose from the kitchen table. The day outside was cold and rainy. She spied Peggy waddling from the shed, carrying a basket-full of carrots, potatoes, and turnips for that evening's dinner. Ellen's heart was full of gratitude as she looked at her friend. She had slowed down a bit in the past couple of years, but she was still mentally sound, and sharp as a tack.

'Lord, but that's a beggar of an evening!' Peggy shook the rain from her hat and stamped her boots on the mat in an effort to rid them of the worst of the mud she had brought in from the garden. She put down the basket and started struggling to take off her mantle with arthritic fingers. It wasn't really fair to ask Peggy to mind all the children while she went out to work, but she didn't have an alternative. That's if anyone would give her a job. She had very little experience. She didn't want to go back to singing in the alehouse. Her heart gave a jolt as she remembered Larry.

Over the years, she had tried to blot out his memory as it caused her nothing but pain. How different her life would have been if she had married him instead of Nicholas. God only knew where he was now, if he was even still alive. Ellen had heard stories about the cruel labour prisoners were subjected to in the Australian jail houses. Apparently, a person could be burned to a crisp out there, the sun was that hot. And the place was full of poisonous snakes and spiders. She had a feeling that he *was* still alive, but she didn't know if that was just wishful thinking. Shaking her head to dispel the image of his face, she focused instead on Peggy who was now washing the vegetables at the kitchen sink.

'Peggy, let me do that. You sit down and rest yourself for a few minutes.'

'Aye lass. I won't say no to a bit of a sit down.'

Peggy collapsed onto a chair beside the range, looking exhausted and distracted. Regarding her face, Ellen pledged to get to the bottom of whatever was bothering her friend, for something surely was. But, first, she had a family to feed. A ravenous family. She would concentrate on the act of preparing a meal and figure it all out later.

CHAPTER 46

Tommy

Tommy looked at his mother's face. It was still very beautiful but was pinched and drawn. There were deep, dark shadows under her eyes. Now he knew what the expression 'haunted' meant. He was no great shakes himself. He couldn't really remember a time when he had felt peace. He was tired. Tired of pretending to be strong and jolly. He remembered the crab he had found one day on the beach. It had a hard shell, but inside, it was soft and very easily damaged. Just like he was.

Ever since his world had shattered when his Da had drowned, life had been one long battle. He had watched his Mam nearly fall apart with grief. Then, there was a brief period of happiness when Larry had been around. Tommy had started to think of him as a good friend. Not a new Da, but he had liked him well enough. He had been a bit scared doing the secret message deliveries for him, but he had done it at the time, as he had wanted to help his Mam. Then Larry had disappeared from their lives – shipped off to the other side of the world. And after that, well, life had taken a rotten turn when his Mam had married that yoke, Nicholas Clinton. Every time she had a baby growing in her belly, she seemed to get sicker and sicker, until she spent most of her time in bed. When little

Michael had been born, Tommy had been delighted to have a brother, even though he was a way older. He had done a little dance in private when Nicholas died. He knew it was very wrong and he would probably go to hell for it, but he hadn't been able to help himself. His Mam had seemed to be happier, despite being a widow for the second time. Well, up until she had discovered that they had to sell the mill.

'Tommy, I need to speak to you about university,' his Mam had said. After Nicholas had died, and they'd found out how bad things were, she had told him then that she was so very, very sorry, but he wouldn't be able to go now, as they couldn't afford it, what with the mill having to be sold. It had broken his heart at the time, but he had tried his best not to show it. He had so badly wanted to be a writer, ever since a poem he had written when he was in fourth class had made the school master cry. He had been amazed that words could have such power. But that dream would have to be put on hold. He would have to just continue scribbling away on his jotter whenever he had a few spare minutes, instead of spending all day immersing himself in all those gorgeous books up in the Maynooth University library.

'You really don't mind?' his Mam had said.

'No Mam. I really don't mind. It's alright. Honestly. I'll get a job.'

'You are such a good boy. I mean, man. I must have done something right. The woman that gets you will be so lucky!'

Tommy had swallowed down the lump in his throat. He didn't think he would ever marry. He would have to let Josie down gently. She had been giving him the eye for months. From behind her fruit stall in the market, he could feel her eyes following him as he made his way from place to place. He just couldn't make himself feel *that* way about her. He wondered if he would ever feel like he was supposed to about a girl. There *was* someone that occupied his thoughts day and night. Tommy felt a sick to his stomach as the familiar rising panic and despair took hold.

'Did you know that, Tommy?' Tommy could hear his Mam's voice speaking to him urgently as she gripped his arm. He was jerked back to reality. His Mam was asking him something.

'Sorry Mam, I was miles away. Did I know what?'

'We have to move out of the house.'

'This house? Why? What?'

No wonder his Mam had looked so anxious lately.

'I don't understand?' Tommy's mind was whirling.

'Nicholas mortgaged the house to try and save the mill. It has to be sold to pay off the debt. Shanleys are buying it as well as the mill.'

'The bloody man has left us virtually homeless.'

'But why didn't you tell me about the house?' He took her hand in his. She glanced at him.

'Ah Tommy, because I feel such a bloody fool. How could I know so little about the financial situation we were all in? What sort of a sorry excuse for a woman am I? I was hoping that I might be able to hold onto the house even if we had to sell the mill. How are we all going to fare when we're out on the street?' A strangled wail escaped her lips, and she seemed to deflate in front of his eyes.

'Don't worry Mam, we'll think of something. At least you're rid of him now. He can't hurt you anymore.'

Ellen cleared her throat and looked out the kitchen window. It was a Sunday afternoon, and Peggy was out in the garden with all the little ones. Her cheery voice and the squeals of the little ones wafted in on the breeze. Alice was somewhere, Lord only knew where. Probably lying behind one of the hedges with a faraway look in her eyes.

'Don't be so hard on yourself. It must have been difficult to stand up to him. You seemed to be always so sick. And there was always another baby on the way. And then Michael.....'

Tommy could see his Mam's eyes fill with tears. She threw her arms around him. They hugged long and hard and he could feel her ribs and her backbone. She really needed to eat some food.

'Thanks son. I am so sorry that you can't go to university.' Ellen wiped her eyes again.

'Mam, I told you. I don't mind. Life throws things at you sometimes and you must figure them out.'

Touching his cheek tenderly, she said 'How did you get to be so wise?'

'I don't know. I must have gotten it from my Da!'

'Cheeky!' She cuffed his ear.

'So, Mam. Tell me about this house. How long before we must leave?' It was time to bring the conversation around to practicalities.

Ellen sighed and began twisting her hands together in her lap. She reached into her pocket and brought out a sprig of lavender, inhaling the scent deeply. She had told him once that it calmed her down whenever she was feeling angry or worried. Tommy suspected that she would need more than they even had outside in the garden to help her over the next few months.

'That bastard Menton. If I could get my hands on him, I'd wring his scrawny bloody neck.' Ellen's eyes flashed fury. Tommy was sure there were people, probably lurking in the alleyways and narrow streets beside the docks, who would be well able to find George Menton. But that required money which was something they no longer had.

'Well Mam, he's gone, and I don't think we should waste any more of our energy thinking about him. We're going to need it for the months ahead. How long have we got?'

'Two weeks.' Ellen exhaled, long and slow.

'Well, that gives us plenty of time to come up with a plan!' Tommy tried to inject some optimism into his voice.

'You think so love? We'll be able to get a house for all seven of us? Tell me, how on earth are we going to pay for it? '

'I'll get a job. And maybe you could get one too? Peggy could mind the young ones. And maybe Alice could get a job? I know she's only thirteen, but she's a big and strong.'

'No! Alice stays at school!' There was a very determined look in Ellen's eyes. 'I don't care how we manage, but all my children are going to get an education. They are not going to becomes skivvies at some factory, or end of cleaning the slops off the floor in some rich eejit's house.'

Tommy couldn't help but laugh at the fierce expression on his Mam's face. That was one of the many things he loved about her. No matter how down she got, she always got back up again, and her love for her children was never, ever in doubt. It had made Tommy feel cocooned down through the years. But now, it was time to step up to the plate, become a man and help his family out. He should probably never had given the university dream any air. Lads like him, who were born on Rope Walk, didn't go anywhere but out to work.

Outside, Peggy was sitting on the low wall that ran down the length of the herb garden with the young ones running around her in delighted circles. She looked like she was wondering how on earth she was going to get back up. Tommy would have to rescue her in a few minutes.

'Peggy is not as young as she used to be.' Ellen's worried look was back again. 'I don't know how she'd fare with all three youngsters to mind, especially Rosena. You have to admit, she's a bit of a firecracker.'

Tommy had to agree. The same thought had crossed his mind. If himself, his Mam and Alice all went out to work, Peggy would be left with the little ones all day on her own. She was over sixty, and the strands of grey were starting to outnumber the red on her head.

'I think she'd be alright Mam. Sure, we have no other option.'

'You're right son. I'll have to put my thinking cap on to see what useless article like me could do for a job!'

'You're not useless! Don't worry, we'll think of something.' Tommy stood up. 'I'd better go and help Peggy to her feet, or she'll be out there all night like a sheep on its back. He made his way out the door into the garden, a smile pasted on his face, even though his heart was heavy with dread.

CHAPTER 47

Ellen

Think, stupid woman, think! There had to be somewhere she could get a job in this town! Ellen was beginning to despair. She banged her head with the heel of her hand, as if to knock her brain into gear. If she had thought her life was a nightmare before, it had been nothing compared to what it was now. Sure, it had been a challenge to cope with Nicholas's volatile moods, and dodge him in the bedroom whenever she could, but she had never gone hungry before. Not even when she had been living in Rope Walk after Jim had died. It seemed that nobody wanted to employ a woman who was the mother of five children. She had also come to realise that Nicholas Clinton wasn't as well liked around Drogheda as he had thought he was. Sure, he had been the big businessman, and on the Corporation. He had been hailed as a great fellow wherever he went, but now, whenever his name was mentioned, Ellen was met with a curl of the lip, a derisory glance.

'Employ the widow of Nicholas Clinton? Not likely!'

'You were married to a cur, Missus. Be glad he's gone.'

'I wouldn't do that blackguard a favour. His offspring can starve as far as I'm concerned!'

The kindest of them, a Mr. Mahon, had looked her up and down, and had said, 'If I were you, Mrs. Clinton, I would see if I could set up home somewhere else. I'm sorry to say, your husband was not liked around this town.' With a sympathetic glance, he had patted her arm and turned away. Whatever Nicholas had done to alienate so many of the businessmen around was a mystery to Ellen. She mentally kicked herself again for not paying more attention to what was going on. Now she couldn't get a start anywhere. She looked up to the sky and shook her fist. 'Damn you, Nicholas Clinton and whatever you did to make everyone despise you so!' She looked down at the ground, thinking that maybe that's where she should be directing her ire. She doubted he was in heaven. More likely to have the flames of hell licking at his feet for all eternity. She threw up a fervent prayer to heaven that none of their young daughters would inherit any of his ways.

Turning around, she made her way down the town towards the market, hoping to pick up a few bits of food at half price, seeing as the trading day was nearly done. They had enough vegetables stored to last another couple of weeks, but the meat was getting scarce. More often than not these days, she went to bed with hunger gnawing her belly. She knew she had lost even more weight and now looked a sight.

Tommy had managed to find himself a job up in the tannery. The fact that he was Jim Cooney's son had stood to him. She felt the familiar pain when she thought of Jim. Now, it was less sharp, more blunted. She could tell that Tommy loathed his new job, as he seemed to have withdrawn into himself. He would arrive home, go straight to the washbasin and try and scrub the smell of the animal hides off his skin. He seemed to have abandoned his writing now that it wasn't possible for him to go to university. This was like a knife piercing Ellen's heart. She had wanted to give her son everything in life. All she had given him was huge responsibility. He was now the man of the house at eighteen, with six mouths to feed as well as his own, and his mother was redundant. They would have to leave their home in less than two weeks and still Ellen hadn't managed to find any work, never mind any other place to live.

She tried to damp down the panic she was feeling. *Come on, Jim. I need a bit of good fortune here. Please, send me something!* Head bowed, she walked briskly, trying to keep the cold rain that had started to fall from making its way down inside her collar. Hunger made her weak, and her legs felt like lead. Turing the corner into West Street, she smacked straight into someone with a broad chest, encased in a wool coat.

'I'm so sorry, begging your pardon,' she muttered, not even looking at the person.

'Ellen, Ellen Cooney, is that you?'

The hunger had made her ears daft. His voice sounded exactly like Larry's. Ellen jerked her head up and focused on the face of the man in front of her. The breath was taken clean out of her lungs, stars burst in front of her eyes, and suddenly the edges of her vision became black. That was the last thing she remembered.

A delicious feeling was wending its way in slow waves throughout Ellen's entire body. She was lying on the beach in the hot July sun. She could hear the gentle sound of the waves as they calmly ebbed and flowed. The sand was soft beneath her body, and she wriggled her toes. She opened her eyes a fraction and could see nothing but an expanse of blue sky with not a cloud in sight. Some gulls were wheeling high above, plaintive and watchful in their flight. She thought she could hear someone calling her name. She was too relaxed to bother trying to see who it was. If she kept her eyes closed, they might go away, whoever they were. But no, this person was being most annoyingly persistent. She heard her name again, this time louder, closer. Then someone was slapping her cheek with a wet towel. What the hell?

'Ellen, Ellen, wake up! Come on now, come back to me.' The voice was rich and warm and held a timbre that stirred Ellen's senses. She opened one eye, and then tentatively opened the other one. She wasn't on the beach in Bettystown. She was on the street in Drogheda. The languorous warmth she had felt had nothing to do with her surroundings as the day was cold and drizzly. Rather, it had to do with the pair of arms that were wrapped around her. She focused on the face that was only inches away from her own. The skin was a ruddy brown. She could see it was freshly shaven and she could smell something lemony that made her stomach flip. The chin was what could be described as 'determined' and the lips, oh, the lips were just right. Not too full and not too thin. Eminently kissable and mobile. As her eyes continued their journey, she could see a strong, straight nose. She seemed to remember kissing the tip of this nose. There were deep lines down the side of it, and her eyes wandered to a thin scar on the left cheek. She finally rested her gaze on the eyes. They were brown in colour - a shade between the colour of autumn leaves and a piece of velvet she had once seen in the dress-makers shop. They held an expression of such tender yearning that Ellen gasped. She drew the cold, damp air into her lungs. When she tried to sit up, she immediately felt dizzy.

The face looked relieved. 'Ellen, *a stór*, you're alright now. I've got you. I've got you.'

Larry. It was Larry.

'Is it really you?' Ellen's voice cracked.

'Yes, it's me Ellen. By God, it's good to see you. I have been dreaming about this moment for eight long years. I didn't think I'd have such an effect on you though! Fainting right away like that. You gave me a bit of a fright.' Ellen righted herself, pulling slightly away from him, wanting to make sure that her eyes weren't playing tricks on her.

'But how did you get here? How...' Larry pressed his finger to Ellen's lips.

'There's plenty of time for explanations. I think the most important thing right now is to get you sitting down somewhere and get you something hot to eat and drink. When was the last time you had a decent meal?'

Ellen could see his eyes raking over her features, and she knew that he would most probably be shocked by her appearance. Her face was skinny, cheekbones, protruding and her hair had lost its usual lustre. A clump of it had come right away in her hand the other day when she was brushing it. Given the stress that she was under, it was probably no surprise. Suddenly shy, she pulled further away from Larry's arms, and immediately became aware of several pairs of curious eyes staring at them. She stood tall, the dizziness finally abating, and straightened her clothes and hat. With a tilt of her chin, she said.

'What was that you mentioned about food?'

Larry chuckled to himself and nodded almost imperceptibly, as if satisfied about something. He offered his arm, and together they picked their way across the market to the nicer of the two little tea shops in the higgledy-piggledy buildings that formed a square in the centre of town. As they walked, Ellen tried to gather herself together. Her mind was swirling, her heart was hammering, and her mouth was dry. But, deep inside, there was a kernel of a feeling that she hadn't felt in a long, long time. She had damped it down eight years ago when she had stood in the oratory, saying her vows to Nicholas. She had tried, over the years, to keep it at bay. Now it was back. She stole a glance at Larry, walking tall beside her and suddenly, that feeling was seeping into her bloodstream, slowly, delightfully making each cell come alive. Larry was back! And more than that, judging by the expression in his eyes, he was just as glad to see her as she was to see him. Yet, part of her was loathe to let him back into her life easily.

Taaffe's Tea House was busy. Mrs. Taaffe was her usual bustling self, moving deftly between all ten of her red and white gingham-clad tables with the poise of a dancer, despite her size. She had a jolly expression that never deserted her, even when she had to deal with contrary customers or vagabonds. The former, she knew how to cajole, and the latter, she ejected from her establishment, but not without first pressing a freshly cooked scone or piece of wheaten bread into a chapped, dirty hand. Today, there was a thin sheen of sweat on her face and some of her red hair was standing to attention in the steamy atmosphere. For a moment, it looked like Ellen and Larry wouldn't get a seat, but then, a mother and her young son got up to leave from a table right at the very back. Quickly claiming the table, Larry ushered Ellen to sit down. She was very glad to do so. The lightness in her head was abating, but the weakness in her knees was causing her to think she couldn't stand a moment longer.

'Right, what do you want to eat Ellen?' Larry perused the menu which didn't take long. 'A nice strong cup of tea, just the way you like it?' *He remembered.* 'And a slice of bread and jam? Or a fruit scone?'

Suddenly, Ellen was absolutely ravenous.

'I think I might like both.'

Larry chuckled and swept his gaze over her face. His expression turned serious.

'Ellen, it's so good to see you.'

'I thought I'd never see you again Larry Clinton! Nicholas told me you were captured and shipped off to prison in Australia.'

'That bastard. He set me up. Sent me away so that you and I couldn't be together. Wanted you all to himself.' Larry's expression was murderous.

'Hold on a minute', Ellen felt winded, and had to take a very deep breath before she could continue. 'Nicholas had you captured?' Tiny pin pricks of light danced in front of her eyes, and she was glad to feel the solid strength of the chair beneath her. 'And sent away? To the other side of the world from me and your baby?'

At that moment, Mrs. Taffe arrived with their tea and a plate with steaming scones, soft butter, two slabs of wheaten bread and a pot of jam. She quickly deposited everything on the table and beat a hasty retreat.

'So, I have a child?' Larry seemed to hold his breath. 'I never knew what had happened...if you had managed to carry...'

Ellen covered his big, rough hand with hers. She noticed tiny little scars that hadn't been there before. The skin was chapped and the knuckles slightly swollen.

'Yes, Larry, you have a daughter called Liberty. She was born fine and healthy.' She could tell by his expression that Larry was remembering the night she had been conceived.

'The memory of that night, of your face, were the only things that kept me sane in that wretch of a place in Australia. '

'I was fully sure I would get to see you in the gaol, but then you just disappeared so quickly, and apparently, no one knew where you were gone. No one would tell me anyway.' Ellen stole a glance at Larry's face which was slowly regaining its colour.

'Larry, the baby was making me so sick. I was so scared at what was to become of me, Tommy and Alice, that the only way I could see out of my predicament was to marry Nicholas. You were gone!' The words tumbled out of Ellen in a torrent. She was trying to convey the absolute wretchedness of the time when she had found herself abandoned, reeling with sickness, with two small children, a baby on the way, and no money to put food on the table. Larry gripped her hand tightly in his. Ellen could see that his was shaking.

'Oh, yes, my brother would not be one to miss a good opportunity. Eat.'

Ellen picked up one of the slices of bread and concentrated on smearing it with butter and jam, all the while trying to get her breathing back to normal. She took a bite. It tasted so good that she took another one.

'Liberty.' You couldn't have thought of a better name for my daughter. Does she look like me?'

'Every day that I look at her face, I see yours staring back at me.'

'And Nicholas took her in as his own?'

'Aye, he did. But he never really had time for her, or her two little sisters. It was when his son came along that he was truly happy.' Ellen could see a range of emotions chase their way across Larry's face.

'So, you had three children for my brother?' he said, through gritted teeth. He closed his eyes and shook his head, as if trying to banish the image of Ellen and Nicholas together. It was all Ellen could do to meet his eyes.

'Yes, I did. But Larry, I had no choice but to be a wife to him. I took my vows, even though my heart was screaming at me not to. You were gone, vanished into thin air.'

'So, you are my sister-in-law.' Larry seemed to slump into his chair. 'I always knew he wanted you, but I never dreamt of the depths to which he'd sink to get you.'

'You knew he wanted me?'

'Oh, yes, with a fervour like you wouldn't believe.'

Suddenly, he sat bolt upright again. 'I insist on seeing my daughter. I have every right. And I don't care what Nicholas says. I will see her, I will.' Anger flashed in Larry's eyes.

He didn't know. How could he not know?

'Larry, just how long have you been back in Drogheda?'

'I got off the boat this morning. I came straight to the market, hoping I might catch a glimpse of you.'

'Oh.' Ellen couldn't stop the dance of delight her insides did on hearing that Larry had been so anxious to find her. But how could he not know about Nicholas?

'Larry, Nicholas died in his sleep last July. So, I am your sister-in-law, but I'm also a widow. Again. At the age of nearly forty, and with six children. Well, five of them living.' Ellen exhaled deeply and she could feel the familiar stab of grief that thinking of Michael always brought. She raised her eyes to Larry's face. It was if he didn't know which piece of information to process first.

'Ah Ellen.' His expression was so tender Ellen thought she might dissolve on the spot. 'You lost a child?'

'Yes, Michael was his name. He wasn't even two years old. He died of brain fever on New Year's Eve, 1874. Nicholas never got over it. I'll never get over it. And then he started to really drink himself into oblivion. Turns out, he left George Menton to look after the mill and the bastard was lining his pocket, and then he skipped off to God only knows where. I've had to sell the mill and the house. We have a week to leave it. I've been looking for a job, but no one will give Nicholas Clinton's widow a start. Turns out your brother wasn't that well liked around this town.'

Larry snorted. 'So, he's dead and gone, that so-called brother of mine?' Good riddance, I say.'

'He didn't make my life very easy.'

Larry closed his eyes at Ellen's words.

'Did he mistreat you, Ellen?' Larry's breathing came faster, and she could sense the tension in his body from across the table. He opened his eyes. The pupils were pinpricks of fury. Ellen's silence said it all. Looking into the corner of the tea shop, he swallowed hard.

'I'm sorry from the bottom of my heart that you were treated so badly at the hands of a Clinton. I will do my utmost to make it up to you.'

'I don't know what I'm going to do. We have nowhere to live.' Ellen continued, covering her mouth, trying to stifle the wail that was threatening to escape. Larry rose quickly, reached across the table, nearly upscuttling all the crockery and took Ellen in his arms.

'Hush now Ellen, I'm back, and now that I've found you again, I'm never going to let you go.'

Ellen stiffened, but then decided to sink into his embrace. Momentarily, she forgot all her worries and just allowed herself to breathe in the scent of the man and let her mind go blank.

'Can I see my daughter? Can I meet Liberty?' Larry mumbled into Ellen's hair.

'Yes, of course you can see her.'

'Does she know about me?' the question was barely audible.

'No, she thinks Nicholas was her father,' Ellen sighed. 'I didn't see the point in telling her otherwise. I thought you were gone forever. We should probably leave it that way for the moment. Until you get used to the fact that you have daughter, and I get used to seeing you come back from the dead, so to speak!'

'So be it Ellen, I'll do as you say. We'll take it slowly. And how is Tommy? He must be a grown man by now?'

'He's eighteen. A fine young man. He's been such a support to me. I must have done something right to raise such a good gasson. He had hopes of becoming a writer. But there's no money now for university.' Ellen felt the usual mixture of overwhelming sadness and guilt that she couldn't give her first born his dream.

'I can't wait to see him again. He has a special place in my heart, that lad.'

The knot that had been permanently lodged in Ellen's gut seemed to unfurl ever so slightly. She didn't know how Larry was going to help, but him just being here was making her feel a spark of hope for the future. The strain of a tune Ellen knew from years before made its way through the noisy tea house. An old man with a fiddle was stopped outside the door. He was playing a tune Jim used to play for Ellen. A lively ditty. She smiled, a proper, wide, joyful one, for the first time in many a long year.

CHAPTER 48

Tommy

Tommy could see that his Mam was doing a bad job of trying to hide her delight about Larry's reappearance. The day before, she had been downcast, weary, looking like she had the weight of the world on her shoulders. He had been fairly surprised when he had returned from work the previous evening and she had told him that Larry was back. He wasn't one hundred per cent sure how he felt about this. He had decided that it was probably a good thing. Larry had done nothing wrong really, not like Nicholas. But it didn't alter the fact that the men in his Mam's life so far hadn't been very reliable. Tommy felt mean thinking that. His Da hadn't drowned on purpose. Nicholas hadn't died in his sleep just to make life awkward for her. Larry had disappeared off to gaol through his involvement in the Fenian movement. Now, that was his own fault. Tommy shivered when he thought of all times he had scuttled nervously through the town, delivering and collecting messages from the other men with whom Larry had associated. Thank God he had never been caught! Now, as a grown-up, he could see the danger that he had been in. But he understood what had driven Larry and the other men to their actions. He did feel a residue of anger at Larry for involving him as a nine-year old boy. But he had really liked Larry too. He had learned about the stars and constellations from him, he had been funny and kind and had certainly brought his Mam back to life after his Da had died.

And now, after all these years, he had returned. His Mam seemed secretly thrilled, and she had definitely been temporarily distracted from the fact that they had less than two weeks to find somewhere else to live. Finding somewhere that wasn't an absolute hovel was going to be a challenge. As the man of the house, Tommy felt that it was up to him to try and sort something out. He loved his little sisters, and Peggy was like his granny. There was every possibility that the family might have to split up, and that was absolutely the last thing he wanted. The prospect was breaking his Mam's heart, he knew. It caused him to lay awake in his bed, night after night, staring dry-eyed at the ceiling. The skin around his right thumb was red raw and it throbbed. He'd have to stop biting it.

Today was Saturday. Larry was coming over for a cup of tea. He'd be here any minute, and his Mam was fussing around like one of the hens in the back yard. She had one of her nicest dresses on today. The red one that suited her so well. But it was kind of hanging on her now. He had caught her frowning as she looked in the mirror the other day. She had spotted a couple of grey hairs. Tommy had seen them a couple of months previously, but he hadn't liked to tell her. It was a wonder her whole head wasn't white with everything she had been through. He took three deep breaths and tried to banish the image of Nicholas from his mind. His Mam no longer had to put up with his moods and tempers. She was safe from him. But now they were in danger of ending up in the workhouse. Even looking at that place gave him the absolute shivers. Any time he had to go near it, he hurried past, head down, eyes averted. It looked like it was probably full of ghosts. The poor people that inhabited it were like the walking dead. Tommy vowed that no one from his family would ever end up there. He just had to figure out a way how.

There was a loud rap on the door and his Mam sprung up from her seat like a Jack-in-the-box.

'Relax Mam. Why are you so bothered? He's been away for nine years.' He knew there was a trace of petulance in his tone, but he couldn't help it.

'I know, son. But he was very special to me. Not as special as your Da, of course, but even so, I did grow to love him. I was very angry at him for a long time for letting himself get caught, but I realise now that he was set up.'

She rested her arm on Tommy's arm and looked at him imploringly. Tommy did understand. Of course, he did. He knew exactly what it was like to yearn for someone. Maybe his Mam might get her happy ending, even though there was no hope of one for himself. If Larry could cheer her up, then it might help get them through this mess they were in.

'Will I go and answer the door?'

'Do love, thanks.'

He bent to kiss his Mam on the cheek and as he straightened up, he said.

'If he hurts you or deserts you again, I will have his guts for garters.'

He left his Mam chuckling nervously as she checked her reflection in the big brass mirror over the fireplace.

Tommy opened the door. Larry had his back to him, and Tommy noticed the beginnings of a bald spot. Larry quickly wheeled around, a smile on his face. Tommy's eyes lingered on the silver scar on his left cheek. Larry stuck out his hand. Tommy took it in his and felt the still-strong grip.

'Tommy! Good to see you again.'

Tommy could see Larry's eyes widen slightly in surprise as he took in the breadth of his shoulders and his height. He was just as tall as Larry now. He could eyeball him, man to man.

'Larry, good to see you too.'

Tommy felt his jaw clench slightly. He tried to keep his expression neutral. Larry's wide smile faltered slightly. Larry placed his hand on Tommy's shoulder and said, 'It really is very good to be back son. I would never have left your mother and you if I'd had any choice in the matter.'

In that moment, Tommy didn't doubt the older man's sincerity.

'Ellen.' Larry moved over towards her like he was a magnet drawn to some iron filings.

I'll be watching you, Larry Clinton, and if you as much as dare look at my mother with anything other than love and adoration, you will have me to reckon with.

Clearing his throat in an effort to break the spell the two of them seemed to be under, Tommy walked towards his Mam and Larry and suggested that they move into the kitchen where Peggy had freshly baked scones cooling on the rack. That woman was a miracle. She'd disappear into town with an empty basket and return a couple of hours later with enough raw ingredients for a family meal or two. He could see that she wasn't feeding herself properly, and he was fairly sure his Mam wasn't eating right either. Both women had lost weight and whatever about Peggy, his Mam couldn't afford to. A tight knot of tension started to form in Tommy's belly. He knew he would have to get another job. He may have to resort to begging for work and that was something that didn't sit right with him. Because he'd been able to stay at school longer than most his age, he knew that people regarded him as spoilt and a bit of a cissy. With two jobs, he wouldn't have very much time for his writing. He'd have to squeeze it in somewhere. He would get published, he would. Tommy was determined about that. Even if it took him ten years, he would get his name on the spine of a book. He could see it now. *'Thomas Cooney'* in gold script on dark green leather.

Tommy could see that Peggy was eyeing Larry warily as he walked into the kitchen.

'Good to see you again Peggy.' Larry nodded his greeting.

Peggy didn't move from her perch on the high stool beside the window.

'Aye, nice to see you again, lad.'

Tommy smiled to himself. Larry was hardly a 'lad.'

'So, can I ask, where in the name of blazes have you been for the past nine years?'

Tommy couldn't help but laugh. Peggy didn't mince her words.

'Peggy, I told you....' Ellen threw her friend a look of annoyance.

Larry looked from Peggy to Tommy and back again. Then his eyes rested on Ellen. He spoke and it was as if there was no one in the room except the two of them.

'I was ripped from Drogheda and everything I held dear. That bastard I called my brother was the one responsible. There was a trap that night, and I ran straight into it. My feet barely had time to touch the ground in the gaol when I was taken off to England.'

'You couldn't find a piece of paper to write home, I don't suppose?' Peggy sniffed.

'I begged the prison warders to let me write a letter, but they just laughed at me. Then after a few months, I was shipped away to the other side of the world. Such a long journey! There were times I thought that we were destined for a watery grave. There were times when I wouldn't have minded. The sea did its very best to topple that ship, but somehow or other, it never quite managed it. I met some good men on board, from all over Ireland. All had been caught fighting for our cause.' Larry took a breath and looked at them all in turn.

'Nine long years I spent labouring on building roads in the heat and the dust in Australia. Christ, you have no idea how hot it was.' For a moment, Larry seemed lost in remembrance. He snapped back into the present. Focusing once more on Ellen, he said. 'Every minute of every day, I was wishing I was back here in Drogheda with you, Ellen. Not knowing what had become of you, Tommy and Alice and my baby was ripping my heart asunder. To the prison warders, we were worse than the dirt under their shoes. There didn't seem to be any hope at all of me getting out of that hellhole, but then myself and another man from Cork hatched an escape plan. It was risky. We were relying on others to help. It took ages to come to pass. But escape we did. For a while I thought we were to be captured again, but we got on board a whaling ship that brought us to America. I've been there the past couple of months arranging my passage back to Ireland. You have no idea how many times I wanted to put pen to paper to write to you, but I wanted to try and speak to you face to face.' Larry let out a deep sigh and Tommy felt that the older man had scars that ran much deeper than the ones on his cheek and hands.

'How did you survive in America?' Tommy's curiosity was genuinely piqued as he stared at Larry.

'We landed in the port of New York. It's a fine, fine city. You'd like it there, Tommy. You too Ellen. It's brim-full of all sorts of people. If you are prepared to work hard, you will never be idle. There's plenty of honest labour on the buildings for the Irish. So, I worked hard, saved up enough for my fare home. And there are some honourable men and women in America who are sympathetic to our cause. I was never short of a bed to lie on and always had a full belly.' Larry's eyes were shining as he breathed 'I'd love to take you there some day, Ellen. You too, Tommy' he glanced in Tommy's direction.

Tommy snorted. He couldn't help it. The notion of him going to New York was about as possible as him flying to the moon. Peggy met his gaze across Ellen and Larry's heads. She threw her eyes up to heaven. She had no time for rubbish talk of flights of fancy.

Ellen's voice was thin and reedy from months of exhaustion and worry.

'That sounds lovely Larry. But we can't even afford the price of a trip to Bettystown at the moment, never mind the fare to New York.'

She sighed, and it seemed to come from her boots. She slouched back in the chair, closed her eyes and when she opened them, her expression was one that tore Tommy's insides asunder. It was panic mixed with desperation and a hint of resignation. It was the resignation that worried him the most. His Mam had never given up, no matter what life threw at her.

'So, you see Larry, this particular family is up the creek without a paddle. I have been trying to get a job these past couple of weeks, but no one wants to know the widow of Nicholas Clinton, never mind come to her aid. That man is ruining my life, even from the grave.' The only noises to be heard in the room were the ticking of the clock and the whistle in Peggy's chest.

'And what about you Tommy?' Larry swivelled his head to look at him.

'I have a job, but it doesn't bring in much and we have a fair-sized family!' *One of them is yours, so what are you going to do about that?* Tommy shuffled his feet, looking down at the floor.

'Tommy has had to give up his dream of becoming a writer.'

'Don't worry Mam. It's alright. I don't really mind.' Tommy forced a smile onto his face.

'But I do worry son. I want all your dreams to come true.'

The pure sorrow on his Mam's face was almost Tommy's undoing. He quickly swallowed a giant lump in his throat.

Larry looked from Ellen to Tommy and back again, slightly ashen faced, even with the tan. He looked like he was thinking very hard about something.

'Is there any chance that I could meet my daughter?' The words were barely more than a whisper.

Tommy knew that Liberty was Larry's daughter as Ellen had told him so when he has sixteen. It had come as a bit of a shock, if he was honest. He didn't like to think of his Mam doing that thing with anyone, but he could just about cope with the image of her and Larry. He bet he'd been kinder to his Mam than the brute who was cold in the ground. He had always wondered why she had married Nicholas so quickly. At the age of sixteen, he had found out. And it had explained why Nicholas, although not particularly kind to his two youngest daughters, had seemed to keep the sharper end of his tongue for Liberty, always finding fault no matter what the child did. He glanced across at Larry. He looked taut as a spring.

Ellen looked at Larry and then nodded at Tommy. This was his cue to go and fetch the girls. Tommy left the kitchen, took a right, crossed the black and white tiled hall and entered the room where his sisters were engrossed in the huge doll's house that had arrived the Christmas Michael died. The familiar pang of loss made Tommy's stomach clench. He shook his head as he tried to erase the image of his baby brother's cold, lifeless body from his mind. Three little heads turned when Tommy walked into the room. Alice was sitting on a chair by the window, a book in her lap, but she looked like she was a million miles away. She often spoke to Tommy about her plans to escape Drogheda and cross the sea. She constantly had her nose stook in books set in France, Italy and America. Tommy had no doubt that she would go places, given half a chance. But they had to find some way of making sure that she could stay at school. Tommy knew that learning was the path to freedom.

'Who was at the door Tommy?' Gladys was the first to run over to him. He ruffled her curls as she looked up at him. Her freckles stood out in stark contrast to her pale skin and her dimples were deep.

'It's a friend of your Mam's and mine. Larry is his name. He's come all the way from Australia, the other side of the world, to see us. Now, wasn't that kind of him? He's very keen to meet all of you, so pat yourselves down, straighten your clothes and walk nicely with me to the kitchen.'

Alice's ears had pricked up at the prospect of meeting someone who had been somewhere so exotic. She jumped off the chair, her book falling to the floor, and was out the door like a shot. Satisfied that his little sisters were all presentable, Tommy led the way back to the kitchen where he found Alice introducing herself to Larry. She had been three when Larry had left. He had never been mentioned by their Mam from that day to this, so it was really like she was meeting him for the first time. Tommy himself remembered Larry in different ways. His kindness at taking the time to tell him all about the stars and constellations, the fun they'd had had on the trip to the seaside that summer he was nine. But then, he also remembered the anxiety he had felt at bringing messages around town before Larry's capture. Tommy was realising that everyone has both good things and bad things about them.

Larry's face was a picture as he extracted his hand from Alice's and looked at the three little girls standing in a straight line before him. They eyed him in three different ways. Liberty held herself straight and looked him boldly in the eye. Gladys looked a bit afraid, and Rosena looked like she couldn't care less who this stranger was who had arrived suddenly. She ran to her Mam and Ellen picked her up and placed her gently on her lap where the little girl cuddled in and began to suck her thumb.

'Well, girls, it certainly is a pleasure to meet you. What four pretty lasses! Your Mam is a very lucky woman to have you all.' He beamed at them, including Alice in his words. She was still staring at him.

'You look very like Nicholas.' She had never called Nicholas 'Father'.

'Well,' Larry chuckled, 'that's because he and I were brothers.'

'Brothers?' a slight frown creased Alice's brow. 'He never mentioned a brother.'

'I'll bet he didn't. Your mother and I were friends before she met Nicholas. And now I've come back to visit.'

'You were in Australia?'

'Aye, and America too.'

Alice's eyes sparked with interest. Her smile, when it came, lit up the room. She looked at Larry in awe.

'Well, Mr. Larry Clinton, I think you and I are going to get along just fine.'

The adults all laughed at this pronouncement. It was obvious to Tommy that Alice had absolutely no memory of Larry. That was fine. If he was going to become a fixture in their lives, and it was becoming increasingly likely judging by the way he and his Mam were looking at each other, then it was just as well she didn't remember everything about him. He, Tommy, on the other hand, had reason to be wary.

'So, who have we here?' Larry had a wide smile on his face.

Liberty decided she would do the introductions.

'This is Gladys, she's eight. Over there, with Mam, is Rosena, and she's seven, and I am Liberty Clinton, and I'm nine.'

It was announced with such clarity and confidence. Tommy could see Larry stifling a laugh as he glanced at Ellen. She looked mightily proud of her brood and her face was temporarily relieved of its worried expression.

'Thank you very much for that lovely introduction, Liberty. I am very pleased to make your acquaintance. Do you young ladies go to school?'

Tommy could see that Larry was trying to divide his attention equally between all the girls, but his eyes lingered on Liberty. It looked like he was trying to drink her face in. His daughter laughed and said of course they did as if this was the silliest question ever.

'How else are we supposed to learn things and get jobs when we're older?'

This answer seemed to please Larry.

'Very true, young lady. And may I ask what teacher you and your sisters have?'

'Gladys and I both have Sister Gerard. She's very nice, but she doesn't like it when we talk in class.'

'I should think not. And what might you have to be talking about when you're supposed to be learning?'

'Ah, just things.'

'Like what?'

Liberty hesitated before answering, like she was weighing up whether to be truthful or not.

'Things like what we want to be when we grow up. Why the sky is blue, how machines work. Things like that.'

Tommy could see that Larry was lit with pride from within as he looked at his daughter.

Tommy would never have a child. He knew he wasn't natural. Sometimes he wished he could just disappear off this earth, but he knew that would break his Mam's heart. And she'd had enough heartache for one lifetime already.

Maybe Larry coming back was a good thing. He intended to keep a very close eye on him. Tommy was just as tall as him and he had youth on his side. He could take him if he had to. He would have to earn his place in the family if he wanted to be by Ellen's side. If he could come up with some solution to help them out of their pickle, then Tommy might give him a bit of leeway. For now, Tommy was just glad to see a smile on his Mam's face.

CHAPTER 49

Ellen

Something had shifted inside Ellen. The days, even the dull ones, seemed a bit brighter, her bones didn't ache as much and the darkness inside her was lifting slightly. She was still hugely anxious about how on earth she was going to look after her family and terribly guilty about the fact that she couldn't send Tommy to University. She hurried along Harpur's Lane with Larry. She didn't usually frequent this part of town which consisted of a warren of streets that snaked their way up the hill from the quay. Usually populated with shady looking characters, it was an area to be avoided. Ellen could see a row of run-down shacks. Some had timber doors, some were made of rusty iron, and they were all secured with locks and chains. It looked like a good kick would defeat most of them. She patted the key in her pocket, just to make sure it was still there. It had been a huge surprise to find it tucked away in a secret compartment in the drawer of Nicholas's desk. She had been tearing the office asunder from top to bottom, hoping to find something - she didn't know what -maybe some money stashed away somewhere. She hadn't found any notes, but she had found a solid brass key, secreted behind a drawer. A piece of paper had fluttered to the ground with the words '17 HL' written in Nicholas's distinctive scrawl. Herself and

Tommy had wracked their brains trying to think what it might mean. And now, here she was, with Larry, making their way towards number seventeen Harpur's Lane. They could be on a wild goose chase, but she was desperate.

The stench from the river and the tannery were particularly strong. She shuddered as a huge rat ran right across their path. Probably a female with her belly full of babies. A scrawny cat with half of its grey fur missing miaowed piteously from the top of one of the shacks.

'Shut your whiny mouth!' yelled a rough looking middle-aged man as he picked up a stone and aimed it at the cat. It missed and the cat ran off with its tail swishing angrily. The man eyed them curiously but continued with his task which seemed to involve hauling a heavy sack into his shack. Ellen darted her eyes about. The gathering dusk made the place look threatening. It was full of little nooks and crannies where shadows lurked, and things scurried.

'Nearly there', Larry said.

In the week since he had come home, Larry had visited her every day. Bit by bit, she told him of how her life had been for the nine years of her marriage to his brother. A little muscle jumped in his cheek every time she mentioned his brother's moods and tempers. She had broken down when she told him about Michael. He had gone with her to Michael's grave in the Cord cemetery, where Nicholas was also buried. He had stood there while she quietly wept and had put his arm gingerly around her shoulders. She had leaned into him and felt something inside her soften and melt. She had told him about how Nicholas had seemed to lose the will to live after Michael had died. About his sudden and unexpected death of a suspected heart-attack in his sleep. George Menton, and his thieving, which they had only discovered after he scarpered. How she had had to face the bank manager where she learned of all

Nicholas's debt. Her efforts to keep the mill going and make sure that none of the workers lost their jobs. The hunt for a buyer when she realised that to sell it was the only way she could pay off what she now owed, courtesy of her dead husband. The fact that they would soon have nowhere to live. Her disappointment that Tommy had to go to work to keep them fed even though he had plans to go to Maynooth University. Her despair as to what was to become of them all. Listening without interrupting, he had held her hand. It had felt so good to unburden everything to him. The way Larry had looked at her had made her feel that she was amazing to have come through all she had endured, still be alive, and be full of resolve to protect her family no matter what.

Ellen consulted the map that she had in her hand.

'I think this is it. Number seventeen.'

They were stopped in front of a shack which looked exactly like most of the others on the lane. It had bare walls and a door with red peeling paint. The lock that secured a thick chain was newish looking - not rusted like so many of the others. She took the key from her pocket, and looking up and down the alleyway to make sure they were not about to be set upon, she lifted the lock and inserted the key. She held her breath until she heard a click. So, they were on the right track. Nicholas must have owned this shack, although he had never, ever mentioned it to her. Her eyes met Larry's. Would there be anything of worth in this hovel? Ellen tried not to let her hopes up. Larry removed the chain, opened the door and stood back to let Ellen enter.

'After you.'

He closed the door behind them, and they stood stock still for a moment, allowing their eyes to adjust to the gloom inside. The air was damp and musty, the inside measured about twelve feet by twelve. Two small windows above the door allowed some fading light in. Ellen could make out a row of shelves at waist height all around the interior. There were some sacks sitting on the shelves. She counted about twenty in all. She moved toward them, jumping slightly as something tickled her face. Realising it was only a cobweb, she pulled it away. Larry walked over to the shelves where he poked one of the sacks. It seemed to be tightly packed with something. He turned to Ellen and raised his eyebrows.

'Want to see what's inside?'

'I suppose so,' she answered.

Larry took out a pocket-knife and started making a slit in one of the sacks. He peered in at what had been revealed, and then made the slit a bit bigger. He took the knife to the next sack, then the next.

'Yes!'

'What? What's in them?'

'It's linen.'

'Linen?' Ellen was perplexed. 'Where did that come from?'

'Well, the dear departed Nicholas must have been putting some aside for a rainy day. He always was a canny devil.' Larry whistled softly under his breath. 'I count twenty sacks. There must be at least one hundred yards in each one. How much would you get for that?' He looked over at Ellen who had a disbelieving expression on her face.

'Enough to get us out of the hole we're in.' Ellen breathed. 'Jesus and all the saints, if I had known this was here...'

A smile was beginning to form on her lips. It would be enough to pay for a year's rent on a cottage somewhere for them all. And who knew what might turn up in the meantime. She might be able to get a job. If she moved away from Drogheda, maybe to Collon, or some other village, where Nicholas's name wasn't so sullied, she might find work.

'Oh, Larry, thank God, thank my devious dead husband!' She couldn't contain her delight and did a little jig on the spot. 'Is this really all mine?'

'Well, your debts are cleared with the bank, aren't they? You don't owe anyone else any money?' Ellen shook her head. 'Well, then, it's all yours.'

'I'll be able to rent somewhere for us to live. And I won't have to worry about having enough to feed us all for a couple of months at least.'

Larry was looking at her with a funny glint in his eye.

'Aye, Ellen. That's true. That's true.'

He took a deep breath and caught her around the waist. His nearness made her senses swim.

'Hear me out. I have a plan.'

'What do you mean 'a plan'?'

'A plan for a new life for you, me and your family.'

'Hold your horses, Larry Clinton. I'm in your plans now, am I?' Ellen laughed, pulling away from him slightly.

'Ellen Clinton, you have been in my every thought, dream and plan since the first moment I clapped eyes on you in that alehouse. As I crossed the seas, on that convict ship, all the years I spent in gaol, there you were. You even invaded my dreams at night. I can't imagine a life without you. There. It's as simple as that.'

'So, what's this plan you have for me, Mr. Clinton?' Ellen arched one dark eyebrow at him.

'Ellen, come with me to America!'

'What?' spluttered Ellen. She tried to loosen Larry's grip on her waist as she stared into his face.

'You would love it! It's such a fantastic place. The sights, the sounds, the opportunities! You and me could go over, get jobs. No one has heard of Nicholas Clinton over there. You could be anyone you want to be. We could set up a home and then send for the children and Peggy. We could see if Tommy could get a job with a newspaper. Please, Ellen, please consider it.'

Ellen laughed out loud. Her head was spinning with the excitement in Larry's voice and the enormity of what he was asking her to do. Cross the Atlantic Ocean, set up home with him, leave her children behind. Was he clean mad? He was still talking.

'There's something about the place that makes you feel that absolutely anything is possible if you work hard enough. I know you're not afraid of it and neither am I.'

Ellen tried to open her mouth to protest, but he cut her off again.

'There's Central Park, like a forest in the middle of the city, the nicest place ever to have a stroll. There's Times Square, all the tall buildings, higher than St. Peter's spire, thousands of people, all colours, all creeds, bustling around, going about their business, making money, making a life for themselves. There're loads of Irish there too. We wouldn't be short of someone to chat with. Please, Ellen, please don't say no until you've had a good think about it.'

Larry's expression was so pleading that Ellen couldn't bring herself to say an outright 'no' to his face. She had no intention of haring off across the Atlantic without her children, no matter what kind of a picture Larry painted. It did sound like a wondrous place, though. No, she couldn't. Could she? Ellen's imagination wandered into the not-too-distant future. She saw herself, traipsing from door to door, looking for work, Tommy coming home in the evening, exhausted from his labours, too tired to even think about writing. Peggy, with even more grey streaks in her frizzy red hair, getting older and stiffer. Hunger pangs gnawing at her own stomach as she tried to sleep. A constant black cloud over her family, never sure where the next meal was going to come from. Alice and three little ones to take care of. She wanted to do her very best for her daughters. Keep them in school as long as possible so that they could make something of themselves. Liberty was definitely smart enough to be a teacher. Hell, to be anything she wanted. She just needed to figure out a way. *And maybe this was the way*? Ellen shook her head. No, Larry was half, if not fully, mad. She had never been outside Drogheda, save for her honeymoon in Wicklow. How on earth could she contemplate crossing the wild, churning Atlantic Ocean? Even with Larry by her side, it would be daunting. The light was fading fast in the shack. A chill suddenly rattled down her spine. She grabbed Larry's hand.

'Let's get out of here Larry. This place is giving me the shivers.' As she began to make her way towards the door, he tightened his grip on her hand so that she had to stop. The planes of Larry's face were handsome in the half-light.

'Just promise me you'll think about it Ellen. Please. I want you. That's non-negotiable. If you really want to stay here in Ireland, then I will stay too. But I think we could be something wonderful in New York. And I always wanted a big family,' he broke into a grin and despite everything, Ellen's heart twisted with love.

'I don't have much in the line of money to my name, but I do have a small pension from the army. I love you, Ellen. Will you make a life with me?'

'Larry Clinton, that sounded very much like a proposal!'

Ellen's stomach did a somersault as she took in the enormity of what he was asking. All of a sudden, Larry was down on one knee in the dusty, grimy shack. He still had a hold of her left hand. He turned it over, traced a heart shape on the inside of her palm and raised his eyes to her face. Ellen's heart began to thud.

'Well, I had planned for slightly prettier surroundings than this to ask you the question, but yes, Ellen Sarsfield Cooney Clinton, love of my life, will you do me the honour of becoming my wife?'

Ellen opened and closed her mouth.

Larry rose to his feet.

'It's too soon. I'm sorry I should have waited a while. Until we got to know each other again. Sorry Ellen. It's just that I couldn't wait to ask.'

'And I am very honoured that you asked me. I just need a little time to think about it all. It's not that I want anyone else, but I just want to be me for a while. Not someone's wife. Can you understand that?'

Ellen wasn't sure he would. She just didn't want to pin all her hopes on one person again.

With a sigh, Larry gathered her to him and rocked her back and forth.

'Yes, I can. You've been through so much, *a stór*. Your heart needs time to mend and your head needs time to recover. I'll be here. I'm not going anywhere.'

'I promise I will think about going to America. It's just so far away...'

'Yes, but I will be there with you every step of the way. Just think of all the things we could do; what Tommy and the girls could become. I'm telling you Ellen, it's a land like no other.'

A warm, sure feeling suddenly suffused Ellen. An image of Jim floated into her mind. He was smiling at her. He blew her a kiss, waved, turned, and walked away, growing smaller and smaller until he disappeared.

CHAPTER 50

Peggy

Skerries Co. Dublin, July 1877

Peggy sat on a wooden chair in the shade of a big oak tree in the back garden of the rented house in Skerries. My, but it was a stinker of a day! The summer so far had been one big, long parade of blue skies, day after day, week after week. She should be grateful, she supposed, but the older she got, the less she was inclined to like the heat. It sapped the energy out of a body. Especially one that was sixty-three years old. Peggy lifted her hand to swat away a wasp that seemed to have taken a liking to her hair. The heat was having its usual effect on her frizzy mop. Now more grey than red, it still had a mind of its own. She could feel a trickle of sweat on her temple and another was making its way down between her bosoms. She welcomed the slight breeze that wound its way around her neck. She closed her eyes and sighed deeply, surrendering to the moment. It wouldn't be long before Ellen and the girls were back from their walk on the beach, and she knew she would need all her strength then.

Lordy, but she didn't know what she felt about Ellen's plans. Peggy shifted in the seat and opened her eyes slightly, squinting against the glare of the sun. She regarded the white stone house in front of her, with its sturdy chimney pots and its gleaming windows. She had been up the walls when she found out that Nicholas and his bad decisions had left the family homeless. Like Ellen, she had spent many sleepless nights wondering just where on earth they were going to go. She had a bit saved from her days as the local 'Handywoman', but she had been dipping into it to help Ellen keep the family fed after the income from the mill dried up. A little shiver of unease settled on Peggy every time she thought of Nicholas and the way he had died. For a couple of years before she found him cold in the bed, she had been giving him St. John's Wort and a touch of Valerian in his food and drink unbeknownst to him, or to anyone else in the house. It had been in an effort to keep the louser quiet, and to get him to leave Ellen alone. Would it have built up in his system and caused his heart to stop? The worry of it had worn a track in her brain. Still, she comforted herself with the thought that Ellen was better off without him. The whole family was. He had been a bad-tempered git. But the thought that she might have been responsible for another person's death caused her insides to curl up in a little ball.

Looking at the house in which they now lived never failed to give her a little thrill. All her life, she had dreamed of living by the sea and now, here she was in this pretty little village, about twenty miles down the coast from Drogheda. But it might as well have been a different world. If Peggy turned her head to the right, she could see the rocky islands after which the town was named. The house faced the street, but at the bottom of the back garden, there was a green wooden gate that opened out onto the beach. The children were in heaven. When they lived in Drogheda, a trip to the seaside in Laytown, Bettystown or Clogherhead was a treat that happened once a year or so, depending on the mood Nicholas had been in. But now, they could run to the sand any time their hearts desired, exclaiming over the funny shaped shells, shrieking as the cold waves splashed over their feet, playing catch in the dunes, and turning as brown as berries. It was lucky they didn't have the type of skin that burned easily.

She filled her lungs with the fresh air. Here, there was just the tang of the sea. She had lived all her life side by side with the smells and the hustle and bustle of the busy port that was Drogheda, but she found that this little fishing village was very much to her liking. Even though she wasn't getting any younger, she seemed to have developed a new lease of life since the move. She still had creaky joints, and her gout bothered her from time to time, but she felt like she still had a few more years left in her yet. The children were keeping her young. And she would need to keep feeling young by the looks of it! She had a busy time in store. A slight frown creased her brow, and she sighed heavily again.

Her mind wandered to Ellen and Larry. Lord but the lass had bloomed since he had come back on the scene. She hadn't been best pleased to see him, *the convict*, come back into Ellen's life. She had always liked the man but had never been able to bring herself to completely trust him. She had known Ellen was falling for him all those years ago, but then, he had disappeared, and Ellen had been bereft once more. Peggy shifted in her seat as two gulls wheeled overhead, sounding like they were having an argument. She continued her reminiscing. Lo and behold, Larry had swanned back into their lives, apparently proclaiming his love for Ellen and wanting them all to be a family. He had certainly brought an air of jollity to the place. His visits had become more frequent, and the little ones seemed to knock great fun out of him. She could see the special way he looked at Liberty, although he included all the little girls in his playacting. Peggy wondered when and if Ellen would ever tell the girl who her Daddy really was. She was a bit too young for that kind of a revelation yet. Alice, at nearly thirteen, usually held herself aloof from the shenanigans, but occasionally, she lapsed into girlish giggles. Peggy had caught her looking at Tony Clancy, the local coachman's lad in a very forward fashion the other day.

After a bit of a cool reception, Tommy seemed to be welcoming Larry into the family again. He was a good lad, Tommy. If only they could find some way to help him get to the university, where he could write his stories. Peggy knew that he was putting on a brave face of it. His work in the tannery had been backbreaking and filthy. At least now, since the move to Skerries, he had a slightly more pleasant job, although being a dogsbody for the gardener at the local big house was still hard, physical work. The muscles on him now! Peggy had jokingly told him he could get a job as a strong man at the circus, and he had replied quietly that he was certainly enough of a freak. There had been something off about his tone when he had said that. Peggy had filed it in her brain for later examination. Right now, she had enough on her mind.

The stash of linen that Nicholas had hidden had fetched a good price. That and the money Tommy was bringing in meant that Ellen and the family had enough to survive on, just about, for the next year. She brought her gaze again to the house and admired the clematis growing around the back door. The house was only rented, but it was much better than anything they could have hoped to afford in Drogheda. Aye, she had come a long way from Rope Walk! But, sure, she was as good as Ellen's Mam. And she was like a granny to the children. The only granny they had. Their real grandmother was still living in fear of angering her bully of a husband. She would live and die a cowering wreck. A short time after her marriage to Nicholas, Ellen's father had arrived at the door of the house in Drogheda, but Nicholas had sent him off with a flea in his ear. Ellen had been too sick to notice or care. That was the last they had seen of him or his miserable wife. And no loss. Of course, there had been no sign of them when Nicholas had died, and Ellen had once again found herself on her uppers. Tommy and Alice knew about their granny and granddad Sarsfield, but they had shown absolutely no desire to get in touch with them.

Peggy closed her eyes. A five-minute nap wouldn't hurt. She'd be up and about again as soon as those wee lassies got back from their walk on the beach. No doubt they'd be full of chatter, and they would, all three of them, try to climb onto her lap at the same time, covered in sand. Peggy would need all her energy for the onslaught that awaited her. She chuckled to herself. By God, but she loved those children.

Even though she was sitting in the shade, the day was very hot, and Peggy welcomed the soft breeze that had sprung up and was now cooling her forehead. She sighed once more and relaxed into the chair. Her thoughts drifted to Larry. He really could have gotten himself a good job, enough to support them all, but no, he was hell bent on going back to New York and bringing them all with him. He had a small bit of money aside from his army pension and it seemed he had persuaded Ellen to use some of the linen money to buy a fare for herself. They were to travel in two weeks-time. The plan was that they would stay with some of the Fenian sympathisers in New York until they found their feet. They would get a place to live, jobs, school for the girls and then, when they were properly set up, Ellen would come back, and they would all leave Ireland to go and make a life in New York. Peggy had been horrified at first when Ellen had suggested the plan. Her, Peggy Murphy, widow, sixty-three years old, uprooting herself to go and live across the ocean? Never to see her homeland again? Facing facts, if she did go, it was highly unlikely that she would ever return. But the idea had grown on her. Sure, Ellen and her family were her world. There would be no life for her in Drogheda if they weren't there. She had no children or grandchildren of her own, so there was nothing really keeping her here except sentimentality for the town in which she had spent all her life. So, she had agreed to the plan. She was to stay and mind the little ones, with Tommy and Alice to help, until Ellen came back for them. All going well, it wouldn't be too long.

Peggy was on the brink of dozing off when she suddenly felt a tingling at the base of her spine. Despite the heat of the day, a cold clamminess started to sweep over her, and she felt dizzy, floaty. Bad cess to it, was she having another one of her *'visions'*? Her last one had been just before little Michael had died. She had thought she was done with them for good. She opened her eyes and felt herself stiffen, a feeling of such sadness and anguish washing over her. The pretty clematis around the door had disappeared, and instead, she was looking at a vision of Tommy dressed in the finest suit she had ever seen. He looked a few years older than he was now and he was standing on a bridge looking down into a river of dark, rushing water. It was night-time and she could see some bright lights reflected in the water. The look on his face was what nearly stopped Peggy's heart. He looked so desperately sad, broken, resigned. Then, with one swift movement, he jumped up onto the edge of the wall, teetering on the edge. *'NO! Tommy, NO!'* Peggy shouted and then the vision disappeared. The house swam back into view. The clematis was still there, the gulls were still wheeling around doing their acrobatics in the sky. Her heart was thumping, and she felt weak, spent. What on earth had this one meant? Was there something going on with Tommy that would make him want to drown himself? For that's how it had seemed to her. She had been in no doubt that she had foreseen the lad about to take his own life. What could possibly make him feel like that? He was a sunny-natured lad with a good friend in Johnny. He had lots of girls after him, but none that stuck around for very long. As her heart rate gradually returned to normal, Peggy vowed that she would keep a close eye on Tommy. She wouldn't tell Ellen about her '*vision*'. Lord knew the lass had enough on her plate.

She turned her head when she heard the sound of squeals coming closer. Ellen, Larry and the girls were on their way back. So much for having a little snooze. She sat up, made a huge effort to try and assemble her features into something approaching jolliness and braced herself for the three little bodies that would soon hurl themselves upon her. She would have to make sure she was on the ball for the next few months. Looking after the wee lassies and keeping an eye on Alice, even with the help of Tommy, would be a challenge. Come September time, she could have a snooze in the mornings after they went to school. And hopefully, it wouldn't be too long before Ellen and Larry got themselves set up in New York and then they would all be off on a big adventure. Peggy still wasn't one hundred percent sure she was definitely going. She would have to give it some serious thought over the coming weeks. For now, she chose to live in the moment. She braced herself and threw out her arms in welcome as the girls started to run across the lawn towards her.

CHAPTER 51

Ellen

Drogheda Quayside, September 1877

It was a good job that her big strong son had her in his arms, as Ellen's knees suddenly gave way.

'You're alright, Mam, I've got you. Don't be worrying yourself about this crew. Me and Peggy will look after them.' Despite the rumpus that surrounded them, Ellen could hear Tommy's voice, loud and clear. She looked up into the handsome face of her first-born who seemed on the verge of tears.

'Tommy lad. I will miss you. Do you know that you are the best, kindest, most lovable son that any mother could hope to have? I am so proud of the man you have grown to be.'

'Ah, stop now Mam, you're embarrassing me!' Tommy's face broke into a grin.

'I mean it. I would never have survived when your Da perished if it weren't for you. The thoughts of you and Alice kept me from going down to the river. You know that I will never forget him, don't you? Please, don't think for a minute that I ever could.'

'I know, Mam. It's ok. You don't have to explain.' Tommy stole a glance at Larry who was keeping the girls occupied a few feet away in order to give him and his Mam a few private moments together.

'If there's one thing I've learned in this life, it's that you have to seize whatever bit of happiness you can find.'

'Do you know what, son, you are absolutely right. You know, after your Da, I thought I would never find anyone again. I dreamed about him the other night. He was smiling at me and telling me to be happy. I suppose that was him giving me his blessing? What do you think?' She looked anxiously up at Tommy as a shadow had crossed his face.

'Mam, if anyone deserves happiness, it's you. After all you've been through. Don't worry about the little ones. We'll all be just fine and will be over to join you before you know it. Just make sure you get a nice house for us all!'

Ellen reached up and ruffled his hair like she had done since he was a little boy.

'I will do my very best. Now, I'd better dry these eyes, paste on a happy smile and say my final goodbyes to the girls. You won't forget to bring them to the fair?'

'As if they'd let me', Tommy said wryly.

The trip to the fair was to try and take the sting out of saying goodbye to their Mam. Alice had been particularly put out at not being allowed to accompany her mother on the journey.

'Good lad.' Ellen hugged Tommy tightly, breathing in the scent of him. 'Time to go now.'

She had caught Larry's eye and could see that the '*RMS Leinster*' on which they were to travel to Liverpool was nearly ready to leave. They would go from there to New York on the '*Royal William.*' The tickets for the entire journey had been purchased in Dooleys in Drogheda and their meagre luggage was already on board. It would take a day, and most of the night to get to Liverpool. The seating area was reasonably comfortable, and provided the water wasn't too choppy, the journey should be pleasant enough. The onward trip to New York would take four weeks. Ellen wasn't too sure she was looking forward to that. She was still haunted by visions of Jim lying somewhere at the bottom of the sea. She knew that crossings could be sometimes risky due to unpredictable weather, but Larry assured her that ships these days were very safe. Especially the big passenger ones that crossed the Atlantic many times each year. Despite her sorrow at leaving her children behind, Ellen felt a frisson of excitement. She wanted so much for Tommy and the girls. A life better than what lay ahead of them if they stayed in Ireland. She felt a stab of sorrow when she thought about little Michael as he lay in his grave in the Cord Road. He was resting with his father, but it still weighed heavy on her heart that she was moving away, moving on with her life. She vowed that she would make enough money to cross the sea as many times as she wanted in the years to come.

Placing her hand in her pocket, to make sure for the umpteenth time that her travel papers were there, she turned towards Larry. With just one glance, he seemed to tell her that he understood how hard this parting from her children was for her. There was something else there that made her shiver. They would be travelling as man and wife from the minute they set foot on the steam packet. They had the same surname, so no one would be any the wiser.

'Now, my lovely little girlies. Have you a kiss for your Mam before she goes?' Ellen tried to keep her tone light, although she could feel a sob rising in her throat.

'I'm not a little girlie.' This was Alice, of course.

'You're quite correct Alice. I will need you to help Peggy in whatever way you can. Do you promise?'

'Yes Mam.' Ellen could see that Alice was fighting with her emotions. She was trying to be a grown-up, but she was still just a little girl. The three younger ones all launched themselves at Ellen at the same time.

'Mam, Mam, we don't want you to go! Please don't leave, please!' Their high-pitched wails could be heard even above the racket on the quayside.

'Now, girls, we've discussed this already. I'm only going to find us a nice house to live in, Larry and I will get jobs, and we will find you a lovely school to go to. You'll all have your very own bed with a doll's house, and we might even be able to get a puppy!' Ellen reminded them of the bargain she had struck with them.

'You just need to be patient, good girls, and I will send for you when we have everything ready. Alright? And you're going to the fair today. Isn't that exciting?' Ellen kissed them all and hugged them tight to her chest, one at a time. Placated for the moment, the girls let go of Ellen and she was able to turn to Peggy. She took the older woman in a bear hug.

'What can I say Peggy' she whispered in her ear. 'You have been my mother, the grandmother to my children. I don't know how I would have survived without you. Please, please, look after yourself and the girls. I expect to come back and bring you on that ship. Don't let me down!'

Ellen looked into the dear face of her old friend who still had a proud twinkle in her slightly faded eyes. Ellen hoped with all her heart that Peggy would agree to move with the family, for she truly loved her.

'Aye, lass, I'll think on it. Now, you look after yourself and tell Larry that he'll have me to deal with if doesn't do right by you.'

'I don't think you have anything to worry about on that score Peggy. It's not the same as Jim. It's different, but it's good, really good.'

'I'm glad to hear it. You be safe now pet. I'll see you soon.'

Ellen couldn't stop the tears any longer. She left Peggy's embrace and blindly walked over to Larry.

'Quick, get me onto that boat before I change my mind', she hissed.

Larry took her hand. A sense of calm came over her as she felt its firm warmth. They walked up the gang plank, the sound of their heels hitting the wood lost in the din of the busy quayside. Ellen turned and looked at her family one last time. There they were, huddled together, Tommy, tall and lean with his arm around Peggy - Alice standing slightly apart from everyone else - Liberty, Gladys and Rosena, clinging to Peggy's skirts, but at least it seemed they were no longer crying. Ellen gripped the side rail of the steam packet as the boat started to push away from the quay wall. She started to wave, and her family waved back. Peggy was conversing with a strange man who looked like he had just disembarked from the steamer, a small travel bag in his left hand, and a letter in his right. Ellen's arm grew tired, her vision blurred by tears that just wouldn't stop. Larry placed his hand gently on her shoulder.

'They'll be fine, Ellen.'

She buried her head in his shoulder and sobbed. After a few minutes, they found a spot on one of the hard benches and sat down. Ellen felt spent. After she had finally fully made up her mind to try her luck with Larry in America, the last few weeks had been a whirlwind, getting travel papers organised, packing, trying to console the girls. Drying her eyes, she cast a look at their fellow passengers. Some were well dressed, most probably businessmen on their way to do a deal. There was a family sitting on the ground in one corner, the children looked skinny, pale, and wide-eyed. On a bench just over to Ellen's left, a young woman was crying quietly into a handkerchief. The steamer slowly made its way down the river Boyne to where it met the Irish sea at Mornington. On and on they chugged towards Liverpool. Ellen's heartbeat gradually slowed, and her breathing became more even. She felt the roughness of Larry's wool coat against her cheek as she closed her eyes and tried to focus on the life to come that they would build together. And then, she would return, on the tide, to *Tredagh*, for her children.

Martin Cooper breathed a sigh of relief. He seemed to be getting somewhere in his quest to find a home for the letter which had been like a hot potato in his bag all the way over to Drogheda from Liverpool. His dying mother, Freda, had beseeched him, two weeks earlier, before she had sunk into her final decline, to make sure that no matter what, he found these two women to whom her letter was addressed. Hating to see her so anxious, he had hushed her, reassured her that he would find them, even if it took him years to do so. The expression on her gaunt face had relaxed, and she had seemed to breathe a little easier. The gratitude in her fading eyes had tugged at his heartstrings. Finding a home for this letter was the least he owed her after what she had done for him all those years ago, by paying his debts, and getting those thugs off his back. He hadn't gambled since. His close shave had made him realise it was a mug's game. He had never figured out how his mother had managed to get the money together. The job in the nursing home where she had worked in Lytham St. Annes hadn't paid that much. Around the time his mother had bailed him out, she had withdrawn into herself. It had seemed as if there was something eating her up. And her insides had been literally eaten up this past year, as she had contracted the wasting disease. And now she was gone.

He glanced at the envelope again which bore the names *Clarice and Sarah Clinton*. His mother had simply written 'Drogheda' for the address. For the umpteenth time, he wondered why his she had been so anxious to get this letter to these Clinton women when he had never, ever heard her mention them until just before she died. Who were they, and what did his mother have to say to them so urgently?

So, having made sure that she had received a decent burial, he had crossed the water to Drogheda to fulfil her final wish. It had been a hard task not to steam the envelope open, for he was very curious to know what it contained. Now, he seemed to have struck lucky. On the noisy, smelly Irish quayside, he had approached an elderly woman whose red hair was shot through with streaks of white, and who was surrounded by a bevy of children of various ages. She had looked at him with a curious expression when he'd approached her, bearing the letter in his hand. After regarding him warily, she confirmed that she did indeed know the Misses Clinton, although they were both married now and had different surnames. She also asked him, her blue eyes burning with curiosity, why he wanted to find them.

With the September sun glancing off his salt and pepper hair, he had taken in a deep breath of the salty, tangy air and had begun to explain.

Epilogue

17th August 1877.Lytham St. Annes, England.

To Clarice and Sarah, daughters of Nicholas Clinton and the late Mrs. Rosemary Clinton, Drogheda, Ireland.

My name is Freda Cooper, and I worked at St. Jude's Nursing Home in Lytham St. Annes for many long years. You are, no doubt, reading this letter with great curiosity, wondering why a complete stranger is corresponding with you. What I am about to tell you will probably come as a huge shock, as my understanding is that you believed your mother to be dead since you were both little girls. In fact, she only died in 1867. She was a patient at St. Jude's for nigh on twenty years.

Your mother, Rosemary Clinton suffered from a severe form of melancholia and spent most of her conscious hours in a world of her own, gazing out the window. She was one of the patients that I looked after. When she came in first, she was a beautiful, if frail- looking woman. Your father came to see her, usually just once a year. I was always told to make sure she received her medication. It never seemed to make her better.

Then one day, in March of 1867, your father arrived at St Jude's. He asked me to do something that I have lived to regret, something has gnawed away at my insides ever since. I can't expect you to understand why I did it, but my only excuse is that I was desperate. You see, my eldest son had gotten in with a bad crowd in Manchester and owed a lot of money. Your father paid me handsomely to hasten your mother's exit from this world. He told me at the time that he was to be married again and that his bride-to-be wanted everything 'tidied up', so to speak before they got married. I used a pillow. It was quick.

I have lived to bitterly regret the madness that made me agree to his suggestion, but what can I say? I am a mother, and my son was in trouble. The payment your father gave me was enough to get the thugs off my son's back.

I have lived with the enormity of what I did for years. I am now paying the price as I have the wasting disease, and the doctor tells me that I have only a couple of weeks left to live. I have confessed my mortal sin in church and am hoping that a merciful God will allow me into his kingdom when my time comes. I feel it won't be long now.

I needed to let you know that I am so very, very sorry for the terrible wrong I committed. Your mother was a lovely woman. She was a beauty when she arrived here, and she muttered your names every now and then. She loved you both, of that, I have no doubt. She didn't deserve to die the way she did.

I am haunted every day by what I did. You can get me thrown in jail if you want. It's what I deserve. But any sentence they could give me would be short-lived at this stage. My real sentence has been served by the guilt I have lived with every day of my life since I committed that terrible act, and the knowledge that I may burn in hell forever.

I am hoping that one day, you can forgive me, for it truly was a most heinous crime committed on an innocent, sick woman.

A friend of mine from St. Jude's has a daughter who lives in Drogheda and often chatters about the news from there. I am aware that your father has passed away and that he had a second family. I believe you are both married and settled, and I hope you have long, happy and healthy lives.

Yours in repentance,

Freda Cooper.

This was the tenth time Clarice Clinton Matthews had read the letter. The sense of shock was beginning to be replaced by a red-hot poker of anger that was threatening to make her breakfast come back up, and her head explode. Could it be true? Was this Cooper woman away with the fairies? Had her mother been alive all those years when herself and Sarah thought she was dead? How had she ended up in a nursing home across the Irish sea? She must have been an embarrassment to their father if she was suffering from her nerves. But, to deprive her and Sarah of their mother for all those years! And to have her killed so that he could marry the Cooney wench? If it was true, it was all that bitch's fault. She had made eyes at their father and cast a spell on him. Why else would he have resorted to such an act as to have their mother done away with? It was there in black and white in Freda Cooper's letter. Ellen Cooney had more or less told him to do it, had probably black-mailed him.

Word on the street was that Ellen was gone to seek her fortune in New York with Uncle Larry. What sort of a woman took up with her own brother-in-law, when her husband, and her second one at that, was barely cold in the ground? There had been nothing left in their father's will for her or Sarah. And the mill had been sold. Bile rose in Clarice's throat at the injustice of it all. No doubt Ellen had run the business into the ground with her demands for finery, and with having to support all the children she kept popping out. Clarice and Sarah had not been invited to the wedding, which still stung a bit, and had never bothered to get to know their half-siblings. They were probably spoilt little brats. And then, her father had been worried into an early grave, no doubt, trying to satisfy his young wife's many, many demands. Her and Sarah's dowries had been reasonable, she supposed, although, if her own husband had his way, what was left would all be piddled down the drain in no time. He was far too fond of the drink. She'd have to give him a serious talking to. That was another day's work. She could feel one of her headaches coming on.

Clarice called her maid to get her carriage ready and strode angrily to the hallway of her large, comfortable farmhouse to find her mantle. She would go over to Sarah's place. Her sister needed to read this letter. Together they would decide what to do. For, until there was no more breath left in her body, she would make that Cooney woman pay for what had been done to their mother and father.

Acknowledgements

"Everyone has a book in them" – so the saying goes. It took me a long number of years to transform the vague ambition of "writing a novel" to an actual physical book. I have discovered a newfound respect for every single author who manages to get their ideas onto paper, bring their characters to life, finish their manuscript and get the whole thing edited, proof-read, formatted and published. It's no easy feat!

My mother grew up in Collon, a small village in Co. Louth, on the east coast of Ireland. She was an only child with no aunts, uncles or cousins on her paternal side, and was told growing up that all her Da's relations were "either dead or in America." It tuns out quite a lot of them did travel across the Atlantic. We know this because, around the year 2000, my sister, Louise, started to research our maternal family history. She uncovered a tragedy which I used to form the kernel of this story. My imagination took over and "As the Tide Turns at Tredagh" (the old name for the town of Drogheda) blossomed from there. Thank you, Louise, for your dogged detective skills!

I was inspired to start writing this story during a "Creative Writing for Publication" course with Maynooth University in 2019. There, I found fantastically encouraging tutors, and a like-minded tribe of fellow scribblers who are still firm friends! Without this safe space to express myself and test my writing skills, I would never have had the confidence to finish this book. Thank you, especially to Karen who gave me such valuable feedback. To my dear friends, and early readers, Marie, Mary, the eagle-eyed Assumpta, and Sinead – thank you for making me believe I could do it! To all my siblings, extended family and many other beloved friends who constantly cheer me on – life would not be the same without ye in it.

And to Seamus, James and Carl – thank you for all the hugs. Keep them coming!

And most of all, thank ***you,*** dear reader.